*Great Short Works*
*of*
# Mark Twain

*Old Times on the Mississippi*
*The Mysterious Stranger*
*The Man That Corrupted Hadleyburg*
The Jumping Frog
Jim Baker's Bluejay Yarn
Letter to the Earth
To the Person Sitting in Darkness
The Private History of a Campaign That Failed

# Great Short Works

## of

# Mark Twain

*Edited, with an Introduction, by*

Justin Kaplan

PERENNIAL LIBRARY

Harper & Row, Publishers
New York, Cambridge, Philadelphia, San Francisco
London, Mexico City, São Paulo, Singapore, Sydney

BY
$\left(\begin{array}{c}\text{S. L. CLEMENS.}\\ \text{MARK TWAIN.}\end{array}\right)$
TRADE MARK.

[TRADE MARK.]

GREAT SHORT WORKS OF MARK TWAIN
Copyright © 1967 by Justin Kaplan.
Copyright 1910, 1917, 1923, 1946, 1962 The Mark Twain Company.
Copyright 1917, 1918, 1922 by Clara Clemens Samossoud.

*Designed by Darlene Starr Carbone. Text set in Baskerville Linotype with Goudy Open Face display. Printed in the United States of America.*

PERENNIAL CLASSICS are published by Harper & Row, Publishers, Inc., 10 East 53rd Street, New York, N.Y. 10022.

ISBN: 0-06-083075-1

95 OPM 30 29 28 27 26 25

# CONTENTS

# INTRODUCTION

In January of 1870 Samuel Clemens was about to marry Olivia Langdon, heiress to an upstate New York coal fortune, and thereby to complete at least the first stage of his transition from river-rat and sagebrush Bohemian to Victorian householder, from itinerant journalist to man of letters, from purely local to world celebrity, and from the "Golden Age" of his remembered boyhood to the "Gilded Age" of his maturity. His travel book *The Innocents Abroad* continued to be something of an historic success, selling one hundred thousand copies in two years, and he had prospered as a humorist on lecture circuits in the East and the Middle West. He was only thirty-four years old, but already he had the habit of his old age of viewing his life in long perspectives and looking for turning points, crucial links in his life's chain forged by the collision of circumstance and temperament. One of these turning points, certainly, had occurred in February of 1863, when for the first time he signed the name "Mark Twain" to a travel letter for the Virginia City *Territorial Enterprise* and thereby committed himself to the identity and obligations of a humorist.

Now, on the eve of his marriage, Clemens remembered another of those turning points as the depressed winter of 1864–1865. He had been broke, out of work as a newspaper reporter and if not exactly a fugitive from the San Francisco police, at least sufficiently unpopular with them to want to leave the city for the mother-lode country. There he lived in a primitive cabin on Jackass Hill and tried to scratch out a living as a gold-miner. "It makes my heart ache yet to call to mind some of those days" he wrote to Jim Gillis, the owner of the cabin:

> Still, it shouldn't—for right in the depths of their poverty and their pocket-hunting vagabondage lay the germ of my coming good fortune. You remember the one gleam of jollity that shot across our dismal sojourn in the rain and mud of Angels' Camp—I mean that day we sat around the tavern stove and heard that chap tell about the frog and how they filled him with shot.

And Clemens had made this entry in his notebook:

Coleman with his jumping frog—bet a stranger $50.
—Stranger had no frog and C. got him one:—In the
meantime stranger filled C's frog full of shot and he
couldn't jump. The stranger's frog won.

Shortly afterwards Clemens told the story to the leading
American humorist of the time, Artemus Ward, who urged
him to write it down and send it East. That October, apparently on the strength of having done this, Clemens announced to his brother that he had finally discovered his
true vocation: "seriously scribbling to excite the *laughter*
of God's creatures." The story, then entitled "Jim Smiley
and his Jumping Frog," was published in *The Saturday
Press* of New York on the 18th of November in 1865, and
soon after, by way of the newspaper exchanges, it was
reprinted all over the country. In May of 1867 it became
the foundation stone of Mark Twain's first book, *The
Celebrated Jumping Frog of Calaveras County, and Other
Sketches.*

But it was not until *The Innocents Abroad* that the
author was finally as celebrated as his frog, and during all
that time his regard for the story had fluctuated from extreme to extreme. It was "a villainous backwoods sketch" he
said early in 1866. At the end of 1868 he was begging Olivia
Langdon not to read it or anything else in "that infamous
volume." By December of 1869 he had taken another position altogether. "Between you and I, privately, Livy dear,"
he wrote, "it is the best humorous sketch America has produced yet, and I must read it in public some day, in order
that people may know what there is in it." Looking back in
January of 1870 to Angels' Camp, Mark Twain had every
reason to believe that the story that he had heard told
around the tavern stove was the beginning of his fame and
fortune.

The "Jumping Frog" did more than to confirm Mark
Twain in his vocation. A complex, mature and completely
assured performance that remains among his best work, it
served as the model for much of what he was to do for the
rest of his life. It became, along with his famous ghost tale
"The Golden Arm," an epitome of his preferred and almost
instinctive form, the oral, humorous story, which, he said,
was distinctly American. It relies for its effectiveness on the

manner of the telling instead of the outcome, as with a comic story. It is delivered gravely and unsuspectingly, with no overt cues for laughter, and it may wander around as much as it pleases. All of this applies to the "Jumping Frog." "Good-natured, garrulous old Simon Wheeler" wears an "expression of winning gentleness and simplicity upon his tranquil countenance," and even when he delivers his irrelevant but unexpendable digression about Jim Smiley's bull-pup named Andrew Jackson, he never betrays "the slightest suspicion of enthusiasm" or the slightest hint that there was anything "ridiculous or funny about his story." And to all of this the bookish, straight-man narrator listens with imperturbable boredom, and he repeats it in the same way.

"Any lecture of mine," Mark Twain once said, "ought to be a running narrative-plank, with square holes in it, six inches apart, all the length of it, and then in my mental shop I ought to have plugs (half marked 'serious' and the others marked 'humorous') to select from and jam into these holes according to the temper of the audiences." This became, in an important sense, the principle of composition of his travel books, from *The Innocents Abroad* on, and even of some of his novels. In order to fill the requisite six hundred pages of the standard travel book of his day, he wrote on purely linear principles, stringing out episode after episode until he reached the end. Sentence by sentence and paragraph by paragraph Mark Twain was an entirely deliberate and conscious craftsman. He insisted that the difference between the nearly right word and the right word was the difference between the lightning bug and the lightning. His ear for the rhythms of speech was unsurpassed, and he demanded in dialect, social notation, description and timing nothing short of perfection. But his large structural methods were often inspirational and intuitive, and sometimes purely accidental. His difficulty as a novelist was as inevitable as his ease in shorter forms.

Mark Twain began *Tom Sawyer* with no clear idea of where it would end. His characteristic method of improvising from chapter to chapter soon proved to have its pitfalls. One day's failure of invention coupled with the absence of an over-all plan could mean that a book would come to a dead stop, sometimes for years. He abandoned *Tom Sawyer* after a summer's work in 1874, returned to it the following summer and even then, as he was finishing, was undecided if he were writing a book for adults or for boys. And with *Huckleberry Finn* the process of creation was considerably more painful and wayward. He began his masterpiece during the summer of 1876, finished only half of it and was only half satisfied with it. His tank ran dry, as he had feared, and although he did not burn the manuscript, as he threatened, he did pigeonhole it for two years. He worked on it again in 1879 or in 1880, pigeonholed it again and finally finished it in 1884, eight years and seven books after he first began it. All of this is a book-length story in itself—Walter Blair's *Mark Twain & Huck Finn*.

In *Pudd'nhead Wilson* (1894) Mark Twain put aside his customary reticence about sex and portrayed the one mature and explicitly sexual woman in all his fiction, Roxy, the slave, and dealt squarely with the intertwined themes of miscegenation and the corruptive effect of slavery. This short book is a sustained and powerful satire in which, as a novelist, Mark Twain took his last long look at America. But, again illustrative of his structural difficulties, he began the book as a farce of mistaken identity about Siamese twins, a subject that had long fascinated him and that offers suggestive parallels to the relationship between Mark Twain and Samuel Clemens. The book "changed itself from a farce to a tragedy" he said, explaining the painful process—the rewritings nearly killed him—by which *The Tragedy of Pudd'nhead Wilson* came to be equipped with a relatively inconsequential pendant piece called *The Comedy of Those Extraordinary Twins*. "I pulled one of the stories out by the roots, and left the other one—a kind of literary Caesarian operation."

The same painful process, surrounded this time by a cloud of indecision and uncertainty, was repeated in the writing of *The Mysterious Stranger*. First published in 1916, six years after Mark Twain's death, it was composed between 1897 and 1908 in several, quite different versions, one of which was set in Hannibal, another in a print shop. In a recent study entitled *Mark Twain and Little Satan* (1963), John S. Tuckey analyses the three extant versions and concludes that the published, or "Eseldorf," version, "does not represent Mark Twain's intention." Albert Bigelow Paine, Mark Twain's authorized biographer and his literary executor,

apparently took a long unfinished manuscript that had been
discarded by Mark Twain in 1900 and without comment
added to it, with a few revisions, a concluding chapter from
another version altogether, hence the contradictions and in-
consistencies that many readers have found in *The Mysterious Stranger* as published. Even with these doubtful origins,
however, and until a "true" text can be established, the
present version is the most important fictional writing of
Mark Twain's late years.

Throughout his life Mark Twain's imagination remained
wedded to his training as a journalist and to the oral story,
the brief unit of narrative, the chunk of reminiscence, the
polemic. Embedded in *A Tramp Abroad* (1880), a European
travel book that he had so much trouble writing that he
ended by despising it, is the wholly self-contained "Jim
Baker's Bluejay Yarn," a brilliant return to the mode and
manner of "The Jumping Frog." The difficulty that Mark
Twain had in finishing any of his books, travel books as well
as novels, is illuminated by the ease with which he wrote
the magazine series entitled *Old Times on the Mississippi*
(1875), the heart and forebearer of the much longer, later
and more dilute *Life on the Mississippi* (1883).

Mark Twain's first contribution to *The Atlantic Monthly*,
the most prestigious magazine of its time in America, had
been a short story about slave life published in the
November issue of 1874. William Dean Howells, the editor
of the magazine, wanted more from him immediately, but
Clemens was overwhelmed by the confusions of finishing
and moving into his Hartford mansion. It was impossible
for him to get back to work. "It's no use" he wrote to
Howells on the 24th of October in 1874: "I find I can't. We
are in such a state of weary and endless confusion that my
head won't 'go'. So I give it up."

But later that day he sent a second letter to Howells. He
had been talking to his friend, the clergyman Joseph H.
Twichell, about "old Mississippi days of steamboating glory
and grandeur as I saw them (during 5 years) *from the pilot
house*. He said 'What a virgin subject to hurl into a magazine! I hadn't thought of that before.'" What was new was
only the magazine idea. For years Mark Twain had been
planning a book about the river, a book that he was sure
would become "a standard work." The book that did grow

out of the idea, *Life on the Mississippi,* was not to be finished and published until 1883, by which time its author was utterly exasperated. "I never had such a fight over a book in my life before" he told Howells; and a little later, when the book was on press, he told his nephew and publishing agent "I will not interest myself in *any*thing connected with this wretched God-damned book."

Nevertheless, in 1874, with the idea fresh in his mind and the pages of the *Atlantic* open to him, he planned to write a series that would run just as long as his material held out, for him an ideal method of working. The past came rushing in on him. The first of seven installments of *Old Times on the Mississippi* was in proof by the end of November. "The piece about the Mississippi is capital" Howells wrote: "it almost made the water in our ice-pitcher muddy as I read it." And from the poet and journalist, former secretary to Lincoln and future Secretary of State, John Hay, who had been born and raised in Warsaw in Illinois, fifty miles up the river from Hannibal, Clemens received a tribute of the same order:

I have just read with delight your article in the Atlantic. It is perfect—no more, no less. I don't see how you do it. I knew all that, every word of it—passed as much time on the levee as you ever did, knew the same crowd and saw the same scenes—but I could not have remembered one word of it. You have the two greatest gifts of the writer, memory and imagination.

Faithful readers of the *Atlantic* would not have been surprised to find in the January issue of 1875 two poems by Professor Longfellow and an essay by Dr. Holmes, nor would the excerpt from the junior Henry James's *Roderick Hudson* have seemed a departure from normal editorial practice. But, beginning on page 69 of that issue, with the first pages of the first installment of *Old Times on the Mississippi,* those readers heard a new voice and should have been electrified by it, just as, in what is surely one of the great passages in American literature, Hannibal, "the white town drowsing in the sunshine of a summer's morning," is electrified into life by the cry of "S-t-e-a-m-boat a-comin'!" The gaudy packet, flying a flag from its

jackstaff and tumbling clouds of black smoke from its
fancy chimney, its paddle wheel churning the water to
foam, pent steam screaming through the valves, was Mark
Twain reasserting his arrival and declaring once and for
all that his surge of power and spectacle derived not from
such streams as the meandering Charles or the sweet Thames
but from "the great Mississippi, the majestic, the magnificent Mississippi, rolling its mile-wide tide along, shining
in the sun".

Justin Kaplan

Cambridge, Massachusetts

# A NOTE ON THE TEXT

With the exceptions of *Old Times on the Mississippi* (reprinted here from seven issues of the *Atlantic Monthly* for
1875) and "Letter to the Earth" (reprinted from *Letters
from the Earth*), the texts followed in this collection are
those of the "Definitive Edition" of *The Writings of Mark
Twain*, edited by Albert Bigelow Paine (New York,
1922–25). Two paragraphs added by Paine to the end of
"The Story of a Speech" have been omitted.

# OLD TIMES ON THE MISSISSIPPI

## I.

When I was a boy, there was but one permanent ambition among my comrades in our village on the west bank of the Mississippi River. That was, to be a steamboatman. We had transient ambitions of other sorts, but they were only transient. When a circus came and went, it left us all burning to become clowns; the first negro minstrel show that came to our section left us all suffering to try that kind of life; now and then we had a hope that if we lived and were good, God would permit us to be pirates. These ambitions faded out, each in its turn; but the ambition to be a steamboatman always remained.

Once a day a cheap, gaudy packet arrived upward from St. Louis, and another downward from Keokuk. Before these events had transpired, the day was glorious with expectancy; after they had transpired, the day was a dead and empty thing. Not only the boys, but the whole village, felt this. After all these years I can picture that old time to myself now, just as it was then: the white town drowsing in the sunshine of a summer's morning; the streets empty, or pretty nearly so; one or two clerks sitting in front of the Water Street stores, with their splint-bottomed chairs tilted back against the wall, chins on breasts, hats slouched over their faces, asleep—with shingle-shavings enough around to show what broke them down; a sow and a litter of pigs loafing along the sidewalk, doing a good business in water-melon rinds and seeds; two or three lonely little freight piles scattered about the "levee;" a pile of "skids" on the slope of the stone-paved wharf, and the fragrant town drunkard asleep in the shadow of them; two or three wood flats at the head of the wharf, but nobody to listen to the peaceful lapping of the wavelets against them; the great Mississippi, the majestic, the magnificent Mississippi, rolling its mile-wide tide along, shining in the sun; the dense forest away on the other side; the "point" above the town, and the "point" below, bounding the river-glimpse and turning it into a sort of sea, and withal a very still and brilliant and lonely one. Presently a film of dark smoke appears above one of those remote "points;" instantly a negro drayman, famous for his quick eye and prodigious voice, lifts up the cry, "S-t-e-a-m-boat a-comin'!" and the scene changes! The town drunkard stirs, the clerks wake up, a furious clatter of drays follows, every house and store pours out a human contribution, and all in a twinkling the dead town is alive and moving. Drays, carts, men, boys, all go hurrying from many quarters to a common centre, the wharf. Assembled there, the people fasten their eyes upon the coming boat as upon a wonder they are seeing for the first time. And the boat *is* rather a handsome sight, too. She is long and sharp and trim and pretty; she has two tall, fancy-topped chimneys, with a gilded device of some kind swung between them; a fanciful pilot-house, all glass and "gingerbread," perched on top of the "texas" deck behind them; the paddle-boxes are gorgeous with a picture or with gilded rays above the boat's name; the boiler deck, the hurricane deck, and the texas deck are fenced and ornamented with clean white railings; there is a flag gallantly flying from the jack-staff; the furnace doors are open and the fires glaring bravely; the upper decks are black with passengers; the captain stands by the big bell, calm, imposing, the envy of all; great volumes of the blackest smoke are rolling and tumbling out of the chimneys—a husbanded grandeur created with a bit of pitch pine just before arriving at a town; the crew are grouped on the forecastle; the broad stage is run far out over the port bow, and an envied deck-hand stands picturesquely on the end of it with a coil of rope in his hand; the pent steam is screaming through the gauge-cocks; the captain lifts his hand, a bell rings, the wheels stop; then they turn back, churning the water to foam, and the steamer is at rest. Then such a scramble as there is to get aboard, and to get ashore, and to take in freight and to discharge freight, all at once and the same time; and such a yelling and cursing as the mates facilitate it all with! Ten minutes later the steamer is under way again, with no flag on the jack-staff and no black smoke issuing from the chimneys. After ten more minutes the town is dead again, and the town drunkard asleep by the skids once more.

My father was a justice of the peace, and I supposed he possessed the power of life and death over all men and could hang anybody that offended him. This was distinction enough for me as a general thing; but the desire to be a steamboatman kept intruding, nevertheless. I first wanted to be a cabin-boy, so that I could come out with a white apron on and shake a table-cloth over the side, where all my old comrades could see me; later I thought I would rather be the deck-hand who stood on the end of the stage-plank with the coil of rope in his hand, because he was particularly conspicuous. But these were only daydreams—they were too heavenly to be contemplated as real possibilities. By and by one of our boys went away. He was not heard of for a long time. At last he turned up as apprentice engineer or "striker" on a steamboat. This thing shook the bottom out of all my Sunday-school teachings. That boy had been notoriously worldly, and I just the reverse; yet he was exalted to this eminence, and I left in obscurity and misery. There was nothing generous about this fellow in his greatness. He would always manage to have a rusty bolt to scrub while his boat tarried at our town, and he would sit on the inside guard and scrub it, where we could all see him and envy him and loathe him. And whenever his boat was laid up he would come home and swell around the town in his blackest and greasiest clothes, so that nobody could help remembering that he was a steamboatman; and he used all sorts of steamboat technicalities in his talk, as if he were so used to them that he forgot common people could not understand them. He would speak of the "labboard" side of a horse in an easy, natural way that would make one wish he was dead. And he was always talking about "St. Looy" like an old citizen; he would refer casually to occasions when he "was coming down Fourth Street," or when he was "passing by the Planter's House," or when there was a fire and he took a turn on the brakes of "the old Big Missouri;" and then he would go on and lie about how many towns the size of ours were burned down there that day. Two or three of the boys had long been persons of consideration among us because they had been to St. Louis once and had a vague general knowledge of its wonders, but the day of their glory was over now. They lapsed into a humble silence, and learned to disappear when the ruthless "cub"-engineer approached. This fellow had money, too, and hair oil. Also an ignorant silver watch and a showy brass watch chain. He wore a leather belt and used no suspenders. If ever a youth was cordially admired and hated by his comrades, this one was. No girl could withstand his charms. He "cut out" every boy in the village. When his boat blew up at last, it diffused a tranquil contentment among us such as we had not known for months. But when he came home the next week, alive, renowned, and appeared in church all battered up and bandaged, a shining hero, stared at and wondered over by everybody, it seemed to us that the partiality of Providence for an undeserving reptile had reached a point where it was open to criticism.

This creature's career could produce but one result, and it speedily followed. Boy after boy managed to get on the river. The minister's son became an engineer. The doctor's and the postmaster's sons became "mud clerks;" the whole-sale liquor dealer's son became a bar-keeper on a boat; four sons of the chief merchant, and two sons of the county judge, became pilots. Pilot was the grandest position of all. The pilot, even in those days of trivial wages, had a princely salary—from a hundred and fifty to two hundred and fifty dollars a month, and no board to pay. Two months of his wages would pay a preacher's salary for a year. Now some of us were left disconsolate. We could not get on the river—at least our parents would not let us.

So by and by I ran away. I said I never would come home again till I was a pilot and could come in glory. But somehow I could not manage it. I went meekly aboard a few of the boats that lay packed together like sardines at the long St. Louis wharf, and very humbly inquired for the pilots, but got only a cold shoulder and short words from mates and clerks. I had to make the best of this sort of treatment for the time being, but I had comforting day-dreams of a future when I should be a great and honored pilot, with plenty of money, and could kill some of these mates and clerks and pay for them.

Months afterward the hope within me struggled to a re-luctant death, and I found myself without an ambition. But I was ashamed to go home. I was in Cincinnati, and I set to work to map out a new career. I had been reading about the recent exploration of the river Amazon by an expedi-tion sent out by our government. It was said that the expedition, owing to difficulties, had not thoroughly explored a part of the country lying about the head-waters, some four thousand miles from the mouth of the river. It was only about fifteen hundred miles from Cincinnati to New Orleans, where I could doubtless get a ship. I had thirty dollars left; I would go and complete the exploration of the Amazon. This was all the thought I gave to the subject. I never was great in matters of detail. I packed my valise, and took passage on an ancient tub called the Paul Jones, for New Orleans. For the sum of sixteen dollars I had the scarred and tarnished splendors of "her" main saloon principally to myself, for she was not a creature to attract the eye of wiser travelers.

When we presently got under way and went poking down the broad Ohio, I became a new being, and the subject of my own admiration. I was a traveler! A word never had tasted so good in my mouth before. I had an exultant sense of being bound for mysterious lands and distant climes which I never have felt in so uplifting a degree since. I was in such a glorified condition that all ignoble feelings departed out of me, and I was able to look down and pity the untraveled with a compassion that had hardly a trace of contempt in it. Still, when we stopped at villages and wood-yards, I could not help lolling carelessly upon the railings of the boiler deck to enjoy the envy of the country boys on the bank. If they did not seem to discover me, I presently sneezed to attract their attention, or moved to a position where they could not help seeing me. And as soon as I knew they saw me I gaped and stretched, and gave other signs of being mightily bored with traveling.

I kept my hat off all the time, and stayed where the wind and the sun could strike me, because I wanted to get the bronzed and weather-beaten look of an old traveler. Before the second day was half gone, I experienced a joy which filled me with the purest gratitude; for I saw that the skin had begun to blister and peel off my face and neck. I wished that the boys and girls at home could see me now.

We reached Louisville in time—at least the neighborhood of it. We stuck hard and fast on the rocks in the middle of the river and lay there four days. I was now beginning to feel a strong sense of being a part of the boat's family, a sort of infant son to the captain and younger brother to the officers. There is no estimating the pride I took in this grandeur, or the affection that began to swell and grow in me for those people. I could not know how the lordly steamboatman scorns that sort of presumption in a mere landsman. I particularly longed to acquire the least trifle of notice from the big stormy mate, and I was on the alert for an opportunity to do him a service to that end. It came at last. The riotous powwow of setting a spar was going on down on the forecastle, and I went down there and stood around in the way—or mostly skipping out of it—till the mate suddenly roared a general order for somebody to bring him a capstan bar. I sprang to his side and said: "Tell me where it is—I'll fetch it!"

If a rag-picker had offered to do a diplomatic service for the Emperor of Russia, the monarch could not have been more astounded than the mate was. He even stopped swearing. He stood and stared down at me. It took him ten seconds to scrape his disjointed remains together again. Then he said impressively: "Well, if this don't beat hell!" and turned to his work with the air of a man who had been confronted with a problem too abstruse for solution.

I crept away, and courted solitude for the rest of the day. I did not go to dinner; I stayed away from supper until everybody else had finished. I did not feel so much like a member of the boat's family now as before. However, my spirits returned, in installments, as we pursued our way down the river. I was sorry I hated the mate so, because it was not in (young) human nature not to admire him. He was huge and muscular, his face was bearded and whiskered all over; he had a red woman and a blue woman tattooed on his right arm,—one on each side of a blue anchor with a red rope to it; and in the matter of profanity he was perfect. When he was getting out cargo at a landing, I was always where I could see and hear. He felt all the sublimity of his great position, and made the world feel it, too. When he gave even the simplest order, he discharged it like a blast of lightning, and sent a long, reverberating peal of profanity thundering after it. I could not help contrasting the way in which the average landsman would give an order, with the mate's way of doing it. If the landsman should wish the gangplank moved a foot farther forward, he would probably say: "James, or William, one of you push that plank forward, please;" but put the mate in his place, and he would roar out: "Here, now, start that gang-plank for'ard! Lively, now! *What*'re you about! Snatch it! *snatch* it! There! there! Aft again! aft again! Don't you hear me? Dash it to dash! are you going to *sleep* over it! 'Vast heaving. 'Vast heaving, I tell you! Going to heave it clear astern? WHERE're you going with that barrel! *for'ard* with it 'fore I make you swallow it, you dash-dash-dash-*dashed* split between a tired mud-turtle and a crippled hearse-horse!"

I wished I could talk like that.

When the soreness of my adventure with the mate had somewhat worn off, I began timidly to make up to the humblest official connected with the boat—the night watchman. He snubbed my advances at first, but I presently ventured to offer him a new chalk pipe, and that softened him. So he allowed me to sit with him by the big bell on the hurricane deck, and in time he melted into conversation. He could not well have helped it, I hung with such homage on his words and so plainly showed that I felt honored by his notice. He told me the names of dim capes and shadowy islands as we glided by them in the solemnity of the night, under the winking stars, and by and by got to talking about himself. He seemed oversentimental for a man whose salary was six dollars a week—or rather he might have seemed so to an older person than I. But I drank in his words hungrily, and with a faith that might have moved mountains if it had been applied judiciously. What was it to me that he was soiled and seedy and fragrant with gin? What was it to me that his grammar was bad, his construction worse, and his profanity so void of art that it was an element of weakness rather than strength in his conversation? He was a wronged man, a man who had seen trouble, and that was enough for me. As he mellowed into his plaintive history his tears dripped upon the lantern in his lap, and I cried, too, from sympathy. He said he was the son of an English nobleman—either an earl or an alderman, he could not remember which, but believed he was both; his father, the nobleman, loved him, but his mother hated him from the cradle; and so while he was still a little boy he was sent to "one of them old, ancient colleges"—he couldn't remember which; and by and by his father died and his mother seized the property and "shook" him, as he phrased it. After his mother shook him, members of the nobility with whom he was acquainted used

their influence to get him the position of "loblolly-boy in
a ship;" and from that point my watchman threw off all
trammels of date and locality and branched out into a
narrative that bristled all along with incredible adventures;
a narrative that was so reeking with bloodshed and so
crammed with hair-breadth escapes and the most engaging
and unconscious personal villainies, that I sat speechless,
enjoying, shuddering, wondering, worshiping.

It was a sore blight to find out afterwards that he was a
low, vulgar, ignorant, sentimental, half-witted humbug,
an untraveled native of the wilds of Illinois, who had
absorbed wildcat literature and appropriated its marvels,
until in time he had woven odds and ends of the mess
into this yarn, and then gone on telling it to fledgelings
like me, until he had come to believe it himself.

## II.

## [A "Cub" Pilot's Experience;
or, Learning the River.]

What with lying on the rocks four days at Louisville, and
some other delays, the poor old Paul Jones fooled away
about two weeks in making the voyage from Cincinnati to
New Orleans. This gave me a chance to get acquainted with
one of the pilots, and he taught me how to steer the boat,
and thus made the fascination of river life more potent
than ever for me.

It also gave me a chance to get acquainted with a youth
who had taken deck passage—more's the pity; for he
easily borrowed six dollars of me on a promise to return
to the boat and pay it back to me the day after we should
arrive. But he probably died or forgot, for he never came.
It was doubtless the former, since he had said his parents
were wealthy, and he only traveled deck passage because it
was cooler.[1]

I soon discovered two things. One was that a vessel would
not be likely to sail for the mouth of the Amazon under
ten or twelve years; and the other was that the nine or
ten dollars still left in my pocket would not suffice for so
imposing an exploration as I had planned, even if I could

[1] "Deck" passage—i.e., steerage passage.

afford to wait for a ship. Therefore it followed that I must contrive a new career. The Paul Jones was now bound for St. Louis. I planned a siege against my pilot, and at the end of three hard days he surrendered. He agreed to teach me the Mississippi River from New Orleans to St. Louis for five hundred dollars, payable out of the first wages I should receive after graduating. I entered upon the small enterprise of "learning" twelve or thirteen hundred miles of the great Mississippi River with the easy confidence of my time of life. If I had really known what I was about to require of my faculties, I should not have had the courage to begin. I supposed that all a pilot had to do was to keep his boat in the river, and I did not consider that that could be much of a trick, since it was so wide.

The boat backed out from New Orleans at four in the afternoon, and it was "our watch" until eight. Mr. B——, my chief, "straightened her up," plowed her along past the sterns of the other boats that lay at the Levee, and then said, "Here, take her; shave those steamships as close as you'd peel an apple." I took the wheel, and my heart went down into my boots; for it seemed to me that we were about to scrape the side off every ship in the line, we were so close. I held my breath and began to claw the boat away from the danger; and I had my own opinion of the pilot who had known no better than to get us into such peril, but I was too wise to express it. In half a minute I had a wide margin of safety intervening between the Paul Jones and the ships; and within ten seconds more I was set aside in disgrace, and Mr. B—— was going into danger again and flaying me alive with abuse of my cowardice. I was stung, but I was obliged to admire the easy confidence with which my chief loafed from side to side of his wheel, and trimmed the ships so closely that disaster seemed ceaselessly imminent. When he had cooled a little he told me that the easy water was close ashore and the current outside, and therefore we must hug the bank, up-stream, to get the benefit of the former, and stay well out, down-stream, to take advantage of the latter. In my own mind I resolved to be a down-stream pilot and leave the up-streaming to people dead to prudence.

Now and then Mr. B—— called my attention to certain things. Said he, "This is Six-Mile Point." I assented. It was pleasant enough information, but I could not see the bearing of it. I was not conscious that it was a matter of any interest to me. Another time he said, "This is Nine-Mile Point." Later he said, "This is Twelve-Mile Point." They were all about level with the water's edge; they all looked about alike to me; they were monotonously unpicturesque. I hoped Mr. B—— would change the subject. But no; he would crowd up around a point, hugging the shore with affection, and then say: "The slack water ends here, abreast this bunch of China-trees; now we cross over." So he crossed over. He gave me the wheel once or twice, but I had no luck. I either came near chipping off the edge of a sugar plantation, or else I yawed too far from shore, and so I dropped back into disgrace again and got abused.

The watch was ended at last, and we took supper and went to bed. At midnight the glare of a lantern shone in my eyes, and the night watchman said:—

"Come! turn out!"

And then he left. I could not understand this extraordinary procedure; so I presently gave up trying to, and dozed off to sleep. Pretty soon the watchman was back again, and this time he was gruff. I was annoyed. I said:—

"What do you want to come bothering around here in the middle of the night for? Now as like as not I'll not get to sleep again to-night."

The watchman said:—

"Well, if this an't good, I'm blest."

The "off-watch" was just turning in, and I heard some brutal laughter from them, and such remarks as "Hello, watchman! an't the new cub turned out yet? He's delicate, likely. Give him some sugar in a rag and send for the chambermaid to sing rock-a-by-baby to him."

About this time Mr. B—— appeared on the scene. Something like a minute later I was climbing the pilot-house steps with some of my clothes on and the rest in my arms. Mr. B—— was close behind, commenting. Here was something fresh—this thing of getting up in the middle of the night to go to work. It was a detail in piloting that had never occurred to me at all. I knew that boats ran all night, but somehow I had never happened to reflect that somebody had to get up out of a warm bed to run them. I began to fear that piloting was not quite so romantic as I had imagined it was; there was something very real and work-like about this new phase of it.

It was a rather dingy night, although a fair number of stars were out. The big mate was at the wheel, and he had the old tub pointed at a star and was holding her straight up the middle of the river. The shores on either hand were not much more than a mile apart, but they seemed wonderfully far away and ever so vague and indistinct. The mate said:—

"We've got to land at Jones's plantation, sir."

The vengeful spirit in me exulted. I said to myself, I wish you joy of your job, Mr. B——; you'll have a good time finding Mr. Jones's plantation such a night as this; and I hope you never *will* find it as long as you live.

Mr. B—— said to the mate:—

"Upper end of the plantation, or the lower?"

"Upper."

"I can't do it. The stumps there are out of water at this stage. It's no great distance to the lower, and you'll have to get along with that."

"All right, sir. If Jones don't like it he'll have to lump it, I reckon."

And then the mate left. My exultation began to cool and my wonder to come up. Here was a man who not only proposed to find this plantation on such a night, but to find either end of it you preferred. I dreadfully wanted to ask a question, but I was carrying about as many short answers as my cargo-room would admit of, so I held my peace. All I desired to ask Mr. B—— was the simple question whether he was ass enough to really imagine he was going to find that plantation on a night when all plantations were exactly alike and all the same color. But I held in. I used to have fine inspirations of prudence in those days.

Mr. B—— made for the shore and soon was scraping it, just the same as if it had been daylight. And not only that, but singing—

"Father in heaven the day is declining," etc.

It seemed to me that I had put my life in the keeping of a peculiarly reckless outcast. Presently he turned on me and said:—

"What's the name of the first point above New Orleans?"

I was gratified to be able to answer promptly, and I did. I said I didn't know.

"Don't *know?*"

This manner jolted me. I was down at the foot again, in a moment. But I had to say just what I had said before.

"Well, you're a smart one," said Mr. B——. "What's the name of the *next* point?"

Once more I didn't know.

"Well this beats anything. Tell me the name of *any* point or place I told you."

I studied a while and decided that I couldn't.

"Look-a-here! What do you start out from, above Twelve-Mile Point, to cross over?"

"I—I—don't know."

"You—you—don't know?" mimicking my drawling manner of speech. "What *do* you know?"

"I—I—nothing, for certain."

"By the great Cæsar's ghost I believe you! You're the stupidest dunderhead I ever saw or ever heard of, so help me Moses! The idea of *you* being a pilot—*you!* Why, you don't know enough to pilot a cow down a lane."

Oh, but his wrath was up! He was a nervous man, and he shuffled from one side of his wheel to the other as if the floor was hot. He would boil a while to himself, and then overflow and scald me again.

"Look-a-here! What do you suppose I told you the names of those points for?"

I tremblingly considered a moment, and then the devil of temptation provoked me to say:—

"Well—to—to—be entertaining, I thought."

This was a red rag to the bull. He raged and stormed so (he was crossing the river at the time) that I judge it made him blind, because he ran over the steering-oar of a trading-scow. Of course the traders sent up a volley of red-hot profanity. Never was a man so grateful as Mr. B—— was: because he was brim full, and here were subjects who would *talk back.* He threw open a window, thrust his head out, and such an irruption followed as I never had heard before. The fainter and farther away the scowmen's curses drifted, the higher Mr. B—— lifted his voice and the weightier his adjectives grew. When he closed the window he was empty. You could have drawn a seine through his system and not caught curses enough to disturb your mother with. Presently he said to me in the gentlest way:—

"My boy, you must get a little memorandum-book, and every time I tell you a thing, put it down right away. There's only one way to be a pilot, and that is to get this entire river by heart. You have to know it just like A B C."

That was a dismal revelation to me; for my memory was never loaded with anything but blank cartridges. However, I did not feel discouraged long. I judged that it was best to make some allowances, for doubtless Mr. B—— was "stretching." Presently he pulled a rope and struck a few strokes on the big bell. The stars were all gone, now, and the night was as black as ink. I could hear the wheels churn along the bank, but I was not entirely certain that I could see the shore. The voice of the invisible watchman called up from the hurricane deck:—

"What's this, sir?"

"Jones's plantation."

I said to myself, I wish I might venture to offer a small bet that it isn't. But I did not chirp. I only waited to see. Mr. B—— handled the engine bells, and in due time the boat's nose came to the land, a torch glowed from the forecastle, a man skipped ashore, a darky's voice on the bank said, "Gimme de carpet-bag, Mars' Jones," and the next moment we were standing up the river again, all serene. I reflected deeply a while, and then said,—but not aloud,—Well, the finding of that plantation was the luckiest accident that ever happened; but it couldn't happen again in a hundred years. And I fully believed it *was* an accident, too.

By the time we had gone seven or eight hundred miles up the river, I had learned to be a tolerably plucky up-stream steersman, in daylight, and before we reached St. Louis I had made a trifle of progress in night-work, but only a trifle. I had a note-book that fairly bristled with the names of towns, "points," bars, islands, bends, reaches, etc.; but the information was to be found only in the note-book —none of it was in my head. It made my heart ache to think I had only got half of the river set down; for as our watch was four hours off and four hours on, day and night, there was a long four-hour gap in my book for every time I had slept since the voyage began.

My chief was presently hired to go on a big New Orleans boat, and I packed my satchel and went with him. She was a grand affair. When I stood in her pilot-house I was so far above the water that I seemed perched on a mountain; and her decks stretched so far away, fore and aft, below me, that I wondered how I could ever have considered the little Paul Jones a large craft. There were other differences, too. The Paul Jones's pilot-house was a cheap, dingy, battered rattle-trap, cramped for room: but here was a sumptuous glass temple; room enough to have a dance in; showy red and gold window-curtains; an imposing sofa; leather cushions and a back to the high bench where visiting pilots sit, to spin yarns and "look at the river;" bright, fanciful "cuspadores" instead of a broad wooden box filled with sawdust; nice new oil-cloth on the floor; a hospitable big stove for winter; a wheel as high as my head, costly with inlaid work; a wire tiller-rope; bright brass knobs for the bells; and a tidy, white-aproned, black "texas-tender," to bring up tarts and ices and coffee during mid-watch, day and night. Now this was "something like;" and so I began to take heart once more to believe that piloting was a romantic sort of occupation after all. The moment we were under way I began to prowl about the great steamer and fill myself with joy. She was as clean and as dainty as a drawing-room; when I looked down her long, gilded saloon, it was like gazing through a splendid tunnel; she had an oil-picture, by some gifted sign-painter, on every state-room door; she glittered with no end of prism-fringed chandeliers; the clerk's office was elegant, the bar was marvelous, and the bar-keeper had been barbered and upholstered at incredible cost. The boiler deck (*i.e.*, the second story of the boat, so to speak) was as spacious as a church, it seemed to me; so with the forecastle; and there was no pitiful handful of deckhands, firemen, and roust-abouts down there, but a whole battalion of men. The fires were fiercely glaring from a long row of furnaces, and over them were eight huge boilers! This was unutterable pomp. The mighty engines—but enough of this. I had never felt so fine before. And when I found that the regiment of natty servants respectfully "sir'd" me, my satisfaction was complete.

When I returned to the pilot-house St. Louis was gone and I was lost. Here was a piece of river which was all down in my book, but I could make neither head nor tail of it: you understand, it was turned around. I had seen it, when coming up-stream, but I had never faced about to see how it looked when it was behind me. My heart broke again, for it was plain that I had got to learn this troublesome river *both ways*.

The pilot-house was full of pilots, going down to "look at the river." What is called the "upper river" (the two hundred miles between St. Louis and Cairo, where the Ohio comes in) was low; and the Mississippi changes its channel so constantly that the pilots used to always find it necessary to run down to Cairo to take a fresh look, when their boats were to lie in port a week, that is, when the water was at a low stage. A deal of this "looking at the river" was done by poor fellows who seldom had a berth, and whose only hope of getting one lay in their being always freshly posted and therefore ready to drop into the shoes of some reputable pilot, for a single trip, on account of such pilot's sudden illness, or some other necessity. And a good many of them constantly ran up and down inspecting the river, not because they ever really hoped to get a berth, but because (they being guests of the boat) it was cheaper to "look at the river" than stay ashore and pay board. In time these fellows grew dainty in their tastes, and only infested boats that had an established reputation for setting good tables. All visiting pilots were useful, for they were always ready and willing, winter or summer, night or day, to go out in the yawl and help buoy the channel or assist the boat's pilots in any way they could. They were likewise welcome because all pilots are tireless talkers, when gathered together, and as they talk only about the river they are always understood and are always interesting. Your true pilot cares nothing about anything on earth but the river, and his pride in his occupation surpasses the pride of kings.

We had a fine company of these river-inspectors along, this trip. There were eight or ten; and there was abundance of room for them in our great pilot-house. Two or three of them wore polished silk hats, elaborate shirt-fronts, diamond breastpins, kid gloves, and patent-leather boots. They were choice in their English, and bore themselves with a dignity proper to men of solid means and prodigious reputation as pilots. The others were more or less loosely clad, and wore upon their heads tall felt cones that were suggestive of the days of the Commonwealth.

I was a cipher in this august company, and felt subdued, not to say torpid. I was not even of sufficient consequence to assist at the wheel when it was necessary to put the tiller hard down in a hurry; the guest that stood nearest did that when occasion required—and this was pretty much all the time, because of the crookedness of the channel and the scant water. I stood in a corner; and the talk I listened to took the hope all out of me. One visitor said to another:—

"Jim, how did you run Plum Point, coming up?"

"It was in the night, there, and I ran it the way one of the boys on the Diana told me; started out about fifty yards above the wood pile on the false point, and held on the cabin under Plum Point till I raised the reef—quarter less twain—then straightened up for the middle bar till I got well abreast the old one-limbed cotton-wood in the bend, then got my stern on the cotton-wood and head on the low place above the point, and came through a-booming —nine and a half."

"Pretty square crossing, ain't it?"

"Yes, but the upper bar's working down fast."

Another pilot spoke up and said:—

"I had better water than that, and ran it lower down; started out from the false point—mark twain—raised the second reef abreast the big snag in the bend, and had quarter less twain."

One of the gorgeous ones remarked: "I don't want to find fault with your leadsmen, but that's a good deal of water for Plum Point, it seems to me."

There was an approving nod all around as this quiet snub dropped on the boaster and "settled" him. And so they went on talk-talk-talking. Meantime, the thing that was running in my mind was, "Now if my ears hear aright, I have not only to get the names of all the towns and islands and bends, and so on, by heart, but I must even get up a warm personal acquaintanceship with every old snag and one-limbed cotton-wood and obscure wood pile that ornaments the banks of this river for twelve hundred miles; and more than that, I must actually know where these things are in the dark, unless these guests are gifted with eyes that can pierce through two miles of solid blackness; I wish the piloting business was in Jericho and I had never thought of it."

At dusk Mr. B—— tapped the big bell three times (the signal to land), and the captain emerged from his drawing-room in the forward end of the texas, and looked up inquiringly. Mr. B—— said:—

"We will lay up here all night, captain."

"Very well, sir."

That was all. The boat came to shore and was tied up for the night. It seemed to me a fine thing that the pilot could do as he pleased without asking so grand a captain's permission. I took my supper and went immediately to bed, discouraged by my day's observations and experiences. My late voyage's note-booking was but a confusion of meaningless names. It had tangled me all up in a knot every time I had looked at it in the daytime. I now hoped for respite in sleep; but no, it reveled all through my head till sunrise again, a frantic and tireless nightmare.

Next morning I felt pretty rusty and low-spirited. We went booming along, taking a good many chances, for we were anxious to "get out of the river" (as getting out to Cairo was called) before night should overtake us. But Mr. B——'s partner, the other pilot, presently grounded the boat, and we lost so much time getting her off that it was plain the darkness would overtake us a good long way above the mouth. This was a great misfortune, especially to certain of our visiting pilots, whose boats would have to wait for their return, no matter how long that might be. It sobered the pilot-house talk a good deal. Coming up-stream, pilots did not mind low water or any kind of darkness; nothing stopped them but fog. But down-stream work was different; a boat was too nearly helpless, with a stiff current pushing behind her; so it was not customary to run down-stream at night in low water.

There seemed to be one small hope, however; if we could

get through the intricate and dangerous Hat Island crossing
before night, we could venture the rest, for we would have
plainer sailing and better water. But it would be insanity
to attempt Hat Island at night. So there was a deal of looking at watches all the rest of the day, and a constant cipher-
ing upon the speed we were making; Hat Island was the
eternal subject; sometimes hope was high and sometimes we
were delayed in a bad crossing, and down it went again.
For hours all hands lay under the burden of this suppressed
excitement; it was even communicated to me, and I got to
feeling so solicitous about Hat Island, and under such an
awful pressure of responsibility, that I wished I might have
five minutes on shore to draw a good, full, relieving breath,
and start over again. We were standing no regular watches.
Each of our pilots ran such portions of the river as he
had run when coming up-stream, because of his greater
familiarity with it; but both remained in the pilot-house
constantly.

An hour before sunset, Mr. B—— took the wheel
and Mr. W—— stepped aside. For the next thirty minutes
every man held his watch in his hand and was restless,
silent, and uneasy. At last somebody said, with a doomful
sigh:

"Well, yonder's Hat Island—and we can't make it."

All the watches closed with a snap, everybody sighed and
muttered something about its being "too bad, too bad—ah,
if we could *only* have got here half an hour sooner!" and
the place was thick with the atmosphere of disappointment.
Some started to go out, but loitered, hearing no bell-tap to
land. The sun dipped behind the horizon, the boat went on.
Inquiring looks passed from one guest to another; and one
who had his hand on the doorknob, and had turned it,
waited, then presently took away his hand and let the knob
turn back again. We bore steadily down the bend. More
looks were exchanged, and nods of surprised admiration—
but no words. Insensibly the men drew together behind Mr.
B—— as the sky darkened and one or two dim stars came
out. The dead silence and sense of waiting became oppres-
sive. Mr. B—— pulled the cord, and two deep, mellow notes

from the big bell floated off on the night. Then a pause, and one more note was struck. The watchman's voice followed, from the hurricane deck:—

"Labboard lead, there! Stabboard lead!"

The cries of the leadsmen began to rise out of the distance, and were gruffly repeated by the word-passers on the hurricane deck.

"M-a-r-k three! M-a-r-k three! Quarter-less-three! Half-twain! Quarter twain! M-a-r-k twain! Quarter-less"—

Mr. B—— pulled two bell-ropes, and was answered by faint jinglings far below in the engine-room, and our speed slackened. The steam began to whistle through the gauge-cocks. The cries of the leadsmen went on—and it is a weird sound, always, in the night. Every pilot in the lot was watching, now, with fixed eyes, and talking under his breath. Nobody was calm and easy but Mr. B——. He would put his wheel down and stand on a spoke, and as the steamer swung into her (to me) utterly invisible marks—for we seemed to be in the midst of a wide and gloomy sea—he would meet and fasten her there. Talk was going on, now, in low voices:—

"There; she's over the first reef all right!"

After a pause, another subdued voice:—

"Her stern's coming down just *exactly* right, by *George*! Now she's in the marks; over she goes!"

Somebody else muttered:—

"Oh, it was done beautiful—*beautiful!*"

Now the engines were stopped altogether, and we drifted with the current. Not that I could see the boat drift, for I could not, the stars being all gone by this time. This drifting was the dismalest work; it held one's heart still. Presently I discovered a blacker gloom than that which surrounded us. It was the head of the island. We were closing right down upon it. We entered its deeper shadow, and so imminent seemed the peril that I was likely to suffocate; and I had the strongest impulse to do *something*, anything, to save the vessel. But still Mr. B—— stood by his wheel, silent, intent as a cat, and all the pilots stood shoulder to shoulder at his back.

"She'll not make it!" somebody whispered.

The water grew shoaler and shoaler by the leadsmen's cries, till it was down to—

"Eight-and-a-half! E-i-g-h-t feet! E-i-g-h-t feet! Seven-and"—

Mr. B—— said warningly through his speaking tube to the engineer:—

"Stand by, now!"

"Aye-aye, sir."

"Seven-and-a-half! Seven feet! *Six*-and"—

We touched bottom! Instantly Mr. B—— set a lot of bells ringing, shouted through the tube, "*Now* let her have it—every ounce you've got!" then to his partner, "Put her hard down! snatch her! snatch her!" The boat rasped and ground her way through the sand, hung upon the apex of disaster a single tremendous instant, and then over she went! And such a shout as went up at Mr. B——'s back never loosened the roof of a pilot-house before!

There was no more trouble after that. Mr. B—— was a hero that night; and it was some little time, too, before his exploit ceased to be talked about by river men.

Fully to realize the marvelous precision required in laying the great steamer in her marks in that murky waste of water, one should know that not only must she pick her intricate way through snags and blind reefs, and then shave the head of the island so closely as to brush the overhanging foliage with her stern, but at one place she must pass almost within arm's reach of a sunken and invisible wreck that would snatch the hull timbers from under her if she should strike it, and destroy a quarter of a million dollars' worth of steamboat and cargo in five minutes, and maybe a hundred and fifty human lives into the bargain.

The last remark I heard that night was a compliment to Mr. B——, uttered in soliloquy and with unction by one of our guests. He said:—

"By the Shadow of Death, but he's a lightning pilot!"

# III.
# [The Continued Perplexities
of "Cub" Piloting.]

At the end of what seemed a tedious while, I had managed to pack my head full of islands, towns, bars, "points,"
and bends; and a curiously inanimate mass of lumber it
was, too. However, inasmuch as I could shut my eyes and
reel off a good long string of these names without leaving
out more than ten miles of river in every fifty, I began to
feel that I could take a boat down to New Orleans if I
could make her skip those little gaps. But of course my
complacency could hardly get start enough to lift my nose
a trifle into the air, before Mr. B—— would think of something to fetch it down again. One day he turned on me
suddenly with this settler:—

"What is the shape of Walnut Bend?"

He might as well have asked me my grandmother's opinion of protoplasm. I reflected respectfully, and then said
I didn't know it had any particular shape. My gunpowdery
chief went off with a bang, of course, and then went on
loading and firing until he was out of adjectives.

I had learned long ago that he only carried just so many
rounds of ammunition, and was sure to subside into a very
placable and even remorseful old smooth-bore as soon as
they were all gone. That word "old" is merely affectionate;
he was not more than thirty-four. I waited. By and by he
said,—

"My boy, you've got to know the *shape* of the river perfectly. It is all there is left to steer by on a very dark night.
Everything else is blotted out and gone. But mind you, it
hasn't the same shape in the night that it has in the daytime."

"How on earth am I ever going to learn it, then?"

"How do you follow a hall at home in the dark? Because you know the shape of it. You can't see it."

"Do you mean to say that I've got to know all the million

trifling variations of shape in the banks of this interminable river as well as I know the shape of the front hall at home?"

"On my honor you've got to know them *better* than any man ever did know the shapes of the halls in his own house."

"I wish I was dead!"

"Now I don't want to discourage you, but"—

"Well, pile it on me; I might as well have it now as another time."

"You see, this has got to be learned; there isn't any getting around it. A clear starlight night throws such heavy shadows that if you didn't know the shape of a shore perfectly you would claw away from every bunch of timber, because you would take the black shadow of it for a solid cape; and you see you would be getting scared to death every fifteen minutes by the watch. You would be fifty yards from shore all the time when you ought to be within twenty feet of it. You can't see a snag in one of those shadows, but you know exactly where it is, and the shape of the river tells you when you are coming to it. Then there's your pitch dark night; the river is a very different shape on a pitch dark night from what it is on a starlight night. All shores seem to be straight lines, then, and mighty dim ones, too; and you'd *run* them for straight lines, only you know better. You boldly drive your boat right into what seems to be a solid, straight wall (you knowing very well that in reality there is a curve there), and that wall falls back and makes way for you. Then there's your gray mist. You take a night when there's one of these grisly, drizzly, gray mists, and then there isn't *any* particular shape to a shore. A gray mist would tangle the head of the oldest man that ever lived. Well, then, different kinds of *moonlight* change the shape of the river in different ways. You see"—

"Oh, don't say any more, please! Have I got to learn the shape of the river according to all these five hundred thousand different ways? If I tried to carry all that cargo in my head it would make me stoop-shouldered."

"*No!* you only learn *the* shape of the river; and you learn it with such absolute certainty that you can always steer by the shape that's *in your head,* and never mind the one that's before your eyes."

"Very well, I'll try it; but after I have learned it can I depend on it? Will it keep the same form and not go fooling around?"

Before Mr. B—— could answer, Mr. W—— came in to take the watch, and he said,—

"B——, you'll have to look out for President's Island and all that country clear away up above the Old Hen and Chickens. The banks are caving and the shape of the shores changing like everything. Why, you wouldn't know the point above 40. You can go up inside the old sycamore snag, now." [1]

So that question was answered. Here were leagues of shore changing shape. My spirits were down in the mud again. Two things seemed pretty apparent to me. One was, that in order to be a pilot a man had got to learn more than any one man ought to be allowed to know; and the other was, that he must learn it all over again in a different way every twenty-four hours.

That night we had the watch until twelve. Now it was an ancient river custom for the two pilots to chat a bit when the watch changed. While the relieving pilot put on his gloves and lit his cigar, his partner, the retiring pilot, would say something like this:—

"I judge the upper bar is making down a little at Hale's Point; had quarter twain with the lower lead and mark twain[2] with the other."

"Yes, I thought it was making down a little, last trip. Meet any boats?"

"Met one abreast the head of 21, but she was away over hugging the bar, and I couldn't make her out entirely. I took her for the Sunny South—hadn't any skylights forward of the chimneys."

And so on. And as the relieving pilot took the wheel his partner[3] would mention that we were in such-and-such a bend, and say we were abreast of such-and-such a man's wood-yard or plantation. This was courtesy; I supposed it was *necessity*. But Mr. W—— came on watch full twelve minutes late, on this particular night—a tremendous breach

---

[1] It may not be necessary, but still it can do no harm to explain that "inside" means between the snag and the shore.
[2] Two fathoms. Quarter twain is 2¼ fathoms, 13½ feet. Mark three is three fathoms.
[3] "Partner" is technical for "the other pilot."

of etiquette; in fact, it is the unpardonable sin among pilots. So Mr. B—— gave him no greeting whatever, but simply surrendered the wheel and marched out of the pilot-house without a word. I was appalled; it was a villainous night for blackness, we were in a particularly wide and blind part of the river, where there was no shape or substance to anything, and it seemed incredible that Mr. B—— should have left that poor fellow to kill the boat trying to find out where he was. But I resolved that I would stand by him any way. He should find that he was not wholly friendless. So I stood around, and waited to be asked where we were. But Mr. W—— plunged on serenely through the solid firmament of black cats that stood for an atmosphere, and never opened his mouth. Here is a proud devil, thought I; here is a limb of Satan that would rather send us all to destruction that put himself under obligations to me, because I am not yet one of the salt of the earth and privileged to snub captains and lord it over everything dead and alive in a steamboat. I presently climbed up on the bench; I did not think it was safe to go to sleep while this lunatic was on watch.

However, I must have gone to sleep in the course of time, because the next thing I was aware of was the fact that day was breaking, Mr. W—— gone, and Mr. B—— at the wheel again. So it was four o'clock and all well—but me; I felt like a skinful of dry bones and all of them trying to ache at once.

Mr. B—— asked me what I had stayed up there for. I confessed that it was to do Mr. W—— a benevolence: tell him where he was. It took five minutes for the entire preposterousness of the thing to filter into Mr. B——'s system, and then I judge it filled him nearly up to the chin; because he paid me a compliment—and not much of a one either. He said,—

"Well, taking you by-and-large, you do seem to be more different kinds of an ass than any creature I ever saw before. What did you suppose he wanted to know for?"

I said I thought it might be a convenience to him.

"Convenience! Dash! Didn't I tell you that a man's got to know the river in the night the same as he'd know his own front hall?"

"Well, I can follow the front hall in the dark if I know it *is* the front hall; but suppose you set me down in the middle of it in the dark and not tell me which hall it is; how am *I* to know?"

"Well, you've *got* to, on the river!"

"All right. Then I'm glad I never said anything to Mr. W——."

"I should say so. Why, he'd have slammed you through the window and utterly ruined a hundred dollars' worth of window-sash and stuff."

I was glad this damage had been saved, for it would have made me unpopular with the owners. They always hated anybody who had the name of being careless, and injuring things.

I went to work, now, to learn the shape of the river; and of all the eluding and ungraspable objects that ever I tried to get mind or hands on, that was the chief. I would fasten my eyes upon a sharp, wooded point that projected far into the river some miles ahead of me, and go to laboriously photographing its shape upon my brain; and just as I was beginning to succeed to my satisfaction, we would draw up toward it and the exasperating thing would begin to melt away and fold back into the bank! If there had been a conspicuous dead tree standing upon the very point of the cape, I would find that tree inconspicuously merged into the general forest, and occupying the middle of a straight shore, when I got abreast of it! No prominent hill would stick to its shape long enough for me to make up my mind what its form really was, but it was as dissolving and changeful as if it had been a mountain of butter in the hottest corner of the tropics. Nothing ever had the same shape when I was coming down-stream that it had borne when I went up. I mentioned these little difficulties to Mr. B——. He said,—

"That's the very main virtue of the thing. If the shapes didn't change every three seconds they wouldn't be of any use. Take this place where we are now, for instance. As long as that hill over yonder is only one hill, I can boom right along the way I'm going; but the moment it splits at the top and forms a V, I know I've got to scratch to starboard in a hurry, or I'll bang this boat's brains out against a rock; and then the moment one of the prongs of the V swings behind the other, I've got to waltz to larboard again, or I'll have a misunderstanding with a snag that would snatch the keelson out of this steamboat as neatly as if it were a sliver in your hand. If that hill didn't change its shape on bad nights there would be an awful steamboat grave-yard around here inside of a year."

It was plain that I had got to learn the shape of the river in all the different ways that could be thought of,— upside down, wrong end first, inside out, fore-and-aft, and "thortships,"—and then know what to do on gray nights when it hadn't any shape at all. So I set about it. In the course of time I began to get the best of this knotty lesson, and my self-complacency moved to the front once more. Mr. B—— was all fixed, and ready to start it to the rear again. He opened on me after this fashion:—

"How much water did we have in the middle crossing at Hole-in-the-Wall, trip before last?"

I considered this an outrage. I said:

"Every trip, down and up, the leadsmen are singing through that tangled place for three quarters of an hour on a stretch. How do you reckon I can remember such a mess as that?"

"My boy, you've got to remember it. You've got to remember the exact spot and the exact marks the boat lay in when we had the shoalest water, in every one of the two thousand shoal places between St. Louis and New Orleans; and you mustn't get the shoal soundings and marks of one trip mixed up with the shoal soundings and marks of another, either, for they're not often twice alike. You must keep them separate."

When I came to myself again, I said,—

"When I get so that I can do that, I'll be able to raise the dead, and then I won't have to pilot a steamboat in order to make a living. I want to retire from this business. I want a slushbucket and a brush; I'm only fit for a roustabout. I haven't got brains enough to be a pilot; and if I had I wouldn't have strength enough to carry them around, unless I went on crutches."

"Now drop that! When I say I'll learn[1] a man the river, I mean it. And you can depend on it I'll learn him or kill him."

There was no use in arguing with a person like this. I promptly put such a strain on my memory that by and

[1] "Teach" is not in the river vocabulary.

by even the shoal water and the countless crossing-marks began to stay with me. But the result was just the same. I never could more than get one knotty thing learned before another presented itself. Now I had often seen pilots gazing at the water and pretending to read it as if it were a book; but it was a book that told me nothing. A time came at last, however, when Mr. B—— seemed to think me far enough advanced to bear a lesson on water-reading. So he began:—

"Do you see that long slanting line on the face of the water? Now that's a reef. Moreover, it's a bluff reef. There is a solid sand-bar under it that is nearly as straight up and down as the side of a house. There is plenty of water close up to it, but mighty little on top of it. If you were to hit it you would knock the boat's brains out. Do you see where the line fringes out at the upper end and begins to fade away?"

"Yes, sir."

"Well, that is a low place; that is the head of the reef. You can climb over there, and not hurt anything. Cross over, now, and follow along close under the reef—easy water there—not much current."

I followed the reef along till I approached the fringed end. Then Mr. B—— said,—

"Now get ready. Wait till I give the word. She won't want to mount the reef; a boat hates shoal water. Stand by—wait—wait—keep her well in hand. *Now* cramp her down! Snatch her! snatch her!"

He seized the other side of the wheel and helped to spin it around until it was hard down, and then we held it so. The boat resisted and refused to answer for a while, and next she came surging to starboard, mounted the reef, and sent a long, angry ridge of water foaming away from her bows.

"Now watch her; watch her like a cat, or she'll get away from you. When she fights strong and the tiller slips a little, in a jerky, greasy sort of way, let up on her a trifle; it is the way she tells you at night that the water is too shoal; but keep edging her up, little by little, toward the point. You are well up on the bar, now; there is a bar under every point, because the water that comes down around it forms an eddy and allows the sediment to sink. Do you see those fine lines on the face of the water that branch

out like the ribs of a fan? Well, those are little reefs; you
want to just miss the ends of them, but run them pretty
close. Now look out—look out! Don't you crowd that slick,
greasy-looking place; there ain't nine feet there; she won't
stand it. She begins to smell it; look sharp, I tell you! Oh
blazes, there you go! Stop the starboard wheel! Quick! Ship
up to back! Set her back!"

The engine bells jingled and the engines answered
promptly, shooting white columns of steam far aloft out
of the scape pipes, but it was too late. The boat had
"smelt" the bar in good earnest; the foamy ridges that
radiated from her bows suddenly disappeared, a great dead
swell came rolling forward and swept ahead of her, she
careened far over to larboard, and went tearing away toward the other shore as if she were about scared to death.
We were a good mile from where we ought to have been,
when we finally got the upper hand of her again.

During the afternoon watch the next day, Mr. B——
asked me if I knew how to run the next few miles. I said:—

"Go inside the first snag above the point, outside the
next one, start out from the lower end of Higgins's wood-
yard, make a square crossing and"—

"That's all right. I'll be back before you close up on
the next point."

But he wasn't. He was still below when I rounded it
and entered upon a piece of river which I had some misgivings about. I did not know that he was hiding behind
a chimney to see how I would perform. I went gayly along,
getting prouder and prouder, for he had never left the
boat in my sole charge such a length of time before. I even
got to "setting" her and letting the wheel go, entirely,
while I vaingloriously turned my back and inspected the
stern marks and hummed a tune, a sort of easy indifference
which I had prodigiously admired in B—— and other
great pilots. Once I inspected rather long, and when I
faced to the front again my heart flew into my mouth so
suddenly that if I hadn't clapped my teeth together I
would have lost it. One of those frightful bluff reefs was
stretching its deadly length right across our bows! My
head was gone in a moment; I did not know which end
I stood on; I gasped and could not get my breath; I spun
the wheel down with such rapidity that it wove itself together like a spider's web; the boat answered and turned

square away from the reef, but the reef followed her!
I fled, and still it followed—still it kept right across my
bows! I never looked to see where I was going, I only fled.
The awful crash was imminent—why didn't that villain
come! If I committed the crime of ringing a bell, I might
get thrown overboard. But better that than kill the boat.
So in blind desperation I started such a rattling "shivaree"
down below as never had astounded an engineer in this
world before, I fancy. Amidst the frenzy of the bells the
engines began to back and fill in a furious way, and my
reason forsook its throne—we were about to crash into the
woods on the other side of the river. Just then Mr. B——
stepped calmly into view on the hurricane deck. My soul
went out to him in gratitude. My distress vanished; I
would have felt safe on the brink of Niagara, with Mr.
B—— on the hurricane deck. He blandly and sweetly took
his tooth-pick out of his mouth between his fingers, as if
it were a cigar,—we were just in the act of climbing an
overhanging big tree, and the passengers were scudding
astern like rats,—and lifted up these commands to me
ever so gently:—

"Stop the starboard. Stop the larboard. Set her back on
both."

The boat hesitated, halted, pressed her nose among the
boughs a critical instant, then reluctantly began to back
away.

"Stop the larboard. Come ahead on it. Stop the starboard. Come ahead on it. Point her for the bar."

I sailed away as serenely as a summer's morning. Mr.
B—— came in and said, with mock simplicity,—

"When you have a hail, my boy, you ought to tap the
big bell three times before you land, so that the engineers
can get ready."

I blushed under the sarcasm, and said I hadn't had
any hail.

"Ah! Then it was for wood, I suppose. The officer of the
watch will tell you when he wants to wood up."

I went on consuming, and said I wasn't after wood.

"Indeed? Why, what could you want over here in the
bend, then? Did you ever know of a boat following a bend
up-stream at this stage of the river?"

"No, sir,—and *I* wasn't trying to follow it. I was getting
away from a bluff reef."

"No, it wasn't a bluff reef; there isn't one within three miles of where you were."

"But I saw it. It was as bluff as that one yonder."

"Just about. Run over it!"

"Do you give it as an order?"

"Yes. Run over it."

"If I don't, I wish I may die."

"All right; I am taking the responsibility."

I was just as anxious to kill the boat, now, as I had been to save her before. I impressed my orders upon my memory, to be used at the inquest, and made a straight break for the reef. As it disappeared under our bows I held my breath; but we slid over it like oil.

"Now don't you see the difference? It wasn't anything but a wind reef. The wind does that."

"So I see. But it is exactly like a bluff reef. How am I ever going to tell them apart?"

"I can't tell you. It is an instinct. By and by you will just naturally *know* one from the other, but you never will be able to explain why or how you know them apart."

It turned out to be true. The face of the water, in time, became a wonderful book—a book that was a dead language to the uneducated passenger, but which told its mind to me without reserve, delivering its most cherished secrets as clearly as if it uttered them with a voice. And it was not a book to be read once and thrown aside, for it had a new story to tell every day. Throughout the long twelve hundred miles there was never a page that was void of interest, never one that you could leave unread without loss, never one that you would want to skip, thinking you could find higher enjoyment in some other thing. There never was so wonderful a book written by man; never one whose interest was so absorbing, so unflagging, so sparklingly renewed with every re-perusal. The passenger who could not read it was charmed with a peculiar sort of faint dimple on its surface (on the rare occasions when he did not overlook it altogether); but to the pilot that was an *italicized* passage; indeed, it was more than that, it was a legend of the largest capitals with a string of shouting exclamation points at the end of it; for it meant that a wreck or a rock was buried there that could tear the life out of the strongest vessel that ever floated. It is the faintest and simplest expression the water ever makes, and the most hideous to a pilot's eye. In truth, the passenger who could not read this book saw nothing but all manner of pretty pictures in it, painted by the sun and shaded by the clouds, whereas to the trained eye these were not pictures at all, but the grimmest and most dead-earnest of reading-matter.

Now when I had mastered the language of this water and had come to know every trifling feature that bordered the great river as familiarly as I knew the letters of the alphabet, I had made a valuable acquisition. But I had lost something, too. I had lost something which could never be restored to me while I lived. All the grace, the beauty, the poetry had gone out of the majestic river! I still keep in mind a certain wonderful sunset which I witnessed when steamboating was new to me. A broad expanse of the river was turned to blood; in the middle distance the red hue brightened into gold, through which a solitary log came floating, black and conspicuous; in one place a long, slanting mark lay sparkling upon the water; in another the surface was broken by boiling, tumbling rings, that were as many-tinted as an opal; where the ruddy flush was faintest, was a smooth spot that was covered with graceful circles and radiating lines, ever so delicately traced; the shore on our left was densely wooded, and the sombre shadow that fell from this forest was broken in one place by a long, ruffled trail that shone like silver; and high above the forest wall a clean-stemmed dead tree waved a single leafy bough that glowed like a flame in the unobstructed splendor that was flowing from the sun. There were graceful curves, reflected images, woody heights, soft distances; and over the whole scene, far and near, the dissolving lights drifted steadily, enriching it. every passing moment, with new marvels of coloring.

I stood like one bewitched. I drank it in, in a speechless rapture. The world was new to me, and I had never seen anything like this at home. But as I have said, a day came when I began to cease noting the glories and the charms which the moon and the sun and the twilight wrought upon the river's face; another day came when I ceased altogether to note them. Then, if that sunset scene had been repeated, I would have looked upon it without rapture, and would have commented upon it, inwardly, after this fashion: This sun means that we are going to have wind to-morrow; that floating log means that the river is rising, small thanks to it; that slanting mark on the water refers to a bluff reef which is going to kill somebody's steamboat one of these nights, if it keeps on stretching out like that; those tumbling "boils" show a dissolving bar and a changing channel there; the lines and circles in the slick water over yonder are a warning that that execrable place is shoaling up dangerously; that silver streak in the shadow of the forest is the "break" from a new snag, and he has located himself in the very best place he could have found to fish for steamboats; that tall, dead tree, with a single living branch, is not going to last long, and then how is a body ever going to get through this blind place at night without the friendly old landmark?

No, the romance and the beauty were all gone from the river. All the value any feature of it had for me now was the amount of usefulness it could furnish toward compassing the safe piloting of a steamboat. Since those days, I have pitied doctors from my heart. What does the lovely flush in a beauty's cheek mean to a doctor but a "break" that ripples above some deadly disease? Are not all her visible charms sown thick with what are to him the signs and symbols of hidden decay? Does he ever see her beauty at all, or doesn't he simply view her professionally, and comment upon her unwholesome condition all to himself? And doesn't he sometimes wonder whether he has gained most or lost most by learning his trade?

## IV.

## [The "Cub" Pilot's Education Nearly Completed.]

Whosoever has done me the courtesy to read my chapters which have preceded this may possibly wonder that I deal so minutely with piloting as a science. It was the prime purpose of these articles; and I am not quite done yet. I wish to show, in the most patient and painstaking way, what a wonderful science it is. Ship channels are buoyed and lighted, and therefore it is a comparatively easy undertaking to learn to run them; clear-water rivers, with gravel bottoms, change their channels very gradually, and therefore one needs to learn them but once; but piloting becomes another matter when you apply it to vast streams like the Mississippi and the Missouri, whose alluvial banks cave and change constantly, whose snags are always hunting up new quarters, whose sand-bars are never at rest, whose channels are forever dodging and shirking, and whose obstructions must be confronted in all nights and all weathers without the aid of a single light-house or a single buoy; for there is neither light nor buoy to be found anywhere in all this three or four thousand miles of villainous river. I feel justified in enlarging upon this great science for the reason that I feel sure no one has ever yet written a paragraph about it who had piloted a steamboat himself, and so had a practical knowledge of the subject. If the theme were hackneyed, I should be obliged to deal gently with the reader; but since it is wholly new, I have felt at liberty to take up a considerable degree of room with it.

When I had learned the name and position of every visible feature of the river; when I had so mastered its shape that I could shut my eyes and trace it from St. Louis to New Orleans; when I had learned to read the face of the water as one would cull the news from the morning paper; and finally, when I had trained my dull memory to treasure up an endless array of soundings and crossing-marks, and keep fast hold of them, I judged that my education was complete: so I got to tilting my cap to the side of my head, and wearing a tooth-pick in my mouth at the wheel. Mr. B—— had his eye on these airs. One day he said,—

"What is the height of that bank yonder, at Burgess's?"

"How can I tell, sir? It is three quarters of a mile away."

"Very poor eye—very poor. Take the glass."

I took the glass, and presently said,—

"I can't tell. I suppose that that bank is about a foot and a half high."

"Foot and a half! That's a six-foot bank. How high was the bank along here last trip?"

"I don't know; I never noticed."

"You didn't? Well, you must always do it hereafter."

"Why?"

"Because you'll have to know a good many things that it tells you. For one thing, it tells you the stage of the river—tells you whether there's more water or less in the river along here than there was last trip."

"The leads tell me that." I rather thought I had the advantage of him there.

"Yes, but suppose the leads lie? The bank would tell you so, and then you'd stir those leadsmen up a bit. There was a ten-foot bank here last trip, and there is only a six-foot bank now. What does that signify?"

"That the river is four feet higher than it was last trip."

"Very good. Is the river rising or falling?"

"Rising."

"No it ain't."

"I guess I am right, sir. Yonder is some drift-wood floating down the stream."

"A rise *starts* the drift-wood, but then it keeps on floating a while after the river is done rising. Now the bank will tell you about this. Wait till you come to a place where it shelves a little. Now here; do you see this narrow belt of fine sediment? That was deposited while the water was higher. You see the drift-wood begins to strand, too. The bank helps in other ways. Do you see that stump on the false point?"

"Ay, ay, sir."

"Well, the water is just up to the roots of it. You must make a note of that."

"Why?"

"Because that means that there's seven feet in the chute of 103."

"But 103 is a long way up the river yet."

"That's where the benefit of the bank comes in. There is water enough in 103 *now*, yet there may not be by the time we get there; but the bank will keep us posted all along. You don't run close chutes on a falling river, up-stream, and there are precious few of them that you are allowed to run at all down-stream. There's a law of the United States against it. The river may be rising by the time we get to 103, and in that case we'll run it. We are drawing—how much?"

"Six feet aft,—six and a half forward."

"Well, you do seem to know something."

"But what I particularly want to know is, if I have got to keep up an everlasting measuring of the banks of this river, twelve hundred miles, month in and month out?"

"Of course!"

My emotions were too deep for words for a while. Presently I said,—

"And how about these chutes? Are there many of them?"

"I should say so. I fancy we shan't run any of the river this trip as you've ever seen it run before—so to speak. If the river begins to rise again, we'll go up behind bars that you've always seen standing out of the river, high and dry like the roof a house; we'll cut across low places that you've never noticed at all, right through the middle of bars that cover fifty acres of river; we'll creep through cracks where you've always thought was solid land; we'll dart through the woods and leave twenty-five miles of river off to one side; we'll see the hind-side of every island between New Orleans and Cairo."

"Then I've got to go to work and learn just as much more river as I already know."

"Just about twice as much more, as near as you can come at it."

"Well, one lives to find out. I think I was a fool when I went into this business."

"Yes, that is true. And you are yet. But you'll not be when you've learned it."

"Ah, I never can learn it."

"I will see that you *do*."

By and by I ventured again:—

"Have I got to learn all this thing just as I know the rest of the river—shapes and all—and so I can run it at night?"

"Yes. And you've got to have good fair marks from one end of the river to the other, that will help the bank tell you when there is water enough in each of these countless places,—like that stump, you know. When the river first begins to rise, you can run half a dozen of the deepest of them; when it rises a foot more you can run another dozen; the next foot will add a couple of dozen, and so on: so you see you have to know your banks and marks to a dead moral certainty, and never get them mixed; for when you start through one of those cracks, there's no backing out again, as there is in the big river; you've got to go through, or stay there six months if you get caught on a falling river. There are about fifty of these cracks which you can't run at all except when the river is brim full and over the banks."

"This new lesson is a cheerful prospect."

"Cheerful enough. And mind what I've just told you; when you start into one of those places you've got to go through. They are too narrow to turn around in, too crooked to back out of, and the shoal water is always *up at the head;* never elsewhere. And the head of them is always likely to be filling up, little by little, so that the marks you reckon their depth by, this season, may not answer for next."

"Learn a new set, then, every year?"

"Exactly. Cramp her up to the bar! What are you standing up through the middle of the river for?"

The next few months showed me strange things. On the same day that we held the conversation above narrated, we met a great rise coming down the river. The whole vast face of the stream was black with drifting dead logs, broken boughs, and great trees that had caved in and been washed away. It required the nicest steering to pick one's way through this rushing raft, even in the day-time, when crossing from point to point; and at night the difficulty was mightily increased; every now and then a huge log, lying deep in the water, would suddenly appear right under our bows, coming head-on; no use to try to avoid it then; we could only stop the engines, and one wheel would walk over that log from one end to the other, keeping up a thundering racket and careening the boat in a way that was very uncomfortable to passengers. Now and then we would hit one of these sunken logs a rattling bang, dead in the centre, with a full head of steam, and it would stun the boat as if she had hit a continent. Sometimes this log would lodge and stay right across our nose, and back the Mississippi up before it; we would have to do a little craw-fishing, then, to get away from the obstruction. We often hit *white* logs, in the dark, for we could not see them till we were right on them; but a black log is a pretty distinct object at night. A white snag is an ugly customer when the daylight is gone.

Of course, on the great rise, down came a swarm of prodigious timber-rafts from the head waters of the Mississippi, coal barges from Pittsburgh, little trading scows from everywhere, and broadhorns from "Posey County," Indiana, freighted with "fruit and furniture"—the usual term for describing it, though in plain English the freight thus aggrandized was hoop-poles and pumpkins. Pilots bore a mortal hatred to these craft; and it was returned with usury. The law required all such helpless traders to keep a light burning, but it was a law that was often broken. All of a sudden, on a murky night, a light would hop up, right under our bows, almost, and an agonized voice, with the backwoods "whang" to it, would wail out:

"Whar 'n the —— you goin' to! Cain't you see nothin', you dash-dashed aig-suckin', sheep-stealin', one-eyed son of a stuffed monkey!"

Then for an instant, as we whistled by, the red glare from our furnaces would reveal the scow and the form of the gesticulating orator as if under a lightning-flash, and in that instant our firemen and deck-hands would send and receive a tempest of missiles and profanity, one of our wheels would walk off with the crashing fragments of a steering-oar, and down the dead blackness would shut again. And that flatboatman would be sure to go into New Orleans and sue our boat, swearing stoutly that he had a light burning all the time, when in truth his gang had the lantern down below to sing and lie and drink and gamble by, and no watch on deck. Once, at night, in one of those forest-bordered crevices (behind an island) which steamboatmen intensely describe with the phrase "as dark as the inside of a cow," we should have eaten up a Posey County family, fruit, furniture, and all, but that they happened to be fiddling down below and we just caught the sound of the music in time to sheer off, doing no serious damage, unfortunately, but coming so near it that we had good hopes for a moment. Those people brought up their lantern, then, of course; and as we backed and filled to get away, the precious family stood in the light of it—both sexes and various ages—and cursed us till everything turned blue. Once a coal-boatman sent a bullet through our pilot-house when we borrowed a steering-oar of him, in a very narrow place.

During this big rise these small-fry craft were an intolerable nuisance. We were running chute after chute,—a new world to me,—and if there was a particularly cramped place in a chute, we would be pretty sure to meet a broadhorn there; and if he failed to be there, we would find him in a still worse locality, namely, the head of the chute, on the shoal water. And then there would be no end of profane cordialities exchanged.

Sometimes, in the big river, when we would be feeling our way cautiously along through a fog, the deep hush would suddenly be broken by yells and a clamor of tin pans, and all in an instant a log raft would appear vaguely through the webby veil, close upon us; and then we did not wait to swap knives, but snatched our engine bells out by the roots and piled on all the steam we had, to scramble out of the way! One doesn't hit a rock or a solid log raft with a steamboat when he can get excused.

You will hardly believe it, but many steamboat clerks always carried a large assortment of religious tracts with them in those old departed steamboating days. Indeed they did. Twenty times a day we would be cramping up around a bar, while a string of these small-fry rascals were drifting down into the head of the bend away above and beyond us a couple of miles. Now a skiff would dart away from one of them and come fighting its laborious way across the desert of water. It would "ease all," in the shadow of our forecastle, and the panting oarsmen would shout, "Gimme a pa-a-per!" as the skiff drifted swiftly astern. The clerk would throw over a file of New Orleans journals. If these were picked up *without comment,* you might notice that now a dozen other skiffs had been drifting down upon us without saying anything. You understand, they had been waiting to see how No. 1 was going to fare. No. 1 making no comment, all the rest would bend to their oars and come on, now; and as fast as they came the clerk would heave over neat bundles of religious tracts tied to shingles. The amount of hard swearing which twelve packages of religious literature will command when impartially divided up among twelve raftsmen's crews, who have pulled a heavy skiff two miles on a hot day to get them, is simply incredible.

As I have said, the big rise brought a new world under my vision. By the time the river was over its banks we had forsaken our old paths and were hourly climbing over bars that had stood ten feet out of water before; we were shaving stumpy shores, like that at the foot of Madrid Bend, which I had always seen avoided before; we were clattering through chutes like that of 82, where the opening at the foot was an unbroken wall of timber till our nose was almost at the very spot. Some of these chutes were utter solitudes. The dense, untouched forest overhung both banks of the crooked little crack, and one could believe that human creatures had never intruded there before. The swinging grape-vines, the grassy nooks and vistas glimpsed as we swept by, the flowering creepers waving their red blossoms from the tops of dead trunks, and all the spend-thrift richness of the forest foliage, were wasted and thrown away there. The chutes were lovely places to steer in; they were deep, except at the head; the current was gentle; under the "points" the water was absolutely dead, and the in-visible banks so bluff that where the tender willow thickets projected you could bury your boat's broadside in them as you tore along, and then you seemed fairly to fly.

Behind other islands we found wretched little farms, and wretcheder little log-cabins; there were crazy rail fences sticking a foot or two above the water, with one or two jeans-clad, chills-racked, yellow-faced male miserables roost-ing on the top-rail, elbows on knees, jaws in hands, grinding tobacco and discharging the result at floating chips through crevices left by lost milk-teeth; while the rest of the family and the few farm-animals were huddled together in an empty wood-flat riding at her moorings close at hand. In this flatboat the family would have to cook and eat and sleep for a lesser or greater number of days (or possibly weeks), until the river should fall two or three feet and let them get back to their log-cabin and their chills again— chills being a merciful provision of an all-wise Providence to enable them to take exercise without exertion. And this sort of watery camping out was a thing which these people were rather liable to be treated to a couple of times a year: by the December rise out of the Ohio, and the June rise out of the Mississippi. And yet these were kindly dis-pensations, for they at least enabled the poor things to rise from the dead now and then, and look upon life when a steamboat went by. They appreciated the blessing, too, for they spread their mouths and eyes wide open and made the most of these occasions. Now what *could* these banished creatures find to do to keep from dying of the blues during the low-water season!

Once, in one of these lovely island chutes, we found our course completely bridged by a great fallen tree. This will serve to show how narrow some of the chutes were. The passengers had an hour's recreation in a virgin wilderness, while the boat-hands chopped the bridge away; for there was no such thing as turning back, you comprehend.

From Cairo to Baton Rouge, when the river is over its banks, you have no particular trouble in the night, for the thousand-mile wall of dense forest that guards the two banks all the way is only gapped with a farm or wood-yard opening at intervals, and so you can't "get out of the river" much easier than you could get out of a fenced lane; but from Baton Rouge to New Orleans it is a different matter. The river is more than a mile wide, and very deep —as much as two hundred feet, in places. Both banks, for a good deal over a hundred miles, are shorn of their timber and bordered by continuous sugar plantations, with only here and there a scattering sapling or row of ornamental China-trees. The timber is shorn off clear to the rear of the plantations, from two to four miles. When the first frost threatens to come, the planters snatch off their crops in a hurry. When they have finished grinding the cane, they form the refuse of the stalks (which they call *bagasse*) into great piles and set fire to them, though in other sugar countries the bagasse is used for fuel in the furnaces of the sugar mills. Now the piles of damp bagasse burn slowly, and smoke like Satan's own kitchen.

An embankment ten or fifteen feet high guards both banks of the Mississippi all the way down that lower end of the river, and this embankment is set back from the edge of the shore from ten to perhaps a hundred feet, according to circumstances; say thirty or forty feet, as a general thing. Fill that whole region with an impenetrable gloom of smoke from a hundred miles of burning bagasse piles, when the river is over the banks, and turn a steamboat loose along there at midnight and see how she will feel. And see how you will feel, too! You find yourself away out in the midst of a vague dim sea that is shoreless, that fades out and loses itself in the murky distances; for you cannot discern the thin rib of embankment, and you are always imagining you see a straggling tree when you don't. The plantations themselves are transformed by the smoke and look like a part of the sea. All through your watch you are tortured with the exquisite misery of uncertainty. You hope you are keeping in the river, but you do not know. All that you are sure about is that you are likely to be within six feet of the bank *and* destruction, when you think you are a good half-mile from shore. And you are sure, also, that if you chance suddenly to fetch up against the embankment and topple your chimneys overboard, you will have the small comfort of knowing that it is about what you were expecting to do. One of the great Vicksburg packets darted out into a sugar plantation one night, at such a time, and had to stay there a week. But there was no novelty about it; it had often been done before.

I thought I had finished this number, but I wish to add a curious thing, while it is in my mind. It is only relevant in that it is connected with piloting. There used to be an excellent pilot on the river, a Mr. X., who was a somnambulist. It was said that if his mind was troubled about a bad piece of river, he was pretty sure to get up and walk in his sleep and do strange things. He was once fellow-pilot for a trip or two with George E——, on a great New Orleans passenger packet. During a considerable part of the first trip George was uneasy, but got over it by and by, as X. seemed content to stay in his bed when asleep. Late one night the boat was approaching Helena, Arkansas; the water was low, and the crossing above the town in a very blind and tangled condition. X. had seen the crossing since E—— had, and as the night was particularly drizzly, sullen, and dark, E—— was considering whether he had not better have X. called to assist in running the place, when the door opened and X. walked in. Now on very dark nights, light is a deadly enemy to piloting; you are aware that if you stand in a lighted room, on such a night, you cannot see things in the street to any purpose; but if you put out the lights and stand in the gloom you can make out objects in the street pretty well. So, on very dark nights, pilots do not smoke; they allow no fire in the pilot-house stove if there is a crack which can allow the least ray to escape; they order the furnaces to be curtained with huge tarpaulins and the sky-lights to be closely blinded. Then no light whatever issues from the boat. The undefinable shape that now entered the pilot-house had Mr. X.'s voice. This said,—

"Let me take her, Mr. E——; I've seen this place since you have, and it is so crooked that I reckon I can run it myself easier than I could tell you how to do it."

"It is kind of you, and I swear *I* am willing. I haven't

got another drop of perspiration left in me. I have been spinning around and around the wheel like a squirrel. It is so dark I can't tell which way she is swinging till she is coming around like a whirligig."

So E——— took a seat on the bench, panting and breathless. The black phantom assumed the wheel without saying anything, steadied the waltzing steamer with a turn or two, and then stood at ease, coaxing her a little to this side and then to that, as gently and as sweetly as if the time had been noonday. When E——— observed this marvel of steering, he wished he had not confessed! He stared, and wondered, and finally said,—

"Well, I thought I knew how to steer a steamboat, but that was another mistake of mine."

X. said nothing, but went serenely on with his work. He rang for the leads; he rang to slow down the steam; he worked the boat carefully and neatly into invisible marks, then stood at the centre of the wheel and peered blandly out into the blackness, fore and aft, to verify his position; as the leads shoaled more and more, he stopped the engines entirely, and the dead silence and suspense of "drifting" followed; when the shoalest water was struck, he cracked on the steam, carried her handsomely over, and then began to work her warily into the next system of shoal marks; the same patient, heedful use of leads and engines followed, the boat slipped through without touching bottom, and entered upon the third and last intricacy of the crossing; imperceptibly she moved through the gloom, crept by inches into her marks, drifted tediously till the shoalest water was cried, and then, under a tremendous head of steam, went swinging over the reef and away into deep water and safety!

E——— let his long-pent breath pour out in a great, relieving sigh, and said:

"That's the sweetest piece of piloting that was ever done on the Mississippi River! I wouldn't believe it could be done, if I hadn't seen it."

There was no reply, and he added:—

"Just hold her five minutes longer, partner, and let me run down and get a cup of coffee."

A minute later E——— was biting into a pie, down in the "texas," and comforting himself with coffee. Just then the night watchman happened in, and was about to happen out again, when he noticed E—— and exclaimed,—

"Who is at the wheel, sir?"

"X."

"Dart for the pilot-house, quicker than lightning!"

The next moment both men were flying up the pilot-house companion-way, three steps at a jump! Nobody there! The great steamer was whistling down the middle of the river at her own sweet will! The watchman shot out of the place again; E—— seized the wheel, set an engine back with power, and held his breath while the boat reluctantly swung away from a "towhead" which she was about to knock into the middle of the Gulf of Mexico!

By and by the watchman came back and said,—

"Didn't that lunatic tell you he was asleep, when he first came up here?"

"No."

"Well, he was. I found him walking along on top of the railings, just as unconcerned as another man would walk a pavement; and I put him to bed; now just this minute there he was again, away astern, going through that sort of tight-rope deviltry the same as before."

"Well, I think I'll stay by, next time he has one of those fits. But I hope he'll have them often. You just ought to have seen him take this boat through Helena crossing. *I* never saw anything so gaudy before. And if he can do such gold-leaf, kid-glove, diamond-breastpin piloting when he is sound asleep, what *couldn't* he do if he was dead!"

# V.

## [ "Sounding." Faculties Peculiarly Necessary to a Pilot. ]

When the river is very low, and one's steamboat is "drawing all the water" there is in the channel,—or a few inches more, as was often the case in the old times,—one must be painfully circumspect in his piloting. We used to have to "sound" a number of particularly bad places almost every trip when the river was at a very low stage.

Sounding is done in this way. The boat ties up at the shore, just above the shoal crossing; the pilot not on watch

takes his "cub" or steersman and a picked crew of men
(sometimes an officer also), and goes out in the yawl—provided the boat has not that rare and sumptuous luxury, a
regularly-devised "sounding-boat"—and proceeds to hunt
for the best water, the pilot on duty watching his movements through a spy-glass, meantime, and in some instances
assisting by signals of the boat's whistle, signifying "try
higher up" or "try lower down;" for the surface of the
water, like an oil-painting, is more expressive and intel-
ligible when inspected from a little distance than very
close at hand. The whistle signals are seldom necessary,
however; never, perhaps, except when the wind confuses
the significant ripples upon the water's surface. When the
yawl has reached the shoal place, the speed is slackened,
the pilot begins to sound the depth with a pole ten or
twelve feet long, and the steersman at the tiller obeys the
order to "hold her up to starboard;" or "let her fall off to
larboard;" [1] or "steady—steady as you go."

When the measurements indicate that the yawl is approaching the shoalest part of the reef, the command is
given to "ease all!" Then the men stop rowing and the
yawl drifts with the current. The next order is, "Stand by
with the buoy!" The moment the shallowest point is
reached, the pilot delivers the order, "Let go the buoy!"
and over she goes. If the pilot is not satisfied, he sounds
the place again; if he finds better water higher up or
lower down, he removes the buoy to that place. Being
finally satisfied, he gives the order, and all the men stand
their oars straight up in the air, in line; a blast from the
boat's whistle indicates that the signal has been seen; then
the men "give way" on their oars and lay the yawl alongside the buoy; the steamer comes creeping carefully down,
is pointed straight at the buoy, husbands her power for the
coming struggle, and presently, at the critical moment,
turns on all her steam and goes grinding and wallowing
over the buoy and the sand, and gains the deep water beyond. Or maybe she doesn't; maybe she "strikes and
swings." Then she has to while away several hours (or days)
sparring herself off.

Sometimes a buoy is not laid at all, but the yawl goes
ahead, hunting the best water, and the steamer follows

---

[1] The term "larboard" is never used at sea, now, to signify the
left hand; but was always used on the river in my time.

along in its wake. Often there is a deal of fun and excitement about sounding, especially if it is a glorious summer day, or a blustering night. But in winter the cold and the peril take most of the fun out of it.

A buoy is nothing but a board four or five feet long, with one end turned up; it is a reversed boot-jack. It is anchored on the shoalest part of the reef by a rope with a heavy stone made fast to the end of it. But for the resistance of the turned-up end, the current would pull the buoy under water. At night a paper lantern with a candle in it is fastened on top of the buoy, and this can be seen a mile or more, a little glimmering spark in the waste of blackness.

Nothing delights a cub so much as an opportunity to go out sounding. There is such an air of adventure about it; often there is danger; it is so gaudy and man-of-war-like to sit up in the stern-sheets and steer a swift yawl; there is something fine about the exultant spring of the boat when an experienced old sailor crew throw their souls into the oars; it is lovely to see the white foam stream away from the bows; there is music in the rush of the water; it is deliciously exhilarating, in summer, to go speeding over the breezy expanses of the river when the world of wavelets is dancing in the sun. It is such grandeur, too, to the cub, to get a chance to give an order; for often the pilot will simply say, "Let her go about!" and leave the rest to the cub, who instantly cries, in his sternest tone of command, "Ease starboard! Strong on the larboard! Starboard give way! With a will, men!" The cub enjoys sounding for the further reason that the eyes of the passengers are watching all the yawl's movements with absorbing interest, if the time be daylight; and if it be night he knows that those same wondering eyes are fastened upon the yawl's lantern as it glides out into the gloom and fades away in the remote distance.

One trip a pretty girl of sixteen spent her time in our pilot-house with her uncle and aunt, every day and all day long. I fell in love with her. So did Mr. T——'s cub, Tom G——. Tom and I had been bosom friends until this time; but now a coolness began to arise. I told the girl a good many of my river adventures, and made myself out a good deal of a hero; Tom tried to make himself appear to be a hero, too, and succeeded to some extent, but then he al-

ways had a way of embroidering. However, virtue is its own
reward, so I was a barely perceptible trifle ahead in the
contest. About this time something happened which promised handsomely for me: the pilots decided to sound the
crossing at the head of 21. This would occur about nine or
ten o'clock at night, when the passengers would be still up;
it would be Mr. T——'s watch, therefore my chief would
have to do the sounding. We had a perfect love of a sounding-boat—long, trim, graceful, and as fleet as a greyhound;
her thwarts were cushioned; she carried twelve oarsmen;
one of the mates was always sent in her to transmit orders
to her crew, for ours was a steamer where no end of "style"
was put on.

We tied up at the shore above 21, and got ready. It was
a foul night, and the river was so wide, there, that a landsman's uneducated eyes could discern no opposite shore
through such a gloom. The passengers were alert and interested; everything was satisfactory. As I hurried through
the engine-room, picturesquely gotten up in storm toggery,
I met Tom, and could not forbear delivering myself of a
mean speech:—

"Ain't you glad *you* don't have to go out sounding?"

Tom was passing on, but he quickly turned, and said,—

"Now just for that, you can go and get the sounding-pole
yourself. I was going after it, but I'd see you in Halifax,
now, before I'd do it."

"Who wants you to get it? *I* don't. It's in the sounding-
boat."

"It ain't, either. It's been new-painted; and it's been up
on the lady's-cabin guards two days, drying."

I flew back, and shortly arrived among the crowd of
watching and wondering ladies just in time to hear the
command:

"Give way, men!"

I looked over, and there was the gallant sounding-boat
booming away, the unprincipled Tom presiding at the
tiller, and my chief sitting by him with the sounding-pole
which I had been sent on a fool's errand to fetch. Then
that young girl said to me,—

"Oh, how awful to have to go out in that little boat on
such a night! Do you think there is any danger?"

I would rather have been stabbed. I went off, full of
venom, to help in the pilot-house. By and by the boat's

lantern disappeared, and after an interval a wee spark glimmered upon the face of the water a mile away. Mr. T—— blew the whistle, in acknowledgment, backed the steamer out, and made for it. We flew along for a while, then slackened steam and went cautiously gliding toward the spark. Presently Mr. T—— exclaimed,—

"Hello, the buoy-lantern's out!"

He stopped the engines. A moment or two later he said,—

"Why, there it is again!"

So he came ahead on the engines once more, and rang for the leads. Gradually the water shoaled up, and then began to deepen again! Mr. T—— muttered:

"Well, I don't understand this. I believe that buoy has drifted off the reef. Seems to be a little too far to the left. No matter, it is safest to run over it, anyhow."

So, in that solid world of darkness, we went creeping down on the light. Just as our bows were in the act of plowing over it, Mr. T—— seized the bell-ropes, rang a startling peal, and exclaimed,—

"My soul, it's the sounding-boat!"

A sudden chorus of wild alarms burst out far below—a pause—and then a sound of grinding and crashing followed. Mr. T—— exclaimed,—

"There! the paddle-wheel has ground the sounding-boat to lucifer matches! Run! See who is killed!"

I was on the main deck in the twinkling of an eye. My chief and the third mate and nearly all the men were safe. They had discovered their danger when it was too late to pull out of the way; then, when the great guards overshadowed them a moment later, they were prepared and knew what to do; at my chief's order they sprang at the right instant, seized the guard, and were hauled aboard. The next moment the sounding-yawl swept aft to the wheel and was struck and splintered to atoms. Two of the men, and the cub Tom, were missing—a fact which spread like wild-fire over the boat. The passengers came flocking to the forward gangway, ladies and all, anxious-eyed, white-faced, and talked in awed voices of the dreadful thing. And often and again I heard them say, "Poor fellows! poor boy, poor boy!"

By this time the boat's yawl was manned and away, to search for the missing. Now a faint call was heard, off to the left. The yawl had disappeared in the other direction.

Half the people rushed to one side to encourage the
swimmer with their shouts; the other half rushed the other
way to shriek to the yawl to turn about. By the callings,
the swimmer was approaching, but some said the sound
showed failing strength. The crowd massed themselves
against the boiler-deck railings, leaning over and staring
into the gloom; and every faint and fainter cry wrung from
them such words as "Ah, poor fellow, poor fellow! is there
*no* way to save him?"

But still the cries held out, and drew nearer, and presently the voice said pluckily,—

"I can make it! Stand by with a rope!"

What a rousing cheer they gave him! The chief mate
took his stand in the glare of a torch-basket, a coil of rope
in his hand, and his men grouped about him. The next
moment the swimmer's face appeared in the circle of light,
and in another one the owner of it was hauled aboard, limp
and drenched, while cheer on cheer went up. It was that
devil Tom.

The yawl crew searched everywhere, but found no sign
of the two men. They probably failed to catch the guard,
tumbled back, and were struck by the wheel and killed.
Tom had never jumped for the guard at all, but had
plunged head-first into the river and dived under the wheel.
It was nothing; I could have done it easy enough, and I
said so; but everybody went on just the same, making a
wonderful to-do over that ass, as if he had done something
great. That girl couldn't seem to have enough of that pitiful
"hero" the rest of the trip; but little I cared; I loathed her,
any way.

The way we came to mistake the sounding-boat's lantern
for the buoy-light was this. My chief said that after laying
the buoy he fell away and watched it till it seemed to be
secure; then he took up a position a hundred yards below it and a little to one side of the steamer's course, headed
the sounding-boat up-stream, and waited. Having to wait
some time, he and the officer got to talking; he looked up
when he judged that the steamer was about on the reef;
saw that the buoy was gone, but supposed that the steamer
had already run over it; he went on with his talk; he
noticed that the steamer was getting very close down on
him, but that was the correct thing; it was her business to
shave him closely, for convenience in taking him aboard;

he was expecting her to sheer off, until the last moment; then it flashed upon him that she was trying to run him down, mistaking his lantern for the buoy-light; so he sang out, "Stand by to spring for the guard, men!" and the next instant the jump was made.

But I am wandering from what I was intending to do, that is, make plainer than perhaps appears in my previous papers, some of the peculiar requirements of the science of piloting. First of all, there is one faculty which a pilot must incessantly cultivate until he has brought it to absolute perfection. Nothing short of perfection will do. That faculty is memory. He cannot stop with merely thinking a thing is so and so; he must *know* it; for this is eminently one of the "exact" sciences. With what scorn a pilot was looked upon, in the old times, if he ever ventured to deal in that feeble phrase "I think," instead of the vigorous one "I know!" One cannot easily realize what a tremendous thing it is to know every trivial detail of twelve hundred miles of river and know it with absolute exactness. If you will take the longest street in New York, and travel up and down it, conning its features patiently until you know every house and window and door and lamp-post and big and little sign by heart, and know them so accurately that you can instantly name the one you are abreast of when you are set down at random in that street in the middle of an inky black night, you will then have a tolerable notion of the amount and the exactness of a pilot's knowledge who carries the Mississippi River in his head. And then if you will go until you know every street crossing, the character, size, and position of the crossing-stones, and the varying depth of mud in each of those numberless places, you will have some idea of what the pilot must know in order to keep a Mississippi steamer out of trouble. Next, if you will take half of the signs in that long street, and *change their places* once a month, and still manage to know their new positions accurately on dark nights, and keep up with these repeated changes without making any mistakes, you will understand what is required of a pilot's peerless memory by the fickle Mississippi.

I think a pilot's memory is about the most wonderful thing in the world. To know the Old and New Testaments by heart, and be able to recite them glibly, forward or backward, or begin at random anywhere in the book and recite both ways and never trip or make a mistake, is no extravagant mass of knowledge, and no marvelous facility, compared to a pilot's massed knowledge of the Mississippi and his marvelous facility in the handling of it. I make this comparison deliberately, and believe I am not expanding the truth when I do it. Many will think my figure too strong, but pilots will not.

And how easily and comfortably the pilot's memory does its work; how placidly effortless is its way! how *unconsciously* it lays up its vast stores, hour by hour, day by day, and never loses or mislays a single valuable package of them all! Take an instance. Let a leadsman cry, "Half twain! half twain! half twain! half twain! half twain!" until it becomes as monotonous as the ticking of a clock; let conversation be going on all the time, and the pilot be doing his share of the talking, and no longer listening to the leadsman; and in the midst of this endless string of half twains let a single "quarter twain!" be interjected, without emphasis, and then the half twain cry go on again, just as before: two or three weeks later that pilot can describe with precision the boat's position in the river when that quarter twain was uttered, and give you such a lot of head-marks, stern-marks, and side-marks to guide you, that you ought to be able to take the boat there and put her in that same spot again yourself! The cry of quarter twain did not really take his mind from his talk, but his trained faculties instantly photographed the bearings, noted the change of depth, and laid up the important details for future reference without requiring any assistance from *him* in the matter. If you were walking and talking with a friend, and another friend at your side kept up a monotonous repetition of the vowel sound A, for a couple of blocks, and then in the midst interjected an R, thus, A, A, A, A, A, R, A, A, A, etc., and gave the R no emphasis, you would not be able to state, two or three weeks afterward, that the R had been put in, nor be able to tell what objects you were passing at the moment it was done. But you could if your memory had been patiently and laboriously trained to do that sort of thing mechanically.

Give a man a tolerably fair memory to start with, and piloting will develop it into a very colossus of capability. But *only in the matters it is daily drilled in.* A time would come when the man's faculties could not help noticing landmarks and soundings, and his memory could not help holding on to them with the grip of a vice; but if you asked that same man at noon what he had had for breakfast, it would be ten chances to one that he could not tell you. Astonishing things can be done with the human memory if you will devote it faithfully to one particular line of business.

At the time that wages soared so high on the Missouri River, my chief, Mr. B——, went up there and learned more than a thousand miles of that stream with an ease and rapidity that were astonishing. When he had seen each division *once* in the daytime and *once* at night, his education was so nearly complete that he took out a "daylight" license; a few trips later he took out a full license, and went to piloting day and night—and he ranked A 1, too.

Mr. B—— placed me as steersman for a while under a pilot whose feats of memory were a constant marvel to me. However, his memory was born in him, I think, not built. For instance, somebody would mention a name. Instantly Mr. J—— would break in:—

"Oh, I knew *him*. Sallow-faced, red-headed fellow, with a little scar on the side of his throat like a splinter under the flesh. He was only in the Southern trade six months. That was thirteen years ago. I made a trip with him. There was five feet in the upper river then; the Henry Blake grounded at the foot of Tower Island, drawing four and a half; the George Elliott unshipped her rudder on the wreck of the Sunflower"—

"Why, the Sunflower didn't sink until"—

"*I* know when she sunk; it was three years before that, on the 2d of December; Asa Hardy was captain of her, and his brother John was first clerk; and it was his first trip in her, too; Tom Jones told me these things a week afterward in New Orleans; he was first mate of the Sunflower. Captain Hardy stuck a nail in his foot the 6th of July of the next year, and died of the lockjaw on the 15th. His brother John died two years after,—3rd of March,— erysipelas. I never saw either of the Hardys,—they were Alleghany River men,—but people who knew them told me all these things. And they said Captain Hardy wore yarn socks winter and summer just the same, and his first wife's name was Jane Shook,—she was from New England, —and his second one died in a lunatic asylum. It was in the blood. She was from Lexington, Kentucky. Name was Horton before she was married."

And so on, by the hour, the man's tongue would go. He could *not* forget anything. It was simply impossible. The most trivial details remained as distinct and luminous in his head, after they had lain there for years, as the most memorable events. His was not simply a pilot's memory; its grasp was universal. If he were talking about a trifling letter he had received seven years before, he was pretty sure to deliver you the entire screed from memory. And then, without observing that he was departing from the true line of his talk, he was more than likely to hurl in a long-drawn parenthetical biography of the writer of that letter; and you were lucky indeed if he did not take up that writer's relatives, one by one, and give you their biographies, too.

Such a memory as that is a great misfortune. To it, all occurrences are of the same size. Its possessor cannot distinguish an interesting circumstance from an uninteresting one. As a talker, he is bound to clog his narrative with tiresome details and make himself an insufferable bore. Moreover, he cannot stick to his subject. He picks up every little-grain of memory he discerns in his way, and so is led aside. Mr. J—— would start out with the honest intention of telling you a vastly funny anecdote about a dog. He would be "so full of laugh" that he could hardly begin; then his memory would start with the dog's breed and personal appearance; drift into a history of his owner; of his owner's family, with descriptions of weddings and burials that had occurred in it, together with recitals of congratulatory verses and obituary poetry provoked by the same; then this memory would recollect that one of these events occurred during the celebrated "hard winter" of such and such a year, and a minute description of that winter would follow, along with the names of people who were frozen to death, and statistics showing the high figures which pork and hay went up to. Pork and hay would suggest corn and fodder; corn and fodder would suggest cows and horses; the latter would suggest the circus and certain celebrated bare-back riders; the transition from the circus to the menagerie was easy and natural; from the elephant to equatorial Africa was but a step; then of course the heathen savages would suggest religion; and at the end of three or four hours' tedious jaw, the watch would change and J—— would go out of the pilot-house muttering extracts from sermons he had heard years before about the efficacy of prayer as a means of grace. And the original first mention would be all you had learned about that dog, after all this waiting and hungering.

A pilot must have a memory; but there are two higher qualities which he must also have. He must have good and quick judgment and decision, and a cool, calm courage that no peril can shake. Give a man the merest trifle of pluck to start with, and by the time he has become a pilot he cannot be unmanned by any danger a steamboat can get into; but one cannot quite say the same for judgment. Judgment is a matter of brains, and a man must *start* with a good stock of that article or he will never succeed as a pilot.

The growth of courage in the pilot-house is steady all the time, but it does not reach a high and satisfactory condition until some time after the young pilot has been "standing his own watch," alone and under the staggering weight of all the responsibilities connected with the position. When an apprentice has become pretty thoroughly acquainted with the river, he goes clattering along so fearlessly with his steamboat, night or day, that he presently begins to imagine that it is *his* courage that animates him; but the first time the pilot steps out and leaves him to his own devices he finds out it was the other man's. He discovers that the article has been left out of his own cargo altogether. The whole river is bristling with exigencies in a moment; he is not prepared for them; he does not know how to meet them; all his knowledge forsakes him; and within fifteen minutes he is as white as a sheet and scared almost to death. Therefore pilots wisely train these cubs by various strategic tricks to look danger in the face a little more calmly. A favorite way of theirs is to play a friendly swindle upon the candidate.

Mr. B—— served me in this fashion once, and for years afterward I used to blush even in my sleep when I thought of it. I had become a good steersman; so good, indeed, that I had all the work to do on our watch, night and day; Mr. B—— seldom made a suggestion to me; all he ever did was to take the wheel on particularly bad nights or in particularly bad crossings, land the boat when she needed to be landed, play gentleman of leisure nine tenths of the watch, and collect the wages. The lower river was about bank-full, and if anybody had questioned my ability to run any crossing between Cairo and New Orleans without help or instruction, I should have felt irreparably hurt. The idea of being afraid of any crossing in the lot, in the *daytime,* was a thing too preposterous for contemplation. Well, one matchless summer's day I was bowling down the bend above island 66, brim full of self-conceit and carrying my nose as high as a giraffe's, when Mr. B—— said,—

"I am going below a while. I suppose you know the next crossing?"

This was almost an affront. It was about the plainest and simplest crossing in the whole river. One couldn't come to any harm, whether he ran it right or not; and as for depth, there never had been any bottom there. I knew all this, perfectly well.

"Know how to *run* it? Why, I can run it with my eyes shut."

"How much water is there in it?"

"Well, that is an odd question. I couldn't get bottom there with a church steeple."

"You think so, do you?"

The very tone of the question shook my confidence. That was what Mr. B—— was expecting. He left, without saying anything more. I began to imagine all sorts of things. Mr. B——, unknown to me, of course, sent somebody down to the forecastle with some mysterious instruction to the leadsmen, another messenger was sent to whisper among the officers, and then Mr. B—— went into hiding behind a smoke-stack where he could observe results. Presently the captain stepped out on the hurricane deck; next the chief mate appeared; then a clerk. Every moment or two a straggler was added to my audience; and before I got to the head of the island I had fifteen or twenty people assembled down there under my nose. I began to wonder what the trouble was. As I started across, the captain glanced aloft at me and said, with a sham uneasiness in his voice,—

"Where is Mr. B——?"

"Gone below, sir."

But that did the business for me. My imagination began to construct dangers out of nothing, and they multiplied faster than I could keep the run of them. All at once

I imagined I saw shoal water ahead! The wave of coward agony that surged through me then came near dislocating every joint in me. All my confidence in that crossing vanished. I seized the bell-rope; dropped it, ashamed; seized it again; dropped it once more; clutched it tremblingly once again, and pulled it so feebly that I could hardly hear the stroke myself. Captain and mate sang out instantly, and both together,—

"Starboard lead there! and quick about it!"

This was another shock. I began to climb the wheel like a squirrel; but I would hardly get the boat started to port before I would see new dangers on that side, and away I would spin to the other; only to find perils accumulating to starboard, and be crazy to get to port again. Then came the leadsman's sepulchral cry:—

"D-e-e-p four!"

Deep four in a bottomless crossing! The terror of it took my breath away.

"M-a-r-k three! M-a-r-k three! Quarter less three! Half twain!"

This was frightful! I seized the bellropes and stopped the engines.

"Quarter twain! Quarter twain! *Mark* twain!"

I was helpless. I did not know what in the world to do. I was quaking from head to foot, and I could have hung my hat on my eyes, they stuck out so far.

"Quarter *less* twain! Nine and a *half!*"

We were *drawing* nine! My hands were in a nerveless flutter. I could not ring a bell intelligibly with them. I flew to the speaking-tube and shouted to the engineer,—

"Oh, Ben, if you love me, *back* her! Quick, Ben! Oh, back the immortal *soul* out of her!"

I heard the door close gently. I looked around, and there stood Mr. B——, smiling a bland, sweet smile. Then the audience on the hurricane deck sent up a shout of humiliating laughter. I saw it all, now, and I felt meaner than the meanest man in human history. I laid in the lead, set the boat in her marks, came ahead on the engines, and said,—

"It was a fine trick to play on an orphan, *wasn't* it? I suppose I'll never hear the last of how I was ass enough to heave the lead at the head of 66."

"Well, no, you won't, maybe. In fact I hope you won't;

nt you to learn something by that experience.
you *know* there was no bottom in that crossing?"
es, sir, I did."

"Very well, then. You shouldn't have allowed me or
anybody else to shake your confidence in that knowledge.
Try to remember that. And another thing: when you get
into a dangerous place, don't turn coward. That isn't going to help matters any."

It was a good enough lesson, but pretty hardly learned.
Yet about the hardest part of it was that for months I so
often had to hear a phrase which I had conceived a particular distaste for. It was, "Oh, Ben, if you love me, back
her!"

## VI.

## [Official Rank and Dignity of a Pilot. The Rise and Decadence of the Pilots' Association.]

In my preceding articles I have tried, by going into the
minutiæ of the science of piloting, to carry the reader step
by step to a comprehension of what the science consists of;
and at the same time I have tried to show him that it is a
very curious and wonderful science, too, and very worthy
of his attention. If I have seemed to love my subject, it is
no surprising thing, for I loved the profession far better
than any I have followed since, and I took a measureless
pride in it. The reason is plain: a pilot, in those days, was
the only unfettered and entirely independent human being that lived in the earth. Kings are but the hampered
servants of parliament and people; parliaments sit in chains
forged by their constituency; the editor of a newspaper
cannot be independent, but must work with one hand tied
behind him by party and patrons, and be content to utter
only half or two thirds of his mind; no clergyman is a free
man and may speak the whole truth, regardless of his par-
ish's opinions; writers of all kinds are manacled servants
of the public. We write frankly and fearlessly, but then
we "modify" before we print. In truth, every man and
woman and child has a master, and worries and frets in
servitude; but in the day I write of, the Mississippi pilot
had *none*. The captain could stand upon the hurricane

deck, in the pomp of a very brief authority, and give him five or six orders, while the vessel backed into the stream, and then that skipper's reign was over. The moment that the boat was under way in the river, she was under the sole and unquestioned control of the pilot. He could do with her exactly as he pleased, run her when and whither he chose, and tie her up to the bank whenever his judgment said that that course was best. His movements were entirely free; he consulted no one, he received commands from nobody, he promptly resented even the merest suggestions. Indeed, the law of the United States forbade him to listen to commands or suggestions, rightly considering that the pilot necessarily knew better how to handle the boat than anybody could tell him. So here was the novelty of a king without a keeper, an absolute monarch who was absolute in sober truth and not by a fiction of words. I have seen a boy of eighteen taking a great steamer serenely into what seemed almost certain destruction, and the aged captain standing mutely by, filled with apprehension but powerless to interfere. His interference, in that particular instance, might have been an excellent thing, but to permit it would have been to establish a most pernicious precedent. It will easily be guessed, considering the pilot's boundless authority, that he was a great personage in the old steamboating days. He was treated with marked courtesy by the captain and with marked deference by all the officers and servants; and this deferential spirit was quickly communicated to the passengers, too. I think pilots were about the only people I ever knew who failed to show, in some degree, embarrassment in the presence of traveling foreign princes. But then, people in one's own grade of life are not usually embarrassing objects.

By long habit, pilots came to put all their wishes in the form of commands. It "gravels" me, to this day, to put my will in the weak shape of a request, instead of launching it in the crisp language of an order.

In those old days, to load a steamboat at St. Louis, take her to New Orleans and back, and discharge cargo, consumed about twenty-five days, on an average. Seven or eight of these days the boat spent at the wharves of St. Louis and New Orleans, and every soul on board was hard at work, except the two pilots; *they* did nothing but play gentleman, up town, and receive the same wages for it as if they had been on duty. The moment the boat touched the wharf at either city, they were ashore; and they were not likely to be seen again till the last bell was ringing and everything in readiness for another voyage.

When a captain got hold of a pilot of particularly high reputation, he took pains to keep him. When wages were four hundred dollars a month on the Upper Mississippi, I have known a captain to keep such a pilot in idleness, under full pay, three months at a time, while the river was frozen up. And one must remember that in those cheap times four hundred dollars was a salary of almost inconceivable splendor. Few men on shore got such pay as that, and when they did they were mightily looked up to. When pilots from either end of the river wandered into our small Missouri village, they were sought by the best and the fairest, and treated with exalted respect. Lying in port under wages was a thing which many pilots greatly enjoyed and appreciated; especially if they belonged in the Missouri River in the heyday of that trade (Kansas times), and got nine hundred dollars a trip, which was equivalent to about eighteen hundred dollars a month. Here is a conversation of that day. A chap out of the Illinois River, with a little stern-wheel tub, accosts a couple of ornate and gilded Missouri River pilots:—

"Gentlemen, I've got a pretty good trip for the up-country, and shall want you about a month. How much will it be?"

"Eighteen hundred dollars apiece."

"Heavens and earth! You take my boat, let me have your wages, and I'll divide!"

I will remark, in passing, that Mississippi steamboatmen were important in landsmen's eyes (and in their own, too, in a degree) according to the dignity of the boat they were on. For instance, it was a proud thing to be of the crew of such stately craft as the Aleck Scott or the Grand Turk. Negro firemen, deck hands, and barbers belonging to those boats were distinguished personages in their grade of life, and they were well aware of that fact, too. A stalwart darkey once gave offense at a negro ball in New Orleans by putting on a good many airs. Finally one of the managers bustled up to him and said,—

"Who *is* you, any way? Who *is* you? dat's what *I* wants to know!"

The offender was not disconcerted in the least, but swelled himself up and threw that into his voice which showed that he knew he was not putting on all those airs on a stinted capital.

"Who *is* I? Who *is* I? I let you know mighty quick who I is! I want you niggers to understan' dat I fires de middle do' [1] on de Aleck Scott!"

That was sufficient.

The barber of the Grand Turk was a spruce young negro, who aired his importance with balmy complacency, and was greatly courted by the circle in which he moved. The young colored population of New Orleans were much given to flirting, at twilight, on the pavements of the back streets. Somebody saw and heard something like the following, one evening, in one of those localities. A middle-aged negro woman projected her head through a broken pane and shouted (very willing that the neighbors should hear and envy), "You Mary Ann, come in de house dis minute! Stannin' out dah foolin' 'long wid dat low trash, an' heah's de barber off 'n de Gran' Turk wants to conwerse wid you!"

My reference, a moment ago, to the fact that a pilot's peculiar official position placed him out of the reach of criticism or command, brings Stephen W—— naturally to my mind. He was a gifted pilot, a good fellow, a tireless talker, and had both wit and humor in him. He had a most irreverent independence, too, and was deliciously easy-going and comfortable in the presence of age, official dignity, and even the most august wealth. He always had work, he never saved a penny, he was a most persuasive borrower, he was in debt to every pilot on the river, and to the majority of the captains. He could throw a sort of splendor around a bit of harum-scarum, devil-may-care piloting, that made it almost fascinating—but not to everybody. He made a trip with good old gentle-spirited Captain Y—— once, and was "relieved" from duty when the boat got to New Orleans. Somebody expressed surprise at the discharge. Captain Y—— shuddered at the mere mention of Stephen. Then his poor, thin old voice piped out something like this:—

"Why, bless me! I wouldn't have such a wild creature on my boat for the world—not for the whole world! He

[1] Door.

swears, he sings, he whistles, he yells—I never saw such an Injun to yell. All times of the night—it never made any difference to him. He would just yell that way, not for anything in particular, but merely on account of a kind of devilish comfort he got out of it. I never could get into a sound sleep but he would fetch me out of bed, all in a cold sweat, with one of those dreadful war-whoops. A queer being,—very queer being; no respect for anything or anybody. Sometimes he called me '*Johnny*.' And he kept a fiddle, and a cat. He played execrably. This seemed to distress the cat, and so the cat would howl. Nobody could sleep where that man—and his family—was. And reckless? There never was anything like it. Now you may believe it or not, but as sure as I am sitting here, he brought my boat a-tilting down through those awful snags at Chicot under a rattling head of steam, and the wind a-blowing like the very nation, at that! My officers will tell you so. They saw it. And, sir, while he was a-tearing right down through those snags, and I a-shaking in my shoes and praying, I wish I may never speak again if he did n't pucker up his mouth and go to *whistling!* Yes, sir; whistling 'Buffalo gals, can't you come out to-night, can't you come out to-night, can't you come out to-night;' and doing it as calmly as if we were attending a funeral and weren't related to the corpse. And when I remonstrated with him about it, he smiled down on me as if I was his child, and told me to run in the house and try to be good, and not be meddling with my superiors!" [1]

Once a pretty mean captain caught Stephen in New Orleans out of work and as usual out of money. He laid steady siege to Stephen, who was in a very "close place," and finally persuaded him to hire with him at one hundred and twenty-five dollars per month, just half wages, the captain agreeing not to divulge the secret and so bring down the contempt of all the guild upon the poor fellow. But the boat was not more than a day out of New Orleans before Stephen discovered that the captain was boasting of his exploit, and that all the officers had been told. Stephen winced, but said nothing. About the middle of the afternoon the captain stepped out on the hurricane deck, cast

[1] Considering a captain's ostentatious but hollow chieftainship, and a pilot's real authority, there was something impudently apt and happy about that way of phrasing it.

his eye around, and looked a good deal surprised. He glanced inquiringly aloft at Stephen, but Stephen was whistling placidly, and attending to business. The captain stood around a while in evident discomfort, and once or twice seemed about to make a suggestion; but the etiquette of the river taught him to avoid that sort of rashness, and so he managed to hold his peace. He chafed and puzzled a few minutes longer, then retired to his apartments. But soon he was out again, and apparently more perplexed than ever. Presently he ventured to remark, with deference,—

"Pretty good stage of the river now, ain't it, sir?"

"Well, I should say so! Bank-full *is* a pretty liberal stage."

"Seems to be a good deal of current here."

"Good deal don't describe it! It's worse than a mill-race."

"Isn't it easier in toward shore than it is out here in the middle?"

"Yes, I reckon it is; but a body can't be too careful with a steamboat. It's pretty safe out here; can't strike any bottom here, you can depend on that."

The captain departed, looking rueful enough. At this rate, he would probably die of old age before his boat got to St. Louis. Next day he appeared on deck and again found Stephen faithfully standing up the middle of the river, fighting the whole vast force of the Mississippi, and whistling the same placid tune. This thing was becoming serious. In by the shore was a slower boat clipping along in the easy water and gaining steadily; she began to make for an island chute; Stephen stuck to the middle of the river. Speech was *wrung* from the captain. He said,—

"Mr. W——, don't that chute cut off a good deal of distance?"

"I think it does, but I don't know."

"Don't know! Well, isn't there water enough in it now to go through?"

"I expect there is, but I am not certain."

"Upon my word this is odd! Why, those pilots on that boat yonder are going to try it. Do you mean to say that you don't know as much as they do?"

"*They!* Why, *they* are two-hundred-and-fifty-dollar pilots! But don't you be uneasy; I know as much as any man can afford to know for a hundred and twenty-five!"

Five minutes later Stephen was bowling through the

chute and showing the rival boat a two-hundred-and-fifty-
dollar pair of heels.

One day, on board the Aleck Scott, my chief, Mr. B——,
was crawling carefully through a close place at Cat Island,
both leads going, and everybody holding his breath. The
captain, a nervous, apprehensive man, kept still as long as
he could, but finally broke down and shouted from the
hurricane deck,—

"For gracious' sake, give her steam, Mr. B——! give her
steam! She'll never raise the reef on this headway!"

For all the effect that was produced upon Mr. B——, one
would have supposed that no remark had been made. But
five minutes later, when the danger was past and the leads
laid in, he burst instantly into a consuming fury, and gave
the captain the most admirable cursing I ever listened to.
No bloodshed ensued; but that was because the captain's
cause was weak; for ordinarily he was not a man to take
correction quietly.

Having now set forth in detail the nature of the science
of piloting, and likewise described the rank which the pilot
held among the fraternity of steamboatmen, this seems a
fitting place to say a few words about an organization
which the pilots once formed for the protection of their
guild. It was curious and noteworthy in this, that it was
perhaps the compactest, the completest, and the strongest
commercial organization ever formed among men.

For a long time wages had been two hundred and fifty
dollars a month; but curiously enough, as steamboats multiplied and business increased, the wages began to fall, little by little. It was easy to discover the reason of this. Too
many pilots were being "made." It was nice to have a
"cub," a steersman, to do all the hard work for a couple
of years, gratis, while his master sat on a high bench and
smoked; all pilots and captains had sons or brothers who
wanted to be pilots. By and by it came to pass that nearly
every pilot on the river had a steersman. When a steersman
had made an amount of progress that was satisfactory to
any two pilots in the trade, they could get a pilot's license
for him by signing an application directed to the United
States Inspector. Nothing further was needed; usually no
questions were asked, no proofs of capacity required.

Very well, this growing swarm of new pilots presently
began to undermine the wages, in order to get berths. Too

late—apparently—the knights of the tiller perceived their mistake. Plainly, something had to be done, and quickly; but what was to be the needful thing? A close organization. Nothing else would answer. To compass this seemed an impossibility; so it was talked, and talked, and then dropped. It was too likely to ruin whoever ventured to move in the matter. But at last about a dozen of the boldest—and some of them the best—pilots on the river launched themselves into the enterprise and took all the chances. They got a special charter from the legislature, with large powers, under the name of the Pilots' Benevolent Association; elected their officers, completed their organization, contributed capital, put "association" wages up to two hundred and fifty dollars at once—and then retired to their homes, for they were promptly discharged from employment. But there were two or three unnoticed trifles in their by-laws which had the seeds of propagation in them. For instance, all idle members of the association, in good standing, were entitled to a pension of twenty-five dollars per month. This began to bring in one straggler after another from the ranks of the new-fledged pilots, in the dull (summer) season. Better have twenty-five dollars than starve; the initiation fee was only twelve dollars, and no dues required from the unemployed.

Also, the widows of deceased members in good standing could draw twenty-five dollars per month, and a certain sum for each of their children. Also, the said deceased would be buried at the association's expense. These things resurrected all the superannuated and forgotten pilots in the Mississippi Valley. They came from farms, they came from interior villages, they came from everywhere. They came on crutches, on drays, in ambulances,—any way, so they got there. They paid in their twelve dollars, and straightway began to draw out twenty-five dollars a month and calculate their burial bills.

By and by, all the useless, helpless pilots, and a dozen first-class ones, were in the association, and nine tenths of the best pilots out of it and laughing at it. It was the laughing-stock of the whole river. Everybody joked about the by-law requiring members to pay ten per cent. of their wages, every month, into the treasury for the support of the association, whereas all the members were outcast and tabooed, and no one would employ them. Everybody was

derisively grateful to the association for taking all the
worthless pilots out of the way and leaving the whole field
to the excellent and the deserving; and everybody was not
only jocularly grateful for that, but for a result which
naturally followed, namely, the gradual advance of wages
as the busy season approached. Wages had gone up from
the low figure of one hundred dollars a month to one hundred and twenty-five, and in some cases to one hundred
and fifty; and it was great fun to enlarge upon the fact
that this charming thing had been accomplished by a body
of men not one of whom received a particle of benefit from
it. Some of the jokers used to call at the association rooms
and have a good time chaffing the members and offering
them the charity of taking them as steersmen for a trip, so
that they could see what the forgotten river looked like.
However, the association was content; or at least it gave
no sign to the contrary. Now and then it captured a pilot
who was "out of luck," and added him to its list; and
these later additions were very valuable, for they were good
pilots; the incompetent ones had all been absorbed before.
As business freshened, wages climbed gradually up to two
hundred and fifty dollars—the association figure—and became firmly fixed there; and still without benefiting a member of that body, for no member was hired. The hilarity
at the association's expense burst all bounds, now. There
was no end to the fun which that poor martyr had to put
up with.

However, it is a long lane that has no turning. Winter
approached, business doubled and trebled, and an ava-
lanche of Missouri, Illinois, and Upper Mississippi River
boats came pouring down to take a chance in the New
Orleans trade. All of a sudden, pilots were in great demand, and were correspondingly scarce. The time for revenge was come. It was a bitter pill to have to accept association pilots at last, yet captains and owners agreed that
there was no other way. But none of these outcasts offered!
So there was a still bitterer pill to be swallowed: they must
be sought out and asked for their services. Captain ——
was the first man who found it necessary to take the dose,
and he had been the loudest derider of the organization.
He hunted up one of the best of the association pilots and
said,—

"Well, you boys have rather got the best of us for a little

while, so I'll give in with as good a grace as I can. I've come to hire you; get your trunk aboard right away I want to leave at twelve o'clock."

"I don't know about that. Who is your other pilot?"

"I 've got I. S——. Why?"

"I can't go with him. He don't belong to the association."

"What!"

"It 's so."

"Do you mean to tell me that you won't turn a wheel with one of the very best and oldest pilots on the river because he don't belong to your association?"

"Yes, I do."

"Well, if this isn't putting on airs! I supposed I was doing you a benevolence; but I begin to think that I am the party that wants a favor done. Are you acting under a law of the concern?"

"Yes."

"Show it to me."

So they stepped into the association rooms, and the secretary soon satisfied the captain, who said,—

"Well, what am I to do? I have hired Mr. S—— for the entire season."

"I will provide for you," said the secretary. "I will detail a pilot to go with you, and he shall be on board at twelve o'clock."

"But if I discharge S——, he will come on me for the whole season's wages."

"Of course that is a matter between you and Mr. S——, captain. We cannot meddle in your private affairs."

The captain stormed, but to no purpose. In the end he had to discharge S——, pay him about a thousand dollars, and take an association pilot in his place. The laugh was beginning to turn the other way, now. Every day, thenceforward, a new victim fell; every day some outraged captain discharged a non-association pet, with tears and profanity, and installed a hated association man in his berth. In a very little while, idle non-associationists began to be pretty plenty, brisk as business was, and much as their services were desired. The laugh was shifting to the other side of their mouths most palpably. These victims, together with the captains and owners, presently ceased to laugh altogether, and began to rage about the revenge they would take when the passing business "spurt" was over.

Soon all the laughers that were left were the owners and crews of boats that had two non-association pilots. But their triumph was not very long-lived. For this reason: It was a rigid rule of the association that its members should never, under any circumstances whatever, give information about the channel to any "outsider." By this time about half the boats had none but association pilots, and the other half had none but outsiders. At the first glance one would suppose that when it came to forbidding information about the river these two parties could play equally at that game; but this was not so. At every good-sized town from one end of the river to the other, there was a "wharf-boat" to land at, instead of a wharf or a pier. Freight was stored in it for transportation, waiting passengers slept in its cabins. Upon each of these wharf-boats the association's officers placed a strong box, fastened with a peculiar lock which was used in no other service but one—the United States mail service. It was the letter-bag lock, a sacred governmental thing. By dint of much beseeching the government had been persuaded to allow the association to use this lock. Every association man carried a key which would open these boxes. That key, or rather a peculiar way of holding it in the hand when its owner was asked for river information by a stranger,—for the success of the St. Louis and New Orleans association had now bred tolerably thriving branches in a dozen neighboring steamboat trades,—was the association man's sign and diploma of membership; and if the stranger did not respond by producing a similar key and holding it in a certain manner duly prescribed, his question was politely ignored. From the association's secretary each member received a package of more or less gorgeous blanks, printed like a bill-head, on handsome paper, properly ruled in columns; a bill-head worded something like this:—

### STEAMER GREAT REPUBLIC.
#### JOHN SMITH, MASTER.
*Pilots, John Jones and Thos. Brown.*

| Crossing. | Soundings. | Marks. | Remarks. |
| --- | --- | --- | --- |

These blanks were filled up, day by day, as the voyage progressed, and deposited in the several wharf-boat boxes.

For instance, as soon as the first crossing, out from St. Louis, was completed, the items would be entered upon the blank, under the appropriate headings, thus:

"St. Louis. Nine and a half (feet). Stern on court-house, head on dead cottonwood above wood-yard, until you raise the first reef, then pull up square." Then under head of Remarks: "Go just outside the wrecks; this is important. New snag just where you straighten down; go above it."

The pilot who deposited that blank in the Cairo box (after adding to it the details of every crossing all the way down from St. Louis) took out and read half a dozen fresh reports (from upward bound steamers) concerning the river between Cairo and Memphis, posted himself thoroughly, returned them to the box, and went back aboard his boat again so armed against accident that he could not possibly get his boat into trouble without bringing the most ingenious carelessness to his aid.

Imagine the benefits of so admirable a system in a piece of river twelve or thirteen hundred miles long, whose channel was shifting every day! The pilot who had formerly been obliged to put up with seeing a shoal place once or possibly twice a month, had a hundred sharp eyes to watch it for him, now, and bushels of intelligent brains to tell him how to run it. His information about it was seldom twenty-four hours old. If the reports in the last box chanced to leave any misgivings on his mind concerning a treacherous crossing, he had his remedy; he blew his steam-whistle in a peculiar way as soon as he saw a boat approaching; the signal was answered in a peculiar way if that boat's pilots were association men; and then the two steamers ranged alongside and all uncertainties were swept away by fresh information furnished to the inquirer by word of mouth and in minute detail.

The first thing a pilot did when he reached New Orleans or St. Louis was to take his final and elaborate report to the association parlors and hang it up there,—*after* which he was free to visit his family. In these parlors a crowd was always gathered together, discussing changes in the channel, and the moment there was a fresh arrival, everybody stopped talking till this witness had told the newest news and settled the latest uncertainty. Other craftsmen can "sink the shop," sometimes, and interest themselves in other matters. Not so with a pilot; he must devote himself wholly to his profession and talk of nothing else; for it would be small gain to be perfect one day and imperfect the next. He has no time or words to waste if he would keep "posted."

But the outsiders had a hard time of it. No particular place to meet and exchange information, no wharf-boat reports, none but chance and unsatisfactory ways of getting news. The consequence was that a man sometimes had to run five hundred miles of river on information that was a week or ten days old. At a fair stage of the river that might have answered; but when the dead low water came it was destructive.

Now came another perfectly logical result. The outsiders began to ground steamboats, sink them, and get into all sorts of trouble, whereas accidents seemed to keep entirely away from the association men. Wherefore even the owners and captains of boats furnished exclusively with outsiders, and previously considered to be wholly independent of the association and free to comfort themselves with brag and laughter, began to feel pretty uncomfortable. Still, they made a show of keeping up the brag, until one black day when every captain of the lot was formally ordered immediately to discharge his outsiders and take association pilots in their stead. And who was it that had the gaudy presumption to do that? Alas, it came from a power behind the throne that was greater than the throne itself. It was the underwriters!

It was no time to "swap knives." Every outsider had to take his trunk ashore at once. Of course it was supposed that there was collusion between the association and the underwriters, but this was not so. The latter had come to comprehend the excellence of the "report" system of the association and the safety it secured, and so they had made their decision among themselves and upon plain business principles.

There was weeping and wailing and gnashing of teeth in the camp of the outsiders now. But no matter, there was but one course for them to pursue, and they pursued it. They came forward in couples and groups, and proffered their twelve dollars and asked for membership. They were surprised to learn that several new by-laws had been long ago added. For instance, the initiation fee had been raised to fifty dollars; that sum must be tendered, and also ten

per cent. of the wages which the applicant had received
each and every month since the founding of the association. In many cases this amounted to three or four hundred
dollars. Still, the association would not entertain the application until the money was present. Even then a single
adverse vote killed the application. Every member had to
vote yes or no in person and before witnesses; so it took
weeks to decide a candidacy, because many pilots were so
long absent on voyages. However, the repentant sinners
scraped their savings together, and one by one, by our tedious voting process, they were added to the fold. A time
came, at last, when only about ten remained outside. They
said they would starve before they would apply. They remained idle a long while, because of course nobody could
venture to employ them.

By and by the association published the fact that upon
a certain date the wages would be raised to five hundred
dollars per month. All the branch associations had grown
strong, now, and the Red River one had advanced wages
to seven hundred dollars a month. Reluctantly the ten outsiders yielded, in view of these things, and made application. There was *another* new by-law, by this time, which
required them to pay dues not only on all the wages they
had received since the association was born, but also on
what they would have received if they had continued at
work up to the time of their application, instead of going
off to pout in idleness. It turned out to be a difficult matter to elect them, but it was accomplished at last. The most
virulent sinner of this batch had stayed out and allowed
"dues" to accumulate against him so long that he had to
send in six hundred and twenty-five dollars with his application.

The association had a good bank account now, and was
very strong. There was no longer an outsider. A by-law
was added forbidding the reception of any more cubs or
apprentices for five years; after which time a limited number would be taken, not by individuals, but by the association, upon these terms: the applicant must not be less
than eighteen years old, of respectable family and good
character; he must pass an examination as to education,
pay a thousand dollars in advance for the privilege of becoming an apprentice, and must remain under the commands of the association until a great part of the mem-

bership (more than half, I think) should be willing to sign his application for a pilot's license.

All previously-articled apprentices were now taken away from their masters and adopted by the association. The president and secretary detailed them for service on one boat or another, as they chose, and changed them from boat to boat according to certain rules. If a pilot could show that he was in infirm health and needed assistance, one of the cubs would be ordered to go with him.

The widow and orphan list grew, but so did the association's financial resources. The association attended its own funerals in state, and paid for them. When occasion demanded, it sent members down the river upon searches for the bodies of brethren lost by steamboat accidents; a search of this kind sometimes cost a thousand dollars.

The association procured a charter and went into the insurance business, also. It not only insured the lives of its members, but took risks on steamboats.

The organization seemed indestructible. It was the tightest monopoly in the world. By the United States law, no man could become a pilot unless two duly licensed pilots signed his application; and now there was nobody outside of the association competent to sign. Consequently the making of pilots was at an end. Every year some would die and others become incapacitated by age and infirmity; there would be no new ones to take their places. In time, the association could put wages up to any figure it chose; and as long as it should be wise enough not to carry the thing too far and provoke the national government into amending the licensing system, steamboat owners would have to submit, since there would be no help for it.

The owners and captains were the only obstruction that lay between the association and absolute power; and at last this one was removed. Incredible as it may seem, the owners and captains deliberately did it themselves. When the pilots' association announced, months beforehand, that on the first day of September, 1861, wages would be advanced to five hundred dollars per month, the owners and captains instantly put freights up a few cents, and explained to the farmers along the river the necessity of it, by calling their attention to the burdensome rate of wages about to be established. It was a rather slender argument, but the farmers did not seem to detect it. It looked reasonable to them that to add five cents freight on a bushel of corn was justifiable under the circumstances, overlooking the fact that this advance on a cargo of forty thousand sacks was a good deal more than necessary to cover the new wages.

So straightway the captains and owners got up an association of their own, and proposed to put captains' wages up to five hundred dollars, too, and move for another advance in freights. It was a novel idea, but of course an effect which had been produced once could be produced again. The new association decreed (for this was before all the outsiders had been taken into the pilots' association) that if any captain employed a non-association pilot, he should be forced to discharge him, and also pay a fine of five hundred dollars. Several of these heavy fines were paid before the captains' organization grew strong enough to exercise full authority over its membership; but that all ceased, presently. The captains tried to get the pilots to decree that no member of their corporation should serve under a non-association captain; but this proposition was declined. The pilots saw that they would be backed up by the captains and the underwriters anyhow, and so they wisely refrained from entering into entangling alliances.

As I have remarked, the pilots' association was now the compactest monopoly in the world, perhaps, and seemed simply indestructible. And yet the days of its glory were numbered. First, the new railroad stretching up through Mississippi, Tennessee, and Kentucky, to Northern railway centres, began to divert the passenger travel from the steamers; next the war came and almost entirely annihilated the steamboating industry during several years, leaving most of the pilots idle, and the cost of living advancing all the time; then the treasurer of the St. Louis association put his hand into the till and walked off with every dollar of the ample fund; and finally, the railroads intruding everywhere, there was little for steamers to do, when the war was over, but carry freights; so straightway some genius from the Atlantic coast introduced the plan of towing a dozen steamer cargoes down to New Orleans at the tail of a vulgar little tug-boat; and behold, in the twinkling of an eye, as it were, the association and the noble science of piloting were things of the dead and pathetic past!

## VII.

[Leaving Port. Racing. Shortening of the
River by Cut-Offs. A Steamboat's Ghost.
"Stephen's" Plan of "Resumption."]

It was always the custom for the boats to leave New
Orleans between four and five o'clock in the afternoon.
From three o'clock onward they would be burning rosin
and pitch pine (the sign of preparation), and so one had
the picturesque spectacle of a rank, some two or three miles
long, of tall, ascending columns of coal-black smoke; a
colonnade which supported a sable roof of the same smoke
blended together and spreading abroad over the city.
Every outward-bound boat had its flag flying at the jack-
staff, and sometimes a duplicate on the vergè staff astern.
Two or three miles of mates were commanding and swearing with more than usual emphasis; countless processions
of freight barrels and boxes were spinning down the slant
of the levee and flying aboard the stage-planks; belated passengers were dodging and skipping among these frantic
things, hoping to reach the forecastle companion way alive,
but having their doubts about it; women with reticules
and bandboxes were trying to keep up with husbands
freighted with carpet-sacks and crying babies, and making
a failure of it by losing their heads in the whirl and roar
and general distraction; drays and baggage-vans were clattering hither and thither in a wild hurry, every now and
then getting blocked and jammed together, and then during ten seconds one could not see them for the profanity,
except vaguely and dimly; every windlass connected with
every fore-hatch, from one end of that long array of steamboats to the other, was keeping up a deafening whiz and
whir, lowering freight into the hold, and the half-naked
crews of perspiring nègroes that worked them were roaring
such songs as De Las' Sack! De Las' Sack!—inspired to un-
imaginable exaltation by the chaos of turmoil and racket
that was driving everybody else mad. By this time the hurricane and boiler decks of the steamers would be packed
and black with passengers. The "last bells" would begin to
clang, all down the line, and then the powwow seemed to

double; in a moment or two the final warning came,—a simultaneous din of Chinese gongs, with the cry, "All dat ain't goin', please to git asho'!"—and behold, the powwow quadrupled! People came swarming ashore, overturning excited stragglers that were trying to swarm aboard. One more moment later a long array of stage-planks was being hauled in, each with its customary latest passenger clinging to the end of it with teeth, nails, and everything else, and the customary latest procrastinator making a wild spring shoreward over his head.

Now a number of the boats slide backward into the stream, leaving wide gaps in the serried rank of steamers. Citizens crowd the decks of boats that are not to go, in order to see the sight. Steamer after steamer straightens herself up, gathers all her strength, and presently comes swinging by, under a tremendous head of steam, with flag flying, black smoke rolling, and her entire crew of firemen and deck-hands (usually swarthy negroes) massed together on the forecastle, the best "voice" in the lot towering from the midst (being mounted on the capstan), waving his hat or a flag, and all roaring a mighty chorus, while the parting cannons boom and the multitudinous spectators swing their hats and huzza! Steamer after steamer falls into line, and the stately procession goes winging its way up the river.

In the old times, whenever two fast boats started out on a race, with a big crowd of people looking on, it was inspiring to hear the crews sing, especially if the time were night-fall, and the forecastle lit up with the red glare of the torch-baskets. Racing was royal fun. The public always had an idea that racing was dangerous; whereas the very opposite was the case—that is, after the laws were passed which restricted each boat to just so many pounds of steam to the square inch. No engineer was ever sleepy or careless when his heart was in a race. He was constantly on the alert, trying gauge-cocks and watching things. The dangerous place was on slow, popular boats, where the engineers drowsed around and allowed chips to get into the "doctor" and shut off the water supply from the boilers.

In the "flush times" of steamboating, a race between two notoriously fleet steamers was an event of vast importance. The date was set for it several weeks in advance, and from that time forward, the whole Mississippi Valley was in a state of consuming excitement. Politics and the weather were dropped, and people talked only of the coming race. As the time approached, the two steamers "stripped" and got ready. Every incumbrance that added weight, or exposed a resisting surface to wind or water, was removed, if the boat could possibly do without it. The "spars," and sometimes even their supporting derricks, were sent ashore, and no means left to set the boat afloat in case she got aground. When the Eclipse and the A. L. Shotwell ran their great race twenty-two years ago, it was said that pains were taken to scrape the gilding off the fanciful device which hung between the Eclipse's chimneys, and that for that one trip the captain left off his kid gloves and had his head shaved. But I always doubted these things.

If the boat was known to make her best speed when drawing five and a half feet forward and five feet aft, she was carefully loaded to that exact figure—she wouldn't enter a dose of homœopathic pills on her manifest after that. Hardly any passengers were taken, because they not only add weight but they never will "trim boat." They always run to the side when there is anything to see, whereas a conscientious and experienced steamboatman would stick to the centre of the boat and part his hair in the middle with a spirit level.

No way-freights and no way-passengers were allowed, for the racers would stop only at the largest towns, and then it would be only "touch and go." Coal flats and wood flats were contracted for beforehand, and these were kept ready to hitch on to the flying steamers at a moment's warning. Double crews were carried, so that all work could be quickly done.

The chosen date being come, and all things in readiness, the two great steamers back into the stream, and lie there jockeying a moment, and apparently watching each other's slightest movement, like sentient creatures; flags drooping, the pent steam shrieking through safety-valves, the black smoke rolling and tumbling from the chimneys and darkening all the air. People, people everywhere; the shores, the house-tops, the steamboats, the ships, are packed with them, and you know that the borders of the broad Mississippi are going to be fringed with humanity thence northward twelve hundred miles, to welcome these racers. Presently tall columns of steam burst from the 'scape-pipes of both steamers, two guns boom a good-by, two red-shirted heroes mounted on capstans wave their small flags above the massed crews on the forecastles, two plaintive solos linger on the air a few waiting seconds, two mighty choruses burst forth—and here they come! Brass bands bray Hail Columbia, huzza after huzza thunders from the shores, and the stately creatures go whistling by like the wind.

Those boats will never halt a moment between New Orleans and St. Louis, except for a second or two at large towns, or to hitch thirty-cord wood-boats alongside. You should be on board when they take a couple of those wood-boats in tow and turn a swarm of men into each; by the time you have wiped your glasses and put them on, you will be wondering what has become of that wood.

Two nicely matched steamers will stay in sight of each other day after day. They might even stay side by side, but for the fact that pilots are not all alike, and the smartest pilots will win the race. If one of the boats has a "lightning" pilot, whose "partner" is a trifle his inferior, you can tell which one is on watch by noting whether that boat has gained ground or lost some during each four-hour stretch. The shrewdest pilot can delay a boat if he has not a fine genius for steering. Steering is a very high art. One must not keep a rudder dragging across a boat's stern if he wants to get up the river fast.

There is a marvelous difference in boats, of course. For a long time I was on a boat that was so slow we used to forget what year it was we left port in. But of course this was at rare intervals. Ferry-boats used to lose valuable trips because their passengers grew old and died, waiting for us to get by. This was at still rarer intervals. I had the documents for these occurrences, but through carelessness they have been mislaid. This boat, the John J. Roe, was so slow that when she finally sunk in Madrid Bend, it was five years before the owners heard of it. That was always a confusing fact to me, but it is according to the record, any way. She was dismally slow; still, we often had pretty exciting times racing with islands, and rafts, and such things. One trip, however, we did rather well. We went to St. Louis in sixteen days. But even at this rattling gait I think we changed watches three times in Fort Adams reach, which is five miles long. A "reach" is a piece of straight river, and of course the current drives through such a place in a pretty lively way.

That trip we went to Grand Gulf, from New Orleans, in four days (three hundred and forty miles); the Eclipse and Shotwell did it in one. We were nine days out, in the chute of 63 (seven hundred miles); the Eclipse and Shotwell went there in two days.

Just about a generation ago, a boat called the J. M. White went from New Orleans to Cairo in three days, six hours, and forty-four minutes. Twenty-two years ago the Eclipse made the same trip in three days, three hours, and twenty minutes. About five years ago the superb R. E. Lee did it in three days and *one* hour. This last is called the fastest trip on record. I will try to show that it was not. For this reason: the distance between New Orleans and Cairo, when the J. M. White ran it, was about eleven hundred and six miles; consequently her average speed was a trifle over fourteen miles per hour. In the Eclipse's day the distance between the two ports had become reduced to one thousand and eighty miles; consequently her average speed was a shade under fourteen and three eighths miles per hour. In the R. E. Lee's time the distance had diminished to about one thousand and thirty miles; consequently her average was about fourteen and one eighth miles per hour. Therefore the Eclipse's was conspicuously the fastest time that has ever been made.

These dry details are of importance in one particular. They give me an opportunity of introducing one of the Mississippi's oddest peculiarities,—that of shortening its length from time to time. If you will throw a long, pliant apple-paring over your shoulder, it will pretty fairly shape itself into an average section of the Mississippi River; that is, the nine or ten hundred miles stretching from Cairo, Illinois, southward to New Orleans, the same being wonderfully crooked, with a brief straight bit here and there at wide intervals. The two-hundred-mile stretch from Cairo northward to St. Louis is by no means so crooked, that being a rocky country which the river cannot cut much.

The water cuts the alluvial banks of the "lower" river into deep horseshoe curves; so deep, indeed, that in some places if you were to get ashore at one extremity of the horseshoe and walk across the neck, half or three quarters of a mile, you could sit down and rest a couple of hours while your steamer was coming around the long elbow, at a speed of ten miles an hour, to take you aboard again. When the river is rising fast, some scoundrel whose plantation is back in the country, and therefore of inferior value, has only to watch his chance, cut a little gutter across the narrow neck of land some dark night, and turn the water into it, and in a wonderfully short time a miracle has happened: to wit, the whole Mississippi has taken possession of that little ditch, and placed the countryman's plantation on its bank (quadrupling its value), and that other party's formerly valuable plantation finds itself away out yonder on a big island; the old water-course around it will soon shoal up, boats cannot approach within ten miles of it, and down goes its value to a fourth of its former worth. Watches are kept on those narrow necks, at needful times, and if a man happens to be caught cutting a ditch across them, the chances are all against his ever having another opportunity to cut a ditch.

Pray observe some of the effects of this ditching business. Once there was a neck opposite Port Hudson, Louisiana, which was only half a mile across, in its narrowest place. You could walk across there in fifteen minutes; but if you made the journey around the cape on a raft, you traveled thirty-five miles to accomplish the same thing. In 1722 the river darted through that neck, deserted its old bed, and thus shortened itself thirty-five miles. In the same way it shortened itself twenty-five miles at Black Hawk Point in 1699. Below Red River Landing, Raccourci cut-off was made (thirty or forty years ago, I think). This shortened the river twenty-eight miles. In our day, if you travel by river from the southernmost of these three cut-offs to the northernmost, you go only seventy miles. To do the same thing a hundred and seventy-six years ago, one had to go a hundred and fifty-eight miles!—a shortening of eighty-eight miles in that trifling distance. At some forgotten time in the past, cut-offs were made above Vidalia, Louisiana; at island 92; at island 84; and at Hale's Point. These shortened the river, in the aggregate, seventy-seven miles.

Since my own day on the Mississippi, I am informed that cut-offs have been made at Hurricane Island; at island 100; at Napoleon, Arkansas; at Walnut Bend; and at Council Bend. These shortened the river, in the aggregate, sixty-seven miles. In my own time a cut-off was made at American Bend, which shortened the river ten miles or more.

Therefore: the Mississippi between Cairo and New Orleans was twelve hundred and fifteen miles long one hundred and seventy-six years ago. It was eleven hundred and eighty after the cut-off of 1722. It was one thousand and forty after the American Bend cut-off (some sixteen or seventeen years ago.) It has lost sixty-seven miles since. Consequently its length is only nine hundred and seventy-three miles at present.

Now, if I wanted to be one of those ponderous scientific people, and "let on" to prove what had occurred in the remote past by what had occurred in a given time in the recent past, or what will occur in the far future by what has occurred in late years, what an opportunity is here! Geology never had such a chance, nor such exact data to argue from! Nor "development of species," either! Glacial epochs are great things, but they are vague—vague. Please observe:—

In the space of one hundred and seventy-six years the Lower Mississippi has shortened itself two hundred and forty-two miles. That is an average of a trifle over one mile and a third per year. Therefore, any calm person, who is not blind or idiotic, can see that in the Old Oölitic Silurian Period, just a million years ago next November, the Lower Mississippi River was upwards of one million three hundred thousand miles long, and stuck out over the Gulf of Mexico like a fishing-rod. And by the same token any person can see that seven hundred and forty-two years from now the Lower Mississippi will be only a mile and three quarters long, and Cairo and New Orleans will have joined their streets together, and be plodding comfortably along under a single mayor and a mutual board of aldermen. There is something fascinating about science. One gets such wholesale returns of conjecture out of such a trifling investment of fact.

When the water begins to flow through one of those ditches I have been speaking of, it is time for the people thereabouts to move. The water cleaves the banks away like a knife. By the time the ditch has become twelve or fifteen feet wide, the calamity is as good as accomplished, for no power on earth can stop it now. When the width has reached a hundred yards, the banks begin to peel off in slices half an acre wide. The current flowing around the bend traveled formerly only five miles an hour; now it is tremendously increased by the shortening of the distance. I was on board the first boat that tried to go through the cut-off at American Bend, but we did not get through. It was toward midnight, and a wild night it was—thunder, lightning, and torrents of rain. It was estimated that the current in the cut-off was making about fifteen or twenty miles an hour; twelve or thirteen was the best our boat could do, even in tolerably slack water, therefore perhaps we were foolish to try the cut-off. However, Mr. X. was ambitious, and he kept on trying. The eddy running up the bank, under the "point," was about as swift as the current out in the middle; so we would go flying up the shore like a lightning express train, get on a big head of steam, and "stand by for a surge" when we struck the current that was whirling by the point. But all our preparations were useless. The instant the current hit us it spun us around like a top, the water deluged the forecastle, and the boat careened so far over that one could hardly keep his feet. The next instant we were away down the river, clawing with might and main to keep out of the woods. We tried the experiment four times. I stood on the forecastle companion way to see. It was astonishing to observe how suddenly the boat would spin around and turn tail the moment she emerged from the eddy and the current struck her nose. The sounding concussion and the quivering would have been about the same if she had come full speed against a sand-bank. Under the lightning flashes one could see the plantation cabins and the goodly acres tumble into the river; and the crash they made was not a bad effort at thunder. Once, when we spun around, we only missed a house about twenty feet, that had a light burning in the window; and in the same instant that house went overboard. Nobody could stay on our forecastle; the water swept across it in a torrent every time we plunged athwart the current. At the end of our fourth effort we brought up in the woods two miles below the cut-off; all the country there was overflowed, of course. A day or two later the cut-off was three quarters of a mile wide, and boats passed up through it without much difficulty, and so saved ten miles.

The old Raccourci cut-off reduced the river's length twenty-eight miles. There used to be a tradition connected with it. It was said that a boat came along there in the night and went around the enormous elbow the usual way, the pilots not knowing that the cut-off had been made. It was a grisly, hideous night, and all shapes were vague and distorted. The old bend had already begun to fill up, and the boat got to running away from mysterious reefs, and occasionally hitting one. The perplexed pilots fell to swearing, and finally uttered the entirely unnecessary wish that they might never get out of that place. As always happens in such cases, that particular prayer was answered, and the others neglected. So to this day that phantom steamer is still butting around in that deserted river, trying to find her way out. More than one grave watchman has sworn to me that on drizzly, dismal nights, he has glanced fearfully down that forgotten river as he passed the head of the island, and seen the faint glow of the spectre steamer's lights drifting through the distant gloom, and heard the muffled cough of her 'scape-pipes and the plaintive cry of her leadsmen.

In the absence of further statistics, I beg to close this series of Old Mississippi articles with one more reminiscence of wayward, careless, ingenious "Stephen," whom I described in a former paper.

Most of the captains and pilots held Stephen's note for borrowed sums ranging from two hundred and fifty dollars upward. Stephen never paid one of these notes, but he was very prompt and very zealous about renewing them every twelvemonth.

Of course there came a time, at last, when Stephen could no longer borrow of his ancient creditors; so he was obliged to lie in wait for new men who did not know him. Such a victim was good-hearted, simple-natured young Yates (I use a fictitious name, but the real name began, as this one does, with a Y). Young Yates graduated as a pilot, got a berth, and when the month was ended and he stepped up to the clerk's office and received his two hundred and fifty dollars in crisp new bills, Stephen was there! His silvery tongue began to wag, and in a very little while Yates's two hundred and fifty dollars had changed hands. The fact was soon known at pilot headquarters, and the amusement and satisfaction of the old creditors were large and generous. But innocent Yates never suspected that Stephen's promise to pay promptly at the end of the week was a worthless one. Yates called for his money at the stipulated time; Stephen sweetened him up and put him off a week. He called then, according to agreement, and came away sugar-coated again, but suffering under another postponement. So the thing went on. Yates haunted Stephen week after week, to no purpose, and at last gave it up. And then straightway Stephen began to haunt Yates! Wherever Yates appeared, there was the inevitable Stephen. And not only there, but beaming with affection and gushing with apologies for not being able to pay. By and by, whenever poor Yates saw him coming, he would turn and fly, and drag his company with him, if he had company; but it was of no use; his debtor would run him down and corner him. Panting and red-faced, Stephen would come, with outstretched hands and eager eyes, invade the conversation, shake both of Yates's arms loose in their sockets, and begin:—

"My, what a race I've had! I saw you didn't see me, and so I clapped on all steam for fear I'd miss you entirely. And here you are! there, just stand so, and let me look at you! Just the same old noble countenance." [To Yates's friend:] "Just look at him! *Look* at him! Ain't it just *good* to look at him! *Ain't* it now? Ain't he just a picture! *Some* call him a picture; *I* call him a panorama! That's what he is—an entire panorama. And now I'm reminded! How I do wish I could have seen you an hour earlier! For twenty-four hours I've been saving up that two hundred and fifty dollars for you; been looking for you everywhere. I waited at the Planter's from six yesterday evening till two o'clock this morning, without rest or food; my wife says, 'Where have you been all night?' I said, 'This debt lies heavy on my mind.' She says, 'In all my days I never saw a man take a debt to heart the way you do.' I said, 'It's my nature; how can *I* change it?' She says, 'Well, do go to bed and get some rest.' I said, 'Not till that poor, noble man has got his money.' So I set up all night, and this morning out I shot, and the first man I struck told me you had shipped on the Grand Turk and gone to New Orleans. Well, sir, I had to lean up against a building and cry. So help me goodness, I couldn't help it. The man that owned the place come out cleaning up with a rag, and said he didn't like to have people cry against his building, and then it seemed to me that the whole world had turned against me, and it wasn't any use to live any more; and coming along an hour ago, suffering no man knows what agony, I met Jim Wilson and paid him the two hundred and fifty dollars on account; and to think that here you are, now, and I haven't got a cent! But as sure as I am standing here on this ground on this particular brick,—there, I've scratched a mark on the brick to remember it by,—I'll borrow that money and pay it over to you at twelve o'clock sharp, to-morrow! Now, stand so; let me look at you just once more."

And so on. Yates's life became a burden to him. He could not escape his debtor and his debtor's awful sufferings on account of not being able to pay. He dreaded to show himself in the street, lest he should find Stephen lying in wait for him at the corner.

Bogart's billiard saloon was a great resort for pilots in those days. They met there about as much to exchange river news as to play. One morning Yates was there; Stephen was there, too, but kept out of sight. But by and by, when about all the pilots had arrived who were in town, Stephen suddenly appeared in the midst, and rushed for Yates as for a long-lost brother.

"*Oh,* I am so glad to see you! Oh my soul, the sight of you is such a comfort to my eyes! Gentlemen, I owe all of you money; among you I owe probably forty thousand dollars. I want to pay it; I intend to pay it—every last cent of it. You all know, without my telling you, what sorrow it has cost me to remain so long under such deep obligations to such patient and generous friends; but the sharpest pang I suffer—by far the sharpest—is from the debt I owe to this noble young man here; and I have come to this place this morning especially to make the announcement that I have at last found a method whereby I can pay off all my debts! And most especially I wanted *him* to be here when I announced it. Yes, my faithful friend,—my benefactor, I've found the method! I've found the method to pay off *all* my debts, and you'll get your money!" Hope dawned in Yates's eye; then Stephen, beaming benignantly, and placing his hand upon Yates's head, added, "I am going to pay them off in alphabetical order!"

Then he turned and disappeared. The full significance of Stephen's "method" did not dawn upon the perplexed and musing crowd for some two minutes; and then Yates murmured with a sigh:—

"Well, the Y's stand a gaudy chance. He won't get any further than the C's in *this* world, and I reckon that after a good deal of eternity has wasted away in the next one, I'll still be referred to up there as 'that poor, ragged pilot that came here from St. Louis in the early days!'"

# THE JUMPING FROG

[In English. Then in French. Then Clawed
Back into a Civilized Language Once More
by Patient, Unremunerated Toil.]

Even a criminal is entitled to fair play; and certainly when
a man who has done no harm has been unjustly treated, he
is privileged to do his best to right himself. My attention
has just been called to an article some three years old in
a French Magazine entitled, *Revue des Deux Mondes* (Review of Some Two Worlds), wherein the writer treats of
"Les Humoristes Americaines" (These Humorists Americans). I am one of these humorists Americans dissected by
him, and hence the complaint I am making.

This gentleman's article is an able one (as articles go, in
the French, where they always tangle up everything to that
degree that when you start into a sentence you never
know whether you are going to come out alive or not). It
is a very good article, and the writer says all manner of
kind and complimentary things about me—for which I am
sure I thank him with all my heart; but then why should
he go and spoil all his praise by one unlucky experiment?
What I refer to is this: he says my Jumping Frog is a
funny story, but still he can't see why it should ever really
convulse any one with laughter—and straightway proceeds
to translate it into French in order to prove to his nation
that there is nothing so very extravagantly funny about it.
Just there is where my complaint originates. He has not
translated it at all; he has simply mixed it all up; it is no
more like the Jumping Frog when he gets through with it
than I am like a meridian of longitude. But my mere assertion is not proof; wherefore I print the French version,
that all may see that I do not speak falsely; furthermore,
in order that even the unlettered may know my injury and

give me their compassion, I have been at infinite pains
and trouble to retranslate this French version back into
English; and to tell the truth I have well-nigh worn myself out at it, having scarcely rested from my work during
five days and nights. I cannot speak the French language,
but I can translate very well, though not fast, I being self-
educated. I ask the reader to run his eye over the original
English version of the Jumping Frog, and then read the
French or my retranslation, and kindly take notice how the
Frenchman has riddled the grammar. I think it is the
worst I ever saw; and yet the French are called a polished
nation. If I had a boy that put sentences together as they
do, I would polish him to some purpose. Without further
introduction, the Jumping Frog, as I originally wrote it,
was as follows [after it will be found the French version,
and after the latter my retranslation from the French]:

# [The Notorious Jumping Frog of Calaveras County.]

In compliance with the request of a friend of mine, who
wrote me from the East, I called on good-natured, garrulous old Simon Wheeler, and inquired after my friend's
friend, Leonidas W. Smiley, as requested to do, and I
hereunto append the result. I have a lurking suspicion
that *Leonidas W.* Smiley is a myth; that my friend never
knew such a personage; and that he only conjectured that
if I asked old Wheeler about him, it would remind him of
his infamous *Jim* Smiley, and he would go to work and
bore me to death with some exasperating reminiscence of
him as long and as tedious as it should be useless to me. If
that was the design, it succeeded.

I found Simon Wheeler dozing comfortably by the bar-
room stove of the dilapidated tavern in the decayed mining
camp of Angel's, and I noticed that he was fat and bald-
headed, and had an expression of winning gentleness and
simplicity upon his tranquil countenance. He roused up,
and gave me good day. I told him that a friend of mine
had commissioned me to make some inquiries about a
cherished companion of his boyhood named *Leonidas W.*
Smiley—*Rev. Leonidas W.* Smiley, a young minister of the

Gospel, who he had heard was at one time a resident of Angel's Camp. I added that if Mr. Wheeler could tell me anything about this Rev. Leonidas W. Smiley, I would feel under many obligations to him.

Simon Wheeler backed me into a corner and blockaded me there with his chair, and then sat down and reeled off the monotonous narrative which follows this paragraph. He never smiled, he never frowned, he never changed his voice from the gentle-flowing key to which he tuned his initial sentence, he never betrayed the slightest suspicion of enthusiasm; but all through the interminable narrative there ran a vein of impressive earnestness and sincerity, which showed me plainly that, so far from his imagining that there was anything ridiculous or funny about his story, he regarded it as a really important matter, and admired its two heroes as men of transcendent genius in *finesse*. I let him go on in his own way, and never interrupted him once.

"Rev. Leonidas W. H'm, Reverend Le—well, there was a feller here once by the name of *Jim* Smiley, in the winter of '49—or maybe it was the spring of '50—I don't recollect exactly, somehow, though what makes me think it was one or the other is because I remember the big flume warn't finished when he first come to the camp; but anyway, he was the curiousest man about always betting on anything that turned up you ever see, if he could get anybody to bet on the other side; and if he couldn't he'd change sides. Any way that suited the other man would suit *him* —any way just so's he got a bet, *he* was satisfied. But still he was lucky, uncommon lucky; he most always come out winner. He was always ready and laying for a chance; there couldn't be no solit'ry thing mentioned but that feller'd offer to bet on it, and take ary side you please, as I was just telling you. If there was a horse-race, you'd find him flush or you'd find him busted at the end of it; if there was a dog-fight, he'd bet on it; if there was a cat-fight, he'd bet on it; if there was a chicken-fight, he'd bet on it; why, if there was two birds setting on a fence, he would bet you which one would fly first; or if there was a camp-meeting, he would be there reg'lar to bet on Parson Walker, which he judged to be the best exhorter about here, and so he was too, and a good man. If he even see a straddle-bug start to go anywheres, he would bet you how long it would take him to get to—to wherever he was go-

ing to, and if you took him up, he would foller that straddle-bug to Mexico but what he would find out where he
was bound for and how long he was on the road. Lots of
the boys here has seen that Smiley, and can tell you about
him. Why, it never made no difference to *him*—he'd bet on
*any* thing—the dangdest feller. Parson Walker's wife laid
very sick once, for a good while, and it seemed as if they
warn't going to save her; but one morning he come in, and
Smiley up and asked him how she was, and he said she was
considerable better—thank the Lord for his inf'nite mercy
—and coming on so smart that with the blessing of Prov'-
dence she'd get well yet; and Smiley, before he thought,
says, 'Well, I'll resk two-and-a-half she don't anyway.'

"Thish-yer Smiley had a mare—the boys called her the
fifteen-minute nag, but that was only in fun, you know,
because of course she was faster than that—and he used
to win money on that horse, for all she was so slow and always had the asthma, or the distemper, or the consumption,
or something of that kind. They used to give her two or
three hundred yards' start, and then pass her under way;
but always at the fag end of the race she'd get excited and
desperate like, and come cavorting and straddling up, and
scattering her legs around limber, sometimes in the air,
and sometimes out to one side among the fences, and kicking up m-o-r-e dust and raising m-o-r-e racket with her
coughing and sneezing and blowing her nose—and *always*
fetch up at the stand just about a neck ahead, as near as
you could cipher it down.

"And he had a little small bull-pup, that to look at him
you'd think he warn't worth a cent but to set around and
look ornery and lay for a chance to steal something. But as
soon as money was up on him he was a different dog; his
under-jaw'd begin to stick out like the fo'castle of a steamboat, and his teeth would uncover and shine like the
furnaces. And a dog might tackle him and bully-rag him,
and bite him, and throw him over his shoulder two or
three times, and Andrew Jackson—which was the name of
the pup—Andrew Jackson would never let on but what *he*
was satisfied, and hadn't expected nothing else—and the
bets being doubled and doubled on the other side all the
time, till the money was all up; and then all of a sudden he
would grab that other dog jest by the j'int of his hind leg
and freeze to it—not chaw, you understand, but only just

grip and hang on till they throwed up the sponge, if it was a year. Smiley always come out winner on that pup, till he harnessed a dog once that didn't have no hind legs, because they'd been sawed off in a circular saw, and when the thing had gone along far enough, and the money was all up, and he come to make a snatch for his pet holt, he see in a minute how he'd been imposed on, and how the other dog had him in the door, so to speak, and he 'peared surprised, and then he looked sorter discouraged-like, and didn't try no more to win the fight, and so he got shucked out bad. He give Smiley a look, as much as to say his heart was broke, and it was *his* fault, for putting up a dog that hadn't no hind legs for him to take holt of, which was his main dependence in a fight, and then he limped off a piece and laid down and died. It was a good pup, was that Andrew Jackson, and would have made a name for hisself if he'd lived, for the stuff was in him and he had genius— I know it, because he hadn't no opportunities to speak of, and it don't stand to reason that a dog could make such a fight as he could under them circumstances if he hadn't no talent. It always makes me feel sorry when I think of that last fight of his'n, and the way it turned out.

"Well, thish-yer Smiley had rat-tarriers, and chicken cocks, and tomcats and all them kind of things, till you couldn't rest, and you couldn't fetch nothing for him to bet on but he'd match you. He ketched a frog one day, and took him home, and said he cal'lated to educate him; and so he never done nothing for three months but set in his back yard and learn that frog to jump. And you bet you he *did* learn him, too. He'd give him a little punch behind, and the next minute you'd see that frog whirling in the air like a doughnut—see him turn one summerset, or maybe a couple, if he got a good start, and come down flat-footed and all right, like a cat. He got him up so in the matter of ketching flies, and kep' him in practice so constant, that he'd nail a fly every time as fur as he could see him. Smiley said all a frog wanted was education, and he could do 'most anything—and I believe him. Why, I've seen him set Dan'l Webster down here on this floor—Dan'l Webster was the name of the frog—and sing out, 'Flies, Dan'l, flies!' and quicker'n you could wink he'd spring straight up and snake a fly off'n the counter there, and flop down on the floor ag'in as solid as a gob of mud, and fall to scratching the side

of his head with his hind foot as indifferent as if he hadn't
no idea he'd been doin' any more'n any frog might do. You
never see a frog so modest and straight-for'ard as he was,
for all he was so gifted. And when it come to fair and
square jumping on a dead level, he could get over more
ground at one straddle than any animal of his breed you
ever see. Jumping on a dead level was his strong suit, you
understand; and when it come to that, Smiley would ante
up money on him as long as he had a red. Smiley was
monstrous proud of his frog, and well he might be, for
fellers that had traveled and been everywheres all said he
laid over any frog that ever *they* see.

"Well, Smiley kep' the beast in a little lattice box, and he
used to fetch him down-town sometimes and lay for a bet.
One day a feller—a stranger in the camp, he was—come
acrost him with his box, and says:

" 'What might it be that you've got in the box?'

"And Smiley says, sorter indifferent-like, 'It might be a
parrot, or it might be a canary, maybe, but it ain't—it's
only just a frog.'

"And the feller took it, and looked at it careful, and
turned it round this way and that, and says, 'H'm—so 'tis.
Well, what's *he* good for?'

" 'Well,' Smiley says, easy and careless, 'he's good enough
for *one* thing, I should judge—he can outjump any frog in
Calaveras County.'

"The feller took the box again, and took another long,
particular look, and give it back to Smiley, and says, very
deliberate, 'Well,' he says, 'I don't see no p'ints about that
frog that's any better'n any other frog.'

" 'Maybe you don't,' Smiley says. 'Maybe you understand
frogs and maybe you don't understand 'em; maybe you've
had experience, and maybe you ain't only a amature, as it
were. Anyways, I've got *my* opinion, and I'll resk forty
dollars that he can outjump any frog in Calaveras County.'

"And the feller studied a minute, and then says, kinder
sadlike, 'Well, I'm only a stranger here, and I ain't got no
frog; but if I had a frog, I'd bet you.'

"And then Smiley says, 'That's all right—that's all right
—if you'll hold my box a minute, I'll go and get you a
frog.' And so the feller took the box, and put up his forty
dollars along with Smiley's, and set down to wait.

"So he set there a good while thinking and thinking to

himself, and then he got the frog out and prized his mouth open and took a teaspoon and filled him full of quail-shot —filled him pretty near up to his chin—and set him on the floor. Smiley he went to the swamp and slopped around in the mud for a long time, and finally he ketched a frog, and fetched him in, and give him to this feller, and says:

" 'Now, if you're ready, set him alongside of Dan'l, with his fore paws just even with Dan'l's, and I'll give the word.' Then he says, 'One—two—three—*git!*' and him and the feller touched up the frogs from behind, and the new frog hopped off lively, but Dan'l give a heave, and hysted up his shoulders—so—like a Frenchman, but it warn't no use—he couldn't budge; he was planted as solid as a church, and he couldn't no more stir than if he was anchored out. Smiley was a good deal surprised, and he was disgusted too, but he didn't have no idea what the matter was, of course.

"The feller took the money and started away; and when he was going out at the door, he sorter jerked his thumb over his shoulder—so—at Dan'l, and says again, very deliberate, 'Well,' he says, '*I* don't see no p'ints about that frog that's any better'n any other frog.'

"Smiley he stood scratching his head and looking down at Dan'l a long time, and at last he says, 'I do wonder what in the nation that frog throw'd off for—I wonder if there ain't something the matter with him—he 'pears to look mighty baggy, somehow.' And he ketched Dan'l by the nap of the neck, and hefted him, and says, 'Why blame my cats if he don't weigh five pound!' and turned him upside down and he belched out a double handful of shot. And then he see how it was, and he was the maddest man—he set the frog down and took out after that feller, but he never ketched him. And—"

[Here Simon Wheeler heard his name called from the front yard, and got up to see what was wanted.] And turning to me as he moved away, he said: "Just set where you are, stranger, and rest easy—I ain't going to be gone a second."

But, by your leave, I did not think that a continuation of the history of the enterprising vagabond *Jim* Smiley would be likely to afford me much information concerning the Rev. *Leonidas W.* Smiley, and so I started away.

At the door I met the sociable Wheeler returning, and he buttonholed me and recommenced:

"Well, thish-yer Smiley had a yaller one-eyed cow that didn't have no tail, only just a short stump like a ban-nanner, and—"

However, lacking both time and inclination, I did not wait to hear about the afflicted cow, but took my leave.

Now let the learned look upon this picture and say if iconoclasm can further go:

[From the *Revue des Deux Mondes,* of July 15th, 1872.]

## ⌈La Grenouille Sauteuse du Comte de Calaveras.⌉

"—Il y avait une fois ici un individu connu sous le nom de Jim Smiley: c'était dans l'hiver de 49, peut-être bien au printemps de 50, je ne me rapelle pas exactement. Ce qui me fait croire que c'était l'un ou l'autre, c'est que je me souviens que le grand bief n'était pas achevé lorsqu'il arriva au camp pour la première fois, mais de toutes façons il était l'homme le plus friand de paris qui se pût voir, pariant sur tout ce qui se présentait, quand il pouvait trouver un adversaire, et, quand il n'en trouvait pas il passait du côté opposé. Tout ce qui convenait à l'autre lui convenait; pourvu qu'il eût un pari, Smiley était satisfait. Et il avait une chance! une chance inouïe: presque toujours il gagnait. Il faut dire qu'il était toujours prêt à s'exposer, qu'on ne pouvait mentionner la moindre chose sans que ce gaillard offrît de parier là-dessus n'importe quoi et de prendre le côté que l'on voudrait, comme je vous le disais tout à l'heure. S'il y avait des courses, vous le trouviez riche ou ruiné à la fin; s'il y avait un combat de chiens, il apportait son enjeu; il l'apportait pour un combat de chats, pour un combat de coqs;—parbleu! si vous aviez vu deux oiseaux sur une haie, il vous aurait offert de parier lequel s'envolerait le premier, et, s'il y avait *meeting* au camp, il venait parier régulièrement pour le curé Walker, qu'il jugeait être le meilleur prédicateur des environs, et qui l'était en effet, et un brave homme. Il aurait rencontré une punaise de bois en chemin, qu'il aurait parié sur le temps qu'il lui faudrait pour aller où elle voudrait aller, et si vous l'aviez pris au mot, il aurait suivi la punaise jusqu'au Mexique, sans se soucier d'aller si loin, ni du temps qu'il y perdrait. Une fois la femme du curé Walker fut très malade pendant long-temps, il semblait qu'on ne la sauverait pas; mais un matin le curé arrive, et Smiley lui demande comment ella va, et il dit qu'elle est bien mieux, grâce à l'infinie miséricorde, tellement mieux qu'avec la bénédiction de la Providence elle s'en tirerait, et voilà que, sans y penser, Smiley répond: —Eh bien! je gage deux et demi qu'elle mourra tout de même.

"Ce Smiley avait une jument que les gars appelaient le bidet du quart d'heure, mais seulement pour plaisanter, vous comprenez, parce que, bien entendu, elle était plus *vite* que ça! Et il avait coutume de gagner de l'argent avec cette bête, quoiqu'elle fût poussive, cornarde, toujours prise d'asthme, de coliques ou de consomption, ou de quelque chose d'approchant. On lui donnait 2 ou 300 *yards* au départ, puis on la dépassait sans peine; mais jamais à la fin elle ne manquait de s'échauffer, de s'exaspérer, et elle arrivait, s'écartant, se défendant, ses jambes grêles en l'air devant les obstacles, quelquefois les évitant et faisant avec cela plus de poussière qu'aucun cheval, plus de bruit surtout avec ses éternumens et reniflemens,—crac! elle arrivait donc toujours première d'une tête, aussi juste qu'on peut le mesurer. Et il avait un petit bouledogue qui, à le voir, ne valait pas un sou; on aurait cru que parier contre lui c'était voler, tant il était ordinaire; mais aussitôt les enjeux faits, il devenait un autre chien. Sa mâchoire in-férieure commençait à ressortir comme un gaillard d'avant, ses dents se découvraient brillantes commes des fournaises, et un chien pouvait le taquiner, l'exciter, le mordre, le jeter deux ou trois fois par-dessus son épaule, André Jackson, c'était le nom du chien, André Jackson prenait cela tran-quillement, comme s'il ne se fût jamais attendu à autre chose, et quand les paris étaient doublés et redoublés contre lui, il vous saisissait l'autre chien juste à l'articulation de la jambe de derrière, et il ne la lâchait plus, non pas qu'il la mâchât, vous concevez, mais il s'y serait tenu pendu jusqu'à ce qu'on jetât l'éponge en l'air, fallût-il attendre un an. Smiley gagnait toujours avec cette bête-là; mal-heureusement ils ont fini par dresser un chien qui n'avait pas de pattes de derrière, parce qu'on les avait sciées, et quand les choses furent au point qu'il voulait, et qu'il en vint à se jeter sur son morceau favori, le pauvre chien

comprit en un instant qu'on s'était moqué de lui, et que
l'autre le tenait. Vous n'avez jamais vu personne avoir l'air
plus penaud et plus découragé; il ne fit aucun effort pour
gagner le combat et fut rudement secoué, de sorte que,
regardant Smiley comme pour lui dire:—Mon cœur est
brisé, c'est ta faute; pourquoi m'avoir livré à un chien qui
n'a pas de pattes de derrière, puisque c'est par là que je
les bats?—il s'en alla en clopinant, et se coucha pour mourir.
Ah! c'était un bon chien, cet André Jackson, et il se serait
fait un nom, s'il avait vécu, car il y avait de l'étoffe en lui,
il avait du génie, je la sais, bien que de grandes occasions
lui aient manqué; mais il est impossible de supposer qu'un
chien capable de se battre comme lui, certaines circonstances
étant données, ait manqué de talent. Je me sens triste
toutes les fois que je pense à son dernier combat et au
dénoûment qu'il a eu. Eh bien! ce Smiley nourrissait des
terriers à rats, et des coqs combat, et des chats, et toute
sorte de choses, au point qu'il était toujours en mesure de
vous tenir tête, et qu'avec sa rage de paris on n'avait plus
de repos. Il attrapa un jour une grenouille et l'emporta
chez lui, disant qu'il prétendait faire son éducation; vous
me croirez si vous voulez, mais pendant trois mois il n'a
rien fait que lui apprendre à sauter dans une cour retirée
de sa maison. Et je vous réponds qu'il avait réussi. Il
lui donnait un petit coup par derrière, et l'instant d'après
vous voyiez la grenouille tourner en l'air comme un beignet
au-dessus de la poêle, faire une culbute, quelquefois deux,
lorsqu'elle était bien partie, et retomber sur ses pattes
comme un chat. Il l'avait dressée dans l'art de gober des
mouches, et l'y exerçait continuellement, si bien qu'une
mouche, du plus loin qu'elle apparaissait, était une mouche
perdue. Smiley avait coutume de dire que tout ce qui
manquait à une grenouille, c'était l'éducation, qu'avec
l'éducation elle pouvait faire presque tout, et je le crois.
Tenez, je l'ai vu poser Daniel Webster là sur se plancher,—
Daniel Webster était le nom de la grenouille,—et lui
chanter:—Des mouches! Daniel, des mouches!—En un clin
d'œil, Daniel avait bondi et saisi une mouche ici sur le
comptoir, puis sauté de nouveau par terre, où il restait
vraiment à se gratter la tête avec sa patte de derrière,
comme s'il n'avait pas eu la moindre idée de sa supériorité.
Jamais vous n'avez grenouille vu de aussi modeste, aussi
naturelle, douée comme elle l'était! Et quand il s'agissait

de sauter purement et simplement sur terrain plat, elle faisait plus de chemin en un saut qu'aucune bête de son espèce que vous puissiez connaître. Sauter à plat, c'était son fort! Quand il s'agissait de cela, Smiley entassait les enjeux sur elle tant qu'il lui, restait un rouge liard. Il faut le reconnaître, Smiley était monstrueusement fier de sa grenouille, et il en avait le droit, car des gens qui avaient voyagé, qui avaient tout vu, disaient qu'on lui ferait injure de la comparer à une autre; de façon que Smiley gardait Daniel dans une petite boîte à claire-voie qu'il emportait parfois à la ville pour quelque pari.

"Un jour, un individu étranger au camp l'arrête avec sa boîte et lui dit:—Qu'est-ce que vous avez donc serré là dedans?

"Smiley dit d'un air indifférent:—Cela pourrait être un perroquet ou un serin, mais ce n'est rien de pareil, ce n'est qu'une grenouille.

"L'individu la prend, la regarde avec soin, la tourne d'un côté et de l'autre puis il dit:—Tiens! en effet! A quoi est elle bonne?

"—Mon Dieu! répond Smiley, toujours d'un air dégagé, elle est bonne pour une chose à mon avis, elle peut battre en sautant toute grenouille du comté de Calaveras.

"L'individu reprend la boîte, l'examine de nouveau longuement, et la rend à Smiley en disant d'un air délibéré: —Eh bien! je ne vois pas que cette grenouille ait rien de mieux qu'aucune grenouille.

"—Possible que vous ne le voyiez pas, dit Smiley, possible que vous vous entendiez en grenouilles, possible que vous ne vous y entendiez point, possible que vous ayez de l'expérience, et possible que vous ne soyez qu'un amateur. De toute manière, je parie quarante dollars qu'elle battra en sautant n'importe quelle grenouille du comté de Calaveras.

"L'individu réfléchit une seconde et dit comme attristé: —Je ne suis qu'un étranger ici, je n'ai pas de grenouille; mais, si j'en avais une, je tiendrais le pari.

"—Fort bien! répond Smiley. Rien de plus facile. Si vous voulez tenir ma boîte une minute, j'irai vous chercher une grenouille.—Voilà donc l'individu qui garde la boîte, qui met ses quarante dollars sur ceux de Smiley et qui attend. Il attend assez longtemps, réfléchissant tout seul, et figurez-vous qu'il prend Daniel, lui ouvre la bouche de force at avec une cuiller à thé l'emplit de menu plomb de

chasse, mais l'emplit jusqu'au menton, puis il le pose par
terre. Smiley pendant ce temps était à barboter dans une
mare. Finalement il attrape une grenouillè, l'apporte à
cet individu et dit:—Maintenant, si vous êtes prêt, mettez-la
tout contre Daniel, avec leurs pattes de devant sur le même
ligne, et je donnerai le signal;—puis il ajoute:—Un, deux,
trois, sautez!

"Lui et l'individu touchent leurs grenouilles par derrière,
et la grenouille neuve se met à sautiller, mais Daniel se
soulève lourdement, hausse les épaules ainsi, comme un
Français; à quoi bon? il ne pouvait bouger, il était planté
solide comme une enclume, il n'avançait pas plus que si on
l'eût mis à l'ancre. Smiley fut surpris et dégoûté, mais il ne
se doutait pas du tour, bien entendu. L'individu empoche
l'argent, s'en va, et en s'en allant est-ce qu'il ne donne pas
un coup de pouce par-dessus l'épaule, comme ça, au pauvre
Daniel, en disant de son air délibéré:—Eh bien! je ne vois
pas que cette grenouille ait rien de mieux qu'une autre.

"Smiley se gratta longtemps la tête, les yeux fixés sur
Daniel, jusqu'à ce qu'enfin il dit:—Je me demanda comment
diable il se fait que cette bête ait refusé. . . . Est-ce qu'elle
aurait quelque chose? . . . On croirait qu'elle est enflée.

"Il empoigne Daniel par la peau du cou, le soulève et
dit:—Le loup me croque, s'il ne pèse pas cinq livres.

"Il le retourne, et le malheureux crache deux poignées de
plomb. Quand Smiley reconnut ce qui en était, il fut
comme fou. Vous le voyez d'ici poser sa grenouille par terre
et courir après cet individu, mais il ne le rattrapa jamais,
et. . . .

[Translation of the above back from the French.]

## [The Frog Jumping of the County of Calaveras.]

It there was one time here an individual known under
the name of Jim Smiley; it was in the winter of '49, possibly well at the spring of '50, I no me recollect not exactly. This which me makes to believe that it was the one
or the other, it is that I shall remember that the grand
flume is not achieved when he arrives at the camp for the
first time, but of all sides he was the man the most fond of

to bet which one have seen, betting upon all that which
is presented, when he could find an adversary; and when he
not of it could not, he passed to the side opposed. All that
which convenienced to the other, to him convenienced
also; seeing that he had a bet, Smiley was satisfied. And he
had a chance! a chance even worthless; nearly always he
gained. It must to say that he was always near to himself
expose, but one no could mention the least thing without
that this gaillard offered to bet the bottom, no matter
what, and to take the side that one him would, as I you
it said all at the hour (tout à l'heure). If it there was of
races, you him find rich or ruined at the end; if it there is
a combat of dogs, he bring his bet; he himself laid always
for a combat of cats, for a combat of cocks;—by-blue! If
you have see two birds upon a fence, he you should have
offered of to bet which of those birds shall fly the first;
and if there is *meeting* at the camp (*meeting* au camp) he
comes to bet regularly for the curé Walker, which he
judged to be the best predicator of the neighborhood
(prédicateur des environs) and which he was in effect, and
a brave man. He would encounter a bug of wood in the
road, whom he will bet upon the time which he shall take
to go where she would go—and if you him have take at the
word, he will follow the bug as far as Mexique, without
himself caring to go so far; neither of the time which he
there lost. One time the woman of the curé Walker is very
sick during long time, it seemed that one not her saved
not; but one morning the curé arrives, and Smiley him
demanded how she goes, and he said that she is well better,
grace to the infinite misery (lui demande comment elle va,
et il dit qu'elle est bien mieux, grâce à l'infinie miséricorde)
so much better that with the benediction of the Providence
she herself of it would pull out (elle s'en tirerait); and behold that without there thinking Smiley responds: "Well,
I gage two-and-half that she will die all of same."

This Smiley had an animal which the boys called the
nag of the quarter of hour, but solely for pleasantry, you
comprehend, because, well understand, she was more fast
as that! [Now why that exclamation?—M. T.] And it was
custom of to gain of the silver with this beast, notwithstanding she was poussive, cornarde, always taken of
asthma, of colics or of consumption, or something of approaching. One him would give two or three hundred

yards at the departure, then one him passed without pain; but never at the last she not fail of herself échauffer, of herself exasperate, and she arrives herself écartant, se défendant, her legs grêles in the air before the obstacles, something them elevating and making with this more of dust than any horse, more of noise above with his éternumens and reniflemens—crac! she arrives then always first by one head, as just as one can it measure. And he had a small bulldog (bouledogue!) who, to him see, no value, not a cent; one would believe that to bet against him it was to steal, so much he was ordinary; but as soon as the game made, she becomes another dog. Her jaw inferior commence to project like a deck of before, his teeth themselves discover brilliant like some furnaces, and a dog could him tackle (le taquiner), him excite, him murder (le mordre), him throw two or three times over his shoulder, André Jackson—this was the name of the dog—André Jackson takes that tranquilly, as if he not himself was never expecting other thing, and when the bets were doubled and redoubled against him, he you seize the other dog just at the articulation of the leg of behind, and he not it leave more, not that he it masticate, you conceive, but he himself there shall be holding during until that one throws the sponge in the air, must he wait a year. Smiley gained always with this beast-là; unhappily they have finished by elevating a dog who no had not of feet of behind, because one them had sawed; and when things were at the point that he would, and that he came to himself throw upon his morsel favorite, the poor dog comprehended in an instant that he himself was deceived in him, and that the other dog him had. You no have never seen person having the air more penaud and more discouraged; he not made no effort to gain the combat, and was rudely shucked.

Eh bien! this Smiley nourished some terriers à rats, and some cocks of combat, and some cats, and all sorts of things; and with his rage of betting one no had more of repose. He trapped one day a frog and him imported with him (et l'emporta chez lui) saying that he pretended to make his education. You me believe if you will, but during three months he not has nothing done but to him apprehend to jump (apprendre à sauter) in a court retired of her mansion (de sa maison). And I you respond that he have succeeded. He him gives a small blow by behind, and the instant after you shall see the frog turn in the air like a grease-biscuit, make one summersault, sometimes two, when she was well started, and refall upon his feet like a cat. He him had accomplished in the art of to gobble the flies (gober des mouches), and him there exercised continually —so well that a fly at the most far that she appeared was a fly lost. Smiley had custom to say that all which lacked to a frog it was the education, but with the education she could do nearly all—and I him believe. Tenez, I him have seen pose Daniel Webster there upon this plank— Daniel Webster was the name of the frog—and to him sing, "Some flies, Daniel, some flies!"—in a flash of the eye Daniel had bounded and seized a fly here upon the counter, then jumped anew at the earth, where he rested truly to himself scratch the head with his behind foot, as if he no had not the least idea of his superiority. Never you not have seen frog as modest, as natural, sweet as she was. And when he himself agitated to jump purely and simply upon plain earth, she does more ground in one jump than any beast of his species than you can know. To jump plain—this was his strong. When he himself agitated for that, Smiley multiplied the bets upon her as long as there to him remained a red. It must to know, Smiley was monstrously proud of his frog, and he of it was right, for some men who were traveled, who had all seen, said that they to him would be injurious to him compare to another frog. Smiley guarded Daniel in a little box latticed which he carried bytimes to the village for some bet.

One day an individual stranger at the camp him arrested with his box and him said:

"What is this that you have them shut up there within?"

Smiley said, with an air indifferent:

"That could be a paroquet, or a syringe (ou un serin), but this no is nothing of such, it not is but a frog."

The individual it took, it regarded with care, it turned from one side and from the other, then he said:

"Tiens! in effect!—At what is she good?"

"My God!" respond Smiley, always with an air disengaged, "she is good for one thing, to my notice (à mon avis), she can batter in jumping (elle peut battre en sautant) all frogs of the county of Calaveras."

The individual retook the box, it examined of new longly, and it rendered to Smiley in saying with an air deliberate:

"Eh bien! I no saw not that that frog had nothing of better than each frog." (Je ne vois pas que cette grenouille ait rien de mieux qu'aucune grenouille.) [If that isn't grammar gone to seed, then I count myself no judge.—M. T.]

"Possible that you not it saw not," said Smiley, "possible that you—you comprehend frogs; possible that you not you there comprehend nothing; possible that you had of the experience, and possible that you not be but an amateur. Of all manner (De toute manière) I bet forty dollars that she batter in jumping no matter which frog of the county of Calaveras."

The individual reflected a second, and said like sad:

"I not am but a stranger here, I no have not a frog; but if I of it had one, I would embrace the bet."

"Strong well!" respond Smiley; "nothing of more facility. If you will hold my box a minute, I go you to search a frog (j'irai vous chercher)."

Behold, then, the individual, who guards the box, who puts his forty dollars upon those of Smiley, and who attends (et qui attend). He attended enough longtimes, reflecting all solely. And figure you that he takes Daniel, him opens the mouth by force and with a teaspoon him fills with shot of the hunt, even him fills just to the chin, then he him puts by the earth. Smiley during these times was at slopping in a swamp. Finally he trapped (attrape) a frog, him carried to that individual, and said:

"Now if you be ready, put him all against Daniel, with their before feet upon the same line, and I give the signal"—then he added: "One, two, three—advance!"

Him and the individual touched their frogs by behind, and the frog new put to jump smartly, but Daniel himself lifted ponderously, exalted the shoulders thus, like a Frenchman—to what good? he not could budge, he is planted solid like a church, he not advance no more than if one him had put at the anchor.

Smiley was surprised and disgusted, but he not himself doubted not of the turn being intended (mais il ne se doutait pas du tour, bien entendu). The individual empocketed the silver, himself with it went, and of it himself in going is it that he no gives not a jerk of thumb over the shoulder—like that—at the poor Daniel, in saying with his air deliberate—(L'individu empoche l'argent, s'en va et en s'en allant est-ce qu'il ne donne pas un coup de pouce par-dessus l'épaule, comme ca, au pauvre Daniel, en disant de son air délibéré):

"Eh bien! *I no see not that that frog has nothing of better than another.*"

Smiley himself scratched longtimes the head, the eyes fixed upon Daniel, until that which at last he said:

"I me demand how the devil it makes itself that this beast has refused. Is it that she had something? One would believe that she is stuffed."

He grasped Daniel by the skin of the neck, him lifted and said:

"The wolf me bite if he no weigh not five pounds."

He him reversed and the unhappy belched two handfuls of shot (et le malheureux, etc.). When Smiley recognized how it was, he was like mad. He deposited his frog by the earth and ran after that individual, but he not him caught never.

Such is the Jumping Frog, to the distorted French eye. I claim that I never put together such an odious mixture of bad grammar and delirium tremens in my life. And what has a poor foreigner like me done, to be abused and mispresented like this? When I say, "Well, I don't see no p'ints about that frog that's any better'n any other frog," is it kind, is it just, for this Frenchman to try to make it appear that I said, "Eh bien! I no saw not that that frog had nothing of better than each frog"? I have no heart to write more. I never felt so about anything before.

HARTFORD, March, 1875.

# THE GREAT LANDSLIDE CASE

## [from *Roughing It.*]

The mountains are very high and steep about Carson, Eagle, and Washoe Valleys—very high and very steep, and so when the snow gets to melting off fast in the spring and the warm surface-earth begins to moisten and soften, the disastrous landslides commence. The reader cannot know what a landslide is, unless he has lived in that country and seen the whole side of a mountain taken off some fine morning and deposited down in the valley, leaving a vast, treeless, unsightly scar upon the mountain's front to keep the circumstance fresh in his memory all the years that he may go on living within seventy miles of that place.

General Buncombe was shipped out to Nevada in the invoice of territorial officers, to be United States Attorney. He considered himself a lawyer of parts, and he very much wanted an opportunity to manifest it—partly for the pure gratification of it and partly because his salary was territorially meager (which is a strong expression). Now the older citizens of a new territory look down upon the rest cf the world with a calm, benevolent compassion, as long as it keeps out of the way—when it gets in the way they snub it. Sometimes this latter takes the shape of a practical joke.

One morning Dick Hyde rode furiously up to General Buncombe's door in Carson City and rushed into his presence without stopping to tie his horse. He seemed much excited. He told the General that he wanted him to conduct a suit for him and would pay him five hundred dollars if he achieved a victory. And then, with violent gestures and a world of profanity, he poured out his griefs. He said it was pretty well known that for some years he had been farming (or ranching, as the more customary term is) in Washoe District, and making a successful thing of it, and furthermore it was known that his ranch was situated just in the edge of the valley, and that Tom Morgan owned a ranch immediately above it on the mountainside. And now the trouble was, that one of those hated and dreaded landslides had come and slid Morgan's ranch, fences, cabins, cattle, barns, and everything down on top of *his* ranch and exactly covered up every single vestige of his property, to a depth of about thirty-eight feet. Morgan was in possession and refused to vacate the premises—said he was occupying his own cabin and not interfering with anybody else's—and said the cabin was standing on the same dirt and same ranch it had always stood on, and he would like to see anybody make him vacate.

"And when I reminded him," said Hyde, weeping, "that it was on top of my ranch and that he was trespassing, he had the infernal meanness to ask me why didn't I *stay* on my ranch and hold possession when I see him a-coming! Why didn't I *stay* on it, the blathering lunatic—by George, when I heard that racket and looked up that hill it was just like the whole world was a-ripping and a-tearing down that mountainside—splinters and cord-wood, thunder and lightning, hail and snow, odds and ends of haystacks, and awful clouds of dust!—trees going end over end in the air, rocks as big as a house jumping 'bout a thousand feet high and busting into ten million pieces, cattle turned inside out and a-coming head on with their tails hanging out between their teeth!—and in the midst of all that wrack and destruction sot that cussed Morgan on his gatepost, a-wondering why I didn't *stay and hold possession!* Laws bless me, I just took one glimpse, General, and lit out'n the county in three jumps exactly.

"But what grinds me is that that Morgan hangs on there and won't move off'n that ranch—says it's his'n and he's going to keep it—likes it better'n he did when it was higher up the hill. Mad! Well, I've been so mad for two days I couldn't find my way to town—been wandering around in the brush in a starving condition—got anything here to drink, General? But I'm here *now*, and I'm a-going to law. You hear *me!*"

Never in all the world, perhaps, were a man's feelings so outraged as were the General's. He said he had never heard of such high-handed conduct in all his life as this Morgan's. And he said there was no use in going to law

—Morgan had no shadow of right to remain where he was
—nobody in the wide world would uphold him in it, and
no lawyer would take his case and no judge listen to it.
Hyde said that right there was where he was mistaken—
everybody in town sustained Morgan; Hal Brayton, a very
smart lawyer, had taken his case; the courts being in
vacation, it was to be tried before a referee, and ex-Governor
Roop had already been appointed to that office, and would
open his court in a large public hall near the hotel at two
that afternoon.

The General was amazed. He said he had suspected before that the people of that territory were fools, and now
he knew it. But he said rest easy, rest easy and collect
the witnesses, for the victory was just as certain as if the
conflict were already over. Hyde wiped away his tears and
left.

At two in the afternoon referee Roop's Court opened,
and Roop appeared throned among his sheriffs, the witnesses, and spectators, and wearing upon his face a solemnity
so awe-inspiring that some of his fellow-conspirators had
misgivings that maybe he had not comprehended, after all,
that this was merely a joke. An unearthly stillness pre-
vailed, for at the slightest noise the judge uttered sternly
the command:

"Order in the Court!"

And the sheriffs promptly echoed it. Presently the General elbowed his way through the crowd of spectators, with
his arms full of law-books, and on his ears fell an order
from the judge which was the first respectful recognition
of his high official dignity that had ever saluted them, and
it trickled pleasantly through his whole system:

"Way for the United States Attorney!"

The witnesses were called—legislators, high government
officers, ranchmen, miners, Indians, Chinamen, negroes.
Three-fourths of them were called by the defendant Morgan, but no matter, their testimony invariably went in
favor of the plaintiff Hyde. Each new witness only added
new testimony to the absurdity of a man's claiming to own
another man's property because his farm had slid down on
top of it. Then the Morgan lawyers made their speeches,
and seemed to make singularly weak ones—they did really
nothing to help the Morgan cause. And now the General,
with exultation in his face, got up and made an impassioned

effort; he pounded the table, he banged the law-books, he shouted, and roared, and howled, he quoted from everything and everybody, poetry, sarcasm, statistics, history, pathos, bathos, blasphemy, and wound up with a grand war-whoop for free speech, freedom of the press, free schools, the Glorious Bird of America and the principles of eternal justice! [Applause.]

When the General sat down, he did it with the conviction that if there was anything in good strong testimony, a great speech and believing and admiring countenances all around, Mr. Morgan's case was killed. Ex-Governor Roop leaned his head upon his hand for some minutes, thinking, and the still audience waited for his decision. And then he got up and stood erect, with bended head, and thought again. Then he walked the floor with long, deliberate strides, his chin in his hand, and still the audience waited. At last he returned to his throne, seated himself, and began, impressively:

"Gentlemen, I feel the great responsibility that rests upon me this day. This is no ordinary case. On the contrary, it is plain that it is the most solemn and awful that ever man was called upon to decide. Gentlemen, I have listened attentively to the evidence, and have perceived that the weight of it, the overwhelming weight of it, is in favor of the plaintiff Hyde. I have listened also to the remark of counsel, with high interest—and especially will I commend the masterly and irrefutable logic of the distinguished gentleman who represents the plaintiff. But, gentlemen, let us beware how we allow mere human testimony, human ingenuity in argument and human ideas of equity, to influence us at a moment so solemn as this. Gentlemen, it ill becomes us, worms as we are, to meddle with the decrees of Heaven. It is plain to me that Heaven, in its inscrutable wisdom, has seen fit to move this defendant's ranch for a purpose. We are but creatures, and we must submit. If Heaven has chosen to favor the defendant Morgan in this marked and wonderful manner; and if Heaven, dissatisfied with the position of the Morgan ranch upon the mountainside, has chosen to remove it to a position more eligible and more advantageous for its owner, it ill becomes us, insects as we are, to question the legality of the act or inquire into the reasons that prompted it. No—Heaven created the ranches, and it is Heaven's prerogative to rearrange them, to experiment with them, to shift them around at its pleasure. It is for us to submit, without repining. I warn you that this thing which has happened is a thing with which the sacrilegious hands and brains and tongues of men must not meddle. Gentlemen, it is the verdict of this court that the plaintiff, Richard Hyde, has been deprived of his ranch by the visitation of God! And from this decision there is no appeal."

Buncombe seized his cargo of law-books and plunged out of the court-room frantic with indignation. He pronounced Roop to be a miraculous fool, an inspired idiot. In all good faith he returned at night and remonstrated with Roop upon his extravagant decision, and implored him to walk the floor and think for half an hour, and see if he could not figure out some sort of modification of the verdict. Roop yielded at last and got up to walk. He walked two hours and a half, and at last his face lit up happily and he told Buncombe it had occurred to him that the ranch underneath the new Morgan ranch still belonged to Hyde, that his title to the ground was just as good as it had ever been, and therefore he was of opinion that Hyde had a right to dig it out from under there and—

The General never waited to hear the end of it. He was always an impatient and irascible man, that way. At the end of two months the fact that he had been played upon with a joke had managed to bore itself, like another Hoosac Tunnel, through the solid adamant of his understanding.

# JIM BLAINE AND HIS
# GRANDFATHER'S RAM

### [from *Roughing It*.]

Every now and then, in these days, the boys used to tell me I ought to get one Jim Blaine to tell me the stirring story of his grandfather's old ram—but they always added that I must not mention the matter unless Jim was drunk at the time—just comfortably and sociably drunk. They kept this up until my curiosity was on the rack to hear the story. I got to haunting Blaine; but it was of no use, the boys always found fault with his condition; he was often moderately but never satisfactorily drunk. I never watched a man's condition with such absorbing interest, such anxious solicitude; I never so pined to see a man uncompromisingly drunk before. At last, one evening I hurried to his cabin, for I learned that this time his situation was such that even the most fastidious could find no fault with it—he was tranquilly, serenely, symmetrically drunk—not a hiccup to mar his voice, not a cloud upon his brain thick enough to obscure his memory. As I entered, he was sitting upon an empty powder-keg, with a clay pipe in one hand and the other raised to command silence. His face was round, red, and very serious; his throat was bare and his hair tumbled; in general appearance and costume he was a stalwart miner of the period. On the pine table stood a candle, and its dim light revealed "the boys" sitting here and there on bunks, candle-boxes, powder-kegs, etc. They said:

"Sh—! Don't speak—he's going to commence."

### [The Story of the Old Ram.]

I found a seat at once, and Blaine said:

"I don't reckon them times will ever come again. There never was a more bullier old ram than what he was.

Grandfather fetched him from Illinois—got him of a man by the name of Yates—Bill Yates—maybe you might have heard of him; his father was a deacon—Baptist—and he was a rustler, too; a man had to get up ruther early to get the start of old Thankful Yates; it was him that put the Greens up to j'ining teams with my grandfather when he moved west. Seth Green was prob'ly the pick of the flock; he married a Wilkerson—Sarah Wilkerson—good cretur, she was—one of the likeliest heifers that was ever raised in old Stoddard, everybody said that knowed her. She could heft a bar'l of flour as easy as I can flirt a flapjack. And spin? Don't mention it! Independent? Humph! When Sile Hawkins came a-browsing around her, she let him know that for all his tin he couldn't trot in harness alongside of *her*. You see, Sile Hawkins was—no, it warn't Sile Hawkins, after all—it was a galoot by the name of Filkins—I disremember his first name; but he *was* a stump—come into pra'r-meeting drunk, one night, hooraying for Nixon, becuz he thought it was a primary; and old Deacon Ferguson up and scooted him through the window and he lit on old Miss Jefferson's head, poor old filly. She was a good soul—had a glass eye and used to lend it to old Miss Wagner, that hadn't any, to receive company in; it warn't big enough, and when Miss Wagner warn't noticing, it would get twisted around in the socket, and look up, maybe, or out to one side, and every which way, while t'other one was looking as straight ahead as a spyglass. Grown people didn't mind it, but it 'most always made the children cry, it was so sort of scary. She tried packing it in raw cotton, but it wouldn't work, somehow— the cotton would get loose and stick out and look so kind of awful that the children couldn't stand it no way. She was always dropping it out, and turning up her old deadlight on the company empty, and making them oncomfortable, becuz *she* never could tell when it hopped out, being blind on that side, you see. So somebody would have to hunch her and say, 'Your game eye has fetched loose, Miss Wagner, dear'—and then all of them would have to sit and wait till she jammed it in again—wrong side before, as a general thing, and green as a bird's egg, being a bashful cretur and easy sot back before company. But being wrong side before warn't much difference, anyway, becuz her own eye was sky-blue and the glass one was yaller on the front side, so whichever way she turned it it didn't match nohow. Old Miss Wagner was considerable on the borrow, she was. When she had a quilting, or Dorcas S'iety at her house she gen'ally borrowed Miss Higgins's wooden leg to stump around on; it was considerable shorter than her other pin, but much *she* minded that. She said she couldn't abide crutches when she had company, becuz they were so slow; said when she had company and things had to be done, she wanted to get up and hump herself. She was as bald as a jug, and so she used to borrow Miss Jacops's wig—Miss Jacops was the coffin-peddler's wife—a ratty old buzzard, he was, that used to go roosting around where people was sick, waiting for 'em; and there that old rip would sit all day, in the shade, on a coffin that he judged would fit the can'idate; and if it was a slow customer and kind of uncertain, he'd fetch his rations and a blanket along and sleep in the coffin nights. He was anchored out that way, in frosty weather, for about three weeks, once, before old Robbins's place, waiting for him; and after that, for as much as two years, Jacops was not on speaking terms with the old man, on account of his disapp'inting him. He got one of his feet froze, and lost money, too, becuz old Robbins took a favorable turn and got well. The next time Robbins got sick, Jacops tried to make up with him, and varnished up the same old coffin and fetched it along; but old Robbins was too many for him; he had him in, and 'peared to be powerful weak; he bought the coffin for ten dollars and Jacops was to pay it back and twenty-five more besides if Robbins didn't like the coffin after he'd tried it. And then Robbins died, and at the funeral he bursted off the lid and riz up in his shroud and told the parson to let up on the performances, becuz he could *not* stand such a coffin as that. You see he had been in a trance once before, when he was young, and he took the chances on another, cal'lating that if he made the trip it was money in his pocket, and if he missed fire he couldn't lose a cent. And, by George, he sued Jacops for the rhino and got judgment; and he set up the coffin in his back parlor and said he 'lowed to take his time, now. It was always an aggravation to Jacops, the way that miserable old thing acted. He moved back to Indiany pretty soon—went to Wellsville—Wellsville was the place the Hogadorns was from. Mighty fine family. Old Mary-

land stock. Old Squire Hogadorn could carry around more
mixed licker, and cuss better than 'most any man I ever
see. His second wife was the Widder Billings—she that was
Becky Martin; her dam was Deacon Dunlap's first wife.
Her oldest child, Maria, married a missionary and died in
grace—et up by the savages. They et *him*, too, poor feller
—biled him. It warn't the custom, so they say, but they
explained to friends of his'n that went down there to
bring away his things, that they'd tried missionaries every
other way and never could get any good out of 'em—and
so it annoyed all his relations to find out that that man's
life was fooled away just out of a dern'd experiment, so to
speak. But mind you, there ain't anything ever reely lost;
everything that people can't understand and don't see
the reason of does good if you only hold on and give it
a fair shake; Prov'dence don't fire no blank ca'tridges, boys.
That there missionary's substance, unbeknowns to himself,
actu'ly converted every last one of them heathens that
took a chance at the barbecue. Nothing ever fetched them
but that. Don't tell *me* it was an accident that he was
biled. There ain't no such a thing as an accident. When
my Uncle Lem was leaning up again a scaffolding once,
sick, or drunk, or suthin, an Irishman with a hod full of
bricks fell on him out of the third story and broke the old
man's back in two places. People said it was an accident.
Much accident there was about that. He didn't know what
he was there for, but he was there for a good object. If
he hadn't been there the Irishman would have been killed.
Nobody can ever make me believe anything different from
that. Uncle Lem's dog was there. Why didn't the Irishman
fall on the dog? Becuz the dog would 'a' seen him a-coming
and stood from under. That's the reason the dog warn't
app'inted. A dog can't be depended on to carry out a
special prov'dence. Mark my words, it was a put-up thing.
Accidents don't happen, boys. Uncle Lem's dog—I wish
you could 'a' seen that dog. He was a reg'lar shepherd—or
ruther he was part bull and part shepherd—splendid
animal; belonged to Parson Hagar before Uncle Lem got
him. Parson Hagar belonged to the Western Reserve
Hagars; prime family; his mother was a Watson; one of
his sisters married a Wheeler; they settled in Morgan
County, and he got nipped by the machinery in a carpet
factory and went through in less than a quarter of a

minute; his widder bought the piece of carpet that had his remains wove in, and people come a hundred mile to 'tend the funeral. There was fourteen yards in the piece. She wouldn't let them roll him up, but planted him just so— full length. The church was middling small where they preached the funeral, and they had to let one end of the coffin stick out of the window. They didn't bury him— they planted one end, and let him stand up, same as a monument. And they nailed a sign on it and put—put on—put on it—sacred to—the m-e-m-o-r-y—of fourteen y-a-r-d-s—of three-ply—car - - - pet—containing all that was —m-o-r-t-a-l—of—of—W-i-l-l-i-a-m—W-h-e—"

Jim Blaine had been growing gradually drowsy and drowsier—his head nodded, once, twice, three times— dropped peacefully upon his breast, and he fell tranquilly asleep. The tears were running down the boys' cheeks— they were suffocating with suppressed laughter—and had been from the start, though I had never noticed it. I perceived that I was "sold." I learned then that Jim Blaine's peculiarity was that whenever he reached a certain stage of intoxication, no human power could keep him from setting out, with impressive unction, to tell about a wonderful adventure which he had once had with his grandfather's old ram—and the mention of the ram in the first sentence was as far as any man had ever heard him get, concerning it. He always maundered off, interminably, from one thing to another, till his whisky got the best of him, and he fell asleep. What the thing was that happened to him and his grandfather's old ram is a dark mystery to this day, for nobody has ever yet found out.

# A TRUE STORY

## [Repeated Word for Word as I Heard It.]

It was summer-time, and twilight. We were sitting on the porch of the farmhouse, on the summit of the hill, and "Aunt Rachel" was sitting respectfully below our level, on the steps—for she was our servant, and colored. She was of mighty frame and stature; she was sixty years old, but her eye was undimmed and her strength unabated. She was a cheerful, hearty soul, and it was no more trouble for her to laugh than it is for a bird to sing. She was under fire now, as usual when the day was done. That is to say, she was being chaffed without mercy, and was enjoying it. She would let off peal after peal of laughter, and then sit with her face in her hands and shake with throes of enjoyment which she could no longer get breath enough to express. At such a moment as this a thought occurred to me, and I said:

"Aunt Rachel, how is it that you've lived sixty years and never had any trouble?"

She stopped quaking. She paused, and there was a moment of silence. She turned her face over her shoulder toward me, and said, without even a smile in her voice:

"Misto C——, is you in 'arnest?"

It surprised me a good deal; and it sobered my manner and my speech, too. I said:

"Why, I thought—that is, I meant—why, you *can't* have had any trouble. I've never heard you sigh, and never seen your eye when there wasn't a laugh in it."

She faced fairly around now, and was full of earnestness.

"Has I had any trouble? Misto C——, I's gwyne to tell you, den I leave it to you. I was bawn down 'mongst de slaves; I knows all 'bout slavery, 'case I ben one of 'em my own se'f. Well, sah, my ole man—dat's my husban'—he was lovin' an' kind to me, jist as kind as you is to yo' own

106

wife. An' we had chil'en—seven chil'en—an' we loved dem chil'en jist de same as you loves yo' chil'en. Dey was black, but de Lord can't make no chil'en so black but what dey mother loves 'em an' wouldn't give 'em up, no, not for anything dat's in dis whole world.

"Well, sah, I was raised in ole Fo'ginny, but my mother she was raised in Maryland; an' my *souls!* she was turrible when she'd git started! My *lan'!* but she'd make de fur fly! When she'd git into dem tantrums, she always had one word dat she said. She'd straighten herse'f up an' put her fists in her hips an' say, 'I want you to understan' dat I wa'n't bawn in de mash to be fool' by trash! I's one o' de ole Blue Hen's Chickens, *I* is!' 'Ca'se, you see, dat's what folks dat's bawn in Maryland calls deyselves, an' dey's proud of it. Well, dat was her word. I don't ever forgit it, beca'se she said it so much, an' beca'se she said it one day when my little Henry tore his wris' awful, and most busted his head, right up at de top of his forehead, an' de niggers didn't fly aroun' fas' enough to 'tend to him. An' when dey talk' back at her, she up an' she says, 'Look-a-heah!' she says, 'I want you niggers to understan' dat I wa'n't bawn in de mash to be fool' by trash! I's one o' de ole Blue Hen's Chickens, *I* is!' an' den she clar' dat kitchen an' bandage' up de chile herse'f. So I says dat word, too, when I's riled.

"Well, bymeby my ole mistis say she's broke, an' she got to sell all de niggers on de place. An' when I heah dat dey gwyne to sell us all off at oction in Richmon', oh, de good gracious! I know what dat mean!"

Aunt Rachel had gradually risen, while she warmed to her subject, and now she towered above us, black against the stars.

"Dey put chains on us an' put us on a stan' as high as dis po'ch—twenty foot high—an' all de people stood aroun', crowds an' crowds. An' dey'd come up dah an' look at us all roun', an' squeeze our arm, an' make us git up an' walk, an' den say, 'Dis one too ole,' or 'Dis one lame,' or 'Dis one don't 'mount to much.' An' dey sole my ole man, an' took him away, an' dey begin to sell my chil'en an' take *dem* away, an' I begin to cry; an' de man say, 'Shet up yo' damn blubberin',' an' hit me on de mouf wid his han'. An' when de las' one was gone but my little Henry, I grab' *him* clost up to my breas' so, an' I ris up

an' says, 'You sha'n't take him away,' I says; 'I'll kill de
man dat tetches him!' I says. But my little Henry whisper
an' say, 'I gwyne to run away, an' den I work an' buy yo'
freedom.' Oh, bless de chile, he always so good! But dey got
him—dey got him, de men did; but I took and tear de
clo'es mos' off 'em an' beat 'em over de head wid my
chain; an' *dey* give it to *me*, too, but I didn't mine dat.

"Well, dah was my ole man gone, an' all my chil'en, all
my seven chil'en—an' six of 'em I hain't set eyes on ag'in
to dis day, an' dat's twenty-two year ago las' Easter. De
man dat bought me b'long' in Newbern, an' he took me
dah. Well, bymeby de years roll on an' de waw come. My
marster he was a Confedrit colonel, an' I was his family's
cook. So when de Unions took dat town, dey all run away
an' lef' me all by myse'f wid de other niggers in dat
mons'us big house. So de big Union officers move in dah,
an' dey ask me would I cook for *dem*. 'Lord bless you,'
says I, 'dat's what I's *for*.'

"Dey wa'n't no small-fry officers, mine you, dey was de
biggest dey *is;* an' de way dey made dem sojers mosey
roun'! De Gen'l he tole me to boss dat kitchen; an' he
say, 'If anybody come meddlin' wid you, you jist make 'em
walk chalk; don't you be afeared,' he say; 'you's 'mong
frens now.'

"Well, I thinks to myse'f, if my little Henry ever got a
chance to run away, he'd make to de Norf, o' course. So
one day I comes in dah whar de big officers was, in de
parlor, an' I drops a kurtchy, so, an' I up an' tole 'em 'bout
my Henry, dey a-listenin' to my troubles jist de same as if
I was white folks; an' I says, 'What I come for is beca'se
if he got away and got up Norf whar you gemmen comes
from, you might 'a' seen him, maybe, an' could tell me
so as I could fine him ag'in; he was very little, an' he
had a sk-yar on his lef' wris' an' at de top of his forehead.'
Den dey look mournful, an' de Gen'l says, 'How long sence
you los' him?' an' I say, 'Thirteen year.' Den de Gen'l
say, 'He wouldn't be little no mo' now—he's a man!'

"I never thought o' dat befo'! He was only dat little
feller to *me* yit. I never thought 'bout him growin' up an'
bein' big. But I see it den. None o' de gemmen had run
acrost him, so dey couldn't do nothin' for me. But all
dat time, do' *I* didn't know it, my Henry *was* run off to de
Norf, years an' years, an' he was a barber, too, an' worked

for hisse'f. An' bymeby, when de waw come he ups an'
he says: 'I's done barberin',' he says, 'I's gwyne to fine my
ole mammy, less'n she's dead.' So he sole out an' went to
whar dey was recruitin', an' hired hisse'f out to de colonel
for his servant; an' den he went all froo de battles every-
whah, huntin' for his ole mammy; yes, indeedy, he'd hire
to fust one officer an' den another, tell he'd ransacked de
whole Souf; but you see *I* didn't know nuffin 'bout *dis*.
How was *I* gwyne to know it?

"Well, one night we had a big sojer ball; de sojers dah
at Newbern was always havin' balls an' carryin' on. Dey
had 'em in my kitchen, heaps o' times, 'ca'se it was so big.
Mine you, I was *down* on sich doin's; beca'se my place was
wid de officers, an' it rasp me to have dem common sojers
cavortin' roun' my kitchen like dat. But I alway' stood
aroun' an' kep' things straight, I did; an' sometimes dey'd
git my dander up, an' den I'd make 'em clar dat kitchen,
mine I *tell* you!

"Well, one night—it was a Friday night—dey comes a
whole platoon f'm a *nigger* ridgment dat was on guard at
de house—de house was headquarters, you know—an' den
I was jist a-*bilin'!* Mad? I was jist a-*boomin'!* I swelled
aroun', an' swelled aroun'; I jist was a-itchin' for 'em to do
somefin for to start me. *An'* dey was a-waltzin' an' a-dancin'!
*my!* but dey was havin' a time! an' I jist a-swellin' an'
a-swellin' up! Pooty soon, 'long comes *sich* a spruce young
nigger a-sailin' down de room wid a yaller wench roun'
de wais'; an' roun' an' roun' an roun' dey went, enough to
make a body drunk to look at 'em; an' when dey got
abreas' o' me, dey went to kin' o' balacin' aroun' fust on one
leg an' den on t'other, an' smilin' at my big red turban, an'
makin' fun, an' I ups an' says '*Git* along wid you!—rub-
bage!' De young man's face kin' o' changed, all of a sudden,
for 'bout a second, but den he went to smilin' ag'in, same
as he was befo'. Well, 'bout dis time, in comes some niggers
dat played music and b'long' to de ban', an' dey *never*
could git along widout puttin' on airs. An' de very fust
air dey put on da: night, I lit into 'em! Dey laughed, an'
dat made me wuss. De res' o' de niggers got to laughin',
an' den my soul *alive* but I was hot! My eye was jist
a-blazin'! I jist straightened myself up so—jist as I is now,
plum to de ceilin', mos'—an' I digs my fists into my hips,
an' I says, 'Look-a-heah!' I says, 'I want you niggers to

understan' dat I wa'n't bawn in de mash to be fool' by trash! I's one o' de ole Blue Hen's Chickens, *I* is!' an' den I see dat young man stan' a-starin' an' stiff, lookin' kin' o' up at de ceilin' like he fo'got somefin, an' couldn't 'member it no mo'. Well, I jist march' on dem niggers—so, lookin' like a gen'l—an' dey jist cave' away befo' me an' out at de do'. An' as dis young man was a-goin' out, I heah him say to another nigger, 'Jim,' he says, 'you go 'long an' tell de cap'n I be on han' 'bout eight o'clock in de mawnin'; dey's somefin on my mine,' he says; 'I don't sleep no mo' dis night. You go 'long,' he says, 'an' leave me by my own se'f.'

"Dis was 'bout one o'clock in de mawnin'. Well, 'bout seven, I was up an' on han', gittin' de officers' breakfast. I was a-stoopin' down by de stove—jist so, same as if yo' foot was de stove—an' I'd opened de stove do' wid my right han'—so, pushin' it back, jist as I pushes yo' foot— an' I'd jist got de pan o' hot biscuits in my han' an' was 'bout to raise up, when I see a black face come aroun' under mine, an' de eyes a-lookin' up into mine, jist as I's a-lookin' up clost under yo' face now; an' I jist stopped *right dah*, an' never budged! jist gazed an' gazed so; an' de pan begin to tremble, an' all of a sudden I *knowed!* De pan drop' on de flo' an' I grab his lef' han' an' shove back his sleeve—jist so, as I's doin' to you—an' den I goes for his forehead an' push de hair back so, an' 'Boy!' I says, 'if you an't my Henry, what is you doin' wid dis welt on yo' wris' an' dat sk-yar on yo' forehead? De Lord God ob heaven be praise', I got my own ag'in!'

"Oh no, Misto C——, *I* hain't had no trouble. An' no *joy!*"

# ACCIDENT INSURANCE—ETC.

## [Delivered in Hartford, at a Dinner to Cornelius Watford, of London.]

Gentlemen,—I am glad, indeed, to assist in welcoming the distinguished guest of this occasion to a city whose fame as an insurance center has extended to all lands, and given us the name of being a quadruple band of brothers working sweetly hand in hand—the Colt's arms company making the destruction of our race easy and convenient, our life-insurance citizens paying for the victims when they pass away, Mr. Batterson perpetuating their memory with his stately monuments, and our fire-insurance comrades taking care of their hereafter. I am glad to assist in welcoming our guest—first, because he is an Englishman, and I owe a heavy debt of hospitality to certain of his fellow-countrymen; and secondly, because he is in sympathy with insurance, and has been the means of making many other men cast their sympathies in the same direction.

Certainly there is no nobler field for human effort than the insurance line of business—especially accident insurance. Ever since I have been a director in an accident-insurance company I have felt that I am a better man. Life has seemed more precious. Accidents have assumed a kindlier aspect. Distressing special providences have lost half their horror. I look upon a cripple now with affectionate interest—as an advertisement. I do not seem to care for poetry any more. I do not care for politics—even agriculture does not excite me. But to me now there is a charm about a railway collision that is unspeakable.

There is nothing more beneficent than accident insurance. I have seen an entire family lifted out of poverty and into affluence by the simple boon of a broken leg. I have had people come to me on crutches, with tears in their eyes, to bless this beneficent institution. In all my experience of life, I have seen nothing so seraphic as the look that comes

111

into a freshly mutilated man's face when he feels in his vest pocket with his remaining hand and finds his accident ticket all right. And I have seen nothing so sad as the look that came into another splintered customer's face when he found he couldn't collect on a wooden leg.

I will remark here, by way of advertisement, that that noble charity which we have named the HARTFORD ACCIDENT INSURANCE COMPANY[1] is an institution which is peculiarly to be depended upon. A man is bound to prosper who gives it his custom. No man can take out a policy in it and not get crippled before the year is out. Now there was one indigent man who had been disappointed so often with other companies that he had grown disheartened, his appetite left him, he ceased to smile—said life was but a weariness. Three weeks ago I got him to insure with us, and now he is the brightest, happiest spirit in this land— has a good steady income and a stylish suit of new bandages every day, and travels around on a shutter.

I will say, in conclusion, that my share of the welcome to our guest is none the less hearty because I talk so much nonsense, and I know that I can say the same for the rest of the speakers.

[1] The speaker was a director of the company named.

# THE <u>FACTS</u> CONCERNING THE RECENT CARNIVAL OF CRIME IN CONNECTICUT

I was feeling blithe, almost jocund. I put a match to my cigar, and just then the morning's mail was handed in. The first superscription I glanced at was in a handwriting that sent a thrill of pleasure through and through me. It was Aunt Mary's; and she was the person I loved and honored most in all the world, outside of my own household. She had been my boyhood's idol; maturity, which is fatal to so many enchantments, had not been able to dislodge her from her pedestal; no, it had only justified her right to be there, and placed her dethronement permanently among the impossibilities. To show how strong her influence over me was, I will observe that long after everybody else's "*do*-stop-smoking" had ceased to affect me in the slightest degree, Aunt Mary could still stir my torpid conscience into faint signs of life when she touched upon the matter. But all things have their limit in this world. A happy day came at last, when even Aunt Mary's words could no longer move me. I was not merely glad to see that day arrive; I was more than glad—I was grateful; for when its sun had set, the one alloy that was able to mar my enjoyment of my aunt's society was gone. The remainder of her stay with us that winter was in every way a delight. Of course she pleaded with me just as earnestly as ever, after that blessed day, to quit my pernicious habit, but to no purpose whatever; the moment she opened the subject I at once became calmly, peacefully, contentedly indifferent—absolutely, adamantinely indifferent. Consequently the closing weeks of that memorable visit melted away as pleasantly as a dream, they were so freighted for me with tranquil satisfaction. I could not have enjoyed my pet vice more if my gentle tormentor had been a smoker herself, and an advocate of the practice. Well, the sight of her handwriting re-

minded me that I was getting very hungry to see her again.
I easily guessed what I should find in her letter. I opened
it. Good! just as I expected; she was coming! Coming this
very day, too, and by the morning train; I might expect
her any moment.

I said to myself, "I am thoroughly happy and content
now. If my most pitiless enemy could appear before me at
this moment, I would freely right any wrong I may have
done him."

Straightway the door opened, and a shriveled, shabby
dwarf entered. He was not more than two feet high. He
seemed to be about forty years old. Every feature and
every inch of him was a trifle out of shape; and so, while
one could not put his finger upon any particular part and
say, "This is a conspicuous deformity," the spectator perceived that this little person was a deformity as a whole—
a vague, general, evenly blended, nicely adjusted deformity.
There was a fox-like cunning in the face and the sharp
little eyes, and also alertness and malice. And yet, this vile
bit of human rubbish seemed to bear a sort of remote and
ill-defined resemblance to me! It was dully perceptible in
the mean form, the countenance, and even the clothes,
gestures, manner, and attitudes of the creature. He was
a far-fetched, dim suggestion of a burlesque upon me, a
caricature of me in little. One thing about him struck me
forcibly and most unpleasantly: he was covered all over
with a fuzzy, greenish mold, such as one sometimes sees
upon mildewed bread. The sight of it was nauseating.

He stepped along with a chipper air, and flung himself
into a doll's chair in a very free-and-easy way, without waiting to be asked. He tossed his hat into the waste-basket. He
picked up my old chalk pipe from the floor, gave the stem
a wipe or two on his knee, filled the bowl from the tobacco-
box at his side, and said to me in a tone of pert command:

"Gimme a match!"

I blushed to the roots of my hair; partly with indignation, but mainly because it somehow seemed to me that
this whole performance was very like an exaggeration of
conduct which I myself had sometimes been guilty of in my
intercourse with familiar friends—but never, never with
strangers, I observed to myself. I wanted to kick the pygmy
into the fire, but some incomprehensible sense of being
legally and legitimately under his authority forced me to
obey his order. He applied the match to the pipe, took

a contemplative whiff or two, and remarked, in an irritatingly familiar way:

"Seems to me it's devilish odd weather for this time of year."

I flushed again, and in anger and humiliation as before; for the language was hardly an exaggeration of some that I have uttered in my day, and moreover was delivered in a tone of voice and with an exasperating drawl that had the seeming of a deliberate travesty of my style. Now there is nothing I am quite so sensitive about as a mocking imitation of my drawling infirmity of speech. I spoke up sharply and said:

"Look here, you miserable ash-cat! you will have to give a little more attention to your manners, or I will throw you out of the window!"

The manikin smiled a smile of malicious content and security, puffed a whiff of smoke contemptuously toward me, and said, with a still more elaborate drawl:

"Come—go gently now; don't put on *too* many airs with your betters."

This cool snub rasped me all over, but it seemed to subjugate me, too, for a moment. The pygmy contemplated me awhile with his weasel eyes, and then said, in a peculiarly sneering way:

"You turned a tramp away from your door this morning."

I said crustily:

"Perhaps I did, perhaps I didn't. How do *you* know?"

"Well, I know. It isn't any matter *how* I know."

"Very well. Suppose I *did* turn a tramp away from the door—what of it?"

"Oh, nothing; nothing in particular. Only you lied to him."

"I *didn't*! That is, I—"

"Yes, but you did; you lied to him."

I felt a guilty pang—in truth, I had felt it forty times before that tramp had traveled a block from my door—but still I resolved to make a show of feeling slandered; so I said:

"This is a baseless impertinence. I said to the tramp—"

"There—wait. You were about to lie again. *I* know what you said to him. You said the cook was gone down-town and there was nothing left from breakfast. Two lies. You knew the cook was behind the door, and plenty of provisions behind *her*."

This astonishing accuracy silenced me; and it filled me
with wondering speculations, too, as to how this cub could
have got his information. Of course he could have culled
the conversation from the tramp, but by what sort of magic
had he contrived to find out about the concealed cook?
Now the dwarf spoke again:

"It was rather pitiful, rather small, in you to refuse to
read that poor young woman's manuscript the other day,
and give her an opinion as to its literary value; and she
had come so far, too, and *so* hopefully. Now *wasn't* it?"

I felt like a cur! And I had felt so every time the thing
had recurred to my mind, I may as well confess. I flushed
hotly and said:

"Look here, have you nothing better to do than prowl
around prying into other people's business? Did that girl
tell you that?"

"Never mind whether she did or not. The main thing
is, you did that contemptible thing. And you felt ashamed
of it afterward. Aha! you feel ashamed of it *now!*"

This was a sort of devilish glee. With fiery earnestness
I responded:

"I told that girl, in the kindest, gentlest way, that I
could not consent to deliver judgment upon *any* one's
manuscript, because an individual's verdict was worthless.
It might underrate a work of high merit and lose it to the
world, or it might overrate a trashy production and so open
the way for its infliction upon the world. I said that the
great public was the only tribunal competent to sit in judgment upon a literary effort, and therefore it must be best
to lay it before that tribunal in the outset, since in the
end it must stand or fall by that mighty court's decision
anyway."

"Yes, you said all that. So you did, you juggling, small-
souled shuffler! And yet when the happy hopefulness faded
out of that poor girl's face, when you saw her furtively
slip beneath her shawl the scroll she had so patiently and
honestly scribbled at—so ashamed of her darling now, so
proud of it before—when you saw the gladness go out of
her eyes and the tears come there, when she crept away
so humbly who had come so—"

"Oh, peace! peace! peace! Blister your merciless tongue,
haven't all these thoughts tortured me enough without *your*
coming here to fetch them back again!"

Remorse! remorse! It seemed to me that it would eat the very heart out of me! And yet that small fiend only sat there leering at me with joy and contempt, and placidly chuckling. Presently he began to speak again. Every sentence was an accusation, and every accusation a truth. Every clause was freighted with sarcasm and derision, every slow-dropping word burned like vitriol. The dwarf reminded me of times when I had flown at my children in anger and punished them for faults which a little inquiry would have taught me that others, and not they, had committed. He reminded me of how I had disloyally allowed old friends to be traduced in my hearing, and been too craven to utter a word in their defense. He reminded me of many dishonest things which I had done; of many which I had procured to be done by children and other irresponsible persons; of some which I had planned, thought upon, and longed to do, and been kept from the performance by fear of consequences only. With exquisite cruelty he recalled to my mind, item by item, wrongs and unkindnesses I had inflicted and humiliations I had put upon friends since dead, "who died thinking of those injuries, maybe, and grieving over them," he added, by way of poison to the stab.

"For instance," said he, "take the case of your younger brother, when you two were boys together, many a long year ago. He always lovingly trusted in you with a fidelity that your manifold treacheries were not able to shake. He followed you about like a dog, content to suffer wrong and abuse if he might only be with you; patient under these injuries so long as it was your hand that inflicted them. The latest picture you have of him in health and strength must be such a comfort to you! You pledged your honor that if he would let you blindfold him no harm should come to him; and then, giggling and choking over the rare fun of the joke, you led him to a brook thinly glazed with ice, and pushed him in; and how you did laugh! Man, you will never forget the gentle, reproachful look he gave you as he struggled shivering out, if you live a thousand years! Oho! you see it now, you see it *now!*"

"Beast, I have seen it a million times, and shall see it a million more! and may you rot away piecemeal, and suffer till doomsday what I suffer now, for bringing it back to me again!"

The dwarf chuckled contentedly, and went on with his accusing history of my career. I dropped into a moody, vengeful state, and suffered in silence under the merciless lash. At last this remark of his gave me a sudden rouse:

"Two months ago, on a Tuesday, you woke up, away in the night, and fell to thinking, with shame, about a peculiarly mean and pitiful act of yours toward a poor ignorant Indian in the wilds of the Rocky Mountains in the winter of eighteen hundred and—"

"Stop a moment, devil! Stop! Do you mean to tell me that even my very *thoughts* are not hidden from you?"

"It seems to look like that. Didn't you think the thoughts I have just mentioned?"

"If I didn't, I wish I may never breathe again! Look here, friend—look me in the eye. Who *are* you?"

"Well, who do you think?"

"I think you are Satan himself. I think you are the devil."

"No."

"No? Then who *can* you be?"

"Would you really like to know?"

"*Indeed* I would."

"Well, I am your *Conscience!*"

In an instant I was in a blaze of joy and exultation. I sprang at the creature, roaring:

"Curse you. I have wished a hundred million times that you were tangible, and that I could get my hands on your throat once! Oh, but I will wreak a deadly vengeance on—"

Folly! Lightning does not move more quickly than my Conscience did! He darted aloft so suddenly that in the moment my fingers clutched the empty air he was already perched on the top of the high bookcase, with his thumb at his nose in token of derision. I flung the poker at him, and missed. I fired the bootjack. In a blind rage I flew from place to place, and snatched and hurled any missile that came handy; the storm of books, inkstands, and chunks of coal gloomed the air and beat about the manikin's perch relentlessly, but all to no purpose; the nimble figure dodged every shot; and not only that, but burst into a cackle of sarcastic and triumphant laughter as I sat down exhausted. While I puffed and gasped with fatigue and excitement, my Conscience talked to this effect:

"My good slave, you are curiously witless—no, I mean

characteristically so. In truth, you are always consistent, always yourself, always an ass. Otherwise it must have occurred to you that if you attempted this murder with a sad heart and a heavy conscience, I would droop under the burdening influence instantly. Fool, I should have weighed a ton, and could not have budged from the floor; but instead, you are so cheerfully anxious to kill me that your conscience is as light as a feather; hence I am away up here out of your reach. I can almost respect a mere ordinary sort of fool; but *you*—pah!"

I would have given anything, then, to be heavy-hearted, so that I could get this person down from there and take his life, but I could no more be heavy-hearted over such a desire than I could have sorrowed over its accomplishment. So I could only look longingly up at my master, and rave at the ill luck that denied me a heavy conscience the one only time that I had ever wanted such a thing in my life. By and by I got to musing over the hour's strange adventure, and of course my human curiosity began to work. I set myself to framing in my mind some questions for this fiend to answer. Just then one of my boys entered, leaving the door open behind him, and exclaimed:

"My! what *has* been going on here? The bookcase is all one riddle of—"

I sprang up in consternation, and shouted:

"Out of this! Hurry! Jump! Fly! Shut the door! Quick, or my Conscience will get away!"

The door slammed to, and I locked it. I glanced up and was grateful, to the bottom of my heart, to see that my owner was still my prisoner. I said:

"Hang you, I might have lost you! Children are the heedlessest creatures. But look here, friend, the boy did not seem to notice you at all; how is that?"

"For a very good reason. I am invisible to all but you."

I made a mental note of that piece of information with a good deal of satisfaction. I could kill this miscreant now, if I got a chance, and no one would know it. But this very reflection made me so light-hearted that my Conscience could hardly keep his seat, but ˑwas like to float aloft toward the ceiling like a toy balloon. I said, presently:

"Come, my Conscience, let us be friendly. Let us fly a flag of truce for a while. I am suffering to ask you some questions."

"Very well. Begin."

"Well, then, in the first place, why were you never visible to me before?"

"Because you never asked to see me before; that is, you never asked in the right spirit and the proper form before. You were just in the right spirit this time, and when you called for your most pitiless enemy I was that person by a very large majority, though you did not suspect it."

"Well, did that remark of mine turn you into flesh and blood?"

"No. It only made me visible to you. I am unsubstantial, just as other spirits are."

This remark prodded me with a sharp misgiving. If he was unsubstantial, how was I going to kill him? But I dissembled, and said persuasively:

"Conscience, it isn't sociable of you to keep at such a distance. Come down and take another smoke."

This was answered with a look that was full of derision, and with this observation added:

"Come where you can get at me and kill me? The invitation is declined with thanks."

"All right," said I to myself; "so it seems a spirit *can* be killed, after all; there will be one spirit lacking in this world, presently, or I lose my guess." Then I said aloud:

"Friend—"

"There; wait a bit. I am not your friend, I am your enemy; I am not your equal, I am your master. Call me 'my lord,' if you please. You are too familiar."

"I don't like such titles. I am willing to call you *sir*. That is as far as—"

"We will have no argument about this. Just obey, that is all. Go on with your chatter."

"Very well, my lord—since nothing but my lord will suit you—I was going to ask you how long you will be visible to me?"

"Always!"

I broke out with strong indignation: "This is simply an outrage. That is what I think of it. You have dogged, and dogged, and *dogged* me, all the days of my life, invisible. That was misery enough; now to have such a looking thing as you tagging after me like another shadow all the rest of my days is an intolerable prospect. You have my opinion, my lord; make the most of it."

"My lad, there was never so pleased a conscience in this world as I was when you made me visible. It gives me an inconceivable advantage. *Now* I can look you straight in the eye, and call you names, and leer at you, jeer at you, sneer at you; and *you* know what eloquence there is in visible gesture and expression, more especially when the effect is heightened by audible speech. I shall always address you henceforth in your o-w-n s-n-i-v-e-l-i-n-g d-r-a-w-l—baby!"

I let fly with the coal-hod. No result. My lord said:

"Come, come! Remember the flag of truce!"

"Ah, I forgot that. I will try to be civil; and *you* try it, too, for a novelty. The idea of a *civil* conscience! It is a good joke; an excellent joke. All the consciences *I* have ever heard of were nagging, badgering, fault-finding, execrable savages! Yes; and always in a sweat about some poor little insignificant trifle or other—destruction catch the lot of them, *I* say! I would trade mine for the smallpox and seven kinds of consumption, and be glad of the chance. Now tell me, why *is* it that a conscience can't haul a man over the coals once, for an offense, and then let him alone? Why is it that it wants to keep on pegging at him, day and night and night and day, week in and week out, forever and ever, about the same old thing? There is no sense in that, and no reason in it. I think a conscience that will act like that is meaner than the very dirt itself."

"Well, *we* like it; that suffices."

"Do you do it with the honest intent to improve a man?"

That question produced a sarcastic smile, and this reply:

"No, sir. Excuse me. We do it simply because it is 'business.' It is our trade. The *purpose* of it is to improve the man, but *we* are merely disinterested agents. We are appointed by authority, and haven't anything to say in the matter. We obey orders and leave the consequences where they belong. But I am willing to admit this much: we *do* crowd the orders a trifle when we get a chance, which is most of the time. We enjoy it. We are instructed to remind a man a few times of an error; and I don't mind acknowledging that we try to give pretty good measure. And when we get hold of a man of a peculiarly sensitive nature, oh, but we do haze him! I have consciences to come all the way from China and Russia to see a person of that kind put through his paces, on a special occasion. Why, I knew a man of that sort who had accidentally crippled a mulatto baby; the news went abroad, and I wish you may never commit another sin if the consciences didn't flock from all over the earth to enjoy the fun and help his master exorcise him. That man walked the floor in torture for forty-eight hours, without eating or sleeping, and then blew his brains out. The child was perfectly well again in three weeks."

"Well, you are a precious crew, not to put it too strong. I think I begin to see now why you have always been a trifle inconsistent with me. In your anxiety to get all the juice you can out of a sin, you make a man repent of it in three or four different ways. For instance, you found fault with me for lying to that tramp, and I suffered over that. But it was only yesterday that I told a tramp the square truth, to wit, that, it being regarded as bad citizenship to encourage vagrancy, I would give him nothing. What did you do *then?* Why, you made me say to myself, 'Ah, it would have been so much kinder and more blameless to ease him off with a little white lie, and send him away feeling that if he could not have bread, the gentle treatment was at least something to be grateful for!' Well, I suffered all day about *that*. Three days before I had fed a tramp, and fed him freely, supposing it a virtuous act. Straight off you said, 'Oh, false citizen, to have fed a tramp!' and I suffered as usual. I gave a tramp work; you objected to it—*after* the contract was made, of course; you never speak up beforehand. Next, I *refused* a tramp work; you objected to *that*. Next, I proposed to kill a tramp; you kept me awake all night, oozing remorse at every pore. Sure I was going to be right *this* time, I sent the next tramp away with my benediction; and I wish you may live as long as I do, if you didn't make me smart all night again because I didn't kill him. Is there *any* way of satisfying that malignant invention which is called a conscience?"

"Ha, ha! this is luxury! Go on!"

"But come, now, answer me that question. *Is* there any way?"

"Well, none that I propose to tell *you*, my son. Ass! I don't care *what* act you may turn your hand to, I can straightway whisper a word in your ear and make you think you have committed a dreadful meanness. It is my *business* —and my joy—to make you repent of *everything* you do.

If I have fooled away any opportunities it was not intentional; I beg to assure you it was not intentional!"

"Don't worry; you haven't missed a trick that *I* know of. I never did a thing in all my life, virtuous or otherwise, that I didn't repent of in twenty-four hours. In church last Sunday I listened to a charity sermon. My first impulse was to give three hundred and fifty dollars; I repented of that and reduced it a hundred; repented of that and reduced it another hundred; repented of that and reduced it another hundred; repented of that and reduced the remaining fifty to twenty-five; repented of that and came down to fifteen; repented of that and dropped to two dollars and a half; when the plate came around at last, I repented once more and contributed ten cents. Well, when I got home, I did wish to goodness I had that ten cents back again! You never *did* let me get through a charity sermon without having something to sweat about."

"Oh, and I never shall, I never shall. You can always depend on me."

"I think so. Many and many's the restless night I've wanted to take you by the neck. If I could only get hold of you now!"

"Yes, no doubt. But I am not an ass; I am only the saddle of an ass. But go on, go on. You entertain me more than I like to confess."

"I am glad of that. (You will not mind my lying a little, to keep in practice.) Look here; not to be too personal, I think you are about the shabbiest and most contemptible little shriveled-up reptile that can be imagined. I am grateful enough that you are invisible to other people, for I should die with shame to be seen with such a mildewed monkey of a conscience as *you* are. Now if you were five or six feet high, and—"

"Oh, come! who is to blame?"

"*I* don't know."

"Why, you are; nobody else."

"Confound you, I wasn't consulted about your personal appearance."

"I don't care, you had a good deal to do with it, nevertheless. When you were eight or nine years old, I was seven feet high, and as pretty as a picture."

"I wish you had died young! So you have grown the wrong way, have you?"

"Some of us grow one way and some the other. You had a large conscience once; if you've a small conscience now I reckon there are reasons for it. However, both of us are to blame, you and I. You see, you used to be conscientious about a great many things; morbidly so, I may say. It was a great many years ago. You probably do not remember it now. Well, I took a great interest in my work, and I so enjoyed the anguish which certain pet sins of yours afflicted you with that I kept pelting at you until I rather overdid the matter. You began to rebel. Of course I began to lose ground, then, and shrivel a little—diminish in stature, get moldy, and grow deformed. The more I weakened, the more stubbornly you fastened on to those particular sins; till at last the places on my person that represent those vices became as callous as shark-skin. Take smoking, for instance. I played that card a little too long, and I lost. When people plead with you at this late day to quit that vice, that old callous place seems to enlarge and cover me all over like a shirt of mail. It exerts a mysterious, smothering effect; and presently I, your faithful hater, your devoted Conscience, go sound asleep! Sound? It is no name for it. I couldn't hear it thunder at such a time. You have some few other vices—perhaps eighty, or maybe ninety—that affect me in much the same way."

"This is flattering; you must be asleep a good part of your time."

"Yes, of late years. I should be asleep *all* the time but for the help I get."

"Who helps you?"

"Other consciences. Whenever a person whose conscience I am acquainted with tries to plead with you about the vices you are callous to, I get my friend to give his client a pang concerning some villainy of his own, and that shuts off his meddling and starts him off to hunt personal consolation. My field of usefulness is about trimmed down to tramps, budding authoresses, and that line of goods now; but don't you worry—I'll harry you on *them* while they last! Just you put your trust in me."

"I think I can. But if you had only been good enough to mention these facts some thirty years ago, I should have turned my particular attention to sin, and I think that by this time I should not only have had you pretty permanently asleep on the entire list of human vices, but reduced to the size of a homeopathic pill, at that. That

is about the style of conscience *I* am pining for. If I only
had you shrunk down to a homeopathic pill, and could get
my hands on you, would I put you in a glass case for a
keepsake? No, sir. I would give you to a yellow dog! That
is where *you* ought to be—you and all your tribe. You are
not fit to be in society, in my opinion. Now another question. Do you know a good many consciences in this section?"

"Plenty of them."

"I would give anything to see some of them! Could you
bring them here? And would they be visible to me?"

"Certainly not."

"I suppose I ought to have known that without asking.
But no matter, you can describe them. Tell me about my
neighbor Thompson's conscience, please."

"Very well. I know him intimately; have known him
many years. I knew him when he was eleven feet high and
of a faultless figure. But he is very rusty and tough and
misshapen now, and hardly ever interests himself about
anything. As to his present size—well, he sleeps in a cigar-
box."

"Likely enough. There are few smaller, meaner men in
this region than Hugh Thompson. Do you know Robinson's conscience?"

"Yes. He is a shade under four and a half feet high;
used to be a blond; is a brunette now, but still shapely and
comely."

"Well, Robinson is a good fellow. Do you know Tom
Smith's conscience?"

"I have known him from childhood. He was thirteen
inches high, and rather sluggish, when he was two years
old—as nearly all of us are at that age. He is thirty-seven
feet high now, and the stateliest figure in America. His
legs are still racked with growing-pains, but he has a good
time, nevertheless. Never sleeps. He is the most active and
energetic member of the New England Conscience Club;
is president of it. Night and day you can find him pegging
away at Smith, panting with his labor, sleeves rolled up,
countenance all alive with enjoyment. He has got his victim
splendidly dragooned now. He can make poor Smith imagine that the most innocent little thing he does is an
odious sin; and then he sets to work and almost tortures
the soul out of him about it."

"Smith is the noblest man in all this section, and the

purest; and yet is always breaking his heart because he cannot be good! Only a conscience *could* find pleasure in heaping agony upon a spirit like that. Do you know my aunt Mary's conscience?"

"I have seen her at a distance, but am not acquainted with her. She lives in the open air altogether, because no door is large enough to admit her."

"I can believe that. Let me see. Do you know the conscience of that publisher who once stole some sketches of mine for a 'series' of his, and then left me to pay the law expenses I had to incur in order to choke him off?"

"Yes. He has a wide fame. He was exhibited, a month ago, with some other antiquities, for the benefit of a recent Member of the Cabinet's conscience that was starving in exile. Tickets and fares were high, but I traveled for nothing by pretending to be the conscience of an editor, and got in for half-price by representing myself to be the conscience of a clergyman. However, the publisher's conscience, which was to have been the main feature of the entertainment, was a failure—as an exhibition. He was there, but what of that? The management had provided a microscope with a magnifying power of only thirty thousand diameters, and so nobody got to see him, after all. There was great and general dissatisfaction, of course, but—"

Just here there was an eager footstep on the stair; I opened the door, and my aunt Mary burst into the room. It was a joyful meeting and a cheery bombardment of questions and answers concerning family matters ensued. By and by my aunt said:

"But I am going to abuse you a little now. You promised me, the day I saw you last, that you would look after the needs of the poor family around the corner as faithfully as I had done it myself. Well, I found out by accident that you failed of your promise. *Was* that right?"

In simple truth, I never had thought of that family a second time! And now such a splintering pang of guilt shot through me! I glanced up at my Conscience. Plainly, my heavy heart was affecting him. His body was drooping forward; he seemed about to fall from the bookcase. My aunt continued:

"And think how you have neglected my poor *protégé* at the almshouse, you dear, hard-hearted promise-breaker!"

I blushed scarlet, and my tongue was tied. As the sense of my guilty negligence waxed sharper and stronger, my Conscience began to sway heavily back and forth; and when my aunt, after a little pause, said in a grieved tone, "Since you never once went to see her, maybe it will not distress you now to know that that poor child died, months ago, utterly friendless and forsaken!" my Conscience could no longer bear up under the weight of my sufferings, but tumbled headlong from his high perch and struck the floor with a dull, leaden thump. He lay there writhing with pain and quaking with apprehension, but straining every muscle in frantic efforts to get up. In a fever of expectancy I sprang to the door, locked it, placed my back against it, and bent a watchful gaze upon my struggling master. Already my fingers were itching to begin their murderous work.

"Oh, what *can* be the matter!" exclaimed by aunt, shrinking from me, and following with her frightened eyes the direction of mine. My breath was coming in short, quick gasps now, and my excitement was almost uncontrollable. My aunt cried out:

"Oh, do not look so! You appal me! Oh, what can the matter be? What is it you see? Why do you stare so? Why do you work your fingers like that?"

"Peace, woman!" I said, in a hoarse whisper. "Look elsewhere; pay no attention to me; it is nothing—nothing. I am often this way. It will pass in a moment. It comes from smoking too much."

My injured lord was up, wild-eyed with terror, and trying to hobble toward the door. I could hardly breathe, I was so wrought up. My aunt wrung her hands, and said:

"Oh, I knew how it would be; I knew it would come to this at last! Oh, I implore you to crush out that fatal habit while it may yet be time! You must not, you shall not be deaf to my supplications longer!" My struggling Conscience showed sudden signs of weariness! "Oh, promise me you will throw off this hateful slavery of tobacco!" My Conscience began to reel drowsily, and grope with his hands —enchanting spectacle! "I beg you, I beseech you, I implore you! Your reason is deserting you! There is madness in your eye! It flames with frenzy! Oh, hear me, hear me, and be saved! See, I plead with you on my very knees!" As she sank before me my Conscience reeled again, and then drooped languidly to the floor, blinking toward me a last supplication for mercy, with heavy eyes. "Oh, promise, or you are lost! Promise, and be redeemed! Promise! Promise and live!" With a long-drawn sigh my conquered Conscience closed his eyes and fell fast asleep!

With an exultant shout I sprang past my aunt, and in an instant I had my lifelong foe by the throat. After so many years of waiting and longing, he was mine at last. I tore him to shreds and fragments. I rent the fragments to bits. I cast the bleeding rubbish into the fire, and drew into my nostrils the grateful incense of my burnt-offering. At last, and forever, my Conscience was dead!

I was a free man! I turned upon my poor aunt, who was almost petrified with terror, and shouted:

"Out of this with your paupers, your charities, your reforms, your pestilent morals! You behold before you a man whose life-conflict is done, whose soul is at peace; a man whose heart is dead to sorrow, dead to suffering, dead to remorse; a man WITHOUT A CONSCIENCE! In my joy I spare you, though I could throttle you and never feel a pang! Fly!"

She fled. Since that day my life is all bliss. Bliss, unalloyed bliss. Nothing in all the world could persuade me to have a conscience again. I settled all my old outstanding scores, and began the world anew. I killed thirty-eight persons during the first two weeks—all of them on account of ancient grudges. I burned a dwelling that interrupted my view. I swindled a widow and some orphans out of their last cow, which is a very good one, though not thoroughbred, I believe. I have also committed scores of crimes, of various kinds, and have enjoyed my work exceedingly, whereas it would formerly have broken my heart and turned my hair gray, I have no doubt.

In conclusion, I wish to state, by way of advertisement, that medical colleges desiring assorted tramps for scientific purposes, either by the gross, by cord measurement, or per ton, will do well to examine the lot in my cellar before purchasing elsewhere, as these were all selected and prepared by myself, and can be had at a low rate, because I wish to clear out my stock and get ready for the spring trade.

# THE STORY OF A SPEECH

*An address delivered in 1877, and a review of it twenty-nine years later. The original speech was delivered at a dinner given by the publishers of* The Atlantic Monthly *in honor of the seventieth anniversary of the birth of John Greenleaf Whittier, at the Hotel Brunswick, Boston, December 17, 1877.*

## [The Speech.]

This is an occasion peculiarly meet for the digging up of pleasant reminiscences concerning literary folk; therefore I will drop lightly into history myself. Standing here on the shore of the Atlantic and contemplating certain of its largest literary billows, I am reminded of a thing which happened to me thirteen years ago, when I had just succeeded in stirring up a little Nevadian literary puddle myself, whose spume-flakes were beginning to blow thinly Californiaward. I started an inspection tramp through the southern mines of California. I was callow and conceited, and I resolved to try the virtue of my *nom de guerre.*

I very soon had an opportunity. I knocked at a miner's lonely log cabin in the foot-hills of the Sierras just at nightfall. It was snowing at the time. A jaded, melancholy man of fifty, barefooted, opened the door to me. When he heard my *nom de guerre* he looked more dejected than before. He let me in—pretty reluctantly, I thought—and after the customary bacon and beans, black coffee and hot whiskey, I took a pipe. This sorrowful man had not said three words up to this time. Now he spoke up and said, in the voice of one who is secretly suffering, "You're the fourth—I'm going to move." "The fourth what?" said I. "The fourth literary man that has been here in twenty-four hours—I'm going to move." "You don't tell me!" said I; "who were the others?" "Mr. Longfellow, Mr. Emerson, and Mr. Oliver Wendell Holmes—consound the lot!"

You can easily believe I was interested. I supplicated—
three hot whiskies did the rest—and finally the melancholy
miner began. Said he:

"They came here just at dark yesterday evening, and I
let them in, of course. Said they were going to the Yosemite.
They were a rough lot, but that's nothing; everybody looks
rough that travels afoot. Mr. Emerson was a seedy little
bit of a chap, red-headed. Mr. Holmes was as fat as a
balloon; he weighed as much as three hundred, and had
double chins all the way down to his stomach. Mr. Longfellow was built like a prize-fighter. His head was cropped
and bristly, like as if he had a wig made of hair-brushes.
His nose lay straight down his face, like a finger with the
end joint tilted up. They had been drinking, I could see
that. And what queer talk they used! Mr. Holmes inspected
this cabin, then he took me by the buttonhole, and says
he:

> " 'Through the deep caves of thought
>     I hear a voice that sings,
>     Build thee more stately mansions,
>     O my soul!'

"Says I, 'I can't afford it, Mr. Holmes, and moreover I
don't want to.' Blamed if I liked it pretty well, either,
coming from a stranger, that way. However, I started to
get out my bacon and beans, when Mr. Emerson came and
looked on awhile, and then *he* takes me aside by the buttonhole and says:

> " 'Gives me agates for my meat;
>     Gives me cantharids to eat;
>     From air and ocean bring me foods,
>     From all zones and altitudes.'

"Says I, 'Mr. Emerson, if you'll excuse me, this ain't no
hotel.' You see it sort of riled me—I warn't used to the
ways of littery swells. But I went on a-sweating over my
work, and next comes Mr. Longfellow and buttonholes me,
and interrupts me. Says he:

> " 'Honor be to Mudjekeewis!
>     You shall hear how Pau-Puk-Keewis—'

"But I broke in, and says I, 'Beg your pardon, Mr. Long-fellow, if you'll be so kind as to hold your yawp for about five minutes and let me get this grub ready, you'll do me proud.' Well, sir, after they'd filled up I set out the jug. Mr. Holmes looks at it, and then he fires up all of sudden and yells:

> " 'Flash out a stream of blood-red wine!
> For I would drink to other days.'

"By George, I was getting kind of worked up. I don't deny it, I was getting kind of worked up. I turns to Mr. Holmes, and says I, 'Looky here, my fat friend, I'm a-running this shanty, and if the court knows herself, you'll take whisky straight or you'll go dry.' Them's the very words I said to him. Now I don't want to sass such famous littery people, but you see they kind of forced me. There ain't nothing onreasonable 'bout me; I don't mind a passel of guests a-treadin' on my tail three or four times, but when it comes to *standing* on it it's different, 'and if the court knows herself,' I says, 'you'll take whisky straight or you'll go dry.' Well, between drinks they'd swell around the cabin and strike attitudes and spout; and pretty soon they got out a greasy old deck and went to playing euchre at ten cents a corner—on trust. I began to notice some pretty suspicious things. Mr. Emerson dealt, looked at his hand, shook his head, says:

> " 'I am the doubter and the doubt—'

and ca'mly bunched the hands and went to shuffling for a new layout. Says he:

> " 'They reckon ill who leave me out;
> They know not well the subtle ways I keep
> I pass and deal *again!*'

Hang'd if he didn't go ahead and do it, too! Oh, he was a cool one! Well, in about a minute things were running pretty tight, but all of a sudden I see by Mr. Emerson's eye he judged he had 'em. He had already coralled two tricks, and each of the others one. So now he kind of lifts a little in his chair and says:

> " 'I tire of globes and aces!—
>     Too long the game is played!'

—and down he fetched a right bower. Mr. Longfellow smiles as sweet as pie and says:

> " 'Thanks thanks to thee, my worthy friend,
>     For the lesson thou hast taught,'

—and blamed if he didn't down with *another* right bower! Emerson claps his hand on his bowie, Longfellow claps his on his revolver, and I went under a bunk. There was going to be trouble; but that monstrous Holmes rose up, wobbling his double chins, and says he, 'Order, gentlemen; the first man that draws, I'll lay down on him and smother him!' All quiet on the Potomac, you bet!

"They were pretty how-come-you-so by now, and they begun to blow. Emerson says, 'The nobbiest thing I ever wrote was "Barbara Frietchie." ' Says Longfellow, 'It don't begin with my "Biglow Papers." ' Says Holmes, 'My "Thanatopsis" lays over 'em both.' They mighty near ended in a fight. Then they wished they had some more company—and Mr. Emerson pointed to me and says:

> " 'Is yonder squalid peasant all
>     That this proud nursery could breed?'

He was a-whetting his bowie on his boot—so I let it pass. Well, sir, next they took it into their heads that they would like some music; so they made me stand up and sing "When Johnny Comes Marching Home" till I dropped —at thirteen minutes past four this morning. That's what I've been through, my friend. When I woke at seven, they were leaving, thank goodness, and Mr. Longfellow had my only boots on, and his'n under his arm. Says I, 'Hold on, there, Evangeline, what are you going to do with *them?*' He says, 'Going to make tracks with 'em; because:

> " 'Lives of great men all remind us
>     We can make our lives sublime;
>   And, departing, leave behind us
>     Footprints on the sands of time.'

As I said, Mr. Twain, you are the fourth in twenty-four hours—and I'm going to move; I ain't suited to a littery atmosphere."

I said to the miner, "Why, my dear sir, *these* were not the gracious singers to whom we and the world pay loving reverence and homage; these were impostors.'

The miner investigated me with a calm eye for awhile; then said he, "Ah! impostors, were they? Are *you?*"

I did not pursue the subject, and since then I have not traveled on my *nom de guerre* enough to hurt. Such was the reminiscence I was moved to contribute, Mr. Chairman. In my enthusiasm I may have exaggerated the details a little, but you will easily forgive me that fault, since I believe it is the first time I have ever deflected from perpendicular fact on an occasion like this.

---

## [The Story.]

*January* 11, 1906.

Answer to a letter received this morning:

DEAR MRS. H.,—I am forever your debtor for reminding me of that curious passage in my life. During the first year or two after it happened, I could not bear to think of it. My pain and shame were so intense, and my sense of having been an imbecile so settled, established and confirmed, that I drove the episode entirely from my mind—and so all these twenty-eight or twenty-nine years I have lived in the conviction that my performance of that time was coarse, vulgar, and destitute of humor. But your suggestion that you and your family found humor in it twenty-eight years ago moved me to look into the matter. So I commissioned a Boston typewriter to delve among the Boston papers of that bygone time and send me a copy of it.

It came this morning, and if there is any vulgarity about it I am not to discover it. If it isn't innocently and ridiculously funny, I am no judge. I will see to it that you get a copy.

What I have said to Mrs. H. is true. I did suffer during a year or two from the deep humiliations of the episode. But at last, in 1888, in Venice, my wife and I came across

Mr. and Mrs. A. P. C., of Concord, Massachusetts, and a
friendship began then of the sort which nothing but death
terminates. The C.'s were very bright people and in every
way charming and companionable. We were together a
month or two in Venice and several months in Rome,
afterward, and one day that lamented break of mine was
mentioned. And when I was on the point of lathering
those people for bringing it to my mind when I had
gotten the memory of it almost squelched, I perceived with
joy that the C.'s were indignant about the way that my
performance had been received in Boston. They poured
out their opinions most freely and frankly about the frosty
attitude of the people who were present at that performance, and about the Boston newspapers for the position they had taken in regard to the matter. That position
was that I had been irreverent beyond belief, beyond
imagination. Very well; I had accepted that as a fact for
a year or two, and had been thoroughly miserable about
it whenever I thought of it—which was not frequently,
if I could help it. Whenever I thought of it I wondered
how I ever could have been inspired to do so unholy a
thing. Well, the C.'s comforted me, but they did not persuade me to continue to think about the unhappy episode.
I resisted that. I tried to get it out of my mind, and let it
die, and I succeeded. Until Mrs. H.'s letter came, it had
been a good twenty-five years since I had thought of that
matter; and when she said that the thing was funny I
wondered if possibly she might be right. At any rate,
my curiosity was aroused, and I wrote to Boston and got
the whole thing copied, as above set forth.

I vaguely remembered some of the details of that gathering—dimly I can see a hundred people—no, perhaps
fifty—shadowy figures sitting at tables feeding, ghosts now
to me, and nameless forevermore. I don't know who they
were, but I can very distinctly see, seated at the grand
table and facing the rest of us, Mr. Emerson, supernaturally
grave, unsmiling; Mr. Whittier, grave, lovely, his beautiful spirit shining out of his face; Mr. Longfellow, with
his silken white hair and his benignant face; Dr. Oliver
Wendell Holmes, flashing smiles and affection and all good-
fellowship everywhere like a rose-diamond whose facets
are being turned toward the light first one way and then
another—a charming man, and always fascinating, whether

he was talking or whether he was sitting still (what *he* would call still, but what would be more or less motion to other people). I can see those figures with entire distinctness across this abyss of time.

One other feature is clear—Willie Winter (for these past thousand years dramatic editor of the *New York Tribune,* and still occupying that high post in his old age) was there. He was much younger then than he is now, and he showed it. It was always a pleasure to me to see Willie Winter at a banquet. During a matter of twenty years I was seldom at a banquet where Willie Winter was not also present, and where he did not read a charming poem written for the occasion. He did it this time, and it was up to standard: dainty, happy, choicely phrased, and as good to listen to as music, and sounding exactly as if it was pouring unprepared out of heart and brain.

Now at that point ends all that was pleasurable about that notable celebration of Mr. Whittier's seventieth birthday—because *I* got up at that point and followed Winter, with what I have no doubt I supposed would be the gem of the evening—the gay oration above quoted from the Boston paper. I had written it all out the day before and had perfectly memorized it, and I stood up there at my genial and happy and self-satisfied ease, and began to deliver it. Those majestic guests, that row of venerable and still active volcanoes, listened, as did everybody else in the house, with attentive interest. Well, I delivered myself of—we'll say the first two hundred words of my speech. I was expecting no returns from that part of the speech, but this was not the case as regarded the rest of it. I arrived now at the dialogue: "The old miner said, 'You are the fourth, I'm going to move.' 'The fourth what?' said I. He answered, 'The fourth littery man that has been here in twenty-four hours. I am going to move.' 'Why, you don't tell me,' said I. 'Who were the others?' 'Mr. Longfellow, Mr. Emerson, Mr. Oliver Wendell Holmes, consound the lot—' "

Now, then, the house's *attention* continued, but the expression of interest in the faces turned to a sort of black frost. I wondered what the trouble was. I didn't know. I went on, but with difficulty—I struggled along, and entered upon that miner's fearful description of the bogus Emerson, the bogus Holmes, the bogus Longfellow, always hoping—but with a gradually perishing hope—that some-body would laugh, or that somebody would at least smile, but nobody did. I didn't know enough to give it up and sit down, I was too new to public speaking, and so I went on with this awful performance, and carried it clear through to the end, in front of a body of people who seemed turned to stone with horror. It was the sort of expression their faces would have worn if I had been making these remarks about the Deity and the rest of the Trinity; there is no milder way in which to describe the petrified condition and the ghastly expression of those people.

When I sat down it was with a heart which had long ceased to beat. I shall never be as dead again as I was then. I shall never be as miserable again as I was then. I speak now as one who doesn't know what the conditions of things may be in the next world, but in this one I shall never be as wretched again as I was then. Howells, who was near me, tried to say a comforting word, but couldn't get beyond a gasp. There was no use—he understood the whole size of the disaster. He had good intentions, but the words froze before they could get out. It was an atmosphere that would freeze anything. If Benvenuto Cellini's sala-mander had been in that place he would not have sur-vived to be put into Cellini's autobiography. There was a frightful pause. There was an awful silence, a desolating silence. Then the next man on the list had to get up—there was no help for it. That was Bishop—Bishop had just burst handsomely upon the world with a most ac-ceptable novel, which had appeared in *The Atlantic Monthly,* a place which would make any novel respectable and any author noteworthy. In this case the novel itself was recognized as being, without extraneous help, respect-able. Bishop was away up in the public favor, and he was an object of high interest, consequently there was a sort of national expectancy in the air; we may say our Ameri-can millions were standing, from Maine to Texas and from Alaska to Florida, holding their breath, their lips parted, their hands ready to applaud, when Bishop should get up on that occasion, and for the first time in his life speak in public. It was under these damaging conditions that he got up to "make good," as the vulgar say. I had spoken several times before, and that is the reason why I was able to go on without dying in my tracks, as I ought to have done—but Bishop had had no experience. He was up facing those awful deities—facing those other people, those strangers—facing human beings for the first time in his life, with a speech to utter. No doubt it was well packed away in his memory, no doubt it was fresh and usable, until I had been heard from. I suppose that after that, and under the smothering pall of that dreary silence, it began to waste away and disappear out of his head like the rags breaking from the edge of a fog, and presently there wasn't any fog left. He didn't go on—he didn't last long. It was not many sentences after his first before he began to hesitate, and break, and lose his grip, and totter, and wobble, and at last he slumped down in a limp and mushy pile.

Well, the programme for the occasion was probably not more than one-third finished, but it ended there. Nobody rose. The next man hadn't strength enough to get up, and everybody looked so dazed, so stupefied, paralyzed, it was impossible for anybody to do anything, or even try. Nothing could go on in that strange atmosphere. Howells mournfully, and without words, hitched himself to Bishop and me and supported us out of the room. It was very kind—he was most generous. He towed us tottering away into some room in that building, and we sat down there. I don't know what my remark was now, but I know the nature of it. It was the kind of remark you make when you know that nothing in the world can help your case. But Howells was honest—he had to say the heart-breaking things he did say: that there was no help for this calamity, this shipwreck, this cataclysm; that this was the most disastrous thing that had ever happened in anybody's history—and then he added, "That is, for *you*—and consider what you have done for Bishop. It is bad enough in your case, you deserve to suffer. You have committed this crime, and you deserve to have all you are going to get. But here is an innocent man. Bishop had never done you any harm, and see what you have done to him. He can never hold his head up again. The world can never look upon Bishop as being a live person. He is a corpse."

That is the history of that episode of twenty-eight years

ago, which pretty nearly killed me with shame during that first year or two whenever it forced its way into my mind.

Now then, I take that speech up and examine it. As I said, it arrived this morning, from Boston. I have read it twice, and unless I am an idiot, it hasn't a single defect in it from the first word to the last. It is just as good as good can be. It is smart; it is saturated with humor. There isn't a suggestion of coarseness or vulgarity in it anywhere. What could have been the matter with that house? It is amazing, it is incredible, that they didn't shout with laughter, and those deities the loudest of them all. Could the fault have been with me? Did I lose courage when I saw those great men up there whom I was going to describe in such a strange fashion? If that happened, if I showed doubt, that can account for it, for you can't be successfully funny if you show that you are afraid of it. Well, I can't account for it, but if I had those beloved and revered old literary immortals back here now on the platform at Carnegie Hall I would take that same old speech, deliver it, word for word, and melt them till they'd run all over that stage. Oh, the fault must have been with *me*, it is not in the speech at all.

# JIM BAKER'S BLUEJAY YARN

## [from *A Tramp Abroad.*]

Animals talk to each other, of course. There can be no question about that; but I suppose there are very few people who can understand them. I never knew but one man who could. I knew he could, however, because he told me so himself. He was a middle-aged, simple-hearted miner who had lived in a lonely corner of California, among the woods and mountains, a good many years, and had studied the ways of his only neighbors, the beasts and the birds, until he believed he could accurately translate any remark which they made. This was Jim Baker. According to Jim Baker, some animals have only a limited education, and use only very simple words, and scarcely ever a comparison or a flowery figure; whereas, certain other animals have a large vocabulary, a fine command of language and a ready and fluent delivery; consequently these latter talk a great deal; they like it; they are conscious of their talent, and they enjoy "showing off." Baker said, that after long and careful observation, he had come to the conclusion that the bluejays were the best talkers he had found among birds and beasts. Said he:

"There's more *to* a bluejay than any other creature. He has got more moods, and more different kinds of feelings than other creatures; and, mind you, whatever a bluejay feels, he can put into language. And no mere common-place language, either, but rattling, out-and-out book-talk—and bristling with metaphor, too—just bristling! And as for command of language—why *you* never see a bluejay get stuck for a word. No man ever did. They just boil out of him! And another thing: I've noticed a good deal, and there's no bird, or cow, or anything that uses as good grammar as a bluejay. You may say a cat uses good grammar. Well, a cat does—but you let a cat get excited once; you let a cat get to pulling fur with another cat on a shed, nights, and you'll hear grammar that will give you the lockjaw. Ignorant people think it's the *noise* which

fighting cats make that is so aggravating, but it ain't so;
it's the sickening grammar they use. Now I've never heard
a jay use bad grammar but very seldom; and when they
do, they are as ashamed as a human; they shut right down
and leave.

"You may call a jay a bird. Well, so he is, in a measure
—because he's got feathers on him, and don't belong to no
church, perhaps; but otherwise he is just as much a
human as you be. And I'll tell you for why. A jay's gifts,
and instincts, and feelings, and interests, cover the whole
ground. A jay hasn't got any more principle than a
Congressman. A jay will lie, a jay will steal, a jay will
deceive, a jay will betray; and four times out of five, a
jay will go back on his solemnest promise. The sacredness
of an obligation is a thing which you can't cram into no
bluejay's head. Now, on top of all this, there's another
thing; a jay can outswear any gentleman in the mines.
You think a cat can swear. Well, a cat can; but you give a
bluejay a subject that calls for his reserve-powers, and
where is your cat? Don't talk to me—I know too much
about this thing. And there's yet another thing; in the one
little particular of scolding—just good, clean, out-and-out
scolding—a bluejay can lay over anything, human or divine.
Yes, sir, a jay is everything that a man is. A jay can cry,
a jay can laugh, a jay can feel shame, a jay can reason and
plan and discuss, a jay likes gossip and scandal, a jay
has got a sense of humor, a jay knows when he is an ass
just as well as you do—maybe better. If a jay ain't human,
he better take in his sign, that's all. Now I'm going to tell
you a perfectly true fact about some bluejays.

"When I first begun to understand jay language correctly, there was a little incident happened here. Seven
years ago, the last man in this region but me moved away.
There stands his house—been empty ever since; a log
house, with a plank roof—just one big room, and no more;
no ceiling—nothing between the rafters and the floor. Well,
one Sunday morning I was sitting out here in front of my
cabin, with my cat, taking the sun, and looking at the blue
hills, and listening to the leaves rustling so lonely in the
trees, and thinking of the home away yonder in the states,
that I hadn't heard from in thirteen years, when a bluejay
lit on that house, with an acorn in his mouth, and says,
'Hello, I reckon I've struck something.' When he spoke, the

acorn dropped out of his mouth and rolled down the roof, of course, but he didn't care; his mind was all on the thing he had struck. It was a knot-hole in the roof. He cocked his head to one side, shut one eye and put the other one to the hole, like a possum looking down a jug; then he glanced up with his bright eyes, gave a wink or two with his wings—which signifies gratification, you understand—and says, 'It looks like a hole, it's located like a hole—blamed if I don't believe it *is* a hole!'

"Then he cocked his head down and took another look; he glances up perfectly joyful, this time; winks his wings and his tail both, and says, 'Oh, no, this ain't no fat thing, I reckon! If I ain't in luck!—why it's a perfectly elegant hole!' So he flew down and got that acorn, and fetched it up and dropped it in, and was just tilting his head back, with the heavenliest smile on his face, when all of a sudden he was paralyzed into a listening attitude and that smile faded gradually out of his countenance like breath off'n a razor, and the queerest look of surprise took its place. Then he says, 'Why, I didn't hear it fall!' He cocked his eye at the hole again, and took a long look; raised up and shook his head; stepped around to the other side of the hole and took another look from that side; shook his head again. He studied a while, then he just went into the *de*tails—walked round and round the hole and spied into it from every point of the compass. No use. Now he took a thinking attitude on the comb of the roof and scratched the back of his head with his right foot a minute, and finally says, 'Well, it's too many for *me,* that's certain; must be a mighty long hole; however, I ain't got no time to fool around here, I got to 'tend to business; I reckon it's all right—chance it, anyway.'

"So he flew off and fetched another acorn and dropped it in, and tried to flirt his eye to the hole quick enough to see what become of it, but he was too late. He held his eye there as much as a minute; then he raised up and sighed, and says, 'Confound it, I don't seem to understand this thing, no way; however, I'll tackle her again.' He fetched another acorn, and done his level best to see what become of it, but he couldn't. He says, 'Well, *I* never struck no such a hole as this before; I'm of the opinion it's a totally new kind of a hole.' Then he begun to get mad. He held in for a spell, walking up and down the comb of the roof and shaking his head and muttering to himself; but his feelings got the upper hand of him, presently, and he broke loose and cussed himself black in the face. I never see a bird take on so about a little thing. When he got through he walks to the hole and looks in again for half a minute; then he says, 'Well, you're a long hole, and a deep hole, and a mighty singular hole altogether—but I've started in to fill you, and I'm d—d if I *don't* fill you, if it takes a hundred years!'

"And with that, away he went. You never see a bird work so since you was born. He laid into his work like a nigger, and the way he hove acorns into that hole for about two hours and a half was one of the most exciting and astonishing spectacles I ever struck. He never stopped to take a look any more—he just hove 'em in and went for more. Well, at last he could hardly flop his wings, he was so tuckered out. He comes a-drooping down, once more, sweating like an ice-pitcher, drops his acorn in and says, '*Now* I guess I've got the bulge on you by this time!' So he bent down for a look. If you'll believe me, when his head come up again he was just pale with rage. He says, 'I've shoveled acorns enough in there to keep the family thirty years, and if I can see a sign of one of 'em I wish I may land in a museum with a belly full of sawdust in two minutes!'

"He just had strength enough to crawl up on to the comb and lean his back agin the chimbly, and then he collected his impressions and begun to free his mind. I see in a second that what I had mistook for profanity in the mines was only just the rudiments, as you may say.

"Another jay was going by, and heard him doing his devotions, and stops to inquire what was up. The sufferer told him the whole circumstance, and says, 'Now yonder's the hole, and if you don't believe me, go and look for yourself.' So this fellow went and looked, and comes back and says, 'How many did you say you put in there?' 'Not any less than two tons,' says the sufferer. The other jay went and looked again. He couldn't seem to make it out, so he raised a yell, and three more jays come. They all examined the hole, they all made the sufferer tell it over again, then they all discussed it, and got off as many leather-headed opinions about it as an average crowd of humans could have done.

"They called in more jays; then more and more, till pretty soon this whole region 'peared to have a blue flush about it. There must have been five thousand of them; and such another jawing and disputing and ripping and cussing, you never heard. Every jay in the whole lot put his eye to the hole and delivered a more chuckle-headed opinion about the mystery than the jay that went there before him. They examined the house all over, too. The door was standing half open, and at last one old jay happened to go and light on it and look in. Of course, that knocked the mystery galley-west in a second. There lay the acorns, scattered all over the floor. He flopped his wings and raised a whoop. 'Come here!' he says, 'Come here, everybody; hang'd if this fool hasn't been trying to fill up a house with acorns!' They all came a-swooping down like a blue cloud, and as each fellow lit on the door and took a glance, the whole absurdity of the contract that that first jay had tackled hit him home and he fell over backward suffocating with laughter, and the next jay took his place and done the same.

"Well, sir, they roosted around here on the housetop and the trees for an hour, and guffawed over that thing like human beings. It ain't any use to tell me a bluejay hasn't got a sense of humor, because I know better. And memory, too. They brought jays here from all over the United States to look down that hole, every summer for three years. Other birds, too. And they could all see the point, except an owl that come from Nova Scotia to visit the Yo Semite, and he took this thing in on his way back. He said he couldn't see anything funny in it. But then he was a good deal disappointed about Yo Semite, too."

# THE PRIVATE HISTORY OF A
# CAMPAIGN THAT FAILED

You have heard from a great many people who did
something in the war; is it not fair and right that you
listen a little moment to one who started out to do something in it, but didn't? Thousands entered the war, got
just a taste of it, and then stepped out again permanently.
These, by their very numbers, are respectable, and are
therefore entitled to a sort of voice—not a loud one, but
a modest one; not a boastful one, but an apologetic one.
They ought not to be allowed much space among better
people—people who did something. I grant that; but they
ought at least to be allowed to state why they didn't do
anything, and also to explain the process by which they
didn't do anything. Surely this kind of light must have a
sort of value.

Out West there was a good deal of confusion in men's
minds during the first months of the great trouble—a good
deal of unsettledness, of leaning first this way, then that,
then the other way. It was hard for us to get our bearings.
I call to mind an instance of this. I was piloting on the
Mississippi when the news came that South Carolina had
gone out of the Union on the 20th of December, 1860.
My pilot mate was a New-Yorker. He was strong for the
Union; so was I. But he would not listen to me with any
patience; my loyalty was smirched, to his eye, because my
father had owned slaves. I said, in palliation of this dark
fact, that I had heard my father say, some years before
he died, that slavery was a great wrong, and that he would
free the solitary negro he then owned if he could think
it right to give away the property of the family when he
was so straitened in means. My mate retorted that a mere
impulse was nothing—anybody could pretend to a good
impulse; and went on decrying my Unionism and libeling
my ancestry. A month later the secession atmosphere had

144

considerably thickened on the Lower Mississippi, and I became a rebel; so did he. We were together in New Orleans the 26th of January, when Louisiana went out of the Union. He did his full share of the rebel shouting, but was bitterly opposed to letting me do mine. He said that I came of bad stock—of a father who had been willing to set slaves free. In the following summer he was piloting a Federal gunboat and shouting for the Union again, and I was in the Confederate army. I held his note for some borrowed money. He was one of the most upright men I ever knew, but he repudiated that note without hesitation because I was a rebel and the son of a man who owned slaves.

In that summer—of 1861—the first wash of the wave of war broke upon the shores of Missouri. Our state was invaded by the Union forces. They took possession of St. Louis, Jefferson Barracks, and some other points. The Governor, Claib Jackson, issued his proclamation calling out fifty thousand militia to repel the invader.

I was visiting in the small town where my boyhood had been spent—Hannibal, Marion County. Several of us got together in a secret place by night and formed ourselves into a military company. One Tom Lyman, a young fellow of a good deal of spirit but of no military experience, was made captain; I was made second lieutenant. We had no first lieutenant; I do not know why; it was long ago. There were fifteen of us. By the advice of an innocent connected with the organization we called ourselves the Marion Rangers. I do not remember that any one found fault with the name. I did not; I thought it sounded quite well. The young fellow who proposed this title was perhaps a fair sample of the kind of stuff we were made of. He was young, ignorant, good-natured, well-meaning, trivial, full of romance, and given to reading chivalric novels and singing forlorn love-ditties. He had some pathetic little nickel-plated aristocratic instincts, and detested his name, which was Dunlap; detested it, partly because it was nearly as common in that region as Smith, but mainly because it had a plebeian sound to his ear. So he tried to ennoble it by writing it in this way: *d'Unlap*. That contented his eye, but left his ear unsatisfied, for people gave the new name the same old pronunciation— emphasis on the front end of it. He then did the bravest thing that can be imagined—a thing to make one shiver when one remembers how the world is given to resenting shams and affectations; he began to write his name so: *d'Un Lap*. And he waited patiently through the long storm of mud that was flung at this work of art, and he had his reward at last; for he lived to see that name accepted, and the emphasis put where he wanted it by people who had known him all his life, and to whom the tribe of Dunlaps had been as familiar as the rain and the sunshine for forty years. So sure of victory at last is the courage that can wait. He said he had found, by consulting some ancient French chronicles, that the name was rightly and originally written d'Un Lap; and said that if it were translated into English it would mean Peterson: *Lap*, Latin or Greek, he said, for stone or rock, same as the French *pierre*, that is to say, Peter: *d'*, of or from; *un*, a or one; hence, d'Un Lap, of or from a stone or a Peter; that is to say, one who is the son of a stone, the son of a Peter—Peterson. Our militia company were not learned, and the explanation confused them; so they called him Peterson Dunlap. He proved useful to us in his way; he named our camps for us, and he generally struck a name that was "no slouch," as the boys said.

That is one sample of us. Another was Ed Stevens, son of the town jeweler—trim-built, handsome, graceful, neat as a cat; bright, educated, but given over entirely to fun. There was nothing serious in life to him. As far as he was concerned, this military expedition of ours was simply a holiday. I should say that about half of us looked upon it in the same way; not consciously, perhaps, but unconsciously. We did not think; we were not capable of it. As for myself, I was full of unreasoning joy to be done with turning out of bed at midnight and four in the morning for a while; grateful to have a change, new scenes, new occupations, a new interest. In my thoughts that was as far as I went; I did not go into the details; as a rule, one doesn't at twenty-four.

Another sample was Smith, the blacksmith's apprentice. This vast donkey had some pluck, of a slow and sluggish nature, but a soft heart; at one time he would knock a horse down for some impropriety, and at another he would get homesick and cry. However, he had one ultimate credit to his account which some of us hadn't; he stuck to the war, and was killed in battle at last.

Jo Bowers, another sample, was a huge, good-natured, flax-headed lubber; lazy, sentimental, full of harmless brag, a grumbler by nature; an experienced, industrious, ambitious, and often quite picturesque liar, and yet not a successful one, for he had had no intelligent training, but was allowed to come up just any way. This life was serious enough to him, and seldom satisfactory. But he was a good fellow, anyway, and the boys all liked him. He was made orderly sergeant; Stevens was made corporal.

These samples will answer—and they are quite fair ones. Well, this herd of cattle started for the war. What could you expect of them? They did as well as they knew how; but, really, what was justly to be expected of them? Nothing, I should say. That is what they did.

We waited for a dark night, for caution and secrecy were necessary; then, toward midnight, we stole in couples and from various directions to the Griffith place, beyond the town; from that point we set out together on foot. Hannibal lies at the extreme southeastern corner of Marion County, on the Mississippi River; our objective point was the hamlet of New London, ten miles away, in Ralls County.

The first hour was all fun, all idle nonsense and laughter. But that could not be kept up. The steady trudging came to be like work; the play had somehow oozed out of it; the stillness of the woods and the somberness of the night began to throw a depressing influence over the spirits of the boys, and presently the talking died out and each person shut himself up in his own thoughts. During the last half of the second hour nobody said a word.

Now we approached a log farm-house where, according to report, there was a guard of five Union soldiers. Lyman called a halt; and there, in the deep gloom of the overhanging branches, he began to whisper a plan of assault upon that house, which made the gloom more depressing than it was before. It was a crucial moment; we realized, with a cold suddenness, that here was no jest—we were standing face to face with actual war. We were equal to the occasion. In our response there was no hesitation, no indecision: we said that if Lyman wanted to meddle with those soldiers, he could go ahead and do it; but if he waited for us to follow him, he would wait a long time.

Lyman urged, pleaded, tried to shame us, but it had no effect. Our course was plain, our minds were made up: we would flank the farm-house—go out around. And that was what we did.

We struck into the woods and entered upon a rough time, stumbling over roots, getting tangled in vines, and torn by briers. At last we reached an open place in a safe region, and sat down, blown and hot, to cool off and nurse our scratches and bruises. Lyman was annoyed, but the rest of us were cheerful; we had flanked the farm-house, we had made our first military movement, and it was a success; we had nothing to fret about, we were feeling just the other way. Horse-play and laughing began again; the expedition was become a holiday frolic once more.

Then we had two more hours of dull trudging and ultimate silence and depression; then, about dawn, we straggled into New London, soiled, heel-blistered, fagged with our little march, and all of us except Stevens in a sour and raspy humor and privately down on the war. We stacked our shabby old shotguns in Colonel Ralls's barn, and then went in a body and breakfasted with that veteran of the Mexican War. Afterward he took us to a distant meadow, and there in the shade of a tree we listened to an old-fashioned speech from him, full of gunpowder and glory, full of that adjective-piling, mixed metaphor and windy declamation which were regarded as eloquence in that ancient time and that remote region; and then he swore us on the Bible to be faithful to the State of Missouri and drive all invaders from her soil, no matter whence they might come or under what flag they might march. This mixed us considerably, and we could not make out just what service we were embarked in; but Colonel Ralls, the practised politician and phrase-juggler, was not similarly in doubt; he knew quite clearly that he had invested us in the cause of the Southern Confederacy. He closed the solemnities by belting around me the sword which his neighbor, Colonel Brown, had worn at Buena Vista and Molino del Rey; and he accompanied this act with another impressive blast.

Then we formed in line of battle and marched four miles to a shady and pleasant piece of woods on the border of the far-reaching expanses of a flowery prairie.

It was an enchanting region for war—our kind of war.

We pierced the forest about half a mile, and took up a strong position, with some low, rocky, and wooded hills behind us, and a purling, limpid creek in front. Straightway half the command were in swimming and the other half fishing. The ass with the French name gave this position a romantic title, but it was too long, so the boys shortened and simplified it to Camp Ralls.

We occupied an old maple-sugar camp, whose half-rotted troughs were still propped against the trees. A long corn-crib served for sleeping-quarters for the battalion. On our left, half a mile away, were Mason's farm and house; and he was a friend to the cause. Shortly after noon the farmers began to arrive from several directions, with mules and horses for our use, and these they lent us for as long as the war might last, which they judged would be about three months. The animals were of all sizes, all colors, and all breeds. They were mainly young and frisky, and nobody in the command could stay on them long at a time; for we were town boys, and ignorant of horsemanship. The creature that fell to my share was a very small mule, and yet so quick and active that it could throw me without difficulty; and it did this whenever I got on it. Then it would bray—stretching its neck out, laying its ears back, and spreading its jaws till you could see down to its works. It was a disagreeable animal in every way. If I took it by the bridle and tried to lead it off the grounds, it would sit down and brace back, and no one could budge it. However, I was not entirely destitute of military resources, and I did presently manage to spoil this game; for I had seen many a steamboat aground in my time, and knew a trick or two which even a grounded mule would be obliged to respect. There was a well by the corn-crib; so I substituted thirty fathom of rope for the bridle, and fetched him home with the windlass.

I will anticipate here sufficiently to say that we did learn to ride, after some days' practice, but never well. We could not learn to like our animals; they were not choice ones, and most of them had annoying peculiarities of one kind or another. Stevens's horse would carry him, when he was not noticing, under the huge excrescences which form on the trunks of oak-trees, and wipe him out of the saddle; in this way Stevens got several bad hurts. Sergeant

Bowers's horse was very large and tall, with slim, long legs, and looked like a railroad bridge. His size enabled him to reach all about, and as far as he wanted to, with his head; so he was always biting Bowers's legs. On the march, in the sun, Bowers slept a good deal; and as soon as the horse recognized that he was asleep he would reach around and bite him on the leg. His legs were black and blue with bites. This was the only thing that could ever make him swear, but this always did; whenever his horse bit him he always swore, and of course Stevens, who laughed at everything, laughed at this, and would even get into such convulsions over it as to lose his balance and fall off his horse; and then Bowers, already irritated by the pain of the horse-bite, would resent the laughter with hard language, and there would be a quarrel; so that horse made no end of trouble and bad blood in the command.

However, I will get back to where I was—our first afternoon in the sugar-camp. The sugar-troughs came very handy as horse-troughs, and we had plenty of corn to fill them with. I ordered Sergeant Bowers to feed my mule; but he said that if I reckoned he went to war to be a dry-nurse to a mule it wouldn't take me very long to find out my mistake. I believed that this was insubordination, but I was full of uncertainties about everything military, and so I let the thing pass, and went and ordered Smith, the blacksmith's apprentice, to feed the mule; but he merely gave me a large, cold, sarcastic grin, such as an ostensibly seven-year-old horse gives you when you lift his lip and find he is fourteen, and turned his back on me. I then went to the captain, and asked if it were not right and proper and military for me to have an orderly. He said it was, but as there was only one orderly in the corps, it was but right that he himself should have Bowers on his staff. Bowers said he wouldn't serve on anybody's staff; and if anybody thought he could make him, let him try it. So, of course, the thing had to be dropped; there was no other way.

Next, nobody would cook; it was considered a degradation; so we had no dinner. We lazied the rest of the pleasant afternoon away, some dozing under the trees, some smoking cob-pipes and talking sweethearts and war, some playing games. By late supper-time all hands were famished; and to meet the difficulty all hands turned to, on an equal footing, and gathered wood, built fires, and cooked the meal. Afterward everything was smooth for a while; then trouble broke out between the corporal and the sergeant, each claiming to rank the other. Nobody knew which was the higher office; so Lyman had to settle the matter by making the rank of both officers equal. The commander of an ignorant crew like that has many troubles and vexations which probably do not occur in the regular army at all. However, with the song-singing and yarn-spinning around the camp-fire, everything presently became serene again; and by and by we raked the corn down level in one end of the crib, and all went to bed on it, tying a horse to the door, so that he would neigh if any one tried to get in.[1]

We had some horsemanship drill every forenoon; then, afternoons, we rode off here and there in squads a few miles, and visited the farmers' girls, and had a youthful good time, and got an honest good dinner or supper, and then home again to camp, happy and content.

For a time life was idly delicious, it was perfect; there was nothing to mar it. Then came some farmers with an alarm one day. They said it was rumored that the enemy were advancing in our direction from over Hyde's prairie. The result was a sharp stir among us, and general consternation. It was a rude awakening from our pleasant trance. The rumor was but a rumor—nothing definite about it; so, in the confusion, we did not know which way to retreat. Lyman was for not retreating at all in these uncertain circumstances; but he found that if he tried to maintain that attitude he would fare badly, for the command were in no humor to put up with insubordination. So he yielded the point and called a council of war—to

[1] It was always my impression that that was what the horse was there for, and I know that it was also the impression of at least one other of the command, for we talked about it at the time, and admired the military ingenuity of the device; but when I was out West, three years ago, I was told by Mr. A. G. Fuqua, a member of our company, that the horse was his; that the leaving him tied at the door was a matter of mere forgetfulness, and that to attribute it to intelligent invention was to give him quite too much credit. In support of his position he called my attention to the suggestive fact that the artifice was not employed again. I had not thought of that before.

consist of himself and the three other officers; but the
privates made such a fuss about being left out that we had
to allow them to remain, for they were already present,
and doing the most of the talking too. The question was,
which way to retreat; but all were so flurried that nobody
seemed to have even a guess to offer. Except Lyman. He
explained in a few calm words that, inasmuch as the enemy
were approaching from over Hyde's prairie, our course
was simple: all we had to do was not to retreat *toward*
him; any other direction would answer our needs perfectly.
Everybody saw in a moment how true this was, and how
wise; so Lyman got a great many compliments. It was now
decided that we should fall back on Mason's farm.

It was after dark by this time, and as we could not
know how soon the enemy might arrive, it did not seem
best to try to take the horses and things with us; so we
only took the guns and ammunition, and started at once.
The route was very rough and hilly and rocky, and
presently the night grew very black and rain began to
fall; so we had a troublesome time of it, struggling and
stumbling along in the dark; and soon some person slipped
and fell, and then the next person behind stumbled over
him and fell, and so did the rest, one after the other; and
then Bowers came, with the keg of powder in his arms,
while the command were all mixed together, arms and
legs, on the muddy slope; and so he fell, of course, with the
keg, and this started the whole detachment down the hill
in a body, and they landed in the brook at the bottom in
a pile, and each that was undermost pulling the hair and
scratching and biting those that were on top of him; and
those that were being scratched and bitten scratching and
biting the rest in their turn, and all saying they would
die before they would ever go to war again if they ever
got out of this brook this time, and the invader might rot
for all they cared, and the country along with him—and
all such talk as that, which was dismal to hear and take
part in, in such smothered, low voices, and such a grisly
dark place and so wet, and the enemy, maybe, coming any
moment.

The keg of powder was lost, and the guns, too; so the
growling and complaining continued straight along while
the brigade pawed around the pasty hillside and slopped
around in the brook hunting for these things; consequently

we lost considerable time at this; and then we heard a sound, and held our breath and listened, and it seemed to be the enemy coming, though it could have been a cow, for it had a cough like a cow; but we did not wait, but left a couple of guns behind and struck out for Mason's again as briskly as we could scramble along in the dark. But we got lost presently among the rugged little ravines, and wasted a deal of time finding the way again, so it was after nine when we reached Mason's stile at last; and then before we could open our mouths to give the countersign several dogs came bounding over the fence, with great riot and noise, and each of them took a soldier by the slack of his trousers and began to back away with him. We could not shoot the dogs without endangering the persons they were attached to; so we had to look on helpless at what was perhaps the most mortifying spectacle of the Civil War. There was light enough, and to spare, for the Masons had now run out on the porch with candles in their hands. The old man and his son came and undid the dogs without difficulty, all but Bowers's; but they couldn't undo his dog, they didn't know his combination; he was of the bull kind, and seemed to be set with a Yale time-lock; but they got him loose at last with some scalding water, of which Bowers got his share and returned thanks. Peterson Dunlap afterward made up a fine name for this engagement, and also for the night march which preceded it, but both have long ago faded out of my memory.

We now went into the house, and they began to ask us a world of questions, whereby it presently came out that we did not know anything concerning who or what we were running from; so the old gentleman made himself very frank, and said we were a curious breed of soldiers, and guessed we could be depended on to end up the war in time, because no government could stand the expense of the shoe-leather we should cost it trying to follow us around. "Marion *Rangers!* good name, b'gosh!" said he. And wanted to know why we hadn't had a picket-guard at the place where the road entered the prairie, and why we hadn't sent out a scouting party to spy out the enemy and bring us an account of his strength, and so on, before jumping up and stampeding out of a strong position upon a mere vague rumor—and so on, and so forth, till he made us all feel shabbier than the dogs had done, not half so enthusiastically welcome. So we went to bed ashamed and low-spirited; except Stevens. Soon Stevens began to devise a garment for Bowers which could be made to automatically display his battle-scars to the grateful, or conceal them from the envious, according to his occasions; but Bowers was in no humor for this, so there was a fight, and when it was over Stevens had some battle-scars of his own to think about.

Then we got a little sleep. But after all we had gone through, our activities were not over for the night; for about two o'clock in the morning we heard a shout of warning from down the lane, accompanied by a chorus from all the dogs, and in a moment everybody was up and flying around to find out what the alarm was about. The alarmist was a horseman who gave notice that a detachment of Union soldiers was on its way from Hannibal with orders to capture and hang any bands like ours which it could find, and said we had no time to lose. Farmer Mason was in a flurry this time himself. He hurried us out of the house with all haste, and sent one of his negroes with us to show us where to hide ourselves and our telltale guns among the ravines half a mile away. It was raining heavily.

We struck down the lane, then across some rocky pastureland which offered good advantages for stumbling; consequently we were down in the mud most of the time, and every time a man went down he blackguarded the war, and the people that started it, and everybody connected with it, and gave himself the master dose of all for being so foolish as to go into it. At last we reached the wooded mouth of a ravine, and there we huddled ourselves under the streaming trees, and sent the negro back home. It was a dismal and heart-breaking time. We were like to be drowned with the rain, deafened with the howling wind and the booming thunder, and blinded by the lightning. It was, indeed, a wild night. The drenching we were getting was misery enough, but a deeper misery still was the reflection that the halter might end us before we were a day older. A death of this shameful sort had not occurred to us as being among the possibilities of war. It took the romance all out of the campaign, and turned our dreams of glory into a repulsive nightmare. As for doubting that so barbarous an order had been given, not one of us did that.

The long night wore itself out at last, and then the negro came to us with the news that the alarm had manifestly been a false one, and that breakfast would soon be ready. Straightway we were light-hearted again, and the world was bright, and life as full of hope and promise as ever—for we were young then. How long ago that was! Twenty-four years.

The mongrel child of philology named the night's refuge Camp Devastation, and no soul objected. The Masons gave us a Missouri country breakfast, in Missourian abundance, and we needed it: hot biscuits; hot "wheat bread," prettily criss-crossed in a lattice pattern on top; hot corn-pone; fried chicken; bacon, coffee, eggs, milk, buttermilk, etc.; and the world may be confidently challenged to furnish the equal of such a breakfast, as it is cooked in the South.

We stayed several days at Mason's; and after all these years the memory of the dullness, and stillness, and lifelessness of that slumberous farm-house still oppresses my spirit as with a sense of the presence of death and mourning. There was nothing to do, nothing to think about; there was no interest in life. The male part of the household were away in the fields all day, the women were busy and out of our sight; there was no sound but the plaintive wailing of a spinning-wheel, forever moaning out from some distant room—the most lonesome sound in nature, a sound steeped and sodden with homesickness and the emptiness of life. The family went to bed about dark every night, and as we were not invited to intrude any new customs we naturally followed theirs. Those nights were a hundred years long to youths accustomed to being up till twelve. We lay awake and miserable till that hour every time, and grew old and decrepit waiting through the still eternities for the clock-strikes. This was no place for town boys. So at last it was with something very like joy that we received news that the enemy were on our track again. With a new birth of the old warrior spirit we sprang to our places in line of battle and fell back on Camp Ralls.

Captain Lyman had taken a hint from Mason's talk, and he now gave orders that our camp should be guarded against surprise by the posting of pickets. I was ordered to place a picket at the forks of the road in Hyde's prairie. Night shut down black and threatening. I told Sergeant Bowers to go out to that place and stay till midnight; and, just as I was expecting, he said he wouldn't do it. I tried to get others to go, but all refused. Some excused themselves on account of the weather; but the rest were frank enough to say they wouldn't go in any kind of weather. This kind of thing sounds odd now, and impossible, but there was no surprise in it at the time. On the contrary, it seemed a perfectly natural thing to do. There were scores of little camps scattered over Missouri where the same thing was happening. These camps were composed of young men who had been born and reared to a sturdy independence, and who did not know what it meant to be ordered around by Tom, Dick, and Harry, whom they had known familiarly all their lives, in the village or on the farm. It is quite within the probabilities that this same thing was happening all over the South. James Redpath recognized the justice of this assumption, and furnished the following instance in support of it. During a short stay in East Tennessee he was in a citizen colonel's tent one day talking, when a big private appeared at the door, and, without salute or other circumlocution, said to the colonel:

"Say, Jim, I'm a-goin' home for a few days."

"What for?"

"Well, I hain't b'en there for a right smart while, and I'd like to see how things is comin' on."

"How long are you going to be gone?"

" 'Bout two weeks."

"Well, don't be gone longer than that; and get back sooner if you can."

That was all, and the citizen officer resumed his conversation where the private had broken it off. This was in the first months of the war, of course. The camps in our part of Missouri were under Brigadier-General Thomas H. Harris. He was a townsman of ours, a first-rate fellow, and well liked; but we had all familiarly known him as the sole and modest-salaried operator in our telegraph-office, where he had to send about one despatch a week in ordinary times, and two when there was a rush of business; consequently, when he appeared in our midst one day, on the wing, and delivered a military command of some sort, in a large military fashion, nobody was surprised at the response which he got from the assembled soldiery:

"Oh, now, what 'll you take to *don't*, Tom Harris?"

It was quite the natural thing. One might justly imagine that we were hopeless material for war. And so we seemed, in our ignorant state; but there were those among us who afterward learned the grim trade; learned to obey like machines; became valuable soldiers; fought all through the war, and came out at the end with excellent records. One of the very boys who refused to go out on picket duty that night, and called me an ass for thinking he would expose himself to danger in such a foolhardy way, had become distinguished for intrepidity before he was a year older.

I did secure my picket that night—not by authority, but by diplomacy. I got Bowers to go by agreeing to exchange ranks with him for the time being, and go along and stand the watch with him as his subordinate. We stayed out there a couple of dreary hours in the pitchy darkness and the rain, with nothing to modify the dreariness but Bowers's monotonous growlings at the war and the weather; then we began to nod, and presently found it next to impossible to stay in the saddle; so we gave up the tedious job, and went back to the camp without waiting for the relief guard. We rode into camp without interruption or objection from anybody, and the enemy could have done the same, for there were no sentries. Everybody was asleep; at midnight there was nobody to send out another picket, so none was sent. We never tried to establish a watch at night again, as far as I remember, but we generally kept a picket out in the daytime.

In that camp the whole command slept on the corn in the big corn-crib; and there was usually a general row before morning, for the place was full of rats, and they would scramble over the boys' bodies and faces, annoying and irritating everybody; and now and then they would bite some one's toe, and the person who owned the toe would start up and magnify his English and begin to throw corn in the dark. The ears were half as heavy as bricks, and when they struck they hurt. The persons struck would respond, and inside of five minutes every man would be locked in a death-grip with his neighbor. There was a grievous deal of blood shed in the corn-crib, but this was all that was spilt while I was in the war. No, that is not quite true. But for one circumstance it would have been all. I will come to that now.

Our scares were frequent. Every few days rumors would come that the enemy were approaching. In these cases we always fell back on some other camp of ours; we never stayed where we were. But the rumors always turned out to be false; so at last even we began to grow indifferent to them. One night a negro was sent to our corn-crib with the same old warning: the enemy was hovering in our neighborhood. We all said let him hover. We resolved to stay still and be comfortable. It was a fine warlike resolution, and no doubt we all felt the stir of it in our veins—for a moment. We had been having a very jolly time, that was full of horse-play and schoolboy hilarity; but that cooled down now, and presently the fast-waning fire of forced jokes and forced laughs died out altogether, and the company became silent. Silent and nervous. And soon uneasy—worried—apprehensive. We had said we would stay, and we were committed. We could have been persuaded to go, but there was nobody brave enough to suggest it. An almost noiseless movement presently began in the dark by a general but unvoiced impulse. When the movement was completed each man knew that he was not the only person who had crept to the front wall and had his eye at a crack between the logs. No, we were all there; all there with our hearts in our throats, and staring out toward the sugar-troughs where the forest footpath came through. It was late, and there was a deep woodsy stillness everywhere. There was a veiled moonlight, which was only just strong enough to enable us to mark the general shape of objects. Presently a muffled sound caught our ears, and we recognized it as the hoof-beats of a horse or horses. And right away a figure appeared in the forest path; it could have been made of smoke, its mass had so little sharpness of outline. It was a man on horseback, and it seemed to me that there were others behind him. I got hold of a gun in the dark, and pushed it through a crack between the logs, hardly knowing what I was doing, I was so dazed with fright. Somebody said "Fire!" I pulled the trigger. I seemed to see a hundred flashes and hear a hundred reports; then I saw the man fall down out of the saddle. My first feeling was of surprised gratification; my first impulse was an apprentice-sportsman's impulse to run and pick up his game. Somebody said, hardly audibly, "Good—we've got him!—wait for the rest." But the rest did not come. We waited—listened—still no more came. There was not a sound, not the whisper of a leaf; just perfect stillness; an uncanny kind of stillness, which was all the more uncanny on account of the damp, earthy, late-night smells now rising and pervading it. Then, wondering, we crept stealthily out, and approached the man. When we got to him the moon revealed him distinctly. He was lying on his back, with his arms abroad; his mouth was open and his chest heaving with long gasps, and his white shirt-front was all splashed with blood. The thought shot through me that I was a murderer; that I had killed a man—a man who had never done me any harm. That was the coldest sensation that ever went through my marrow. I was down by him in a moment, helplessly stroking his forehead; and I would have given anything then—my own life freely—to make him again what he had been five minutes before. And all the boys seemed to be feeling in the same way; they hung over him, full of pitying interest, and tried all they could to help him, and said all sorts of regretful things. They had forgotten all about the enemy; they thought only of this one forlorn unit of the foe. Once my imagination persuaded me that the dying man gave me a reproachful look out of his shadowy eyes, and it seemed to me that I could rather he had stabbed me than done that. He muttered and mumbled like a dreamer in his sleep about his wife and his child; and I thought with a new despair, "This thing that I have done does not end with him; it falls upon *them* too, and they never did me any harm, any more than he."

In a little while the man was dead. He was killed in war; killed in fair and legitimate war; killed in battle, as you may say; and yet he was as sincerely mourned by the opposing force as if he had been their brother. The boys stood there a half-hour sorrowing over him, and recalling the details of the tragedy, and wondering who he might be, and if he were a spy, and saying that if it were to do over again they would not hurt him unless he attacked them first. It soon came out that mine was not the only shot fired; there were five others—a division of the guilt which was a great relief to me, since it in some degree lightened and diminished the burden I was carrying. There were six shots fired at once; but I was not in my right mind at the time, and my heated imagination had magnified my one shot into a volley.

The man was not in uniform, and was not armed. He was a stranger in the country; that was all we ever found out about him. The thought of him got to preying upon me every night; I could not get rid of it. I could not drive it away, the taking of that unoffending life seemed such a wanton thing. And it seemed an epitome of war; that all war must be just that—the killing of strangers against whom you feel no personal animosity; strangers whom, in other circumstances, you would help if you found them in trouble, and who would help you if you needed it. My campaign was spoiled. It seemed to me that I was not rightly equipped for this awful business; that war was intended for men, and I for a child's nurse. I resolved to retire from this avocation of sham soldiership while I could save some remnant of my self-respect. These morbid thoughts clung to me against reason; for at bottom I did not believe I had touched that man. The law of probabilities decreed me guiltless of his blood; for in all my small experience with guns I had never hit anything I had tried to hit, and I knew I had done my best to hit him. Yet there was no solace in the thought. Against a diseased imagination demonstration goes for nothing.

The rest of my war experience was of a piece with what I have already told of it. We kept monotonously falling back upon one camp or another, and eating up the farmers and their families. They ought to have shot us; on the contrary, they were as hospitably kind and courteous to us as if we had deserved it. In one of these camps we found Ab Grimes, an Upper Mississippi pilot, who afterward became famous as a dare-devil rebel spy, whose career bristled with desperate adventures. The look and style of his comrades suggested that they had not come into the war to play, and their deeds made good the conjecture later. They were fine horsemen and good revolver shots; but their favorite arm was the lasso. Each had one at his pommel, and could snatch a man out of the saddle with it every time, on a full gallop, at any reasonable distance.

In another camp the chief was a fierce and profane old blacksmith of sixty, and he had furnished his twenty recruits with gigantic home-made bowie-knives, to be swung with two hands, like the *machetes* of the Isthmus. It was a grisly spectacle to see that earnest band practising their murderous cuts and slashes under the eye of that remorseless old fanatic.

The last camp which we fell back upon was in a hollow near the village of Florida, where I was born—in Monroe County. Here we were warned one day that a Union colonel was sweeping down on us with a whole regiment at his heel. This looked decidedly serious. Our boys went apart and consulted; then we went back and told the other companies present that the war was a disappointment to us, and we were going to disband. They were getting ready themselves to fall back on some place or other, and were only waiting for General Tom Harris, who was expected to arrive at any moment; so they tried to persuade us to wait a little while, but the majority of us said no, we were accustomed to falling back, and didn't need any of Tom Harris's help; we could get along perfectly well without him—and save time, too. So about half of our fifteen, including myself, mounted and left on the instant; the others yielded to persuasion and stayed—stayed through the war.

An hour later we met General Harris on the road, with two or three people in his company—his staff, probably, but we could not tell; none of them were in uniform; uniforms had not come into vogue among us yet. Harris ordered us back; but we told him there was a Union colonel coming with a whole regiment in his wake, and it looked as if there was going to be a disturbance; so we had concluded to go home. He raged a little, but it was of no use; our minds were made up. We had done our share; had killed one man, exterminated one army, such as it was; let him go and kill the rest, and that would end the war. I did not see that brisk young general again until last year; then he was wearing white hair and whiskers.

In time I came to know that Union colonel whose coming frightened me out of the war and crippled the Southern cause to that extent—General Grant. I came within a few hours of seeing him when he was as unknown as I was myself; at a time when anybody could have said, "Grant?—Ulysses S. Grant? I do not remember hearing the name before." It seems difficult to realize that there was once a time when such a remark could be rationally made;

but there *was*, and I was within a few miles of the place and the occasion, too, though proceeding in the other direction.

The thoughtful will not throw this war paper of mine lightly aside as being valueless. It has this value: it is a not unfair picture of what went on in many and many a militia camp in the first months of the rebellion, when the green recruits were without discipline, without the steadying and heartening influence of trained leaders; when all their circumstances were new and strange, and charged with exaggerated terrors, and before the invaluable experience of actual collision in the field had turned them from rabbits into soldiers. If this side of the picture of that early day has not before been put into history, then history has been to that degree incomplete, for it had and has its rightful place there. There was more Bull Run material scattered through the early camps of this country than exhibited itself at Bull Run. And yet it learned its trade presently, and helped to fight the great battles later. I could have become a soldier myself if I had waited. I had got part of it learned; I knew more about retreating than the man that invented retreating.

# LETTER TO THE EARTH

OFFICE OF THE RECORDING ANGEL
Department of Petitions, Jan. 20

*Abner Scofield*
*Coal Dealer*
*Buffalo, New York*

I have the honor, as per command, to inform you that your recent act of benevolence and self-sacrifice has been recorded upon a page of the Book called *Golden Deeds of Men;* a distinction, I am permitted to remark, which is not merely extraordinary, it is unique.

As regards your prayers, for the week ending the 19th, I have the honor to report as follows:

1. For weather to advance hard coal 15 cents a ton. Granted.

2. For influx of laborers to reduce wages 10 percent. Granted.

3. For a break in rival soft-coal prices. Granted.

4. For a visitation upon the man, or upon the family of the man, who has set up a competing retail coal-yard in Rochester. Granted, as follows: diphtheria, 2, 1 fatal; scarlet fever, 1, to result in deafness and imbecility. NOTE. This prayer should have been directed against this subordinate's principals, the N. Y. Central R. R. Co.

5. For deportation to Sheol of annoying swarms of persons who apply daily for work, or for favors of one sort or another. Taken under advisement for later decision and compromise, this petition appearing to conflict with another one of same date, which will be cited further along.

6. For application of some form of violent death to neighbor who threw brick at family cat, whilst the same was serenading. Reserved for consideration and compromise because of conflict with a prayer of even date to be cited further along.

7. To "damn the missionary cause." Reserved also—as above.

8. To increase December profits of $22,230 to $45,000 for January, and perpetuate a proportionate monthly increase thereafter—"which will satisfy you." The prayer granted; the added remark accepted with reservations.

9. For cyclone, to destroy the works and fill up the mine of the North Pennsylvania Co. NOTE: Cyclones are not kept in stock in the winter season. A reliable article of fire-damp can be furnished upon application.

Especial note is made of the above list, they being of particular moment. The 298 remaining supplications classifiable under the head of Special Providences, Schedule A, for week ending 19th, are granted in a body, except that 3 of the 32 cases requiring immediate death have been modified to incurable disease.

This completes the week's invoice of petitions known to this office under the technical designation of Secret Supplications of the Heart, and which, for a reason which may suggest itself, always receive our first and especial attention.

The remainder of the week's invoice falls under the head of what we term Public Prayers, in which classification we place prayers uttered in Prayer Meeting, Sunday School, Class Meeting, Family Worship, etc. These kinds of prayers have value according to classification of Christian uttering them. By rule of this office, Christians are divided into two grand classes, to wit: (1) Professing Christians; (2) Professional Christians. These, in turn, are minutely subdivided and classified by Size, Species, and Family; and finally, Standing is determined by carats, the minimum being 1, the maximum 1,000.

As per balance sheet for quarter ending Dec. 31st, 1847, you stood classified as follows:

*Grand Classification:* Professing Christian.

*Size:* one-fourth of maximum.

*Species:* Human-Spiritual.

*Family:* A of the Elect, Division 16.

*Standing:* 322 carats fine.

As per balance sheet for quarter just ended—that is to say, forty years later—you stand classified as follows:

*Grand Classification:* Professional Christian.

*Size:* six one-hundredths of maximum.

*Species:* Human-Animal.
*Family:* W of the Elect, Division 1547.
*Standing:* 3 carats fine.

I have the honor to call your attention to the fact that you seem to have deteriorated.

To resume report upon your Public Prayers—with the side remark that in order to encourage Christians of your grade and of approximate grades, it is the custom of this office to grant many things to them which would not be granted to Christians of a higher grade—partly because they would not be asked for:

Prayer for weather mercifully tempered to the needs of the poor and the naked. Denied. This was a Prayer-Meeting prayer. It conflicts with Item 1 of this report, which was a Secret Supplication of the Heart. By a rigid rule of this office, certain sorts of Public Prayers of Professional Christians are forbidden to take precedence of Secret Supplications of the Heart.

Prayer for better times and plentier food "for the hard-handed son of toil whose patient and exhausting labors make comfortable the homes, and pleasant the ways, of the more fortunate, and entitle him to our vigilant and effective protection from the wrongs and injustices which grasping avarice would do him, and to the tenderest offices of our grateful hearts." Prayer-Meeting prayer. Refused. Conflicts with Secret Supplication of the Heart No. 2.

Prayer "that such as in any way obstruct our preferences may be generously blessed, both themselves and their families, we here calling our hearts to witness that in their worldly prosperity we are spiritually blessed, and our joys made perfect." Prayer-Meeting prayer. Refused. Conflicts with Secret Supplications of the Heart Nos. 3 and 4.

"Oh, let none fall heir to the pains of perdition through words or acts of ours." Family Worship. Received fifteen minutes in advance of Secret Supplication of the Heart No. 5, with which it distinctly conflicts. It is suggested that one or the other of these prayers be withdrawn, or both of them modified.

"Be mercifully inclined toward all who would do us offense in our persons or our property." Includes man who threw brick at cat. Family Prayer. Received some minutes in advance of No. 6, Secret Supplications of the Heart. Modification suggested, to reconcile discrepancy.

"Grant that the noble missionary cause, the most precious labor entrusted to the hands of men, may spread and prosper without let or limit in all heathen lands that do as yet reproach us with their spiritual darkness." Uninvited prayer shoved in at meeting of American Board. Received nearly half a day in advance of No. 7, Secret Supplications of the Heart. This office takes no stock in missionaries, and is not connected in any way with the American Board. We should like to grant one of these prayers, but cannot grant both. It is suggested that the American Board one be withdrawn.

This office desires for the twentieth time to call urgent attention to your remark appended to No. 8. It is a chestnut.

Of the 464 specifications contained in your Public Prayers for the week, and not previously noted in this report, we grant 2, and deny the rest. To wit: Granted, (1) "that the clouds may continue to perform their office; (2) and the sun his." It was the divine purpose anyhow; it will gratify you to know that you have not disturbed it. Of the 462 details refused, 61 were uttered in Sunday School. In this connection I must once more remind you that we grant no Sunday School Prayers of Professional Christians of the classification technically known in this office as the John Wanamaker grade. We merely enter them as "words," and they count to his credit according to number uttered within certain limits of time; 3,000 per quarter-minute required, or no score; 4,200 in a possible 5,000 is a quite common Sunday School score, among experts, and counts the same as two hymns and a bouquet furnished by young ladies in the assassin's cell, execution morning. Your remaining 401 details count for wind only. We bunch them and use them for head winds in retarding the ships of improper people, but it takes so many of them to make an impression that we cannot allow anything for their use.

I desire to add a word of my own to this report. When certain sorts of people do a sizable good deed, we credit them up a thousand-fold more for it than we would in the case of a better man—on account of the strain. You stand far away above your classification record here, because of certain self-sacrifices of yours which greatly exceed what could have been expected of you. Years ago, when you were worth only $100,000, and sent $2 to your impoverished cousin the widow when she appealed to you for help, there were many in heaven who were not able to believe it, and many more who believed that the money was counterfeit. Your character went up many degrees when it was shown that these suspicions were unfounded. A year or two later, when you sent the poor girl $4 in answer to another appeal, everybody believed it, and you were all the talk here for days together. Two years later you sent $6, upon supplication, when the widow's youngest child died, and that act made perfect your good fame. Everybody in heaven said, "Have you heard about Abner?"—for you are now affectionately called Abner here. Your increasing donation, every two or three years, has kept your name on all lips, and warm in all hearts. All heaven watches you Sundays, as you drive to church in your handsome carriage; and when your hand retires from the contribution plate, the glad shout is heard even to the ruddy walls of remote Sheol, "Another nickel from Abner!"

But the climax came a few days ago, when the widow wrote and said she could get a school in a far village to teach if she had $50 to get herself and her two surviving children over the long journey; and you counted up last month's clear profit from your three coal mines—$22,230 —and added to it the certain profit for the current month —$45,000 and a possible fifty—and then got down your pen and your checkbook and mailed her *fifteen whole dollars!* Ah, heaven bless and keep you forever and ever, generous heart! There was not a dry eye in the realms of bliss; and amidst the hand-shakings, and embracings, and praisings, the decree was thundered forth from the shining mount, that this deed should outhonor all the historic self-sacrifices of men and angels, and be recorded by itself upon a page of its own, for that the strain of it upon you had been heavier and bitterer than the strain it costs ten thousand martyrs to yield up their lives at the fiery stake; and all said, "What is the giving up of life, to a noble soul, or to ten thousand noble souls, compared with the giving up of fifteen dollars out of the greedy grip of the meanest white man that ever lived on the face of the earth?"

And it was a true word. And Abraham, weeping, shook

out the contents of his bosom and pasted the eloquent label there, "RESERVED"; and Peter, weeping, said, "He shall be received with a torchlight procession when he comes"; and then all heaven boomed, and was glad you were going there. And so was hell.

[Signed]
THE RECORDING ANGEL [SEAL]

By command

# FENIMORE COOPER'S LITERARY OFFENSES

*The Pathfinder and The Deerslayer stand at the head of Cooper's novels as artistic creations. There are others of his works which contain parts as perfect as are to be found in these, and scenes even more thrilling. Not one can be compared with either of them as a finished whole.*

*The defects in both of these tales are comparatively slight. They were pure works of art.*—Prof. Lounsbury.

*The five tales reveal an extraordinary fullness of invention.*

*. . . One of the very greatest characters in fiction, Natty Bumppo. . . .*

*The craft of the woodsman, the tricks of the trapper, all the delicate art of the forest, were familiar to Cooper from his youth up.*—Prof. Brander Matthews.

*Cooper is the greatest artist in the domain of romantic fiction yet produced by America.*—Wilkie Collins.

It seems to me that it was far from right for the Professor of English Literature in Yale, the Professor of English Literature in Columbia, and Wilkie Collins to deliver opinions on Cooper's literature without having read some of it. It would have been much more decorous to keep silent and let persons talk who have read Cooper.

Cooper's art has some defects. In one place in *Deerslayer*, and in the restricted space of two-thirds of a page, Cooper has scored 114 offenses against literary art out of a possible 115. It breaks the record.

There are nineteen rules governing literary art in the domain of romantic fiction—some say twenty-two. In *Deerslayer* Cooper violated eighteen of them. These eighteen require:

1. That a tale shall accomplish something and arrive

somewhere. But the *Deerslayer* tale accomplishes nothing and arrives in the air.

2. They require that the episodes of a tale shall be necessary parts of the tale, and shall help to develop it. But as the *Deerslayer* tale is not a tale, and accomplishes nothing and arrives nowhere, the episodes have no rightful place in the work, since there was nothing for them to develop.

3. They require that the personages in a tale shall be alive, except in the case of corpses, and that always the reader shall be able to tell the corpses from the others. But this detail has often been overlooked in the *Deerslayer* tale.

4. They require that the personages in a tale, both dead and alive, shall exhibit a sufficient excuse for being there. But this detail also has been overlooked in the *Deerslayer* tale.

5. They require that when the personages of a tale deal in conversation, the talk shall sound like human talk, and be talk such as human beings would be likely to talk in the given circumstances, and have a discoverable meaning, also a discoverable purpose, and a show of relevancy, and remain in the neighborhood of the subject in hand, and be interesting to the reader, and help out the tale, and stop when the people cannot think of anything more to say. But this requirement has been ignored from the beginning of the *Deerslayer* tale to the end of it.

6. They require that when the author describes the character of a personage in his tale, the conduct and conversation of that personage shall justify said description. But this law gets little or no attention in the *Deerslayer* tale, as Natty Bumppo's case will amply prove.

7. They require that when a personage talks like an illustrated, gilt-edged, tree-calf, hand-tooled, seven-dollar Friendship's Offering in the beginning of a paragraph, he shall not talk like a negro minstrel in the end of it. But this rule is flung down and danced upon in the *Deerslayer* tale.

8. They require that crass stupidities shall not be played upon the reader as "the craft of the woodsman, the delicate art of the forest," by either the author or the people in the tale. But this rule is persistently violated in the *Deerslayer* tale.

9. They require that the personages of a tale shall confine themselves to possibilities and let miracles alone; or, if they venture a miracle, the author must so plausibly set it forth as to make it look possible and reasonable. But these rules are not respected in the *Deerslayer* tale.

10. They require that the author shall make the reader feel a deep interest in the personages of his tale and in their fate; and that he shall make the reader love the good people in the tale and hate the bad ones. But the reader of the *Deerslayer* tale dislikes the good people in it, is indifferent to the others, and wishes they would all get drowned together.

11. They require that the characters in a tale shall be so clearly defined that the reader can tell beforehand what each will do in a given emergency. But in the *Deerslayer* tale this rule is vacated.

In addition to these large rules there are some little ones. These require that the author shall

12. *Say* what he is proposing to say, not merely come near it.

13. Use the right word, not its second cousin.

14. Eschew surplusage.

15. Not omit necessary details.

16. Avoid slovenliness of form.

17. Use good grammar.

18. Employ a simple and straightforward style.

Even these seven are coldly and persistently violated in the *Deerslayer* tale.

Cooper's gift in the way of invention was not a rich endowment; but such as it was he liked to work it, he was pleased with the effects, and indeed he did some quite sweet things with it. In his little box of stage-properties he kept six or eight cunning devices, tricks, artifices for his savages and woodsmen to deceive and circumvent each other with, and he was never so happy as when he was working these innocent things and seeing them go. A favorite one was to make a moccasined person tread in the tracks of the moccasined enemy, and thus hide his own trail. Cooper wore out barrels and barrels of moccasins in working that trick. Another stage-property that he pulled out of his box pretty frequently was his broken twig. He prized his broken twig above all the rest of his effects, and worked it the hardest. It is a restful chapter in any book of

his when somebody doesn't step on a dry twig and alarm all
the reds and whites for two hundred yards around. Every
time a Cooper person is in peril, and absolute silence is
worth four dollars a minute, he is sure to step on a dry
twig. There may be a hundred handier things to step on,
but that wouldn't satisfy Cooper. Cooper requires him to
turn out and find a dry twig; and if he can't do it, go and
borrow one. In fact, the Leatherstocking Series ought to
have been called the Broken Twig Series.

I am sorry there is not room to put in a few dozen instances of the delicate art of the forest, as practised by
Natty Bumppo and some of the other Cooperian experts.
Perhaps we may venture two or three samples. Cooper was
a sailor—a naval officer; yet he gravely tells us how a vessel, driving toward a lee shore in a gale, is steered for a
particular spot by her skipper because he knows of an *un-
dertow* there which will hold her back against the gale and
save her. For just pure woodcraft, or sailorcraft, or whatever it is, isn't that neat? For several years Cooper was
daily in the society of artillery, and he ought to have
noticed that when a cannon-ball strikes the ground it either
buries itself or skips a hundred feet or so; skips again a
hundred feet or so—and so on, till finally it gets tired and
rolls. Now in one place he loses some "females"—as he always calls women—in the edge of a wood near a plain at
night in a fog, on purpose to give Bumppo a chance to
show off the delicate art of the forest before the reader.
These mislaid people are hunting for a fort. They hear a
cannon-blast, and a cannon-ball presently comes rolling
into the wood and stops at their feet. To the females this
suggests nothing. The case is very different with the admirable Bumppo. I wish I may never know peace again if
he doesn't strike out promptly and *follow the track* of that
cannon-ball across the plain through the dense fog and
find the fort. Isn't it a daisy? If Cooper had any real
knowledge of Nature's ways of doing things, he had a
most delicate art in concealing the fact. For instance: one
of his acute Indian experts, Chingachgook (pronounced
Chicago, I think), has lost the trail of a person he is track-
ing through the forest. Apparently that trail is hopelessly
lost. Neither you nor I could ever have guessed out the
way to find it. It was very different with Chicago. Chicago
was not stumped for long. He turned a running stream

out of its course, and there, in the slush in its old bed, were that person's moccasin tracks. The current did not wash them away, as it would have done in all other like cases—no, even the eternal laws of Nature have to vacate when Cooper wants to put up a delicate job of woodcraft on the reader.

We must be a little wary when Brander Matthews tell us that Cooper's books "reveal an extraordinary fullness of invention." As a rule, I am quite willing to accept Brander Matthews's literary judgments and applaud his lucid and graceful phrasing of them; but that particular statement needs to be taken with a few tons of salt. Bless your heart, Cooper hadn't any more invention than a horse; and I don't mean a high-class horse, either; I mean a clothes-horse. It would be very difficult to find a really clever "situation" in Cooper's books, and still more difficult to find one of any kind which he has failed to render absurd by his handling of it. Look at the episodes of "the caves"; and at the celebrated scuffle between Maqua and those others on the table-land a few days later; and at Hurry Harry's queer water-transit from the castle to the ark; and at Deerslayer's half-hour with his first corpse; and at the quarrel between Hurry Harry and Deerslayer later; and at —but choose for yourself; you can't go amiss.

If Cooper had been an observer his inventive faculty would have worked better; not more interestingly, but more rationally, more plausibly. Cooper's proudest creations in the way of "situations" suffer noticeably from the absence of the observer's protecting gift. Cooper's eye was splendidly inaccurate. Cooper seldom saw anything correctly. He saw nearly all things as through a glass eye, darkly. Of course a man who cannot see the commonest little every-day matters accurately is working at a disadvantage when he is constructing a "situation." In the *Deerslayer* tale Cooper has a stream which is fifty feet wide where it flows out of a lake; it presently narrows to twenty as it meanders along for no given reason, and yet when a stream acts like that it ought to be required to explain itself. Fourteen pages later the width of the brook's outlet from the lake has suddenly shrunk thirty feet, and become "the narrowest part of the stream." This shrinkage is not accounted for. The stream has bends in it, a sure indication that it has alluvial banks and cuts them; yet these

bends are only thirty and fifty feet long. If Cooper had
been a nice and punctilious observer he would have noticed that the bends were oftener nine hundred feet long
than short of it.

Cooper made the exit of that stream fifty feet wide, in
the first place, for no particular reason; in the second
place, he narrowed it to less than twenty to accommodate
some Indians. He bends a "sapling" to the form of an arch
over this narrow passage, and conceals six Indians in its
foliage. They are "laying" for a settler's scow or ark which
is coming up the stream on its way to the lake; it is being
hauled against the stiff current by a rope whose stationary
end is anchored in the lake; its rate of progress cannot be
more than a mile an hour. Cooper describes the ark, but
pretty obscurely. In the matter of dimensions "it was little
more than a modern canal-boat." Let us guess, then, that it
was about one hundred and forty feet long. It was of
"greater breadth than common." Let us guess, then, that it
was about sixteen feet wide. This leviathan had been
prowling down bends which were but a third as long as
itself, and scraping between banks where it had only two
feet of space to spare on each side. We cannot too much
admire this miracle. A low-roofed log dwelling occupies
"two-thirds of the ark's length"—a dwelling ninety feet
long and sixteen feet wide, let us say—a kind of vestibule
train. The dwelling has two rooms—each forty-five feet
long and sixteen feet wide, let us guess. One of them is
the bedroom of the Hutter girls, Judith and Hetty; the
other is the parlor in the daytime, at night it is papa's bed-
chamber. The ark is arriving at the stream's exit now,
whose width has been reduced to less than twenty feet to
accommodate the Indians—say to eighteen. There is a foot
to spare on each side of the boat. Did the Indians notice
that there was going to be a tight squeeze there? Did they
notice that they could make money by climbing down out
of that arched sapling and just stepping aboard when the
ark scraped by? No, other Indians would have noticed
these things, but Cooper's Indians never notice anything.
Cooper thinks they are marvelous creatures for noticing,
but he was almost always in error about his Indians. There
was seldom a sane one among them.

The ark is one hundred and forty-feet long; the dwelling
is ninety feet long. The idea of the Indians is to drop

softly and secretly from the arched sapling to the dwelling as the ark creeps along under it at the rate of a mile an hour, and butcher the family. It will take the ark a minute and a half to pass under. It will take the ninety-foot dwelling a minute to pass under. Now, then, what did the six Indians do? It would take you thirty years to guess, and even then you would have to give it up, I believe. Therefore, I will tell you what the Indians did. Their chief, a person of quite extraordinary intellect for a Cooper Indian, warily watched the canal-boat as it squeezed along under him, and when he had got his calculations fined down to exactly the right shade, as he judged, he let go and dropped. And *missed the house!* That is actually what he did. He missed the house, and landed in the stern of the scow. It was not much of a fall, yet it knocked him silly. He lay there unconscious. If the house had been ninety-seven feet long he would have made the trip. The fault was Cooper's, not his. The error lay in the construction of the house. Cooper was no architect.

There still remained in the roost five Indians. The boat has passed under and is now out of their reach. Let me explain what the five did—you would not be able to reason it out for yourself. No. 1 jumped for the boat, but fell in the water astern of it. Then No. 2 jumped for the boat, but fell in the water still farther astern of it. Then No. 3 jumped for the boat, and fell a good way astern of it. Then No. 4 jumped for the boat, and fell in the water *away* astern. Then even No. 5 made a jump for the boat—for he was a Cooper Indian. In the matter of intellect, the difference between a Cooper Indian and the Indian that stands in front of the cigar-shop is not spacious. The scow episode is really a sublime burst of invention; but it does not thrill, because the inaccuracy of the details throws a sort of air of fictitiousness and general improbability over it. This comes of Cooper's inadequacy as an observer.

The reader will find some examples of Cooper's high talent for inaccurate observation in the account of the shooting-match in *The Pathfinder*.

A common wrought nail was driven lightly into the target, its head having been first touched with paint.

The color of the paint is not stated—an important omission, but Cooper deals freely in important omissions. No, after all, it was not an important omission; for this nail-head is *a hundred yards* from the marksmen, and could not be seen by them at that distance, no matter what its color might be. How far can the best eyes see a common house-fly? A hundred yards? It is quite impossible. Very well; eyes that cannot see a house-fly that is a hundred yards away cannot see an ordinary nail-head at that distance, for the size of the two objects is the same. It takes a keen eye to see a fly or a nail-head at fifty yards—one hundred and fifty feet. Can the reader do it?

The nail was lightly driven, its head painted, and game called. Then the Cooper miracles began. The bullet of the first marksman chipped an edge of the nail-head; the next man's bullet drove the nail a little way into the target—and removed all the paint. Haven't the miracles gone far enough now? Not to suit Cooper; for the purpose of this whole scheme is to show off his prodigy, Deerslayer-Hawk-eye-Long-Rifle-Leatherstocking-Pathfinder-Bumppo  before the ladies.

"Be all ready to clench it, boys!" cried out Pathfinder, stepping into his friend's tracks the instant they were vacant. "Never mind a new nail; I can see that, though the paint is gone, and what I can see I can hit at a hundred yards, though it were only a mosquito's eye. Be ready to clench!"

The rifle cracked, the bullet sped its way, and the head of the nail was buried in the wood, covered by the piece of flattened lead.

There, you see, is a man who could hunt flies with a rifle, and command a ducal salary in a Wild West show to-day if we had him back with us.

The recorded feat is certainly surprising just as it stands; but it is not surprising enough for Cooper. Cooper adds a touch. He has made Pathfinder do this miracle with another man's rifle; and not only that, but Pathfinder did not have even the advantage of loading it himself. He had everything against him, and yet he made that impossible shot; and not only made it, but did it with absolute confidence, saying, "Be ready to clench." Now a person like that would have undertaken that same feat with a brick-bat, and with Cooper to help he would have achieved it, too.

Pathfinder showed off handsomely that day before the ladies. His very first feat was a thing which no Wild West show can touch. He was standing with the group of marksmen, observing—a hundred yards from the target, mind; one Jasper raised his rifle and drove the center of the bull's-eye. Then the Quartermaster fired. The target exhibited no result this time. There was a laugh. "It's a dead miss," said Major Lundie. Pathfinder waited an impressive moment or two; then said, in that calm, indifferent, know-it-all way of his, "No, Major, he has covered Jasper's bullet, as will be seen if any one will take the trouble to examine the target."

Wasn't it remarkable! How *could* he see that little pellet fly through the air and enter that distant bullet-hole? Yet that is what he did; for nothing is impossible to a Cooper person. Did any of those people have any deep-seated doubts about this thing? No; for that would imply sanity, and these were all Cooper people.

The respect for Pathfinder's skill and for his *quickness and accuracy of sight* [the italics are mine] was so profound and general, that the instant he made this declaration the spectators began to distrust their own opinions, and a dozen rushed to the target in order to ascertain the fact. There, sure enough, it was found that the Quartermaster's bullet had gone through the hole made by Jasper's, and that, too, so accurately as to require a minute examination to be certain of the circumstance, which, however, was soon clearly established by discovering one bullet over the other in the stump against which the target was placed.

They made a "minute" examination; but never mind, how could they know that there were two bullets in that hole without digging the latest one out? for neither probe nor eyesight could prove the presence of any more than one bullet. Did they dig? No; as we shall see. It is the Pathfinder's turn now; he steps out before the ladies, takes aim, and fires.

But, alas! here is a disappointment; an incredible, an unimaginable disappointment—for the target's aspect is unchanged; there is nothing there but that same old bullet-hole!

"If one dared to hint at such a thing," cried Major Duncan, "I should say that the Pathfinder has also missed the target!"

As nobody had missed it yet, the "also" was not necessary; but never mind about that, for the Pathfinder is going to speak.

"No, no, Major," said he, confidently, "that *would* be a risky declaration. I didn't load the piece, and can't say what was in it; but if it was lead, you will find the bullet driving down those of the Quartermaster and Jasper, else is not my name Pathfinder."

A shout from the target announced the truth of this assertion.

Is the miracle sufficient as it stands? Not for Cooper. The Pathfinder speaks again, as he "now slowly advances toward the stage occupied by the females":

"That's not all, boys, that's not all; if you find the target touched at all, I'll own to a miss. The Quartermaster cut the wood, but you'll find no wood cut by that last messenger."

The miracle is at last complete. He knew—doubtless *saw* —at the distance of a hundred yards—that his bullet had passed into the hole *without fraying the edges*. There were now three bullets in that one hole—three bullets embedded processionally in the body of the stump back of the target. Everybody knew this—somehow or other—and yet nobody had dug any of them out to make sure. Cooper is not a close observer, but he is interesting. He is certainly always that, no matter what happens. And he is more interesting when he is not noticing what he is about than when he is. This is a considerable merit.

The conversations in the Cooper books have a curious sound in our modern ears. To believe that such talk really ever came out of people's mouths would be to believe that there was a time when time was of no value to a person who thought he had something to say; when it was the custom to spread a two-minute remark out to ten; when a man's mouth was a rolling-mill, and busied itself all day long in turning four-foot pigs of thought into thirty-foot bars of conversational railroad iron by attenuation; when subjects were seldom faithfully stuck to, but the talk wandered all around and arrived nowhere; when conversations consisted mainly of irrelevancies, with here and there a relevancy, a relevancy with an embarrassed look, as not being able to explain how it got there.

Cooper was certainly not a master in the construction of dialogue. Inaccurate observation defeated him here as it defeated him in so many other enterprises of his. He even failed to notice that the man who talks corrupt English six days in the week must and will talk it on the seventh, and can't help himself. In the *Deerslayer* story he lets Deerslayer talk the showiest kind of book-talk sometimes, and at other times the basest of base dialects. For instance, when some one asks him if he has a sweet-heart, and if so, where she abides, this is his majestic answer:

"She's in the forest—hanging from the boughs of the trees, in a soft rain—in the dew on the open grass—the clouds that float about in the blue heavens—the birds that sing in the woods—the sweet springs where I slake my thirst—and in all the other glorious gifts that come from God's Providence!"

And he preceded that, a little before, with this:

"It consarns me as all things that touches a fri'nd consarns a fri'nd."

And this is another of his remarks:

"If I was Injin born, now, I might tell of this, or carry in the scalp and boast of the expl'ite afore the whole tribe; or if my inimy had only been a bear"—[and so on].

We cannot imagine such a thing as a veteran Scotch Commander-in-Chief comporting himself in the field like a windy melodramatic actor, but Cooper could. On one occasion Alice and Cora were being chased by the French through a fog in the neighborhood of their father's fort:

"*Point de quartier aux coquins!*" cried an eager pursuer, who seemed to direct the operations of the enemy. "Stand firm and be ready, my gallant 60ths!" suddenly exclaimed a voice above them; "wait to see the enemy; fire low, and sweep the glacis."

"Father! father" exclaimed a piercing cry from out the mist; "it is I! Alice! thy own Elsie! spare, O! save your daughters!"

"Hold!" shouted the former speaker, in the awful tones of parental agony, the sound reaching even to the woods, and rolling back in solemn echo. " 'Tis she! God has restored me my children! Throw open the sally-port; to the field, 60ths, to the field! pull not a trigger, lest ye kill my lambs! Drive off these dogs of France with your steel!"

Cooper's word-sense was singularly dull. When a person has a poor ear for music he will flat and sharp right along without knowing it. He keeps near the tune, but it is *not* the tune. When a person has a poor ear for words, the result is a literary flatting and sharping; you perceive what he is intending to say, but you also perceive that he doesn't *say* it. This is Cooper. He was not a word-musician. His ear was satisfied with the *approximate* word. I will furnish some circumstantial evidence in support of this charge. My instances are gathered from half a dozen pages of the tale called *Deerslayer*. He uses "verbal" for "oral"; "precision" for "facility"; "phenomena" for "marvels"; "necessary" for "predetermined"; "unsophisticated" for "primitive"; "preparation" for "expectancy"; "rebuked" for "subdued"; "dependent on" for "resulting from"; "fact" for "condition"; "fact" for "conjecture"; "precaution" for "caution"; "explain" for "determine"; "mortified" for "disappointed"; "meretricious" for "factitious"; "materially" for "considerably"; "decreasing" for "deepening"; "increasing" for "disappearing"; "embedded" for "inclosed"; "treacherous" for "hostile"; "stood" for "stooped"; "softened" for "replaced"; "rejoined" for "remarked"; "situation" for "condition"; "different" for "differing"; "insensible" for "unsentient"; "brevity" for "celerity"; "distrusted" for "suspicious"; "mental imbecility" for "imbecility"; "eyes" for "sight"; "counteracting" for "opposing"; "funeral obsequies" for "obsequies."

There have been daring people in the world who claimed that Cooper could write English, but they are all dead now —all dead but Lounsbury. I don't remember that Lounsbury makes the claim in so many words, still he makes it, for he says that *Deerslayer* is a "pure work of art." Pure, in that connection, means faultless—faultless in all details—and language is a detail. If Mr. Lounsbury had only compared Cooper's English with the English which he writes himself—but it is plain that he didn't; and so it is likely that he imagines until this day that Cooper's is as clean and compact as his own. Now I feel sure, deep down in my heart, that Cooper wrote about the poorest English that exists in our language, and that the English of *Deerslayer* is the very worst that even Cooper ever wrote.

I may be mistaken, but it does seem to me that *Deerslayer* is not a work of art in any sense; it does seem to me that it is destitute of every detail that goes to the making of a work of art; in truth, it seems to me that *Deerslayer* is just simply a literary *delirium tremens*.

A work of art? It has no invention; it has no order, system, sequence, or result; it has no life-likeness, no thrill, no stir, no seeming of reality; its characters are confusedly drawn, and by their acts and words they prove that they are not the sort of people the author claims that they are; its humor is pathetic; its pathos is funny, its conversations are —oh! indescribable; its love-scenes odious; its English a crime against the language.

Counting these out, what is left is Art. I think we must all admit that.

# HOW TO TELL A STORY

[The Humorous Story an American
Development.—Its Difference
from Comic and Witty Stories.]

I do not claim that I can tell a story as it ought to be told.
I only claim to know how a story ought to be told, for I
have been almost daily in the company of the most expert
story-tellers for many years.

There are several kinds of stories, but only one difficult
kind—the humorous. I will talk mainly about that one.
The humorous story is American, the comic story is English, the witty story is French. The humorous story depends
for its effect upon the *manner* of the telling; the comic
story and the witty story upon the *matter*.

The humorous story may be spun out to great length, and
may wander around as much as it pleases, and arrive nowhere in particular; but the comic and witty stories must
be brief and end with a point. The humorous story bubbles
gently along, the others burst.

The humorous story is strictly a work of art—high and
delicate art—and only an artist can tell it; but no art is
necessary in telling the comic and the witty story; anybody
can do it. The art of telling a humorous story—understand,
I mean by word of mouth, not print—was created in America, and has remained at home.

The humorous story is told gravely; the teller does his
best to conceal the fact that he even dimly suspects that
there is anything funny about it; but the teller of the
comic story tells you beforehand that it is one of the
funniest things he has ever heard, then tells it with eager
delight, and is the first person to laugh when he gets
through. And sometimes, if he has had good success, he is
so glad and happy that he will repeat the "nub" of it and
glance around from face to face, collecting applause, and
then repeat it again. It is a pathetic thing to see.

Very often, of course, the rambling and disjointed humorous story finishes with a nub, point, snapper, or whatever you like to call it. Then the listener must be alert, for in many cases the teller will divert attention from that nub by dropping it in a carefully casual and indifferent way, with the pretense that he does not know it is a nub.

Artemus Ward used that trick a good deal; then when the belated audience presently caught the joke he would look up with innocent surprise, as if wondering what they had found to laugh at. Dan Setchell used it before him, Nye and Riley and others use it to-day.

But the teller of the comic story does not slur the nub; he shouts it at you—every time. And when he prints it, in England, France, Germany, and Italy, he italicizes it, puts some whooping exclamation-points after it, and sometimes explains it in a parenthesis. All of which is very depressing, and makes one want to renounce joking and lead a better life.

Let me set down an instance of the comic method, using an anecdote which has been popular all over the world for twelve or fifteen hundred years. The teller tells it in this way:

## [The Wounded Soldier.]

In the course of a certain battle a soldier whose leg had been shot off appealed to another soldier who was hurrying by to carry him to the rear, informing him at the same time of the loss which he had sustained; whereupon the generous son of Mars, shouldering the unfortunate, proceeded to carry out his desire. The bullets and cannon-balls were flying in all directions, and presently one of the latter took the wounded man's head off—without, however, his deliverer being aware of it. In no long time he was hailed by an officer, who said:

"Where are you going with that carcass?"

"To the rear, sir—he's lost his leg!"

"His leg, forsooth?" responded the astonished officer; "you mean his head, you booby."

Whereupon the soldier dispossessed himself of his burden, and stood looking down upon it in great perplexity. At length he said:

"It is true, sir, just as you have said." Then after a pause he added, "*But he* TOLD *me* IT WAS HIS LEG! ! ! ! !"

Here the narrator bursts into explosion after explosion of thunderous horse-laughter, repeating that nub from time to time through his gaspings and shriekings and suffocatings.

It takes only a minute and a half to tell that in its comic-story form; and isn't worth the telling, after all. Put into the humorous-story form it takes ten minutes, and is about the funniest thing I have ever listened to—as James Whitcomb Riley tells it.

He tells it in the character of a dull-witted old farmer who has just heard it for the first time, thinks it is unspeakably funny, and is trying to repeat it to a neighbor. But he can't remember it; so he gets all mixed up and wanders helplessly round and round, putting in tedious details that don't belong in the tale and only retard it; taking them out conscientiously and putting in others that are just as useless; making minor mistakes now and then and stopping to correct them and explain how he came to make them; remembering things which he forgot to put in in their proper place and going back to put them in there; stopping his narrative a good while in order to try to recall the name of the soldier that was hurt, and finally remembering that the soldier's name was not mentioned, and remarking placidly that the name is of no real importance, anyway—better, of course, if one knew it, but not essential, after all—and so on, and so on, and so on.

The teller is innocent and happy and pleased with himself, and has to stop every little while to hold himself in and keep from laughing outright; and does hold in, but his body quakes in a jelly-like way with interior chuckles; and at the end of the ten minutes the audience have laughed until they are exhausted, and the tears are running down their faces.

The simplicity and innocence and sincerity and unconsciousness of the old farmer are perfectly simulated, and the result is a performance which is thoroughly charming and delicious. This is art—and fine and beautiful, and only a master can compass it; but a machine could tell the other story.

To string incongruities and absurdities together in a wandering and sometimes purposeless way, and seem innocently unaware that they are absurdities, is the basis of the American art, if my position is correct. Another feature is the slurring of the point. A third is the dropping of a studied remark apparently without knowing it, as if one were thinking aloud. The fourth and last is the pause.

Artemus Ward dealt in numbers three and four a good deal. He would begin to tell with great animation something which he seemed to think was wonderful; then lose confidence, and after an apparently absent-minded pause add an incongruous remark in a soliloquizing way; and that was the remark intended to explode the mine—and it did.

For instance, he would say eagerly, excitedly, "I once knew a man in New Zealand who hadn't a tooth in his head"—here his animation would die out; a silent, reflective pause would follow, then he would say dreamily, and as if to himself, "and yet that man could beat a drum better than any man I ever saw."

The pause is an exceedingly important feature in any kind of story, and a frequently recurring feature, too. It is a dainty thing, and delicate, and also uncertain and treacherous; for it must be exactly the right length—no more and no less—or it fails of its purpose and makes trouble. If the pause is too short the impressive point is passed, and the audience have had time to divine that a surprise is intended—and then you can't surprise them, of course.

On the platform I used to tell a negro ghost story that had a pause in front of the snapper on the end, and that pause was the most important thing in the whole story. If I got it the right length precisely, I could spring the finishing ejaculation with effect enough to make some impressible girl deliver a startled little yelp and jump out of her seat—and that was what I was after. This story was called "The Golden Arm," and was told in this fashion. You can practise with it yourself—and mind you look out for the pause and get it right.

## [The Golden Arm.]

Once 'pon a time dey wuz a monsus mean man, en he live 'way out in de prairie all 'lone by hisself, 'cep'n he had a wife. En bimeby she died, en he tuck en toted her way

out dah in de prairie en buried her. Well, she had a
golden arm—all solid gold, fum de shoulder down. He
wuz pow'ful mean—pow'ful; en dat night he couldn't
sleep, caze he want dat golden arm so bad.

When it come midnight he couldn't stan' it no mo'; so
he git up, he did, en tuck his lantern en shoved out thoo
de storm en dug her up en got de golden arm; en he bent
his head down 'gin de win', en plowed en plowed en
plowed thoo de snow. Den all on a sudden he stop (make
a considerable pause here, and look startled, and take a
listening attitude) en say: "My *lan'*, what's dat?"

En he listen—en listen—en de win' say (set your teeth
together and imitate the wailing and wheezing singsong of
the wind), "Bzzz-z-zzz"—en den, way back yonder whah de
grave is, he hear a *voice!*—he hear a voice all mix' up in de
win'—can't hardly tell 'em 'part—"Bzzz—zzz—W-h-o—g-o-t
—m-y—g-o-l-d-e-n *arm?*" (You must begin to shiver violently
now.)

En he begin to shiver en shake, en say, "Oh, my! *Oh,
my lan'!*" en de win' blow de lantern out, en de snow en
sleet blow in his face en mos' choke him, en he start a-
plowin' knee-deep towards home mos' dead, he so sk'yerd
—en pooty soon he hear de voice agin, en (pause) it 'us
comin' *after* him! "Bzzz—zzz—zzz—W-h-o—g-o-t—m-y—
g-o-l-d-e-n—*arm?*"

When he git to de pasture he hear it agin—closter now,
en a-*comin'!*—a-comin' back dah in de dark en de storm—
(repeat the wind and the voice). When he git to de house
he rush up-stairs en jump in de bed en kiver up, head
and years, en lay dah shiverin' en shakin'—en den way out
dah he hear it *agin!*—en a-*comin'!* En bimeby he hear
(pause—awed, listening attitude)—pat—pat—pat—*hit's a-
comin' up-stairs!* Den he hear de latch, en he *know* it's in
de room!

Den pooty soon he know it's a-*stannin' by de bed!* (Pause.)
Den—he know it's a-*bendin' down over him*—en he cain't
skasely git his breath! Den—den—he seem to feel someth'n'
*c-o-l-d*, right down 'most agin his head! (Pause.)

Den de voice say, *right at his year*—"W-h-o—g-o-t—m-y—
g-o-l-d-e-n *arm?*" (You must wail it out very plaintively and
accusingly; then you stare steadily and impressively into
the face of the farthest-gone auditor—a girl, preferably—
and let that awe-inspiring pause begin to build itself in the

deep hush. When it has reached exactly the right length, jump suddenly at that girl and yell, "*You've* got it!"

If you've got the *pause* right, she'll fetch a dear little yelp and spring right out of her shoes. But you *must* get the pause right; and you will find it the most troublesome and aggravating and uncertain thing you ever undertook.

# CORN-PONE OPINIONS

Fifty years ago, when I was a boy of fifteen and helping to inhabit a Missourian village on the banks of the Mississippi, I had a friend whose society was very dear to me because I was forbidden by my mother to partake of it. He was a gay and impudent and satirical and delightful young black man—a slave—who daily preached sermons from the top of his master's woodpile, with me for sole audience. He imitated the pulpit style of the several clergymen of the village, and did it well, and with fine passion and energy. To me he was a wonder. I believed he was the greatest orator in the United States and would some day be heard from. But it did not happen; in the distribution of rewards he was overlooked. It is the way, in this world.

He interrupted his preaching, now and then, to saw a stick of wood; but the sawing was a pretense—he did it with his mouth; exactly imitating the sound the bucksaw makes in shrieking its way through the wood. But it served its purpose; it kept his master from coming out to see how the work was getting along. I listened to the sermons from the open window of a lumber room at the back of the house. One of his texts was this:

"You tell me whar a man gits his corn pone, en I'll tell you what his 'pinions is."

I can never forget it. It was deeply impressed upon me. By my mother. Not upon my memory, but elsewhere. She had slipped in upon me while I was absorbed and not watching. The black philosopher's idea was that a man is not independent, and cannot afford views which might interfere with his bread and butter. If he would prosper, he must train with the majority; in matters of large moment, like politics and religion, he must think and feel with the bulk of his neighbors, or suffer damage in his social standing and in his business prosperities. He must restrict himself to corn-pone opinions—at least on the surface. He must get his opinions from other people; he must reason out none for himself; he must have no first-hand views.

I think Jerry was right, in the main, but I think he did not go far enough.

1. It was his idea that a man conforms to the majority view of his locality by calculation and intention.

This happens, but I think it is not the rule.

2. It was his idea that there is such a thing as a first-hand opinion; an original opinion; an opinion which is coldly reasoned out in a man's head, by a searching analysis of the facts involved, with the heart unconsulted, and the jury room closed against outside influences. It may be that such an opinion has been born somewhere, at some time or other, but I suppose it got away before they could catch it and stuff it and put it in the museum.

I am persuaded that a coldly-thought-out and independent verdict upon a fashion in clothes, or manners, or literature, or politics, or religion, or any other matter that is projected into the field of our notice and interest, is a most rare thing—if it has indeed ever existed.

A new thing in costume appears—the flaring hoopskirt, for example—and the passers-by are shocked, and the irreverent laugh. Six months later everybody is reconciled; the fashion has established itself; it is admired, now, and no one laughs. Public opinion resented it before, public opinion accepts it now, and is happy in it. Why? Was the resentment reasoned out? Was the acceptance reasoned out? No. The instinct that moves to conformity did the work. It is our nature to conform; it is a force which not many can successfully resist. What is its seat? The inborn requirement of self-approval. We all have to bow to that; there are no exceptions. Even the woman who refuses from first to last to wear the hoopskirt comes under that law and is its slave; she could not wear the skirt and have her own approval; and that she *must* have, she cannot help herself. But as a rule our self-approval has its source in but one place and not elsewhere—the approval of other people. A person of vast consequences can introduce any kind of novelty in dress and the general world will presently adopt it—moved to do it, in the first place, by the natural instinct to passively yield to that vague something recognized as authority, and in the second place by the human instinct to train with the multitude and have its approval. An empress introduced the hoopskirt, and we know the result. A nobody introduced the bloomer, and we know the result. If Eve should come again, in her ripe renown, and reintroduce her quaint styles—well, we know what would happen. And we should be cruelly embarrassed, along at first.

The hoopskirt runs its course and disappears. Nobody reasons about it. One woman abandons the fashion; her neighbor notices this and follows her lead; this influences the next woman; and so on and so on, and presently the skirt has vanished out of the world, no one knows how nor why; nor cares, for that matter. It will come again, by and by; and in due course will go again.

Twenty-five years ago, in England, six or eight wine glasses stood grouped by each person's plate at a dinner party, and they were used, not left idle and empty; to-day there are but three or four in the group, and the average guest sparingly uses about two of them. We have not adopted this new fashion yet, but we shall do it presently. We shall not think it out; we shall merely conform, and let it go at that. We get our notions and habits and opinions from outside influences; we do not have to study them out.

Our table manners, and company manners, and street manners change from time to time, but the changes are not reasoned out; we merely notice and conform. We are creatures of outside influences; as a rule we do not think, we only imitate. We cannot invent standards that will stick; what we mistake for standards are only fashions, and perishable. We may continue to admire them, but we drop the use of them. We notice this in literature. Shakespeare is a standard, and fifty years ago we used to write tragedies which we couldn't tell from—from somebody else's; but we don't do it any more, now. Our prose standard, three quarters of a century ago, was ornate and diffuse; some authority or other changed it in the direction of compactness and simplicity, and conformity followed, without argument. The historical novel starts up suddenly, and sweeps the land. Everybody writes one, and the nation is glad. We had historical novels before; but nobody read them, and the rest of us conformed—without reasoning it out. We are conforming in the other way, now, because it is another case of everybody.

The outside influences are always pouring in upon us, and we are always obeying their orders and accepting their verdicts. The Smiths like the new play; the Joneses go to see it, and they copy the Smith verdict. Morals, religions, politics, get their following from surrounding influences and atmospheres, almost entirely; not from study, not from thinking. A man must and will have his own approval first of all, in each and every moment and circumstance of his life—even if he must repent of a self-approved act the moment after its commission, in order to get his self-approval *again:* but, speaking in general terms, a man's self-approval in the large concerns of life has its source in the approval of the peoples about him, and not in a searching personal examination of the matter. Mohammedans are Mohammedans because they are born and reared among that sect, not because they have thought it out and can furnish sound reasons for being Mohammedans; we know why Catholics are Catholics; why Presbyterians are Presbyterians; why Baptists are Baptists; why Mormons are Mormons; why thieves are thieves; why monarchists are monarchists; why Republicans are Republicans and Democrats, Democrats. We know it is a matter of association and sympathy, not reasoning and examination; that hardly a man in the world has an opinion upon morals, politics, or religion which he got otherwise than through his associations and sympathies. Broadly speaking, there are none but corn-pone opinions. And broadly speaking, corn-pone stands for self-approval. Self-approval is acquired mainly from the approval of other people. The result is conformity. Sometimes conformity has a sordid business interest—the bread-and-butter interest—but not in most cases, I think. I think that in the majority of cases it is unconscious and not calculated; that it is born of the human being's natural yearning to stand well with his fellows and have their inspiring approval and praise—a yearning which is commonly so strong and so insistent that it cannot be effectually resisted, and must have its way.

A political emergency brings out the corn-pone opinion in fine force in its two chief varieties—the pocketbook variety, which has its origin in self-interest, and the bigger variety, the sentimental variety—the one which can't bear to be outside the pale; can't bear to be in disfavor; can't endure the averted face and the cold shoulder; wants to stand well with his friends, wants to be smiled upon, wants to be welcome, wants to hear the precious word, "*He's* on the right track!" Uttered, perhaps by an ass, but still an ass of high degree, an ass whose approval is gold and diamonds to a smaller ass, and confers glory and honor and happiness, and membership in the herd. For these gauds many a man will dump his life-long principles into the street, and his conscience along with them. We have seen it happen. In some millions of instances.

Men think they think upon great political questions, and they do; but they think with their party, not independently; they read its literature, but not that of the other side; they arrive at convictions, but they are drawn from a partial view of the matter in hand and are of no particular value. They swarm with their party, they feel with their party, they are happy in their party's approval; and where the party leads they will follow, whether for right and honor, or through blood and dirt and a mush of mutilated morals.

In our late canvass half of the nation passionately believed that in silver lay salvation, the other half as passionately believed that that way lay destruction. Do you believe that a tenth part of the people, on either side, had any rational excuse for having an opinion about the matter at all? I studied that mighty question to the bottom—came out empty. Half of our people passionately believe in high tariff, and other half believe otherwise. Does this mean study and examination, or only feeling? The latter, I think. I have deeply studied that question, too—and didn't arrive. We all do no end of feeling, and we mistake it for thinking. And out of it we get an aggregation which we consider a boon. Its name is Public Opinion. It is held in reverence. It settles everything. Some think it the Voice of God.

# THE UNITED STATES OF
# LYNCHERDOM

## I.

And so Missouri has fallen, that great state! Certain of her children have joined the lynchers, and the smirch is upon the rest of us. That handful of her children have given us a character and labeled us with a name, and to the dwellers in the four quarters of the earth we are "lynchers," now, and ever shall be. For the world will not stop and think—it never does, it is not its way; its way is to generalize from a single sample. It will not say, "Those Missourians have been busy eighty years in building an honorable good name for themselves; these hundred lynchers down in the corner of the state are not real Missourians, they are renegades." No, that truth will not enter its mind; it will generalize from the one or two misleading samples and say, "The Missourians are lynchers." It has no reflection, no logic, no sense of proportion. With it, figures go for nothing; to it, figures reveal nothing, it cannot reason upon them rationally; it would say, for instance, that China is being swiftly and surely Christianized, since nine Chinese Christians are being made every day; and it would fail, with him, to notice that the fact that 33,000 pagans are *born* there every day, damages the argument. It would say, "There are a hundred lynchers there, therefore the Missourians are lynchers"; the considerable fact that there are two and a half million Missourians who are *not* lynchers would not affect their verdict.

## II.

Oh, Missouri!

The tragedy occurred near Pierce City, down in the southwestern corner of the state. On a Sunday afternoon a young white woman who had started alone from church was found murdered. For there are churches there; in my

time religion was more general, more pervasive, in the
South than it was in the North, and more virile and
earnest, too, I think; I have some reason to believe that
this is still the case. The young woman was found murdered. Although it was a region of churches and schools
the people rose, lynched three negroes—two of them very
aged ones—burned out five negro households, and drove
thirty negro families into the woods.

I do not dwell upon the provocation which moved the
people to these crimes, for that has nothing to do with the
matter; the only question is, does the assassin *take the law
into his own hands?* It is very simple, and very just. If the
assassin be proved to have usurped the law's prerogative
in righting his wrongs, that ends the matter; a thousand
provocations are no defense. The Pierce City people had
bitter provocation—indeed, as revealed by certain of the
particulars, the bitterest of all provocations—but no matter, they took the law into their own hands, when by the
terms of their statutes their victim would certainly hang
if the law had been allowed to take its course, for there
are but few negroes in that region and they are without
authority and without influence in overawing juries.

Why has lynching, with various barbaric accompani-
ments, become a favorite regulator in cases of "the usual
crime" in several parts of the country? Is it because men
think a lurid and terrible punishment a more forcible object lesson and a more effective deterrent than a sober and
colorless hanging done privately in a jail would be? Surely
sane men do not think that. Even the average child should
know better. It should know that any strange and much-
talked-of event is always followed by imitations, the world
being so well supplied with excitable people who only
need a little stirring up to make them lose what is left of
their heads and do mad things which they would not have
thought of ordinarily. It should know that if a man jump
off Brooklyn Bridge another will imitate him; that if a
person venture down Niagara Whirlpool in a barrel another will imitate him; that if a Jack the Ripper make
notoriety by slaughtering women in dark alleys he will be
imitated; that if a man attempt a king's life and the newspapers carry the noise of it around the globe, regicides will
crop up all around. The child should know that one much-
talked-of outrage and murder committed by a negro will

upset the disturbed intellects of several other negroes and produce a series of the very tragedies the community would so strenuously wish to prevent; that each of these crimes will produce another series, and year by year steadily increase the tale of these disasters instead of diminishing it; that, in a word, the lynchers are themselves the worst enemies of their women. The child should also know that by a law of our make, communities, as well as individuals, are imitators; and that a much-talked-of lynching will infallibly produce other lynchings here and there and yonder, and that in time these will breed a mania, a fashion; a fashion which will spread wide and wider, year by year, covering state after state, as with an advancing disease. Lynching has reached Colorado, it has reached California, it has reached Indiana—and now Missouri! I may live to see a negro burned in Union Square, New York, with fifty thousand people present, and not a sheriff visible, not a governor, not a constable, not a colonel, not a clergyman, not a law-and-order representative of any sort.

*Increase in Lynching.*—In 1900 there were eight more cases than in 1899, and probably this year there will be more than there were last year. The year is little more than half gone, and yet there are eighty-eight cases as compared with one hundred and fifteen for all of last year. The four Southern states, Alabama, Georgia, Louisiana, and Mississippi are the worst offenders. Last year there were eight cases in Alabama, sixteen in Georgia, twenty in Louisiana, and twenty in Mississippi—over one-half the total. This year to date there have been nine in Alabama, twelve in Georgia, eleven in Louisiana, and thirteen in Mississippi—again more than one-half the total number in the whole United States.— Chicago *Tribune*.

It must be that the increase comes of the inborn human instinct to imitate—that and man's commonest weakness, his aversion to being unpleasantly conspicuous, pointed at, shunned, as being on the unpopular side. Its other name is Moral Cowardice, and is the commanding feature of the make-up of 9,999 men in the 10,000. I am not offering this as a discovery; privately the dullest of us knows it to be true. History will not allow us to forget or ignore this supreme trait of our character. It persistently and sardonically reminds us that from the beginning of the world no revolt against a public infamy or oppression has ever been begun but by the one daring man in the 10,000, the rest timidly waiting, and slowly and reluctantly joining, under the influence of that man and his fellows from the other ten thousands. The abolitionists remember. Privately the public feeling was with them early, but each man was afraid to speak out until he got some hint that his neighbor was privately feeling as he privately felt himself. Then the boom followed. It always does. It will occur in New York, some day; and even in Pennsylvania.

It has been supposed—and said—that the people at a lynching enjoy the spectacle and are glad of a chance to see it. It cannot be true; all experience is against it. The people in the South are made like the people in the North —the vast majority of whom are right-hearted and compassionate, and would be cruelly pained by such a spectacle —and *would attend it,* and let on to be pleased with it, if the public approval seemed to require it. We are made like that, and we cannot help it. The other animals are not so, but we cannot help that, either. They lack the Moral Sense; we have no way of trading ours off, for a nickel or some other thing above its value. The Moral Sense teaches us what is right, and how to avoid it—when unpopular.

It is thought, as I have said, that a lynching crowd enjoys a lynching. It certainly is not true; it is impossible of belief. It is freely asserted—you have seen it in print many times of late—that the lynching impulse has been misinterpreted; that it is *not* the outcome of a spirit of revenge, but of a "mere atrocious hunger *to look upon human suffering.*" If that were so, the crowds that saw the Windsor Hotel burn down would have enjoyed the horrors that fell under their eyes. Did they? No one will think that of them, no one will make that charge. Many risked their lives to save the men and women who were in peril. Why did they do that? Because *none would disapprove.* There was no restraint; they could follow their natural impulse. Why does a crowd of the same kind of people in Texas, Colorado, Indiana, stand by, smitten to the heart and miserable, and by ostentatious outward signs pretend to enjoy a lynching? Why does it lift no hand or voice in protest? Only because it would be unpopular to do it, I think;

each man is afraid of his neighbor's disapproval—a thing which, to the general run of the race, is more dreaded than wounds and death. When there is to be a lynching the people hitch up and come miles to see it, bringing their wives and children. Really to see it? No—they come only because they are afraid to stay at home, lest it be noticed and offensively commented upon. We may believe this, for we all know how *we* feel about such spectacles—also, how we would act under the like pressure. We are not any better nor any braver than anybody else, and we must not try to creep out of it.

A Savonarola can quell and scatter a mob of lynchers with a mere glance of his eye: so can a Merrill[1] or a Beloat.[2] For no mob has any sand in the presence of a man known to be splendidly brave. Besides, a lynching mob would *like* to be scattered, for of a certainty there are never ten men in it who would not prefer to be somewhere else—and would be, if they but had the courage to go. When I was a boy I saw a brave gentleman deride and insult a mob and drive it away; and afterward, in Nevada, I saw a noted desperado make two hundred men sit still, with the house burning under them, until he gave them permission to retire. A plucky man can rob a whole passenger train by himself; and the half of a brave man can hold up a stagecoach and strip its occupants.

Then perhaps the remedy for lynchings comes to this: station a brave man in each affected community to encourage, support, and bring to light the deep disapproval of lynching hidden in the secret places of its heart—for it is there, beyond question. Then those communities will find something better to imitate—of course, being human, they must imitate something. Where shall these brave men be found? That is indeed a difficulty; there are not three hundred of them in the earth. If merely *physically* brave men would do, then it were easy; they could be furnished by the cargo. When Hobson called for seven volunteers to go with him to what promised to be certain death, four thousand men responded—the whole fleet, in fact. Because *all the world would approve*. They knew that; but

[1] Sheriff of Carroll County, Georgia.
[2] Sheriff, Princeton, Indiana. By that formidable power which lies in an established reputation for cold pluck they faced lynching mobs and securely held the field against them.

if Hobson's project had been charged with the scoffs and jeers of the friends and associates, whose good opinion and approval the sailors valued, he could not have got his seven.

No, upon reflection, the scheme will not work. There are not enough morally brave men in stock. We are out of moral-courage material; we are in a condition of profound poverty. We have those two sheriffs down South who—but never mind, it is not enough to go around; they have to stay and take care of their own communities.

But if we only *could* have three or four more sheriffs of that great breed! Would it help? I think so. For we are all imitators: other brave sheriffs would follow; to be a dauntless sheriff would come to be recognized as the correct and only thing, and the dreaded disapproval would fall to the share of the other kind; courage in this office would become custom, the absence of it a dishonor, just as courage presently replaces the timidity of the new soldier; then the mobs and the lynchings would disappear, and——

However. It can never be done without some starters, and where are we to get the starters? Advertise? Very well, then, let us advertise.

In the meantime, there is another plan. Let us import American missionaries from China, and send them into the lynching field. With 1,511 of them out there converting two Chinamen apiece per annum against an uphill birth rate of 33,000 pagans per day,[1] it will take upward of a million years to make the conversions balance the output and bring the Christianizing of the country in sight to the naked eye; therefore, if we can offer our missionaries as rich a field at home at lighter expense and quite satisfactory in the matter of danger, why shouldn't they find it fair and right to come back and give us a trial? The Chinese are universally conceded to be excellent people, honest, honorable, industrious, trustworthy, kindhearted, and all that—leave them alone, they are plenty

[1] These figures are not fanciful; all of them are genuine and authentic. They are from official missionary records in China. See Doctor Morrison's book on his pedestrian journey across China; he quotes them and gives his authorities. For several years he has been the London *Times's* representative in Peking, and was there through the siege.

good enough just as they are; and besides, almost every convert runs a risk of catching our civilization. We ought to be careful. We ought to think twice before we encourage a risk like that; for, *once civilized, China can never be uncivilized again.* We have not been thinking of that. Very well, we ought to think of it now. Our missionaries will find that we have a field for them—and not only for the 1,511, but for 15,011. Let them look at the following telegram and see if they have anything in China that is more appetizing. It is from Texas:

The negro was taken to a tree and swung in the air. Wood and fodder were piled beneath his body and a hot fire was made. *Then it was suggested that the man ought not to die too quickly, and he was let down to the ground while a party went to Dexter, about two miles distant, to procure coal oil.* This was thrown on the flames and the work completed.

We implore them to come back and help us in our need. Patriotism imposes this duty on them. Our country is worse off than China; they are our countrymen, their motherland supplicates their aid in this her hour of deep distress. They are competent; our people are not. They are used to scoffs, sneers, revilings, danger; our people are not. They have the martyr spirit; nothing but the martyr spirit can brave a lynching mob, and cow it and scatter it. They can save their country, we beseech them to come home and do it. We ask them to read that telegram again, and yet again, and picture the scene in their minds, and soberly ponder it; then multiply it by 115, add 88; place the 203 in a row, allowing 600 feet of space for each human torch, so that there may be viewing room around it for 5,000 Christian American men, women, and children, youths and maidens; make it night, for grim effect; have the show in a gradually rising plain, and let the course of the stakes be uphill; the eye can then take in the whole line of twenty-four miles of blood-and-flesh bonfires unbroken, whereas if it occupied level ground the ends of the line would bend down and be hidden from view by the curvature of the earth. All being ready, now, and the darkness opaque, the stillness impressive—for there should be no sound but the soft moaning of the night wind and the muffled sobbing of the sacrifices—let all the far stretch of kerosened pyres be touched off simultaneously and the glare and the shrieks and the agonies burst heavenward to the Throne.

There are more than a million persons present; the light from the fires flushes into vague outline against the night the spires of five thousand churches. O kind missionary, O compassionate missionary, leave China! come home and convert these Christians!

I believe that if anything can stop this epidemic of bloody insanities it is martial personalities that can face mobs without flinching; and as such personalities are developed only by familiarity with danger and by the training and seasoning which come of resisting it, the likeliest place to find them must be among the missionaries who have been under tuition in China during the past year or two. We have abundance of work for them, and for hundreds and thousands more, and the field is daily growing and spreading. Shall we find them? We can try. In 75,000,000 there must be other Merrills and Beloats; and it is the law of our make that each example shall wake up drowsing chevaliers of the same great knighthood and bring them to the front.

# TO THE PERSON SITTING
# IN DARKNESS

Christmas will dawn in the United States over a
people full of hope and aspiration and good cheer.
Such a condition means contentment and happiness.
The carping grumbler who may here and there go forth
will find few to listen to him. The majority will wonder
what is the matter with him and pass on.—New York
*Tribune,* on Christmas Eve.

From the *Sun,* of New York:

The purpose of this article is not to describe the terrible offenses against humanity committed in the name
of Politics in some of the most notorious East Side dis-
tricts. *They could not be described, even verbally.* But
it is the intention to let the great mass of more or less
careless citizens of this beautiful metropolis of the New
World get some conception of the havoc and ruin
wrought to man, woman, and child in the most densely
populated and least-known section of the city. Name,
date, and place can be supplied to those of little faith—
or to any man who feels himself aggrieved. It is a plain
statement of record and observation, written without
license and without garnish.

Imagine, if you can, a section of the city territory completely dominated by one man, without whose permission neither legitimate nor illegitimate business can be
conducted; *where illegitimate business is encouraged
and legitimate business discouraged;* where the respectable residents have to fasten their doors and windows
summer nights and sit in their rooms with asphyxiating
air and 100-degree temperature, rather than try to catch
the faint whiff of breeze in their natural breathing
places, the stoops of their homes; *where naked women*

201

*dance by night in the streets, and unsexed men prowl
like vultures through the darkness on "business"* not
only permitted but encouraged by the police; *where
the education of infants begins with the knowledge of
prostitution* and the training of little girls is training
in the arts of Phryne; where *American* girls brought up
with the refinements of *American* homes are imported
from small towns up-state, Massachusetts, Connecticut,
and New Jersey, and kept as virtually prisoners as if
they were locked up behind jail bars until they have lost
all semblance of womanhood; *where small boys are
taught to solicit for the women of disorderly houses;*
where there is an organized society of young men *whose
sole business in life is to corrupt young girls and turn
them over to bawdy houses;* where men walking with
their wives along the street are openly insulted; *where
children that have adult diseases are the chief patrons
of the hospitals and dispensaries;* where it is the rule,
rather than the exception, that *murder, rape, robbery,
and theft go unpunished*—in short where the Premium
of the most awful forms of Vice is the Profit of the
politicians.

The following news from China appeared in the *Sun,*
of New York, on Christmas Eve. The italics are mine:

The Rev. Mr. Ament, of the American Board of
Foreign Missions, has returned from a trip which he
made for the purpose of collecting indemnities for
damages done by Boxers. *Everywhere he went he compelled the Chinese to pay.* He says that all his native
Christians are now provided for. He had 700 of them
under his charge, and 300 were killed. He has *collected
300 taels for each* of these murders, and has *compelled
full payment for all the property belonging to Christians*
that was destroyed. He also assessed *fines* amounting to
THIRTEEN TIMES the amount of the indemnity. *This
money will be used for the propagation of the Gospel.*
Mr. Ament declares that the compensation he has collected is *moderate* when compared with the amount
secured by the Catholics, who demand, in addition to
money, *head for head.* They collect 500 taels for each
murder of a Catholic. In the Wenchiu country, 680
Catholics were killed, and for this the European Catholics here demand 750,000 strings of cash and 680 *heads.*
In the course of a conversation, Mr. Ament referred

to the attitude of the missionaries toward the Chinese.
He said:

"I deny emphatically that the missionaries are *vindictive,* that they *generally* looted, or that they have
done anything *since* the siege that *the circumstances did
not demand.* I criticize the Americans. *The soft hand of
the Americans is not as good as the mailed fist of the
Germans.* If you deal with the Chinese with a soft hand
they will take advantage of it.

"The statement that the French government will return the loot taken by the French soldiers is the source
of the greatest amusement here. The French soldiers were
more systematic looters than the Germans, and it is a
fact that to-day *Catholic Christians,* carrying French flags
and armed with modern guns, *are looting villages* in the
Province of Chili."

By happy luck, we get all these glad tidings on Christmas Eve—just in time to enable us to celebrate the day with
proper gayety and enthusiasm. Our spirits soar, and we
find we can even make jokes: Taels, I win, Heads, you
lose.

Our Reverend Ament is the right man in the right place.
What we want of our missionaries out there is, not that
they shall merely represent in their acts and persons the
grace and gentleness and charity and loving-kindness of
our religion, but that they shall also represent the American
spirit. The oldest Americans are the Pawnees. Macallum's
History says:

When a white Boxer kills a Pawnee and destroys his
property, the other Pawnees do not trouble to seek *him*
out, they kill any white person that comes along; also,
they make some white village pay deceased's heirs the
full cash value of deceased, together with full cash value
of the property destroyed; they also make the village
pay, in addition, *thirteen times* the value of that property
into a fund for the dissemination of the Pawnee religion,
which they regard as the best of all religions for the
softening and humanizing of the heart of man. It is their
idea that it is only fair and right that the innocent
should be made to suffer for the guilty, and that it is
better that ninety and nine innocent should suffer than
that one guilty person should escape.

Our Reverend Ament is justifiably jealous of those enterprising Catholics, who not only get big money for each lost convert, but get "head for head" besides. But he should soothe himself with the reflections that the entirety of their exactions are for their own pockets, whereas he, less selfishly, devotes only 300 taels per head to that service, and gives the whole vast thirteen repetitions of the property-indemnity to the service of propagating the Gospel. His magnanimity has won him the approval of his nation, and will get him a monument. Let him be content with these rewards. We all hold him dear for manfully defending his fellow missionaries from exaggerated charges which were beginning to distress us, but so considerably modified that we can now contemplate them without noticeable pain. For now we know that, even before the siege, the missionaries were not "generally" out looting, and that, "since the siege," they have acted quite handsomely, except when "circumstances" crowded them. I am arranging for the monument. Subscriptions for it can be sent to the American Board; designs for it can be sent to me. Designs must allegorically set forth the Thirteen Reduplications of the Indemnity, and the Object for which they were exacted; as Ornaments, the designs must exhibit 680 Heads, so disposed as to give a pleasing and pretty effect; for the Catholics have done nicely, and are entitled to notice in the monument. Mottoes may be suggested, if any shall be discovered that will satisfactorily cover the ground.

Mr. Ament's financial feat of squeezing a thirteen-fold indemnity out of the pauper peasants to square other people's offenses, thus condemning them and their women and innocent little children to inevitable starvation and lingering death, in order that the blood money so acquired might be *"used for the propagation of the Gospel,"* does not flutter my serenity; although the act and the words, taken together, concrete a blasphemy so hideous and so colossal that, without doubt, its mate is not findable in the history of this or of any other age. Yet, if a layman had done that thing and justified it with those words, I should have shuddered, I know. Or, if I had done the thing and said the words myself— However, the thought is unthinkable, irreverent as some imperfectly informed people think me. Sometimes an ordained minister sets out to be blasphemous. When this happens, the layman is out of the running; he stands no chance.

We have Mr. Ament's impassioned assurance that the missionaries are not "vindictive." Let us hope and pray that they will never become so, but will remain in the almost morbidly fair and just and gentle temper which is affording so much satisfaction to their brother and champion to-day.

The following is from the New York *Tribune* of Christmas Eve. It comes from that journal's Tokyo correspondent. It has a strange and impudent sound, but the Japanese are but partially civilized as yet. When they become wholly civilized they will not talk so:

> The missionary question, of course, occupies a foremost place in the discussion. It is now felt as essential that the Western Powers take cognizance of the sentiment here, that religious invasions of Oriental countries by powerful Western organizations are tantamount to filibustering expeditions, and should not only be discountenanced, but that stern measures should be adopted for their suppression. The feeling here is that the missionary organizations constitute a constant menace to peaceful international relations.

*Shall we?* That is, shall we go on conferring our Civilization upon the peoples that sit in darkness, or shall we give those poor things a rest? Shall we bang right ahead in our old-time, loud, pious way, and commit the new century to the game; or shall we sober up and sit down and think it over first? Would it not be prudent to get our Civilization tools together, and see how much stock is left on hand in the way of Glass Beads and Theology, and Maxim Guns and Hymn Books, and Trade Gin and Torches of Progress and Enlightenment (patent adjustable ones, good to fire villages with, upon occasion), and balance the books, and arrive at the profit and loss, so that we may intelligently decide whether to continue the business or sell out the property and start a new Civilization Scheme on the proceeds?

Extending the Blessings of Civilization to our Brother who Sits in Darkness has been a good trade and has paid well, on the whole; and there is money in it yet, if carefully worked—but not enough, in my judgment, to make any considerable risk advisable. The People that Sit in Darkness are getting to be too scarce—too scarce and too shy. And such darkness as is now left is really of but an indifferent quality, and not dark enough for the game. The most of those People that Sit in Darkness have been furnished with more light than was good for them or profitable for us. We have been injudicious.

The Blessings-of-Civilization Trust, wisely and cautiously administered, is a Daisy. There is more money in it, more territory, more sovereignty, and other kinds of emolument, than there is in any other game that is played. But Christendom has been playing it badly of late years, and must certainly suffer by it, in my opinion. She has been so eager to get every stake that appeared on the green cloth, that the People who Sit in Darkness have noticed it —they have noticed it, and have begun to show alarm. They have become suspicious of the Blessings of Civilization. More—they have begun to examine them. This is not well. The Blessings of Civilization are all right, and a good commercial property; there could not be a better, in a dim light. In the right kind of a light, and at a proper distance, with the goods a little out of focus, they furnish this desirable exhibit to the Gentlemen who Sit in Darkness:

| | |
|---|---|
| LOVE, | LAW AND ORDER, |
| JUSTICE, | LIBERTY, |
| GENTLENESS, | EQUALITY, |
| CHRISTIANITY, | HONORABLE DEALING, |
| PROTECTION TO THE WEAK, | MERCY, |
| TEMPERANCE, | EDUCATION, |

—and so on.

There. Is it good? Sir, it is pie. It will bring into camp any idiot that sits in darkness anywhere. But not if we adulterate it. It is proper to be emphatic upon that point. This brand is strictly for Export—apparently. *Apparently.* Privately and confidentially, it is nothing of the kind. Privately and confidentially, it is merely an outside cover, gay and pretty and attractive, displaying the special patterns of our Civilization which we reserve for Home Consumption, while *inside* the bale is the Actual Thing that the Customer Sitting in Darkness buys with his blood and tears and land and liberty. That Actual Thing is, indeed, Civilization, but it is only for Export. Is there a difference between the two brands? In some of the details, yes.

We all know that the Business is being ruined. The reason is not far to seek. It is because our Mr. McKinley, and Mr. Chamberlain, and the Kaiser, and the Tsar and the French have been exporting the Actual Thing *with the outside cover left off.* This is bad for the Game. It shows that these new players of it are not sufficiently acquainted with it.

It is a distress to look on and note the mismoves, they are so strange and so awkward. Mr. Chamberlain manufactures a war out of materials so inadequate and so fanciful that they make the boxes grieve and the gallery laugh, and he tries hard to persuade himself that it isn't purely a private raid for cash, but has a sort of dim, vague respectability about it somewhere, if he could only find the spot; and that, by and by, he can scour the flag clean again after he has finished dragging it through the mud, and make it shine and flash in the vault of heaven once more as it had shone and flashed there a thousand years in the world's respect until he laid his unfaithful hand upon it. It is bad play— bad. For it exposes the Actual Thing to Them that Sit in Darkness, and they say: "What! Christian against Christian? And only for money? Is *this* a case of magnanimity, forbearance, love, gentleness, mercy, protection of the weak—this strange and overshowy onslaught of an elephant upon a nest of field mice, on the pretext that the mice had squeaked an insolence at him—conduct which 'no self-respecting government could allow to pass unavenged'? as Mr. Chamberlain said. Was that a good pretext in a small case, when it had not been a good pretext in a large one?—for only recently Russia had affronted the elephant three times and survived alive and unsmitten. Is this Civilization and Progress? Is it something better than we already possess? These harryings and burnings and desert-makings in the Transvaal—is this an improvement on our darkness? Is it, perhaps, possible that there are two kinds of Civilization—one for home consumption and one for the heathen market?"

Then They that Sit in Darkness are troubled, and shake their heads; and they read this extract from a letter of a

British private, recounting his exploits in one of Methuen's victories, some days before the affair of Magersfontein, and they are troubled again:

> We tore up the hill and into the intrenchments, and the Boers saw we had them; so they dropped their guns and went down on their knees and put up their hands clasped, and begged for mercy. And we gave it them— *with the long spoon.*

The long spoon is the bayonet. See *Lloyd's Weekly,* London, of those days. The same number—and the same column—contained some quite unconscious satire in the form of shocked and bitter upbraidings of the Boers for their brutalities and inhumanities!

Next, to our heavy damage, the Kaiser went to playing the game without first mastering it. He lost a couple of missionaries in a riot in Shantung, and in his account he made an overcharge for them. China had to pay a hundred thousand dollars apiece for them, in money; twelve miles of territory, containing several millions of inhabitants and worth twenty million dollars; and to build a monument, and also a Christian church; whereas the people of China could have been depended upon to remember the missionaries without the help of these expensive memorials. This was all bad play. Bad, because it would not, and could not, and will not now or ever, deceive the Person Sitting in Darkness. He knows that it was an overcharge. He knows that a missionary is like any other man: he is worth merely what you can supply his place for, and no more. He is useful, but so is a doctor, so is a sheriff, so is an editor; but a just Emperor does not charge war prices for such. A diligent, intelligent, but obscure missionary, and a diligent, intelligent country editor are worth much, and we know it; but they are not worth the earth. We esteem such an editor, and we are sorry to see him go; but, when he goes, we should consider twelve miles of territory, and a church, and a fortune, overcompensation for his loss. I mean, if he was a Chinese editor, and we had to settle for him. It is no proper figure for an editor or a missionary; one can get shop-worn kings for less. It was bad play on the Kaiser's part. It got this property, true; but it *produced the Chinese revolt,* the indignant uprising of China's traduced patriots, the Boxers. The results have been expensive to Germany, and to the other Disseminators of Progress and the Blessings of Civilization.

The Kaiser's claim was paid, yet it was bad play, for it could not fail to have an evil effect upon Persons Sitting in Darkness in China. They would muse upon the event, and be likely to say: "Civilization is gracious and beautiful, for such is its reputation; but can we afford it? There are rich Chinamen, perhaps they can afford it; but this tax is not laid upon them, it is laid upon the peasants of Shantung; it is they that must pay this mighty sum, and their wages are but four cents a day. Is this a better civilization than ours, and holier and higher and nobler? Is not this rapacity? Is not this extortion? Would Germany charge America two hundred thousand dollars for two missionaries, and shake the mailed fist in her face, and send warships, and send soldiers, and say: 'Seize twelve miles of territory, worth twenty millions of dollars, as additional pay for the missionaries; and make those peasants build a monument to the missionaries, and a costly Christian church to remember them by?' And later would Germany say to her soldiers: 'March through America and slay, *giving no quarter;* make the German face there, as has been our Hun-face here, a terror for a thousand years; march through the Great Republic and slay, slay, slay, carving a road for our offended religion through its heart and bowels?' Would Germany do like this to America, to England, to France, to Russia? Or only to China, the helpless—imitating the elephant's assault upon the field mice? Had we better invest in this Civilization—this Civilization which called Napoleon a buccaneer for carrying off Venice's bronze horses, but which steals our ancient astronomical instruments from our walls, and goes looting like common bandits—that is, all the alien soldiers except America's; and (Americans again excepted) storms frightened villages and cables the result to glad journals at home every day: 'Chinese losses, 450 killed; ours, *one officer and two men wounded.* Shall proceed against neighboring village to-morrow, where a *massacre* is reported.' Can we afford Civilization?"

And next Russia must go and play the game injudiciously. She affronts England once or twice—with the Person Sitting in Darkness observing and noting; by moral assistance of France and Germany, she robs Japan of her hard-earned spoil, all swimming in Chinese blood—Port Arthur—with

the Person again observing and noting; then she seizes
Manchuria, raids its villages, and chokes its great river
with the swollen corpses of countless massacred peasants—
that astonished Person still observing and noting. And
perhaps he is saying to himself: "It is yet *another* Civilized
Power, with its banner of the Prince of Peace in one hand
and its loot basket and its butcher knife in the other. Is
there no salvation for us but to adopt Civilization and lift
ourselves down to its level?"

And by and by comes America, and our Master of the
Game plays it badly—plays it as Mr. Chamberlain was playing it in South Africa. It was a mistake to do that; also, it
was one which was quite unlooked for in a Master who was
playing it so well in Cuba. In Cuba, he was playing the
usual and regular *American* game, and it was winning, for
there is no way to beat it. The Master, contemplating Cuba,
said: "Here is an oppressed and friendless little nation
which is willing to fight to be free; we go partners, and put
up the strength of seventy million sympathizers and the
resources of the United States: play!" Nothing but Europe
combined could call that hand: and Europe cannot combine on anything. There, in Cuba, he was following our
great traditions in a way which made us very proud of
him, and proud of the deep dissatisfaction which his play
was provoking in continental Europe. Moved by a high
inspiration, he threw out those stirring words which pro-
claimed that forcible annexation would be "criminal ag-
gression"; and in that utterance fired another "shot heard
round the world." The memory of that fine saying will be
outlived by the remembrance of no act of his but one—
that he forgot it within the twelvemonth, and its honorable
gospel along with it.

For, presently, came the Philippine temptation. It was
strong; it was too strong, and he made that bad mistake: he
played the European game, the Chamberlain game. It was
a pity; it was a great pity, that error; that one grievous
error, that irrevocable error. For it was the very place and
time to play the American game again. And at no cost.
Rich winnings to be gathered in, too; rich and permanent;
indestructible; a fortune transmissible forever to the children of the flag. Not land, not money, not dominion—no,
something worth many times more than that dross: our
share, the spectacle of a nation of long harassed and per-

secuted slaves set free through our influence; our posterity's share, the golden memory of that fair deed. The game was in our hands. If it had been played according to the American rules, Dewey would have sailed away from Manila as soon as he had destroyed the Spanish fleet—after putting up a sign on shore guaranteeing foreign property and life against damage by the Filipinos, and warning the Powers that interference with the emancipated patriots would be regarded as an act unfriendly to the United States. The Powers cannot combine, in even a bad cause, and the sign would not have been molested.

Dewey could have gone about his affairs elsewhere, and left the competent Filipino army to starve out the little Spanish garrison and send it home, and the Filipino citizens to set up the form of government they might prefer, and deal with the friars and their doubtful acquisitions according to Filipino ideas of fairness and justice—ideas which have since been tested and found to be of as high an order as any that prevail in Europe or America.

But we played the Chamberlain game, and lost the chance to add another Cuba and another honorable deed to our good record.

The more we examine the mistake, the more clearly we perceive that it is going to be bad for the Business. The Person Sitting in Darkness is almost sure to say: "There is something curious about this—curious and unaccountable. There must be two Americas: one that sets the captive free, and one that takes a once-captive's new freedom away from him, and picks a quarrel with him with nothing to found it on; then kills him to get his land."

The truth is, the Person Sitting in Darkness *is* saying things like that; and for the sake of the Business we must persuade him to look at the Philippine matter in another and healthier way. We must arrange his opinions for him. I believe it can be done; for Mr. Chamberlain has arranged England's opinion of the South African matter, and done it most cleverly and successfully. He presented the facts— some of the facts—and showed those confiding people what the facts meant. He did it statistically, which is a good way. He used the formula: "Twice 2 are 14, and 2 from 9 leaves 35." Figures are effective; figures will convince the elect.

Now, my plan is a still bolder one than Mr. Chamberlain's, though apparently a copy of it. Let us be franker than Mr. Chamberlain; let us audaciously present the whole of the facts, shirking none, then explain them according to Mr. Chamberlain's formula. This daring truthfulness will astonish and dazzle the Person Sitting in Darkness, and he will take the Explanation down before his mental vision has had time to get back into focus. Let us say to him:

"Our case is simple. On the 1st of May, Dewey destroyed the Spanish fleet. This left the Archipelago in the hands of its proper and rightful owners, the Filipino nation. Their army numbered 30,000 men, and they were competent to whip out or starve out the little Spanish garrison; then the people could set up a government of their own devising. Our traditions required that Dewey should now set up his warning sign, and go away. But the Master of the Game happened to think of another plan—the European plan. He acted upon it. This was, to send out an army—ostensibly to help the native patriots put the finishing touch upon their long and plucky struggle for independence, but really to take their land away from them and keep it. That is, in the interest of Progress and Civilization. The plan developed, stage by stage, and quite satisfactorily. We entered into a military alliance with the trusting Filipinos, and they hemmed in Manila on the land side, and by their valuable help the place, with its garrison of 8,000 or 10,000 Spaniards, was captured—a thing which we could not have accomplished unaided at that time. We got their help by—by ingenuity. We knew they were fighting for their independence, and that they had been at it for two years. We knew they supposed that we also were fighting in their worthy cause—just as we had helped the Cubans fight for Cuban independence—and we allowed them to go on thinking so. *Until Manila was ours and we could get along without them.* Then we showed our hand. Of course, they were surprised—that was natural; surprised and disappointed; disappointed and grieved. To them it looked un-American; uncharacteristic; foreign to our established traditions. And this was natural, too; for we were only playing the American Game in public—in private it was the European. It was neatly done, very neatly, and it bewildered them. They could not understand it; for we had been so friendly—so affectionate, even —with those simple-minded patriots! We, our own selves, had brought back out of exile their leader, their hero, their hope, their Washington—Aguinaldo; brought him in a warship, in high honor, under the sacred shelter and hospitality of the flag; brought him back and restored him to his people, and got their moving and eloquent gratitude for it. Yes, we had been so friendly to them, and had heartened them up in so many ways! We had lent them guns and ammunition; advised with them; exchanged pleasant courtesies with them; placed our sick and wounded in their kindly care; intrusted our Spanish prisoners to their humane and honest hands; fought shoulder to shoulder with them against "the common enemy" (our own phrase); praised their courage, praised their gallantry, praised their mercifulness, praised their fine and honorable conduct; borrowed their trenches, borrowed strong positions which they had previously captured from the Spaniards; petted them, lied to them—officially proclaiming that our land and naval forces came to give them their freedom and displace the bad Spanish Government— fooled them, used them until we needed them no longer; then derided the sucked orange and threw it away. We kept the positions which we had beguiled them of; by and by, we moved a force forward and overlapped patriot ground—a clever thought, for we needed trouble, and this would produce it. A Filipino soldier, crossing the ground, where no one had a right to forbid him, was shot by our sentry. The badgered patriots resented this with arms, without waiting to know whether Aguinaldo, who was absent, would approve or not. Aguinaldo did not approve; but that availed nothing. What we wanted, in the interest of Progress and Civilization, was the Archipelago, unencumbered by patriots struggling for independence; and War was what we needed. We clinched our opportunity. It is Mr. Chamberlain's case over again—at least in its motive and intention; and we played the game as adroitly as he played it himself."

At this point in our frank statement of fact to the Person Sitting in Darkness, we should throw in a little trade taffy about the Blessings of Civilization—for a change, and for the refreshment of his spirit—then go on with our tale:

"We and the patriots having captured Manila, Spain's ownership of the Archipelago and her sovereignty over it were at an end—obliterated—annihilated—not a rag or

shred of either remaining behind. It was then that we
conceived the divinely humorous idea of *buying* both of
these specters from Spain! [It is quite safe to confess this
to the Person Sitting in Darkness, since neither he nor any
other sane person will believe it.] In buying those ghosts
for twenty millions, we also contracted to take care of the
friars and their accumulations. I think we also agreed to
propagate leprosy and smallpox, but as to this there is
doubt. But it is not important; persons afflicted with the
friars do not mind other diseases.

"With our Treaty ratified, Manila subdued, and our
Ghosts secured, we had no further use for Aguinaldo and
the owners of the Archipelago. We forced a war, and we
have been hunting America's guest and ally through the
woods and swamps ever since."

At this point in the tale, it will be well to boast a little
of our war work and our heroisms in the field, so as to
make our performance look as fine as England's in South
Africa; but I believe it will not be best to emphasize this
too much. We must be cautious. Of course, we must read
the war telegrams to the Person, in order to keep up our
frankness; but we can throw an air of humorousness over
them, and that will modify their grim eloquence a little,
and their rather indiscreet exhibitions of gory exultation.
Before reading to him the following display heads of the
dispatches of November 18, 1900, it will be well to practice
on them in private first, so as to get the right tang of light-
ness and gayety into them:

## "ADMINISTRATION WEARY OF PROTRACTED HOSTILITIES!"

## "REAL WAR AHEAD FOR FILIPINO REBELS!" [1] "WILL SHOW NO MERCY!"

## "KITCHENER'S PLAN ADOPTED!"

Kitchener knows how to handle disagreeable people who
are fighting for their homes and their liberties, and we
must let on that we are merely imitating Kitchener, and
have no national interest in the matter, further than to get
ourselves admired by the Great Family of Nations, in which

[1] "Rebels!" Mumble that funny word—don't let the Person catch
it distinctly.

august company our Master of the Game has bought a place for us in the back row.

Of course, we must not venture to ignore our General MacArthur's reports—oh, why do they keep on printing those embarrassing things?—we must drop them trippingly from the tongue and take the chances:

> During the last ten months our losses have been 268 killed and 750 wounded; Filipino loss, *three thousand two hundred and twenty-seven killed,* and 694 wounded.

We must stand ready to grab the Person Sitting in Darkness, for he will swoon away at this confession, saying: "Good God! those 'niggers' spare their wounded, and the Americans massacre theirs!"

We must bring him to, and coax him and coddle him, and assure him that the ways of Providence are best, and that it would not become us to find fault with them; and then, to show him that we are only imitators, not originators, we must read the following passage from the letter of an American soldier lad in the Philippines to his mother, published in *Public Opinion,* of Decorah, Iowa, describing the finish of a victorious battle:

"WE NEVER LEFT ONE ALIVE. IF ONE WAS WOUNDED, WE WOULD RUN OUR BAYONETS THROUGH HIM."

Having now laid all the historical facts before the Person Sitting in Darkness, we should bring him to again, and explain them to him. We should say to him:

"They look doubtful, but in reality they are not. There have been lies; yes, but they were told in a good cause. We have been treacherous; but that was only in order that real good might come out of apparent evil. True, we have crushed a deceived and confiding people; we have turned against the weak and the friendless who trusted us; we have stamped out a just and intelligent and well-ordered republic; we have stabbed an ally in the back and slapped the face of a guest; we have bought a Shadow from an enemy that hadn't it to sell; we have robbed a trusting friend of his land and his liberty; we have invited our clean young men to shoulder a discredited musket and do bandits' work under a flag which bandits have been accustomed to fear, not to follow; we have debauched America's honor and blackened her face before the world; but each detail was for the best. We know this. The Head of every State and Sovereignty in Christendom and 90 per cent of every legislative body in Christendom, including our Congress and our fifty state legislatures, are members not only of the church, but also of the Blessings-of-Civilization Trust. This world-girdling accumulation of trained morals, high principles, and justice cannot do an unright thing, an unfair thing, an ungenerous thing, an unclean thing. It knows what it is about. Give yourself no uneasiness; it is all right."

Now then, that will convince the Person. You will see. It will restore the Business. Also, it will elect the Master of the Game to the vacant place in the Trinity of our national gods; and there on their high thrones the Three will sit, age after age, in the people's sight, each bearing the Emblem of his service: Washington, the Sword of the Liberator; Lincoln, the Slave's Broken Chains; the Master, the Chains Repaired.

It will give the Business a splendid new start. You will see.

Everything is prosperous, now; everything is just as we should wish it. We have got the Archipelago, and we shall never give it up. Also, we have every reason to hope that we shall have an opportunity before very long to slip out of our congressional contract with Cuba and give her something better in the place of it. It is a rich country, and many of us are already beginning to see that the contract was a sentimental mistake. But now—right now—is the best time to do some profitable rehabilitating work—work that will set us up and make us comfortable, and discourage gossip. We cannot conceal from ourselves that, privately, we are a little troubled about our uniform. It is one of our prides; it is acquainted with honor; it is familiar with great deeds and noble; we love it, we revere it; and so this errand it is on makes us uneasy. And our flag—another pride of ours, our chiefest! We have worshiped it so; and when we have seen it in far lands—glimpsing it unexpectedly in that strange sky, waving its welcome and benediction to us—we have caught our breaths, and uncovered our heads, and couldn't speak, for a moment, for the thought of what it was to us and the great ideals it stood for. Indeed, we *must* do something about these things; it is easily managed. We can have a special one—our states do it: we can have just our usual flag, with the white stripes painted black and the stars replaced by the skull and cross-bones.

And we do not need that Civil Commission out there. Having no powers, it has to invent them, and that kind of work cannot be effectively done by just anybody; an expert is required. Mr. Croker can be spared. We do not want the United States represented there, but only the Game.

By help of these suggested amendments, Progress and Civilization in that country can have a boom, and it will take in the Persons who are Sitting in Darkness, and we can resume Business at the old stand.

# THE WAR PRAYER

It was a time of great and exalting excitement. The country was up in arms, the war was on, in every breast burned the holy fire of patriotism; the drums were beating, the bands playing, the toy pistols popping, the bunched firecrackers hissing and spluttering; on every hand and far down the receding and fading spread of roofs and balconies a fluttering wilderness of flags flashed in the sun; daily the young volunteers marched down the wide avenue gay and fine in their new uniforms, the proud fathers and mothers and sisters and sweethearts cheering them with voices choked with happy emotion as they swung by; nightly the packed mass meetings listened, panting, to patriot oratory which stirred the deepest deeps of their hearts, and which they interrupted at briefest intervals with cyclones of applause, the tears running down their cheeks the while; in the churches the pastors preached devotion to flag and country, and invoked the God of Battles, beseeching His aid in our good cause in outpouring of fervid eloquence which moved every listener. It was indeed a glad and gracious time, and the half dozen rash spirits that ventured to disapprove of the war and cast a doubt upon its righteousness straightway got such a stern and angry warning that for their personal safety's sake they quickly shrank out of sight and offended no more in that way.

Sunday morning came—next day the battalions would leave for the front; the church was filled; the volunteers were there, their young faces alight with martial dreams —visions of the stern advance, the gathering momentum, the rushing charge, the flashing sabers, the flight of the foe, the tumult, the enveloping smoke, the fierce pursuit, the surrender!—then home from the war, bronzed heroes, welcomed, adored, submerged in golden seas of glory! With the volunteers sat their dear ones, proud, happy, and envied by the neighbors and friends who had no sons and brothers to send forth to the field of honor, there to win for the flag, or, failing, die the noblest of noble deaths. The service proceeded; a war chapter from the Old Testament was read; the first prayer was said; it was followed by an organ burst that shook the building, and with one impulse the house rose, with glowing eyes and beating hearts, and poured out that tremendous invocation—

"God the all-terrible! Thou who ordainest,
      Thunder thy clarion and lightning thy sword!"

Then came the "long" prayer. None could remember the like of it for passionate pleading and moving and beautiful language. The burden of its supplication was, that an ever-merciful and benignant Father of us all would watch over our noble young soldiers, and aid, comfort, and encourage them in their patriotic work; bless them, shield them in the day of battle and the hour of peril, bear them in His mighty hand, make them strong and confident, invincible in the bloody onset; help them to crush the foe, grant to them and to their flag and country imperishable honor and glory—

An aged stranger entered and moved with slow and noiseless step up the main aisle, his eye fixed upon the minister, his long body clothed in a robe that reached to his feet, his head bare, his white hair descending in a frothy cataract to his shoulders, his seamy face unnaturally pale, pale even to ghastliness. With all eyes following him and wondering, he made his silent way; without pausing, he ascended to the preacher's side and stood there, waiting. With shut lids the preacher, unconscious of his presence, continued his moving prayer, and at last finished it with the words, uttered in fervent appeal, "Bless our arms, grant us the victory, O Lord our God, Father and Protector of our land and flag!"

The stranger touched his arm, motioned him to step aside—which the startled minister did—and took his place. During some moments he surveyed the spellbound audience with solemn eyes, in which burned an uncanny light; then in a deep voice he said:

"I come from the Throne—bearing a message from Almighty God!" The words smote the house with a shock; if the stranger perceived it he gave no attention. "He has heard the prayer of His servant your shepherd, and will grant it if such shall be your desire after I, His messenger, shall have explained to you its import—that is to say, its full import. For it is like unto many of the prayers of men, in that it asks for more than he who utters it is aware of—except he pause and think.

"God's servant and yours has prayed his prayer. Has he paused and taken thought? Is it one prayer? No, it is two —one uttered, the other not. Both have reached the ear of Him Who heareth all supplications, the spoken and the unspoken. Ponder this—keep it in mind. If you would beseech a blessing upon yourself, beware! lest without intent you invoke a curse upon a neighbor at the same time. If you pray for the blessing of rain upon your crop which needs it, by that act you are possibly praying for a curse upon some neighbor's crop which may not need rain and can be injured by it.

"You have heard your servant's prayer—the uttered part of it. I am commissioned of God to put into words the other part of it—that part which the pastor—and also you in your hearts—fervently prayed silently. And ignorantly and unthinkingly? God grant that it was so! You heard these words: 'Grant us the victory, O Lord our God!' That is sufficient. The *whole* of the uttered prayer is compact into those pregnant words. Elaborations were not necessary. When you have prayed for victory you have prayed for many unmentioned results which follow victory—*must* follow it, cannot help but follow it. Upon the listening spirit of God the Father fell also the unspoken part of the prayer. He commandeth me to put it into words. Listen!

"O Lord our Father, our young patriots, idols of our hearts, go forth to battle—be Thou near them! With them —in spirit—we also go forth from the sweet peace of our beloved firesides to smite the foe. O Lord our God, help us to tear their soldiers to bloody shreds with our shells; help us to cover their smiling fields with the pale forms of their patriot dead; help us to drown the thunder of the guns with the shrieks of their wounded, writhing in pain; help us to lay waste their humble homes with a hurricane of fire; help us to wring the hearts of their unoffending widows with unavailing grief; help us to turn them out roofless with their little children to wander unfriended the wastes of their desolated land in rags and hunger and thirst, sports of the sun flames of summer and the icy winds of winter, broken in spirit, worn with travail, imploring Thee for the refuge of the grave and denied it—for our sakes who adore Thee, Lord, blast their hopes, blight their lives, protract their bitter pilgrimage, make heavy their steps, water their way with their tears, stain the white snow with the blood of their wounded feet! We ask it, in the spirit of love, of Him Who is the source of Love, and Who is the ever-faithful refuge and friend of all that are sore beset and seek His aid with humble and contrite hearts. Amen."

(*After a pause.*) "Ye have prayed it; if ye still desire it, speak! The messenger of the Most High waits."

It was believed afterward that the man was a lunatic, because there was no sense in what he said.

# THE TURNING-POINT OF MY LIFE

## I.

If I understand the idea, the *Bazar* invites several of us to write upon the above text. It means the change in my life's course which introduced what must be regarded by me as the most *important* condition of my career. But it also implies—without intention, perhaps—that that turning-point *itself* was the creator of the new condition. This gives it too much distinction, too much prominence, too much credit. It is only the *last* link in a very long chain of turning-points commissioned to produce the cardinal result; it is not any more important than the humblest of its ten thousand predecessors. Each of the ten thousand did its appointed share, on its appointed date, in forwarding the scheme, and they were all necessary; to have left out any one of them would have defeated the scheme and brought about *some other* result. I know we have a fashion of saying "such and such an event was the turning-point in my life," but we shouldn't say it. We should merely grant that its place as *last* link in the chain makes it the most *conspicuous* link; in real importance it has no advantage over any one of its predecessors.

Perhaps the most celebrated turning-point recorded in history was the crossing of the Rubicon. Suetonius says:

> Coming up with his troops on the banks of the Rubicon, he halted for a while, and, revolving in his mind the importance of the step he was on the point of taking, he turned to those about him and said, "We may still retreat; but if we pass this little bridge, nothing is left for us but to fight it out in arms."

This was a stupendously important moment. And all the incidents, big and little, of Cæsar's previous life had been leading up to it, stage by stage, link by link. This was the *last* link—merely the last one, and no bigger than the others; but as we gaze back at it through the inflating mists of our imagination, it looks as big as the orbit of Neptune.

You, the reader, have a *personal* interest in that link, and so have I; so has the rest of the human race. It was one of the links in your life-chain, and it was one of the links in mine. We may wait, now, with bated breath, while Cæsar reflects. Your fate and mine are involved in his decision.

While he was thus hesitating, the following incident occurred. A person remarked for his noble mien and graceful aspect appeared close at hand, sitting and playing upon a pipe. When not only the shepherds, but a number of soldiers also, flocked to listen to him, and some trumpeters among them, he snatched a trumpet from one of them, ran to the river with it, and, sounding the advance with a piercing blast, crossed to the other side. Upon this, Cæsar exclaimed: "Let us go whither the omens of the gods and the iniquity of our enemies call us. *The die is cast.*"

So he crossed—and changed the future of the whole human race, for all time. But that stranger was a link in Cæsar's life-chain, too; and a necessary one. We don't know his name, we never hear of him again; he was very casual; he acts like an accident; but he was no accident, he was there by compulsion of *his* life-chain, to blow the electrifying blast that was to make up Cæsar's mind for him, and thence go piping down the aisles of history forever.

If the stranger hadn't been there! But he *was*. And Cæsar crossed. With such results! Such vast events—each a link in the *human race's* life-chain; each event producing the next one, and that one the next one, and so on: the destruction of the republic; the founding of the empire; the breaking up of the empire; the rise of Christianity upon its ruins; the spread of the religion to other lands— and so on: link by link took its appointed place at its appointed time, the discovery of America being one of them; our Revolution another; the inflow of English and other immigrants another; their drift westward (my ancestors among them) another; the settlement of certain of them in Missouri, which resulted in *me*. For I was one of the unavoidable results of the crossing of the Rubicon. If the stranger, with his trumpet blast, had stayed away (which he *couldn't*, for he was an appointed link) Cæsar

would not have crossed. What would have happened, in
that case, we can never guess. We only know that the
things that did happen would not have happened. They
might have been replaced by equally prodigious things, of
course, but their nature and results are beyond our guess-
ing. But the matter that interests me personally is that I
would not be *here* now, but somewhere else; and probably
black—there is no telling. Very well, I am glad he crossed.
And very really and thankfully glad, too, though I never
cared anything about it before.

## II.

To me, the most important feature of my life is its
literary feature. I have been professionally literary something more than forty years. There have been many turning-points in my life, but the one that was the last link in
the chain appointed to conduct me to the literary guild is
the most *conspicuous* link in that chain. *Because* it was the
last one. It was not any more important than its predecessors. All the other links have an inconspicuous look, except
the crossing of the Rubicon; but as factors in making me
literary they are all of the one size, the crossing of the
Rubicon included.

I know how I came to be literary, and I will tell the
steps that led up to it and brought it about.

The crossing of the Rubicon was not the first one, it was
hardly even a recent one; I should have to go back ages
before Cæsar's day to find the first one. To save space I
will go back only a couple of generations and start with
an incident of my boyhood. When I was twelve and a half
years old, my father died. It was in the spring. The summer
came, and brought with it an epidemic of measles. For a
time, a child died almost every day. The village was paralyzed with fright, distress, despair. Children that were not
smitten with the disease were imprisoned in their homes
to save them from the infection. In the homes there were
no cheerful faces, there was no music, there was no singing
but of solemn hymns, no voice but of prayer, no romping
was allowed, no noise, no laughter, the family moved
spectrally about on tiptoe, in a ghostly hush. I was a
prisoner. My soul was steeped in this awful dreariness—
and in fear. At some time or other every day and every

night a sudden shiver shook me to the marrow, and I said to myself, "There, I've got it! and I shall die." Life on these miserable terms was not worth living, and at last I made up my mind to get the disease and have it over, one way or the other. I escaped from the house and went to the house of a neighbor where a playmate of mine was very ill with the malady. When the chance offered I crept into his room and got into bed with him. I was discovered by his mother and sent back into captivity. But I had the disease; they could not take that from me. I came near to dying. The whole village was interested, and anxious, and sent for news of me every day; and not only once a day, but several times. Everybody believed I would die; but on the fourteenth day a change came for the worse and they were disappointed.

This was a turning-point of my life. (Link number one.) For when I got well my mother closed my school career and apprenticed me to a printer. She was tired of trying to keep me out of mischief, and the adventure of the measles decided her to put me into more masterful hands than hers.

I became a printer, and began to add one link after another to the chain which was to lead me into the literary profession. A long road, but I could not know that; and as I did not know what its goal was, or even that it had one, I was indifferent. Also contented.

A young printer wanders around a good deal, seeking and finding work; and seeking again, when necessity commands. N. B. Necessity is a *Circumstance;* Circumstance is man's master—and when Circumstance commands, he must obey; he may argue the matter—that is his privilege, just as it is the honorable privilege of a falling body to argue with the attraction of gravitation—but it won't do any good, he must *obey*. I wandered for ten years, under the guidance and dictatorship of Circumstance, and finally arrived in a city of Iowa, where I worked several months. Among the books that interested me in those days was one about the Amazon. The traveler told an alluring tale of his long voyage up the great river from Para to the sources of the Madeira, through the heart of an enchanted land, a land wastefully rich in tropical wonders, a romantic land where all the birds and flowers and animals were of the museum varieties, and where the alligator and the crocodile and the monkey seemed as much at home as if they were in the Zoo. Also, he told an astonishing tale about *coca*, a vegetable product of miraculous powers, asserting that it was so nourishing and so strength-giving that the natives of the mountains of the Madeira region would tramp up hill and down all day on a pinch of powdered coca and require no other sustenance.

I was fired with a longing to ascend the Amazon. Also with a longing to open up a trade in coca with all the world. During months I dreamed that dream, and tried to contrive ways to get to Para and spring that splendid enterprise upon an unsuspecting planet. But all in vain. A person may *plan* as much as he wants to, but nothing of consequence is likely to come of it until the magician *Circumstance* steps in and takes the matter off his hands. At last Circumstance came to my help. It was in this way. Circumstance, to help or hurt another man, made him lose a fifty-dollar bill in the street; and to help or hurt me, made me find it. I advertised the find, and left for the Amazon the same day. This was another turning-point, another link.

Could Circumstance have ordered another dweller in that town to go to the Amazon and open up a world-trade in coca on a fifty-dollar basis and been obeyed? No, I was the only one. There were other fools there—shoals and shoals of them—but they were not of my kind. I was the only one of my kind.

Circumstance is powerful, but it cannot work alone; it has to have a partner. Its partner is man's *temperament*—his natural disposition. His temperament is not his invention, it is *born* in him, and he has no authority over it, neither is he responsible for its acts. He cannot change it, nothing can change it, nothing can modify it—except temporarily. But it won't stay modified. It is permanent, like the color of the man's eyes and the shape of his ears. Blue eyes are gray in certain unusual lights; but they resume their natural color when that stress is removed.

A Circumstance that will coerce one man will have no effect upon a man of a different temperament. If Circumstance had thrown the bank-note in Cæsar's way, his temperament would not have made him start for the Amazon. His temperament would have compelled him to do something with the money, but not that. It might have made him advertise the note—and *wait*. We can't tell. Also, it might have made him go to New York and buy into the Government, with results that would leave Tweed nothing to learn when it came his turn.

Very well, Circumstance furnished the capital, and my temperament told me what to do with it. Sometimes a temperament is an ass. When that is the case the owner of it is an ass, too, and is going to remain one. Training, experience, association, can temporarily so polish him, improve him, exalt him that people will think he is a mule, but they will be mistaken. Artificially he *is* a mule, for the time being, but at bottom he is an ass yet, and will remain one.

By temperament I was the kind of person that *does* things. Does them, and reflects afterward. So I started for the Amazon without reflecting and without asking any questions. That was more than fifty years ago. In all that time my temperament has not changed, by even a shade. I have been punished many and many a time, and bitterly, for doing things and reflecting afterward, but these tortures have been of no value to me: I still do the thing commanded by Circumstance and Temperament, and reflect afterward. Always violently. When I am reflecting, on those occasions, even deaf persons can hear me think.

I went by the way of Cincinnati, and down the Ohio and Mississippi. My idea was to take ship, at New Orleans, for Para. In New Orleans I inquired, and found there was no ship leaving for Para. Also, that there never had *been* one leaving for Para. I reflected. A policeman came and asked me what I was doing, and I told him. He made me move on, and said if he caught me reflecting in the public street again he would run me in.

After a few days I was out of money. Then Circumstance arrived, with another turning-point of my life—a new link. On my way down, I had made the acquaintance of a pilot. I begged him to teach me the river, and he consented. I became a pilot.

By and by Circumstance came again—introducing the Civil War, this time, in order to push me ahead another stage or two toward the literary profession. The boats stopped running, my livelihood was gone.

Circumstance came to the rescue with a new turning-

point and a fresh link. My brother was appointed secretary
to the new Territory of Nevada, and he invited me to go
with him and help him in his office. I accepted.

In Nevada, Circumstance furnished me the silver fever
and I went into the mines to make a fortune, as I supposed;
but that was not the idea. The idea was to advance me
another step toward literature. For amusement I scribbled
things for the Virginia City *Enterprise*. One isn't a printer
ten years without setting up acres of good and bad literature, and learning—unconsciously at first, consciously later
—to discriminate between the two, within his mental limita-
tions; and meantime he is unconsciously acquiring what
is called a "style." One of my efforts attracted attention,
and the *Enterprise* sent for me and put me on its staff.

And so I became a journalist—another link. By and by
Circumstance and the Sacramento *Union* sent me to the
Sandwich Islands for five or six months, to write up sugar.
I did it; and threw in a good deal of extraneous matter
that hadn't anything to do with sugar. But it was this
extraneous matter that helped me to another link.

It made me notorious, and San Francisco invited me to
lecture. Which I did. And profitably. I had long had a
desire to travel and see the world, and now Circumstance
had most kindly and unexpectedly hurled me upon the
platform and furnished me the means. So I joined the
"Quaker City Excursion."

When I returned to America, Circumstance was waiting
on the pier—with the *last* link—the conspicuous, the con-
summating, the victorious link: I was asked to *write a book*,
and I did it, and called it *The Innocents Abroad*. Thus
I became at last a member of the literary guild. That was
forty-two years ago, and I have been a member ever since.
Leaving the Rubicon incident away back where it belongs,
I can say with truth that the reason I am in the literary
profession is because I had the measles when I was twelve
years old.

## III.

Now what interests me, as regards these details, is not
the details themselves, but the fact that none of them was
foreseen by me, none of them was planned by me, I was
the author of none of them. Circumstance, working in
harness with my temperament, created them all and com-

pelled them all. I often offered help, and with the best intentions, but it was rejected—as a rule, uncourteously. I could never plan a thing and get it to come out the way I planned it. It came out some other way—some way I had not counted upon.

And so I do not admire the human being—as an intellectual marvel—as much as I did when I was young, and got him out of books, and did not know him personally. When I used to read that such and such a general did a certain brilliant thing, I believed it. Whereas it was not so. Circumstance did it by help of his temperament. The circumstance would have failed of effect with a general of another temperament: he might see the chance, but lose the advantage by being by nature too slow or too quick or too doubtful. Once General Grant was asked a question about a matter which had been much debated by the public and the newspapers; he answered the question without any hesitancy. "General, who planned the march through Georgia?" "The enemy!" He added that the enemy usually makes your plans for you. He meant that the enemy by neglect or through force of circumstances leaves an opening for you, and you see your chance and take advantage of it.

Circumstances do the planning for us all, no doubt, by help of our temperaments. I see no great difference between a man and a watch, except that the man is conscious and the watch isn't, and the man *tries* to plan things and the watch doesn't. The watch doesn't wind itself and doesn't regulate itself—these things are done exteriorly. Outside influences, outside circumstances, wind the *man* and regulate him. Left to himself, he wouldn't get regulated at all, and the sort of time he would keep would not be valuable. Some rare men are wonderful watches, with gold case, compensation balance, and all those things, and some men are only simple and sweet and humble Waterburys. I am a Waterbury. A Waterbury of that kind, some say.

A nation is only an individual multiplied. It makes plans and Circumstance comes and upsets them—or enlarges them. Some patriots throw the tea overboard; some other patriots destroy a Bastille. The *plans* stop there; then Circumstance comes in, quite unexpectedly, and turns these modest riots into a revolution.

And there was poor Columbus. He elaborated a deep plan to find a new route to an old country. Circumstance revised his plan for him, and he found a new *world*. And *he* gets the credit of it to this day. He hadn't anything to do with it.

Necessarily the scene of the real turning-point of my life (and of yours) was the Garden of Eden. It was there that the first link was forged of the chain that was ultimately to lead to the emptying of me into the literary guild. Adam's *temperament* was the first command the Deity ever issued to a human being on this planet. And it was the only command Adam would *never* be able to disobey. It said, "Be weak, be water, be characterless, be cheaply persuadable." The later command, to let the fruit alone, was certain to be disobeyed. Not by Adam himself, but by his *temperament*—which he did not create and had no authority over. For the *temperament* is the man; the thing tricked out with clothes and named Man is merely its Shadow, nothing more. The law of the tiger's temperament is, Thou shalt kill; the law of the sheep's temperament is, Thou shalt not kill. To issue later commands requiring the tiger to let the fat stranger alone, and requiring the sheep to imbue its hands in the blood of the lion is not worth while, for those commands *can't* be obeyed. They would invite to violations of the law of *temperament*, which is supreme, and takes precedence of all other authorities. I cannot help feeling disappointed in Adam and Eve. That is, in their temperaments. Not in *them*, poor helpless young creatures—afflicted with temperaments made out of butter; which butter was commanded to get into contact with fire and *be melted*. What I cannot help wishing is, that Adam and Eve had been postponed, and Martin Luther and Joan of Arc put in their place— that splendid pair equipped with temperaments not made of butter, but of asbestos. By neither sugary persuasions nor by hell fire could Satan have beguiled *them* to eat the apple.

There would have been results! Indeed, yes. The apple would be intact to-day; there would be no human race; there would be no *you*; there would be no *me*. And the old, old creation-dawn scheme of ultimately launching me into the literary guild would have been defeated.

# THE
# MAN THAT CORRUPTED
# HADLEYBURG

## I.

It was many years ago. Hadleyburg was the most honest
and upright town in all the region around about. It had
kept that reputation unsmirched during three generations,
and was prouder of it than of any other of its possessions.
It was so proud of it, and so anxious to insure its perpetuation, that it began to teach the principles of honest deal-
ing to its babies in the cradle, and made the like teachings
the staple of their culture thenceforward through all the
years devoted to their education. Also, throughout the
formative years temptations were kept out of the way of
the young people, so that their honesty could have every
chance to harden and solidify, and become a part of their
very bone. The neighboring towns were jealous of this
honorable supremacy, and affected to sneer at Hadleyburg's
pride in it and call it vanity; but all the same they were
obliged to acknowledge that Hadleyburg was in reality an
incorruptible town; and if pressed they would also acknowledge that the mere fact that a young man hailed
from Hadleyburg was all the recommendation he needed
when he went forth from his natal town to seek for responsible employment.

But at last, in the drift of time, Hadleyburg had the ill
luck to offend a passing stranger—possibly without knowing it, certainly without caring, for Hadleyburg was sufficient unto itself, and cared not a rap for strangers or their
opinions. Still, it would have been well to make an exception in this one's case, for he was a bitter man and
revengeful. All through his wanderings during a whole
year he kept his injury in mind, and gave all his leisure
moments to trying to invent a compensating satisfaction
for it. He contrived many plans, and all of them were good,

but none of them was quite sweeping enough; the poorest of them would hurt a great many individuals, but what he wanted was a plan which would comprehend the entire town, and not let so much as one person escape unhurt. At last he had a fortunate idea, and when it fell into his brain it lit up his whole head with an evil joy. He began to form a plan at once, saying to himself, "That is the thing to do—I will corrupt the town."

Six months later he went to Hadleyburg, and arrived in a buggy at the house of the old cashier of the bank about ten at night. He got a sack out of the buggy, shouldered it, and staggered with it through the cottage yard, and knocked at the door. A woman's voice said "Come in," and he entered, and set his sack behind the stove in the parlor, saying politely to the old lady who sat reading the *Missionary Herald* by the lamp:

"Pray keep your seat, madam, I will not disturb you. There—now it is pretty well concealed; one would hardly know it was there. Can I see your husband a moment, madam?"

No, he was gone to Brixton, and might not return before morning.

"Very well, madam, it is no matter. I merely wanted to leave that sack in his care, to be delivered to the rightful owner when he shall be found. I am a stranger; he does not know me; I am merely passing through the town to-night to discharge a matter which has been long in my mind. My errand is now completed, and I go pleased and a little proud, and you will never see me again. There is a paper attached to the sack which will explain everything. Good night, madam."

The old lady was afraid of the mysterious big stranger, and was glad to see him go. But her curiosity was roused, and she went straight to the sack and brought away the paper. It began as follows:

*TO BE PUBLISHED; or, the right man sought out by private inquiry—either will answer. This sack contains gold coin weighing a hundred and sixty pounds four ounces—*

"Mercy on us, and the door not locked!"

Mrs. Richards flew to it all in a tremble and locked it,

then pulled down the window-shades and stood frightened, worried, and wondering if there was anything else she could do toward making herself and the money more safe. She listened awhile for burglars, then surrendered to curiosity and went back to the lamp and finished reading the paper:

*I am a foreigner, and am presently going back to my own country, to remain there permanently. I am grateful to America for what I have received at her hands during my long stay under her flag; and to one of her citizens— a citizen of Hadleyburg—I am especially grateful for a great kindness done me a year or two ago. Two great kindnesses, in fact. I will explain. I was a gambler. I say I WAS. I was a ruined gambler. I arrived in this village at night, hungry and without a penny. I asked for help—in the dark; I was ashamed to beg in the light. I begged of the right man. He gave me twenty dollars—that is to say, he gave me life, as I considered it. He also gave me fortune; for out of that money I have made myself rich at the gaming-table. And finally, a remark which he made to me has remained with me to this day, and has at last conquered me; and in conquering has saved the remnant of my morals; I shall gamble no more. Now I have no idea who that man was, but I want him found, and I want him to have this money, to give away, throw away, or keep, as he pleases. It is merely my way of testifying my gratitude to him. If I could stay, I would find him myself; but no matter, he will be found. This is an honest town, an incorruptible town, and I know I can trust it without fear. This man can be identified by the remark which he made to me; I feel persuaded that he will remember it.*

*And now my plan is this: If you prefer to conduct the inquiry privately, do so. Tell the contents of this present writing to any one who is likely to be the right man. If he shall answer, 'I am the man; the remark I made was so-and-so,' apply the test—to wit: open the sack, and in it you will find a sealed envelope containing that remark. If the remark mentioned by the candidate tallies with it, give him the money, and ask no further questions, for he is certainly the right man.*

*But if you shall prefer a public inquiry, then publish this present writing in the local paper—with these instructions added, to wit: Thirty days from now, let the candidate appear at the town-hall at eight in the evening (Friday), and hand his remark, in a sealed envelope, to the Rev. Mr. Burgess (if he will be kind enough to act); and let Mr. Burgess there and then destroy the seals of the*

*sack, open it, and see if the remark is correct; if correct,*
*let the money be delivered, with my sincere gratitude, to*
*my benefactor thus identified.*

Mrs. Richards sat down, gently quivering with excitement, and was soon lost in thinkings—after this pattern:
"What a strange thing it is! . . . And what a fortune for
that kind man who set his bread afloat upon the waters!
. . . If it had only been my husband that did it!—for we
are so poor, so old and poor! . . ." Then, with a sigh—
"But it was not my Edward; no, it was not he that gave
a stranger twenty dollars. It is a pity, too; I see it now.
. . ." Then, with a shudder—"But it is *gambler's* money!
the wages of sin: we couldn't take it; we couldn't touch it.
I don't like to be near it; it seems a defilement." She moved
to a farther chair. . . . "I wish Edward would come and
take it to the bank; a burglar might come at any moment;
it is dreadful to be here all alone with it."

At eleven Mr. Richards arrived, and while his wife was
saying, "I am *so* glad you've come!" he was saying, "I'm
so tired—tired clear out; it is dreadful to be poor, and
have to make these dismal journeys at my time of life.
Always at the grind, grind, grind, on a salary—another
man's slave, and he sitting at home in his slippers, rich
and comfortable."

"I am so sorry for you, Edward, you know that; but be
comforted: we have our livelihood; we have our good
name—"

"Yes, Mary, and that is everything. Don't mind my talk
—it's just a moment's irritation and doesn't mean anything.
Kiss me—there, it's all gone now, and I am not complaining any more. What have you been getting? What's in the
sack?"

Then his wife told him the great secret. It dazed him
for a moment; then he said:

"It weighs a hundred and sixty pounds? Why, Mary, it's
for-ty thou-sand dollars—think of it—a whole fortune! Not
ten men in this village are worth that much. Give me the
paper."

He skimmed through it and said:

"Isn't it an adventure! Why, it's a romance; it's like the
impossible things one reads about in books, and never sees
in life." He was well stirred up now; cheerful, even gleeful.

He tapped his old wife on the cheek, and said, humorously, "Why, we're rich, Mary, rich; all we've got to do is to bury the money and burn the papers. If the gambler ever comes to inquire, we'll merely look coldly upon him and say: 'What is this nonsense you are talking? We have never heard of you and your sack of gold before'; and then he would look foolish, and—"

"And in the mean time, while you are running on with your jokes, the money is still here, and it is fast getting along toward burglar-time."

"True. Very well, what shall we do—make the inquiry private? No, not that: it would spoil the romance. The public method is better. Think what a noise it will make! And it will make all the other towns jealous; for no stranger would trust such a thing to any town but Hadleyburg, and they know it. It's a great card for us. I must get to the printing-office now, or I shall be too late."

"But stop—stop—don't leave me here alone with it, Edward!"

But he was gone. For only a little while, however. Not far from his own house he met the editor-proprietor of the paper, and gave him the document, and said, "Here is a good thing for you, Cox—put it in."

"It may be too late, Mr. Richards, but I'll see."

At home again he and his wife sat down to talk the charming mystery over; they were in no condition for sleep. The first question was, Who could the citizen have been who gave the stranger the twenty dollars? It seemed a simple one; both answered it in the same breath:

"Barclay Goodson."

"Yes," said Richards, "he could have done it, and it would have been like him, but there's not another in the town."

"Everybody will grant that, Edward—grant it privately, anyway. For six months, now, the village has been its own proper self once more—honest, narrow, self-righteous, and stingy."

"It is what he always called it, to the day of his death— said it right out publicly, too."

"Yes, and he was hated for it."

"Oh, of course; but he didn't care. I reckon he was the best-hated man among us, except the Reverend Burgess."

"Well, Burgess deserves it—he will never get another

congregation here. Mean as the town is, it knows how to
estimate *him.* Edward, doesn't it seem odd that the stranger
should appoint Burgess to deliver the money?"

"Well, yes—it does. That is—that is—"

"Why so much that-*is*-ing? Would *you* select him?"

"Mary, maybe the stranger knows him better than this
village does."

"Much *that* would help Burgess!"

The husband seemed perplexed for an answer; the wife
kept a steady eye upon him, and waited. Finally Richards
said, with the hesitancy of one who is making a statement
which is likely to encounter doubt:

"Mary, Burgess is not a bad man."

His wife was certainly surprised.

"Nonsense!" she exclaimed.

"He is not a bad man. I know. The whole of his un-
popularity had its foundation in that one thing—the thing
that made so much noise."

"That 'one thing,' indeed! As if that 'one thing' wasn't
enough, all by itself."

"Plenty. Plenty. Only he wasn't guilty of it."

"How you talk! Not guilty of it! Everybody knows he
*was* guilty."

"Mary, I give you my word—he was innocent."

"I can't believe it, and I don't. How do you know?"

"It is a confession. I am ashamed, but I will make it.
I was the only man who knew he was innocent. I could
have saved him, and—and—well, you know how the town
was wrought up—I hadn't the pluck to do it. It would
have turned everybody against me. I felt mean, ever so
mean; but I didn't dare; I hadn't the manliness to face
that."

Mary looked troubled, and for a while was silent. Then
she said, stammeringly:

"I—I don't think it would have done for you to—to—
One mustn't—er—public opinion—one has to be so careful
—so—" It was a difficult road, and she got mired; but
after a little she got started again. "It was a great pity,
but— Why, we couldn't afford it, Edward—we couldn't
indeed. Oh, I wouldn't have had you do it for anything!"

"It would have lost us the good will of so many people,
Mary; and then—and then—"

"What troubles me now is, what *he* thinks of us, Edward."

"He? *He* doesn't suspect that I could have saved him."

"Oh," exclaimed the wife, in a tone of relief, "I am glad of that! As long as he doesn't know that you could have saved him, he—he—well, that makes it a great deal better. Why, I might have known he didn't know, because he is always trying to be friendly with us, as little encouragement as we give him. More than once people have twitted me with it. There's the Wilsons, and the Wilcoxes, and the Harknesses, they take a mean pleasure in saying, '*Your friend* Burgess,' because they know it pesters me. I wish he wouldn't persist in liking us so; I can't think why he keeps it up."

"I can explain it. It's another confession. When the thing was new and hot, and the town made a plan to ride him on a rail, my conscience hurt me so that I couldn't stand it, and I went privately and gave him notice, and he got out of the town and staid out till it was safe to come back."

"Edward! If the town had found it out—"

"*Don't!* It scares me yet, to think of it. I repented of it the minute it was done; and I was even afraid to tell you, lest your face might betray it to somebody. I didn't sleep any that night, for worrying. But after a few days I saw that no one was going to suspect me, and after that I got to feeling glad I did it. And I feel glad yet, Mary—glad through and through."

"So do I, now, for it would have been a dreadful way to treat him. Yes, I'm glad; for really you did owe him that, you know. But, Edward, suppose it should come out yet, some day!"

"It won't."

"Why?"

"Because everybody thinks it was Goodson."

"Of course they would!"

"Certainly. And of course *he* didn't care. They persuaded poor old Sawlsberry to go and charge it on him, and he went blustering over there and did it. Goodson looked him over, like as if he was hunting for a place on him that he could despise the most, then he says, 'So you are the Committee of Inquiry, are you?' Sawlsberry said that was about what he was. 'Hm. Do they require particulars, or do you reckon a kind of a *general* answer will do?' 'If they require particulars, I will come back, Mr. Goodson; I will take the general answer first.' 'Very well, then, tell them to go to hell—I reckon that's general enough. And I'll give you some advice, Sawlsberry; when you come back for the particulars, fetch a basket to carry the relics of yourself home in.' "

"Just like Goodson; it's got all the marks. He had only one vanity: he thought he could give advice better than any other person."

"It settled the business, and saved us, Mary. The subject was dropped."

"Bless you, I'm not doubting *that*."

Then they took up the gold-sack mystery again, with strong interest. Soon the conversation began to suffer breaks—interruptions caused by absorbed thinkings. The breaks grew more and more frequent. At last Richards lost himself wholly in thought. He sat long, gazing vacantly at the floor, and by and by he began to punctuate his thoughts with little nervous movements of his hands that seemed to indicate vexation. Meantime his wife too had relapsed into a thoughtful silence, and her movements were beginning to show a troubled discomfort. Finally Richards got up and strode aimlessly about the room, plowing his hands through his hair, much as a somnambulist might do who was having a bad dream. Then he seemed to arrive at a definite purpose; and without a word he put on his hat and passed quickly out of the house. His wife sat brooding, with a drawn face, and did not seem to be aware that she was alone. Now and then she murmured, "Lead us not into t— . . . but—but—we are so poor, so poor! . . . Lead us not into . . . Ah, who would be hurt by it?—and no one would ever know. . . . Lead us . . ." The voice died out in mumblings. After a little she glanced up and muttered in a half-frightened, half-glad way:

"He is gone! But, oh dear, he may be too late—too late. . . . Maybe not—maybe there is still time." She rose and stood thinking, nervously clasping and unclasping her hands. A slight shudder shook her frame, and she said, out of a dry throat, "God forgive me—it's awful to think such things—but . . . Lord, how we are made—how strangely we are made!"

She turned the light low, and slipped stealthily over and kneeled down by the sack and felt of its ridgy sides with her hands, and fondled them lovingly; and there was a gloating light in her poor old eyes. She fell into fits of absence; and came half out of them at times to mutter, "If we had only waited!—oh, if we had only waited a little, and not been in such a hurry!"

Meantime Cox had gone home from his office and told his wife all about the strange thing that had happened, and they had talked it over eagerly, and guessed that the late Goodson was the only man in the town who could have helped a suffering stranger with so noble a sum as twenty dollars. Then there was a pause, and the two became thoughtful and silent. And by and by nervous and fidgety. At last the wife said, as if to herself:

"Nobody knows this secret but the Richardses . . . and us . . . nobody."

The husband came out of his thinkings with a slight start, and gazed wistfully at his wife, whose face was become very pale; then he hesitatingly rose, and glanced furtively at his hat, then at his wife—a sort of mute inquiry. Mrs. Cox swallowed once or twice, with her hand at her throat, then in place of speech she nodded her head. In a moment she was alone, and mumbling to herself.

And now Richards and Cox were hurrying through the deserted streets, from opposite directions. They met, panting, at the foot of the printing-office stairs; by the night light there they read each other's face. Cox whispered:

"Nobody knows about this but us?"

The whispered answer was,

"Not a soul—on honor, not a soul!"

"If it isn't too late to—"

The men were starting up-stairs; at this moment they were overtaken by a boy, and Cox asked:

"Is that you, Johnny?"

"Yes, sir."

"You needn't ship the early mail—nor *any* mail; wait till I tell you."

"It's already gone, sir."

"*Gone?*" It had the sound of an unspeakable disappointment in it.

"Yes, sir. Time-table for Brixton and all the towns beyond changed to-day, sir—had to get the papers in twenty

minutes earlier than common. I had to rush; if I had been
two minutes later—"

The men turned and walked slowly away, not waiting
to hear the rest. Neither of them spoke during ten minutes;
then Cox said, in a vexed tone:

"What possessed you to be in such a hurry, *I* can't make
out."

The answer was humble enough:

"I see it now, but somehow I never thought, you know,
until it was too late. But the next time—"

"Next time be hanged! It won't come in a thousand
years."

Then the friends separated without a good night, and
dragged themselves home with the gait of mortally stricken
men. At their homes their wives sprang up with an eager
"Well?"—then saw the answer with their eyes and sank
down sorrowing, without waiting for it to come in words.
In both houses a discussion followed of a heated sort—a
new thing; there had been discussions before, but not
heated ones, not ungentle ones. The discussions to-night
were a sort of seeming plagiarisms of each other. Mrs.
Richards said,

"If you had only waited, Edward—if you had only
stopped to think; but no, you must run straight to the
printing-office and spread it all over the world."

"It *said* publish it."

"That is nothing; it also said do it privately, if you
liked. There, now—is that true, or not?"

"Why, yes—yes, it is true; but when I thought what a
stir it would make, and what a compliment it was to
Hadleyburg that a stranger should trust it so—"

"Oh, certainly, I know all that; but if you had only
stopped to think, you would have seen that you *couldn't*
find the right man, because he is in his grave, and hasn't
left chick nor child nor relation behind him; and as long
as the money went to somebody that awfully needed it,
and nobody would be hurt by it, and—and—"

She broke down, crying. Her husband tried to think of
some comforting thing to say, and presently came out with
this:

"But after all, Mary, it must be for the best—it *must*
be; we know that. And we must remember that it was so
ordered—"

"Ordered! Oh, everything's *ordered*, when a person has to find some way out when he has been stupid. Just the same, it was *ordered* that the money should come to us in this special way, and it was you that must take it on yourself to go meddling with the designs of Providence—and who gave you the right? It was wicked, that is what it was —just blasphemous presumption, and no more becoming to a meek and humble professor of—"

"But, Mary, you know how we have been trained all our lives long, like the whole village, till it is absolutely second nature to us to stop not a single moment to think when there's an honest thing to be done—"

"Oh, I know it, I know it—it's been one everlasting training and training and training in honesty—honesty shielded, from the very cradle, against every possible temptation, and so it's *artificial* honesty, and weak as water when temptation comes, as we have seen this night. God knows I never had shade nor shadow of a doubt of my petrified and indestructible honesty until now—and now, under the very first big and real temptation, I—Edward, it is my belief that this town's honesty is as rotten as mine is; as rotten as yours is. It is a mean town, a hard, stingy town, and hasn't a virtue in the world but this honesty it is so celebrated for and so conceited about; and so help me, I do believe that if ever the day comes that its honesty falls under great temptation, its grand reputation will go to ruin like a house of cards. There, now, I've made confession, and I feel better; I am a humbug, and I've been one all my life, without knowing it. Let no man call me honest again—I will not have it."

"I—well, Mary, I feel a good deal as you do; I certainly do. It seems strange, too, so strange. I never could have believed it—never."

A long silence followed; both were sunk in thought. At last the wife looked up and said:

"I know what you are thinking, Edward."

Richards had the embarrassed look of a person who is caught.

"I am ashamed to confess it, Mary, but—"

"It's no matter, Edward, I was thinking the same question myself."

"I hope so. State it."

"You were thinking, if a body could only guess out

*what the remark was* that Goodson made to the stranger."

"It's perfectly true. I feel guilty and ashamed. And you?"

"I'm past it. Let us make a pallet here; we've got to stand watch till the bank vault opens in the morning and admits the sack. . . . Oh dear, oh dear—if we hadn't made the mistake!"

The pallet was made, and Mary said:

"The open sesame—what could it have been? I do wonder what that remark could have been? But come; we will get to bed now."

"And sleep?"

"No: think."

"Yes, think."

By this time the Coxes too had completed their spat and their reconciliation, and were turning in—to think, to think, and toss, and fret, and worry over what the remark could possibly have been which Goodson made to the stranded derelict; that golden remark; that remark worth forty thousand dollars, cash.

The reason that the village telegraph-office was open later than usual that night was this: The foreman of Cox's paper was the local representative of the Associated Press. One might say its honorary representative, for it wasn't four times a year that he could furnish thirty words that would be accepted. But this time it was different. His despatch stating what he had caught got an instant answer:

*Send the whole thing—all the details—twelve hundred words.*

A colossal order! The foreman filled the bill; and he was the proudest man in the State. By breakfast-time the next morning the name of Hadleyburg the Incorruptible was on every lip in America, from Montreal to the Gulf, from the glaciers of Alaska to the orange-groves of Florida; and millions and millions of people were discussing the stranger and his money-sack, and wondering if the right man would be found, and hoping some more news about the matter would come soon—right away.

## II.

Hadleyburg village woke up world-celebrated—astonished —happy—vain. Vain beyond imagination. Its nineteen

principal citizens and their wives went about shaking
hands with each other, and beaming, and smiling, and
congratulating, and saying *this* thing adds a new word to
the dictionary—*Hadleyburg*, synonym for *incorruptible*—
destined to live in dictionaries forever! And the minor and
unimportant citizens and their wives went around acting
in much the same way. Everybody ran to the bank to see
the gold-sack; and before noon grieved and envious crowds
began to flock in from Brixton and all neighboring towns;
and that afternoon and next day reporters began to arrive
from everywhere to verify the sack and its history and
write the whole thing up anew, and make dashing free-
hand pictures of the sack, and of Richards's house, and the
bank, and the Presbyterian church, and the Baptist church,
and the public square, and the town-hall where the test
would be applied and the money delivered; and damnable
portraits of the Richardses, and Pinkerton the banker, and
Cox, and the foreman, and Reverend Burgess, and the postmaster—and even of Jack Halliday, who was the loafing,
good-natured, no-account, irreverent fisherman, hunter,
boys' friend, stray-dogs' friend, typical "Sam Lawson" of
the town. The little, mean, smirking, oily Pinkerton showed
the sack to all comers, and rubbed his sleek palms together
pleasantly, and enlarged upon the town's fine old reputation for honesty and upon this wonderful indorsement of
it, and hoped and believed that the example would now
spread far and wide over the American world, and be
epoch-making in the matter of moral regeneration. And
so on, and so on.

By the end of a week things had quieted down again;
the wild intoxication of pride and joy had sobered to a
soft, sweet, silent delight—a sort of deep, nameless, unutterable content. All faces bore a look of peaceful, holy
happiness.

Then a change came. It was a gradual change: so gradual
that its beginnings were hardly noticed; maybe were not
noticed at all, except by Jack Halliday, who always noticed
everything; and always made fun of it, too, no matter
what it was. He began to throw out chaffing remarks about
people not looking quite so happy as they did a day or
two ago; and next he claimed that the new aspect was
deepening to positive sadness; next, that it was taking on
a sick look; and finally he said that everybody was become

so moody, thoughtful, and absent-minded that he could rob the meanest man in town of a cent out of the bottom of his breeches pocket and not disturb his revery.

At this stage—or at about this stage—a saying like this was dropped at bedtime—with a sigh, usually—by the head of each of the nineteen principal households: "Ah, what *could* have been the remark that Goodson made?"

And straightway—with a shudder—came this, from the man's wife:

"Oh, *don't!* What horrible thing are you mulling in your mind? Put it away from you, for God's sake!"

But that question was wrung from those men again the next night—and got the same retort. But weaker.

And the third night the men uttered the question yet again—with anguish, and absently. This time—and the following night—the wives fidgeted feebly, and tried to say something. But didn't.

And the night after that they found their tongues and responded—longingly:

"Oh, if we *could* only guess!"

Halliday's comments grew daily more and more sparklingly disagreeable and disparaging. He went diligently about, laughing at the town, individually and in mass. But his laugh was the only one left in the village: it fell upon a hollow and mournful vacancy and emptiness. Not even a smile was findable anywhere. Halliday carried a cigar-box around on a tripod, playing that it was a camera, and halted all passers and aimed the thing and said, "Ready!— now look pleasant, please," but not even this capital joke could surprise the dreary faces into any softening.

So three weeks passed—one week was left. It was Saturday evening—after supper. Instead of the aforetime Saturday-evening flutter and bustle and shopping and larking, the streets were empty and desolate. Richards and his old wife sat apart in their little parlor—miserable and thinking. This was become their evening habit now: the lifelong habit which had preceded it, of reading, knitting, and contented chat, or receiving or paying neighborly calls, was dead and gone and forgotten, ages ago—two or three weeks ago; nobody talked now, nobody read, nobody visited—the whole village sat at home, sighing, worrying, silent. Trying to guess out that remark.

The postman left a letter. Richards glanced listlessly at

the superscription and the postmark—unfamiliar, both—
and tossed the letter on the table and resumed his might-
have-beens and his hopeless dull miseries where he had
left them off. Two or three hours later his wife got wearily
up and was going away to bed without a good night—custom now—but she stopped near the letter and eyed it
awhile with a dead interest, then broke it open, and began
to skim it over. Richards, sitting there with his chair tilted
back against the wall and his chin between his knees, heard
something fall. It was his wife. He sprang to her side, but
she cried out:

"Leave me alone, I am too happy. Read the letter—
read it!"

He did. He devoured it, his brain reeling. The letter was
from a distant state, and it said:

*I am a stranger to you, but no matter: I have some-
thing to tell. I have just arrived home from Mexico, and
learned about that episode. Of course you do not know
who made that remark, but I know, and I am the only
person living who does know. It was* GOODSON. *I knew
him well, many years ago. I passed through your village
that very night, and was his guest till the midnight train
came along. I overheard him make that remark to the
stranger in the dark—it was in Hale Alley. He and I
talked of it the rest of the way home, and while smoking
in his house. He mentioned many of your villagers in the
course of his talk—most of them in a very uncomplimen-
tary way, but two or three favorably; among these latter
yourself. I say "favorably"—nothing stronger. I remember his saying he did not actually* LIKE *any person in the
town—not one; but that you—I* THINK *he said you—am
almost sure—had done him a very great service once,
possibly without knowing the full value of it, and he
wished he had a fortune, he would leave it to you when
he died, and a curse apiece for the rest of the citizens.
Now, then, if it was you that did him that service, you
are his legitimate heir, and entitled to the sack of gold.
I know that I can trust to your honor and honesty, for
in a citizen of Hadleyburg these virtues are an unfailing
inheritance, and so I am going to reveal to you the
remark, well satisfied that if you are not the right man
you will seek and find the right one and see that poor*

*Goodson's debt of gratitude for the service referred to is
paid. This is the remark:* "YOU ARE FAR FROM BEING A
BAD MAN: GO, AND REFORM."

HOWARD L. STEPHENSON.

"Oh, Edward, the money is ours, and I am so grateful,
*oh,* so grateful—kiss me, dear, it's forever since we kissed
—and we needed it so—the money—and now you are free
of Pinkerton and his bank, and nobody's slave any more;
it seems to me I could fly for joy."

It was a happy half-hour that the couple spent there on
the settee caressing each other; it was the old days come
again—days that had begun with their courtship and lasted
without a break till the stranger brought the deadly money.
By and by the wife said:

"Oh, Edward, how lucky it was you did him that grand
service, poor Goodson! I never liked him, but I love him
now. And it was fine and beautiful of you never to mention it or brag about it." Then, with a touch of reproach,
"But you ought to have told *me,* Edward, you ought to
have told your wife, you know."

"Well, I—er—well, Mary, you see—"

"Now stop hemming and hawing, and tell me about it,
Edward. I always loved you, and now I'm proud of you.
Everybody believes there was only one good generous soul
in this village, and now it turns out that you—Edward, why
don't you tell me?"

"Well—er—er— Why, Mary, I can't!"

"You *can't? Why* can't you?"

"You see, he—well, he—he made me promise I
wouldn't."

The wife looked him over, and said, very slowly:

"Made—you—promise? Edward, what do you tell me
that for?"

"Mary, do you think I would lie?"

She was troubled and silent for a moment, then she laid
her hand within his and said:

"No . . . no. We have wandered far enough from our
bearings—God spare us that! In all your life you have never
uttered a lie. But now—now that the foundations of things
seem to be crumbling from under us, we—we—" She lost
her voice for a moment, then said, brokenly, "Lead us not
into temptation. . . . I think you made the promise,

Edward. Let it rest so. Let us keep away from that ground. Now—that is all gone by; let us be happy again; it is no time for clouds."

Edward found it something of an effort to comply, for his mind kept wandering—trying to remember what the service was that he had done Goodson.

The couple lay awake the most of the night, Mary happy and busy, Edward busy but not so happy. Mary was planning what she would do with the money. Edward was trying to recall that service. At first his conscience was sore on account of the lie he had told Mary—if it was a lie. After much reflection—suppose it *was* a lie? What then? Was it such a great matter? Aren't we always *acting* lies? Then why not *tell* them? Look at Mary—look what she had done. While he was hurrying off on his honest errand, what was she doing? Lamenting because the papers hadn't been destroyed and the money kept! Is theft better than lying?

*That* point lost its sting—the lie dropped into the background and left comfort behind it. The next point came to the front: *Had* he rendered that service? Well, here was Goodson's own evidence as reported in Stephenson's letter; there could be no better evidence than that—it was even *proof* that he had rendered it. Of course. So that point was settled. . . . No, not quite. He recalled with a wince that this unknown Mr. Stephenson was just a trifle unsure as to whether the performer of it was Richards or some other—and, oh dear, he had put Richards on his honor! He must himself decide whither that money must go—and Mr. Stephenson was not doubting that if he was the wrong man he would go honorably and find the right one. Oh, it was odious to put a man in such a situation—ah, why couldn't Stephenson have left out that doubt! What did he want to intrude that for?

Further reflection. How did it happen that *Richards's* name remained in Stephenson's mind as indicating the right man, and not some other man's name? That looked good. Yes, that looked very good. In fact, it went on looking better and better, straight along—until by and by it grew into positive *proof*. And then Richards put the matter at once out of his mind, for he had a private instinct that a proof once established is better left so.

He was feeling reasonably comfortable now, but there was still one other detail that kept pushing itself on his

notice: of course he had done that service—that was settled;
but what *was* that service? He must recall it—he would
not go to sleep till he had recalled it; it would make his
peace of mind perfect. And so he thought and thought. He
thought of a dozen things—possible services, even probable
services—but none of them seemed adequate, none of them
seemed large enough, none of them seemed worth the
money—worth the fortune Goodson had wished he could
leave in his will. And besides, he couldn't remember
having done them, anyway. Now, then—now, then—what
*kind* of a service would it be that would make a man so
inordinately grateful? Ah—the saving of his soul! That
must be it. Yes, he could remember, now, how he once
set himself the task of converting Goodson, and labored
at it as much as—he was going to say three months; but
upon closer examination it shrunk to a month, then to a
week, then to a day, then to nothing. Yes, he remembered
now, and with unwelcome vividness, that Goodson had told
him to go to thunder and mind his own business—*he*
wasn't hankering to follow Hadleyburg to heaven!

So that solution was a failure—he hadn't saved Goodson's soul. Richards was discouraged. Then after a little
came another idea: had he saved Goodson's property? No,
that wouldn't do—he hadn't any. His life? That is it! Of
course. Why, he might have thought of it before. This
time he was on the right track, sure. His imagination-mill
was hard at work in a minute, now.

Thereafter during a stretch of two exhausting hours he
was busy saving Goodson's life. He saved it in all kinds of
difficult and perilous ways. In every case he got it saved
satisfactorily up to a certain point; then, just as he was
beginning to get well persuaded that it had really happened, a troublesome detail would turn up which made
the whole thing impossible. As in the matter of drowning,
for instance. In that case he had swum out and tugged
Goodson ashore in an unconscious state with a great
crowd looking on and applauding, but when he had got
it all thought out and was just beginning to remember all
about it, a whole swarm of disqualifying details arrived
on the ground: the town would have known of the circumstance, Mary would have known of it, it would glare
like a limelight in his own memory instead of being an
inconspicuous service which he had possibly rendered "with-

out knowing its full value." And at this point he remembered that he couldn't swim, anyway.

Ah—*there* was a point which he had been overlooking from the start: it had to be a service which he had rendered "possibly without knowing the full value of it." Why, really, that ought to be an easy hunt—much easier than those others. And sure enough, by and by he found it. Goodson, years and years ago, came near marrying a very sweet and pretty girl, named Nancy Hewitt, but in some way or other the match had been broken off; the girl died, Goodson remained a bachelor, and by and by became a soured one and a frank despiser of the human species. Soon after the girl's death the village found out, or thought it had found out, that she carried a spoonful of negro blood in her veins. Richards worked at these details a good while, and in the end he thought he remembered things concerning them which must have gotten mislaid in his memory through long neglect. He seemed to dimly remember that it was *he* that found out about the negro blood; that it was he that told the village; that the village told Goodson where they got it; that he thus saved Goodson from marrying the tainted girl; that he had done him this great service "without knowing the full value of it," in fact without knowing that he *was* doing it; but that Goodson knew the value of it, and what a narrow escape he had had, and so went to his grave grateful to his benefactor and wishing he had a fortune to leave him. It was all clear and simple now, and the more he went over it the more luminous and certain it grew; and at last, when he nestled to sleep satisfied and happy, he remembered the whole thing just as if it had been yesterday. In fact, he dimly remembered Goodson's *telling* him his gratitude once. Meantime Mary had spent six thousand dollars on a new house for herself and a pair of slippers for her pastor, and then had fallen peacefully to rest.

That same Saturday evening the postman had delivered a letter to each of the other principal citizens—nineteen letters in all. No two of the envelopes were alike, and no two of the superscriptions were in the same hand, but the letters inside were just like each other in every detail but one. They were exact copies of the letter received by Richards—handwriting and all—and were all signed by

Stephenson, but in place of Richards's name each receiver's own name appeared.

All night long eighteen principal citizens did what their caste-brother Richards was doing at the same time—they put in their energies trying to remember what notable service it was that they had unconsciously done Barclay Goodson. In no case was it a holiday job; still they succeeded.

And while they were at this work, which was difficult, their wives put in the night spending the money, which was easy. During that one night the nineteen wives spent an average of seven thousand dollars each out of the forty thousand in the sack—a hundred and thirty-three thousand altogether.

Next day there was a surprise for Jack Halliday. He noticed that the faces of the nineteen chief citizens and their wives bore that expression of peaceful and holy happiness again. He could not understand it, neither was he able to invent any remarks about it that could damage it or disturb it. And so it was his turn to be dissatisfied with life. His private guesses at the reasons for the happiness failed in all instances, upon examination. When he met Mrs. Wilcox and noticed the placid ecstasy in her face, he said to himself, "Her cat has had kittens"—and went and asked the cook: it was not so; the cook had detected the happiness, but did not know the cause. When Halliday found the duplicate ecstasy in the face of "Shadbelly" Billson (village nickname), he was sure some neighbor of Billson's had broken his leg, but inquiry showed that this had not happened. The subdued ecstasy in Gregory Yates's face could mean but one thing—he was a mother-in-law short: it was another mistake. "And Pinkerton—Pinkerton—he has collected ten cents that he thought he was going to lose." And so on, and so on. In some cases the guesses had to remain in doubt, in the others they proved distinct errors. In the end Halliday said to himself, "Anyway it foots up that there's nineteen Hadleyburg families temporarily in heaven: I don't know how it happened; I only know Providence is off duty to-day."

An architect and builder from the next state had lately ventured to set up a small business in this unpromising village, and his sign had now been hanging out a week. Not a customer yet; he was a discouraged man, and sorry he had come. But his weather changed suddenly now. First one and then another chief citizen's wife said to him privately:

"Come to my house Monday week—but say nothing about it for the present. We think of building."

He got eleven invitations that day. That night he wrote his daughter and broke off her match with her student. He said she could marry a mile higher than that.

Pinkerton the banker and two or three other well-to-do men planned country-seats—but waited. That kind don't count their chickens until they are hatched.

The Wilsons devised a grand new thing—a fancy-dress ball. They made no actual promises, but told all their acquaintanceship in confidence that they were thinking the matter over and thought they should give it—"and if we do, you will be invited, of course." People were surprised, and said, one to another, "Why, they are crazy, those poor Wilsons, they can't afford it." Several among the nineteen said privately to their husbands, "It is a good idea: we will keep still till their cheap thing is over, then *we* will give one that will make it sick."

The days drifted along, and the bill of future squanderings rose higher and higher, wilder and wilder, more and more foolish and reckless. It began to look as if every member of the nineteen would not only spend his whole forty thousand dollars before receiving-day, but be actually in debt by the time he got the money. In some cases light-headed people did not stop with planning to spend, they really spent—on credit. They bought land, mortgages, farms, speculative stocks, fine clothes, horses, and various other things, paid down the bonus, and made themselves liable for the rest—at ten days. Presently the sober second thought came, and Halliday noticed that a ghastly anxiety was beginning to show up in a good many faces. Again he was puzzled, and didn't know what to make of it. "The Wilcox kittens aren't dead, for they weren't born; nobody's broken a leg; there's no shrinkage in mother-in-laws; *nothing* has happened—it is an unsolvable mystery."

There was another puzzled man, too—the Rev. Mr. Burgess. For days, wherever he went, people seemed to follow him or to be watching out for him; and if he ever found himself in a retired spot, a member of the nineteen would be sure to appear, thrust an envelope privately into his hand, whisper "To be opened at the town-hall Friday evening," then vanish away like a guilty thing. He was expecting that there might be one claimant for the sack—doubtful, however, Goodson being dead—but it never occurred to him that all this crowd might be claimants. When the great Friday came at last, he found that he had nineteen envelopes.

## III.

The town hall had never looked finer. The platform at the end of it was backed by a showy draping of flags; at intervals along the walls were festoons of flags; the gallery fronts were clothed in flags; the supporting columns were swathed in flags; all this was to impress the stranger, for he would be there in considerable force, and in a large degree he would be connected with the press. The house was full. The 412 fixed seats were occupied; also the 68 extra chairs which had been packed into the aisles; the steps of the platform were occupied; some distinguished strangers were given seats on the platform; at the horse-shoe of tables which fenced the front and sides of the platform sat a strong force of special correspondents who had come from everywhere. It was the best-dressed house the town had ever produced. There were some tolerably expensive toilets there, and in several cases the ladies who wore them had the look of being unfamiliar with that kind of clothes. At least the town thought they had that look, but the notion could have arisen from the town's knowledge of the fact that these ladies had never inhabited such clothes before.

The gold-sack stood on a little table at the front of the platform where all the house could see it. The bulk of the house gazed at it with a burning interest, a mouth-watering interest, a wistful and pathetic interest; a minority of nineteen couples gazed at it tenderly, lovingly, pro-prietarily, and the male half of this minority kept saying over to themselves the moving little impromptu speeches of thankfulness for the audience's applause and congratulations which they were presently going to get up and deliver. Every now and then one of these got a piece of paper out of his vest pocket and privately glanced at it to refresh his memory.

Of course there was a buzz of conversation going on—

there always is; but at last when the Rev. Mr. Burgess rose
and laid his hand on the sack he could hear his microbes
gnaw, the place was so still. He related the curious history
of the sack, then went on to speak in warm terms of
Hadleyburg's old and well-earned reputation for spotless
honesty, and of the town's just pride in this reputation.
He said that this reputation was a treasure of priceless
value; that under Providence its value had now become
inestimably enhanced, for the recent episode had spread
this fame far and wide, and thus had focused the eyes of
the American world upon this village, and made its name
for all time, as he hoped and believed, a synonym for
commercial incorruptibility. [*Applause.*] "And who is to
be the guardian of this noble treasure—the community as
a whole? No! The responsibility is individual, not com-
munal. From this day forth each and every one of you
is in his own person its special guardian, and individually
responsible that no harm shall come to it. Do you—does
each of you—accept this great trust? [*Tumultuous assent.*]
Then all is well. Transmit it to your children and to your
children's children. To-day your purity is beyond reproach
—see to it that it shall remain so. To-day there is not a
person in your community who could be beguiled to touch
a penny not his own—see to it that you abide in this
grace. ["*We will! we will!*"] This is not the place to make
comparisons between ourselves and other communities—
some of them ungracious toward us; they have their ways,
we have ours; let us be content. [*Applause.*] I am done.
Under my hand, my friends, rests a stranger's eloquent
recognition of what we are; through him the world will
always henceforth know what we are. We do not know
who he is, but in your name I utter your gratitude, and
ask you to raise your voices in indorsement."

The house rose in a body and made the walls quake
with the thunders of its thankfulness for the space of a
long minute. Then it sat down, and Mr. Burgess took an
envelope out of his pocket. The house held its breath
while he slit the envelope open and took from it a slip
of paper. He read its contents—slowly and impressively
—the audience listening with tranced attention to this
magic document, each of whose words stood for an ingot
of gold:

"'*The remark which I made to the distressed stranger*

*was this: "You are very far from being a bad man: go, and reform." ' "* Then he continued:

"We shall know in a moment now whether the remark here quoted corresponds with the one concealed in the sack; and if that shall prove to be so—and it undoubtedly will—this sack of gold belongs to a fellow-citizen who will henceforth stand before the nation as the symbol of the special virtue which has made our town famous throughout the land—Mr. Billson!"

The house had gotten itself all ready to burst into the proper tornado of applause; but instead of doing it, it seemed stricken with a paralysis; there was a deep hush for a moment or two, then a wave of whispered murmurs swept the place—of about this tenor: "*Billson!* oh, come, this is *too* thin! Twenty dollars to a stranger—or *anybody—Billson!* tell it to the marines!" And now at this point the house caught its breath all of a sudden in a new access of astonishment, for it discovered that whereas in one part of the hall Deacon Billson was standing up with his head meekly bowed, in another part of it Lawyer Wilson was doing the same. There was a wondering silence now for a while.

Everybody was puzzled, and nineteen couples were surprised and indignant.

Billson and Wilson turned and stared at each other. Billson asked, bitingly:

"Why do *you* rise, Mr. Wilson?"

"Because I have a right to. Perhaps you will be good enough to explain to the house why *you* rise?"

"With great pleasure. Because I wrote that paper."

"It is an impudent falsity! I wrote it myself."

It was Burgess's turn to be paralyzed. He stood looking vacantly at first one of the men and then the other, and did not seem to know what to do. The house was stupefied. Lawyer Wilson spoke up, now, and said,

"I ask the Chair to read the name signed to that paper."

That brought the Chair to itself, and it read out the name:

" 'John Wharton *Billson.*' "

"There!" shouted Billson, "what have you got to say for yourself, now? And what kind of apology are you going to make to me and to this insulted house for the imposture which you have attempted to play here?"

"No apologies are due, sir; and as for the rest of it, I publicly charge you with pilfering my note from Mr. Burgess and substituting a copy of it signed with your own name. There is no other way by which you could have gotten hold of the test-remark; I alone, of living men, possessed the secret of its wording."

There was likely to be a scandalous state of things if this went on; everybody noticed with distress that the short-hand scribes were scribbling like mad; many people were crying "Chair, Chair! Order! order!" Burgess rapped with his gavel, and said:

"Let us not forget the proprieties due. There has evidently been a mistake somewhere, but surely that is all. If Mr. Wilson gave me an envelope—and I remember now that he did—I still have it."

He took one out of his pocket, opened it, glanced at it, looked surprised and worried, and stood silent a few moments. Then he waved his hand in a wandering and mechanical way, and made an effort or two to say something, then gave it up, despondently. Several voices cried out:

"Read it! read it! What is it?"

So he began in a dazed and sleep-walker fashion:

"*'The remark which I made to the unhappy stranger was this: "You are far from being a bad man.* [The house gazed at him, marveling.] *Go, and reform.'"* [*Murmurs:* "Amazing! what can this mean?"] This one," said the Chair, "is signed Thurlow G. Wilson."

"There!" cried Wilson. "I reckon that settles it! I knew perfectly well my note was purloined."

"Purloined!" retorted Billson. "I'll let you know that neither you nor any man of your kidney must venture to—"

*The Chair.* "Order, gentlemen, order! Take your seats, both of you, please."

They obeyed, shaking their heads and grumbling angrily. The house was profoundly puzzled; it did not know what to do with this curious emergency. Presently Thompson got up. Thompson was the hatter. He would have liked to be a Nineteener; but such was not for him: his stock of hats was not considerable enough for the position. He said:

"Mr. Chairman, if I may be permitted to make a sug-

gestion, can both of these gentlemen be right? I put it to
you, sir, can both have happened to say the very same
words to the stranger? It seems to me—"

The tanner got up and interrupted him. The tanner
was a disgruntled man; he believed himself entitled to be
a Nineteener, but he couldn't get recognition. It made him
a little unpleasant in his ways and speech. Said he:

"Sho, *that's* not the point! *That* could happen—twice
in a hundred years—but not the other thing. *Neither* of
them gave the twenty dollars!"

[*A ripple of applause.*]

*Billson.* "I did!"

*Wilson.* "I did!"

Then each accused the other of pilfering.

*The Chair.* "Order! Sit down, if you please—both of
you. Neither of the notes has been out of my possession
at any moment."

*A Voice.* "Good—that settles *that!*"

*The Tanner.* "Mr. Chairman, one thing is now plain:
one of these men has been eavesdropping under the other
one's bed, and filching family secrets. If it is not un-
parliamentary to suggest it, I will remark that both are
equal to it. [*The Chair.* "Order! order!"] I withdraw the
remark, sir, and will confine myself to suggesting that *if*
one of them has overheard the other reveal the test-
remark to his wife, we shall catch him now."

*A Voice.* "How?"

*The Tanner.* "Easily. The two have not quoted the
remark in exactly the same words. You would have noticed
that, if there hadn't been a considerable stretch of time
and an exciting quarrel inserted between the two read-
ings."

*A Voice.* "Name the difference."

*The Tanner.* "The word *very* is in Billson's note, and
not in the other."

*Many Voices.* "That's so—he's right!"

*The Tanner.* "And so, if the Chair will examine the test-
remark in the sack, we shall know which of these two
frauds— [*The Chair.* "Order!"]—which of these two ad-
venturers— [*The Chair.* "Order! order!"]—which of these
two gentlemen—[*laughter and applause*]—is entitled to
wear the belt as being the first dishonest blatherskite ever
bred in this town—which he has dishonored, and which

will be a sultry place for him from now out!" [*Vigorous applause.*]

*Many Voices.* "Open it!—open the sack!"

Mr. Burgess made a slit in the sack, slid his hand in and brought out an envelope. In it were a couple of folded notes. He said:

"One of these is marked, 'Not to be examined until all written communications which have been addressed to the Chair—if any—shall have been read.' The other is marked '*The Test.*' Allow me. It is worded—to wit:

" 'I do not require that the first half of the remark which was made to me by my benefactor shall be quoted with exactness, for it was not striking, and could be forgotten; but its closing fifteen words are quite striking, and I think easily rememberable; unless *these* shall be accurately reproduced, let the applicant be regarded as an impostor. My benefactor began by saying he seldom gave advice to any one, but that it always bore the hall-mark of high value when he did give it. Then he said this—and it has never faded from my memory: *"You are far from being a bad man—"* ' "

*Fifty Voices.* "That settles it—the money's Wilson's! Wilson! Wilson! Speech! Speech!"

People jumped up and crowded around Wilson, wringing his hand and congratulating fervently—meantime the Chair was hammering with the gavel and shouting:

"Order, gentlemen! Order! Order! Let me finish reading, please." When quiet was restored, the reading was resumed —as follows:

" ' "Go, and reform—or, mark my words—some day, for your sins, you will die and go to hell or Hadleyburg—TRY AND MAKE IT THE FORMER." ' "

A ghastly silence followed. First an angry cloud began to settle darkly upon the faces of the citizenship; after a pause the cloud began to rise, and a tickled expression tried to take its place; tried so hard that it was only kept under with great and painful difficulty; the reporters, the Brixtonites, and other strangers bent their heads down and shielded their faces with their hands, and managed to hold in by main strength and heroic courtesy. At this most inopportune time burst upon the stillness the roar of a solitary voice—Jack Halliday's:

"*That's* got the hall-mark on it!"

Then the house let go, strangers and all. Even Mr. Burgess's gravity broke down presently, then the audience considered itself officially absolved from all restraint, and it made the most of its privilege. It was a good long laugh, and a tempestuously whole-hearted one, but it ceased at last—long enough for Mr. Burgess to try to resume, and for the people to get their eyes partially wiped; then it broke out again; and afterward yet again; then at last Burgess was able to get out these serious words:

"It is useless to try to disguise the fact—we find ourselves in the presence of a matter of grave import. It involves the honor of your town, it strikes at the town's good name. The difference of a single word between the test-remarks offered by Mr. Wilson and Mr. Billson was itself a serious thing, since it indicated that one or the other of these gentlemen had committed a theft—"

The two men were sitting limp, nerveless, crushed; but at these words both were electrified into movement, and started to get up—

"Sit down!" said the Chair, sharply, and they obeyed. "That, as I have said, was a serious thing. And it was—but for only one of them. But the matter has become graver; for the honor of *both* is now in formidable peril. Shall I go even further, and say in inextricable peril? *Both* left out the crucial fifteen words." He paused. During several moments he allowed the pervading stillness to gather and deepen its impressive effects, then added: "There would seem to be but one way whereby this could happen. I ask these gentlemen—Was there *collusion?—agreement?*"

A low murmur sifted through the house; its import was, "He's got them both."

Billson was not used to emergencies; he sat in a helpless collapse. But Wilson was a lawyer. He struggled to his feet, pale and worried, and said:

"I ask the indulgence of the house while I explain this most painful matter. I am sorry to say what I am about to say, since it must inflict irreparable injury upon Mr. Billson, whom I have always esteemed and respected until now, and in whose invulnerability to temptation I entirely believed—as did you all. But for the preservation of my own honor I must speak—and with frankness. I confess with shame—and I now beseech your pardon for it—that I said to the ruined stranger all of the words contained in the test-remark, including the disparaging fifteen. [*Sensation.*] When the late publication was made I recalled them, and I resolved to claim the sack of coin, for by every right I was entitled to it. Now I will ask you to consider this point, and weigh it well: that stranger's gratitude to me that night knew no bounds; he said himself that he could find no words for it that were adequate, and that if he should ever be able he would repay me a thousandfold. Now, then, I ask you this: Could I expect—could I believe —could I even remotely imagine—that, feeling as he did, he would do so ungrateful a thing as to add those quite unnecessary fifteen words to his test?—set a trap for me?— expose me as a slanderer of my own town before my own people assembled in a public hall? It was preposterous; it was impossible. His test would contain only the kindly opening clause of my remark. Of that I had no shadow of doubt. You would have thought as I did. You would not have expected a base betrayal from one whom you had befriended and against whom you had committed no offense. And so, with perfect confidence, perfect trust, I wrote on a piece of paper the opening words—ending with 'Go, and reform,'—and signed it. When I was about to put it in an envelope I was called into my back office, and without thinking I left the paper lying open on my desk." He stopped, turned his head slowly toward Billson, waited a moment, then added: "I ask you to note this: when I returned, a little later, Mr. Billson was retiring by my street door." [*Sensation.*]

In a moment Billson was on his feet and shouting:

"It's a lie! It's an infamous lie!"

*The Chair.* "Be seated, sir! Mr. Wilson has the floor."

Billson's friends pulled him into his seat and quieted him, and Wilson went on:

"Those are the simple facts. My note was now lying in a different place on the table from where I had left it. I noticed that, but attached no importance to it, thinking a draught had blown it there. That Mr. Billson would read a private paper was a thing which could not occur to me; he was an honorable man, and he would be above that. If you will allow me to say it, I think his extra word *'very'* stands explained; it is attributable to a defect of memory. I was the only man in the world who could furnish here any detail of the test-remark—by *honorable* means. I have finished."

There is nothing in the world like a persuasive speech to fuddle the mental apparatus and upset the convictions and debauch the emotions of an audience not practised in the tricks and delusions of oratory. Wilson sat down victorious. The house submerged him in tides of approving applause; friends swarmed to him and shook him by the hand and congratulated him, and Billson was shouted down and not allowed to say a word. The Chair hammered and hammered with its gavel, and kept shouting:

"But let us proceed, gentlemen, let us proceed!"

At last there was a measurable degree of quiet, and the hatter said:

"But what is there to proceed with, sir, but to deliver the money?"

*Voices.* "That's it! That's it! Come forward, Wilson!"

*The Hatter.* "I move three cheers for Mr. Wilson, Symbol of the special virtue which—"

The cheers burst forth before he could finish; and in the midst of them—and in the midst of the clamor of the gavel also—some enthusiasts mounted Wilson on a big friend's shoulder and were going to fetch him in triumph to the platform. The Chair's voice now rose above the noise—

"Order! To your places! You forget that there is still a document to be read." When quiet had been restored he took up the document, and was going to read it, but laid it down again, saying, "I forgot; this is not to be read until all written communications received by me have first been read." He took an envelope out of his pocket, removed its inclosure, glanced at it—seemed astonished—held it out and gazed at it—stared at it.

Twenty or thirty voices cried out:

"What is it? Read it! read it!"

And he did—slowly, and wondering:

" 'The remark which I made to the stranger— [*Voices.* "Hello! how's this?"]—was this: "You are far from being a bad man. [*Voices.* "Great Scott!"] Go, and reform." ' [*Voice.* "Oh, saw my leg off!"] Signed by Mr. Pinkerton, the banker."

The pandemonium of delight which turned itself loose now was of a sort to make the judicious weep. Those whose

withers were unwrung laughed till the tears ran down;
the reporters, in throes of laughter, set down disordered
pot-hooks which would never in the world be decipherable;
and a sleeping dog jumped up, scared out of its wits, and
barked itself crazy at the turmoil. All manner of cries were
scattered through the din: "We're getting rich—*two* Symbols of Incorruptibility!—without counting Billson!"
"*Three!*—count Shadbelly in—we can't have too many!"
"All right—Billson's elected!" "Alas, poor Wilson—victim
of *two* thieves!"

*A Powerful Voice.* "Silence! The Chair's fished up something more out of its pocket."

*Voices.* "Hurrah! Is it something fresh? Read it! read!
read!"

*The Chair* [*reading*]. " 'The remark which I made,' etc.:
"You are far from being a bad man. Go,"' etc. Signed,
'Gregory Yates.'"

*Tornado of Voices.* "Four Symbols!" " 'Rah for Yates!"
"Fish again!"

The house was in a roaring humor now, and ready to
get all the fun out of the occasion that might be in it.
Several Nineteeners, looking pale and distressed, got up
and began to work their way toward the aisles, but a score
of shouts went up:

"The doors, the doors—close the doors; no Incorruptible
shall leave this place! Sit down, everybody!"

The mandate was obeyed.

"Fish again! Read! read!"

The Chair fished again, and once more the familiar
words began to fall from its lips—" 'You are far from
being a bad man.'"

"Name! name! What's his name?"

" 'L. Ingoldsby Sargent.'"

"Five elected! Pile up the Symbols! Go on, go on!"

" 'You are far from being a bad—'"

"Name! name!"

" 'Nicholas Whitworth.'"

"Hooray! hooray! it's a symbolical day!"

Somebody wailed in, and began to sing this rhyme (leaving out "it's") to the lovely "Mikado" tune of "When a
man's afraid, a beautiful maid—"; the audience joined in,
with joy; then, just in time, somebody contributed another
line—

And don't this you forget—

The house roared it out. A third line was at once furnished—

Corruptibles far from Hadleyburg are—

The house roared that one too. As the last note died, Jack Halliday's voice rose high and clear, freighted with a final line—

But the Symbols are here, you bet!

That was sung, with booming enthusiasm. Then the happy house started in at the beginning and sang the four lines through twice, with immense swing and dash, and finished up with a crashing three-times-three and a tiger for "Hadleyburg the Incorruptible and all Symbols of it which we shall find worthy to receive the hall-mark to-night."

Then the shoutings at the Chair began again, all over the place:

"Go on! go on! Read! read some more! Read all you've got!"

"That's it—go on! We are winning eternal celebrity!"

A dozen men got up now and began to protest. They said that this farce was the work of some abandoned joker, and was an insult to the whole community. Without a doubt these signatures were all forgeries—

"Sit down! sit down! Shut up! You are confessing. We'll find *your* names in the lot."

"Mr. Chairman, how many of those envelopes have you got?"

The Chair counted.

"Together with those that have been already examined, there are nineteen."

A storm of derisive applause broke out.

"Perhaps they all contain the secret. I move that you open them all and read every signature that is attached to a note of that sort—and read also the first eight words of the note."

"Second the motion!"

It was put and carried—uproariously. Then poor old Richards got up, and his wife rose and stood at his side. Her head was bent down, so that none might see that she was crying. Her husband gave her his arm, and so supporting her, he began to speak in a quavering voice:

"My friends, you have known us two—Mary and me—all our lives, and I think you have liked us and respected us—"

The Chair interrupted him:

"Allow me. It is quite true—that which you are saying, Mr. Richards: this town *does* know you two; it *does* like you; it *does* respect you; more—it honors you and *loves* you—"

Halliday's voice rang out:

"That's the hall-marked truth, too! If the Chair is right, let the house speak up and say it. Rise! Now, then—hip! hip! hip!—all together!"

The house rose in mass, faced toward the old couple eagerly, filled the air with a snow-storm of waving handkerchiefs, and delivered the cheers with all its affectionate heart.

The Chair then continued:

"What I was going to say is this: We know your good heart, Mr. Richards, but this is not a time for the exercise of charity toward offenders. [*Shouts of "Right! right!"*] I see your generous purpose in your face, but I cannot allow you to plead for these men—"

"But I was going to—"

"Please take your seat, Mr. Richards. We must examine the rest of these notes—simple fairness to the men who have already been exposed requires this. As soon as that has been done—I give you my word for this—you shall be heard."

*Many Voices.* "Right!—the Chair is right—no interruption can be permitted at this stage! Go on!—the names! the names!—according to the terms of the motion!"

The old couple sat reluctantly down, and the husband whispered to the wife, "It is pitifully hard to have to wait; the shame will be greater than ever when they find we were only going to plead for *ourselves*."

Straightway the jollity broke loose again with the reading of the names.

"'You are far from being a bad man—' Signature, 'Robert J. Titmarsh.'"

"'You are far from being a bad man—' Signature, 'Eliphalet Weeks.'"

"'You are far from being a bad man—' Signature, 'Oscar B. Wilder '"

At this point the house lit upon the idea of taking the

eight words out of the Chairman's hands. He was not un-thankful for that. Thenceforward he held up each note in its turn, and waited. The house droned out the eight words in a massed and measured and musical deep volume of sound (with a daringly close resemblance to a well-known church chant) — "'You are f-a-r from being a b-a-a-a-d man.'" Then the Chair said, "Signature, 'Archibald Wil-cox.'" And so on, and so on, name after name, and every-body had an increasingly and gloriously good time except the wretched Nineteen. Now and then, when a particularly shining name was called, the house made the Chair wait while it chanted the whole of the test-remark from the beginning to the closing words, "And go to hell or Hadley-burg—try and make it the for-or-m-e-r!" and in these spe-cial cases they added a grand and agonized and imposing "A-a-a-a-*men!*"

The list dwindled, dwindled, dwindled, poor old Richards keeping tally of the count, wincing when a name resembling his own was pronounced, and waiting in miser-able suspense for the time to come when it would be his humiliating privilege to rise with Mary and finish his plea, which he was intending to word thus: ". . . for until now we have never done any wrong thing, but have gone our humble way unreproached. We are very poor, we are old, and have no chick nor child to help us; we were sorely tempted, and we fell. It was my purpose when I got up before to make confession and beg that my name might not be read out in this public place, for it seemed to us that we could not bear it; but I was prevented. It was just; it was our place to suffer with the rest. It has been hard for us. It is the first time we have ever heard our name fall from any one's lips—sullied. Be merciful—for the sake of the better days; make our shame as light to bear as in your charity you can." At this point in his revery Mary nudged him, perceiving that his mind was absent. The house was chanting, "You are f-a-r," etc.

"Be ready," Mary whispered. "Your name comes now; he has read eighteen."

The chant ended.

"Next! next! next!" came volleying from all over the house.

Burgess put his hand into his pocket. The old couple,

trembling, began to rise. Burgess fumbled a moment, then said,

"I find I have read them all."

Faint with joy and surprise, the couple sank into their seats, and Mary whispered:

"Oh, bless God, we are saved!—he has lost ours—I wouldn't give this for a hundred of those sacks!"

The house burst out with its "Mikado" travesty, and sang it three times with ever-increasing enthusiasm, rising to its feet when it reached for the third time the closing line—

> But the Symbols are here, you bet!

and finishing up with cheers and a tiger for "Hadleyburg purity and our eighteen immortal representatives of it."

Then Wingate, the saddler, got up and proposed cheers "for the cleanest man in town, the one solitary important citizen in it who didn't try to steal that money—Edward Richards."

They were given with great and moving heartiness; then somebody proposed that Richards be elected sole guardian and Symbol of the now Sacred Hadleyburg Tradition, with power and right to stand up and look the whole sarcastic world in the face.

Passed, by acclamation; then they sang the "Mikado" again, and ended it with:

> And there's *one* Symbol left, you bet!

There was a pause; then—

*A Voice.* "Now, then, who's to get the sack?"

*The Tanner (with bitter sarcasm).* "That's easy. The money has to be divided among the eighteen Incorruptibles. They gave the suffering stranger twenty dollars apiece —and that remark—each in his turn—it took twenty-two minutes for the procession to move past. Staked the stranger—total contribution, $360. All they want is just the loan back—and interest—forty thousand dollars altogether."

*Many Voices [derisively].* "That's it! Divvy! divvy! Be kind to the poor—don't keep them waiting!"

*The Chair.* "Order! I now offer the stranger's remaining document. It says: 'If no claimant shall appear [*grand chorus of groans*] I desire that you open the sack and count out the money to the principal citizens of your town, they to take it in trust [*cries of "Oh! Oh! Oh!"*], and use it in such ways as to them shall seem best for the propagation and preservation of your community's noble reputation for incorruptible honesty [*more cries*]—a reputation to which their names and their efforts will add a new and far-reaching luster.' [*Enthusiastic outburst of sarcastic applause.*] That seems to be all. No—here is a postscript:

"'P. S.—CITIZENS OF HADLEYBURG: There *is* no test-remark—nobody made one. [*Great sensation.*] There wasn't any pauper stranger, nor any twenty-dollar contribution, nor any accompanying benediction and compliment—these are all inventions. [*General buzz and hum of astonishment and delight.*] Allow me to tell my story—it will take but a word or two. I passed through your town at a certain time, and received a deep offense which I had not earned. Any other man would have been content to kill one or two of you and call it square, but to me that would have been a trivial revenge, and inadequate; for the dead do not *suffer*. Besides, I could not kill you all—and, anyway, made as I am, even that would not have satisfied me. I wanted to damage every man in the place, and every woman—and not in their bodies or in their estate, but in their vanity—the place where feeble and foolish people are most vulnerable. So I disguised myself and came back and studied you. You were easy game. You had an old and lofty reputation for honesty, and naturally you were proud of it—it was your treasure of treasures, the very apple of your eye. As soon as I found out that you carefully and vigilantly kept yourselves and your children *out of temptation,* I knew how to proceed. Why, you simple creatures, the weakest of all weak things is a virtue which has not been tested in the fire. I laid a plan, and gathered a list of names. My project was to corrupt Hadleyburg the Incorruptible. My idea was to make liars and thieves of nearly half a hundred smirchless men and women who had never in their lives uttered a lie or stolen a penny. I was afraid of Goodson. He was neither born nor reared in Hadleyburg. I was afraid that if I started to operate my scheme by getting my letter laid before you, you would say to yourselves, "Goodson is the only man among us who would give away twenty dollars to a poor devil"—and then you might not bite at my bait. But Heaven took Goodson; then I knew I was safe, and I set my trap and baited it. It may be that I shall not catch all the men to whom I mailed the pretended test secret, but I shall catch the most of them, if I know Hadleyburg nature. [*Voices.* "Right—he got every last one of them."] I believe they will even steal ostensible *gamble*-money, rather than miss, poor, tempted, and mistrained fellows. I am hoping to eternally and everlastingly squelch your vanity and give Hadleyburg a new renown—one that will *stick*—and spread far. If I have succeeded, open the sack and summon the Committee on Propagation and Preservation of the Hadleyburg Reputation.' "

*A Cyclone of Voices.* "Open it! Open it! The Eighteen to the front! Committee on Propagation of the Tradition! Forward—the Incorruptibles!"

The Chair ripped the sack wide, and gathered up a handful of bright, broad, yellow coins, shook them together, then examined them—

"Friends, they are only gilded disks of lead!"

There was a crashing outbreak of delight over this news, and when the noise had subsided, the tanner called out:

"By right of apparent seniority in this business, Mr. Wilson is Chairman of the Committee on Propagation of the Tradition. I suggest that he step forward on behalf of his pals, and receive in trust the money."

*A Hundred Voices.* "Wilson! Wilson! Wilson! Speech! Speech!"

*Wilson* [*in a voice trembling with anger*]. "You will allow me to say, and without apologies for my language, *damn* the money!"

*A Voice.* "Oh, and him a Baptist!"

*A Voice.* "Seventeen Symbols left! Step up, gentlemen, and assume your trust!"

There was a pause—no response.

*The Saddler.* "Mr. Chairman, we've got *one* clean man left, anyway, out of the late aristocracy; and he needs money, and deserves it. I move that you appoint Jack Halliday to get up there and auction off that sack of gilt twenty-dollar pieces, and give the result to the right man—the man whom Hadleyburg delights to honor—Edward Richards."

This was received with great enthusiasm, the dog taking a hand again; the saddler started the bids at a dollar, the Brixton folk and Barnum's representative fought hard for it, the people cheered every jump that the bids made, the excitement climbed moment by moment higher and higher, the bidders got on their mettle and grew steadily more and more daring, more and more determined, the jumps went from a dollar up to five, then to ten, then to twenty, then fifty, then to a hundred, then—

At the beginning of the auction Richards whispered in distress to his wife: "O Mary, can we allow it? It—it—you see, it is an honor-reward, a testimonial to purity of character, and—and—can we allow it? Hadn't I better get up and—O Mary, what ought we to do?—what do you think we—[*Halliday's voice. "Fifteen I'm bid!—fifteen for the sack!—twenty!—ah, thanks!—thirty—thanks again! Thirty, thirty, thirty!—do I hear forty?—forty it is! Keep the ball rolling, gentlemen, keep it rolling!—fifty! thanks, noble Roman! going at fifty, fifty, fifty!—seventy!—ninety!—splendid!—a hundred!—pile it up, pile it up!—hundred and twenty—forty!—just in time!—hundred and fifty!—*TWO *hundred!—superb! Do I hear two h— thanks!—two hundred and fifty!—"*]

"It is another temptation, Edward—I'm all in a tremble—but, oh, we've escaped *one* temptation, and that ought to warn us to— [*"Six did I hear?—thanks!—six-fifty, six-f — *SEVEN *hundred!"*] And yet, Edward, when you think—nobody susp— [*"Eight hundred dollars!—hurrah!—make it nine!—Mr. Parsons, did I hear you say—thanks—nine! —this noble sack of virgin lead going at only nine hundred dollars, gilding and all—come! do I hear—a thousand!—gratefully yours!—did some one say eleven?—a sack which is going to be the most celebrated in the whole Uni—"*] O Edward" (beginning to sob), "we are *so* poor!—but—but—do as you think best—do as you think best."

Edward fell—that is, he sat still; sat with a conscience which was not satisfied, but which was overpowered by circumstances.

Meantime a stranger, who looked like an amateur detective gotten up as an impossible English earl, had been watching the evening's proceedings with manifest interest, and with a contented expression in his face; and he had been privately commenting to himself. He was now soliloquizing somewhat like this: "None of the Eighteen are bidding; that is not satisfactory; I must change that—the dramatic unities require it; they must buy the sack they tried to steal; they must pay a heavy price, too—some of them are rich. And another thing, when I make a mistake in Hadleyburg nature the man that puts that error upon me is entitled to a high honorarium, and some one must pay it. This poor old Richards has brought my judgment to shame; he is an honest man:—I don't understand it, but I acknowledge it. Yes, he saw my deuces *and* with a straight flush, and by rights the pot is his. And it shall be a jackpot, too, if I can manage it. He disappointed me, but let that pass."

He was watching the bidding. At a thousand, the market broke; the prices tumbled swiftly. He waited—and still watched. One competitor dropped out; then another, and another. He put in a bid or two, now. When the bids had sunk to ten dollars, he added a five; some one raised him a three; he waited a moment, then flung in a fifty-dollar jump, and the sack was his—at $1,282. The house broke out in cheers—then stopped; for he was on his feet, and had lifted his hand. He began to speak.

"I desire to say a word, and ask a favor. I am a speculator in rarities, and I have dealings with persons interested in numismatics all over the world. I can make a profit on this purchase, just as it stands; but there is a way, if I can get your approval, whereby I can make every one of these leaden twenty-dollar pieces worth its face in gold, and perhaps more. Grant me that approval, and I will give part of my gains to your Mr. Richards, whose invulnerable probity you have so justly and so cordially recognized tonight; his share shall be ten thousand dollars, and I will hand him the money to-morrow. [*Great applause from the house*. But the "invulnerable probity" made the Richardses blush prettily; however, it went for modesty, and did no harm.] If you will pass my proposition by a good majority —I would like a two-thirds vote—I will regard that as the town's consent, and that is all I ask. Rarities are always helped by any device which will rouse curiosity and compel remark. Now if I may have your permission to stamp upon the faces of each of these ostensible coins the names of the eighteen gentlemen who—"

Nine-tenths of the audience were on their feet in a moment—dog and all—and the proposition was carried with a whirlwind of approving applause and laughter.

They sat down, and all the Symbols except "Dr." Clay

Harkness got up, violently protesting against the proposed outrage, and threatening to—

"I beg you not to threaten me," said the stranger, calmly. "I know my legal rights, and am not accustomed to being frightened at bluster." [*Applause.*] He sat down. "Dr." Harkness saw an opportunity here. He was one of the two very rich men of the place, and Pinkerton was the other. Harkness was proprietor of a mint; that is to say, a popular patent medicine. He was running for the legislature on one ticket, and Pinkerton on the other. It was a close race and a hot one, and getting hotter every day. Both had strong appetites for money; each had bought a great tract of land, with a purpose; there was going to be a new railway, and each wanted to be in the legislature and help locate the route to his own advantage; a single vote might make the decision, and with it two or three fortunes. The stake was large, and Harkness was a daring speculator. He was sitting close to the stranger. He leaned over while one or another of the other Symbols was entertaining the house with protests and appeals, and asked, in a whisper:

"What is your price for the sack?"

"Forty thousand dollars."

"I'll give you twenty."

"No."

"Twenty-five."

"No."

"Say thirty."

"The price is forty thousand dollars; not a penny less."

"All right, I'll give it. I will come to the hotel at ten in the morning. I don't want it known: will see you privately."

"Very good." Then the stranger got up and said to the house:

"I find it late. The speeches of these gentlemen are not without merit, not without interest, not without grace; yet if I may be excused I will take my leave. I thank you for the great favor which you have shown me in granting my petition. I ask the Chair to keep the sack for me until to-morrow, and to hand these three five-hundred-dollar notes to Mr. Richards." They were passed up to the Chair. "At nine I will call for the sack, and at eleven will deliver the rest of the ten thousand to Mr. Richards in person, at his home. Good night."

Then he slipped out, and left the audience making a vast noise, which was composed of a mixture of cheers, the "Mikado" song, dog-disapproval, and the chant, "You are f-a-r from being a b-a-a-d man—a-a-a-a-men!"

## IV.

At home the Richardses had to endure congratulations and compliments until midnight. Then they were left to themselves. They looked a little sad, and they sat silent and thinking. Finally Mary sighed and said,

"Do you think we are to blame, Edward—*much* to blame?" and her eyes wandered to the accusing triplet of big bank-notes lying on the table, where the congratulators had been gloating over them and reverently fingering them. Edward did not answer at once; then he brought out a sigh and said, hesitatingly:

"We—we couldn't help it, Mary. It—well, it was ordered. *All* things are."

Mary glanced up and looked at him steadily, but he didn't return the look. Presently she said:

"I thought congratulations and praises always tasted good. But—it seems to me, now—Edward?"

"Well?"

"Are you going to stay in the bank?"

"N-no."

"Resign?"

"In the morning—by note."

"It does seem best."

Richards bowed his head in his hands and muttered:

"Before, I was not afraid to let oceans of people's money pour through my hands, but—Mary, I am so tired, so tired—"

"We will go to bed."

At nine in the morning the stranger called for the sack and took it to the hotel in a cab. At ten Harkness had a talk with him privately. The stranger asked for and got five checks on a metropolitan bank—drawn to "Bearer" —four for $1,500 each, and one for $34,000. He put one of the former in his pocketbook, and the remainder, representing $38,500, he put in an envelope, and with these he added a note, which he wrote after Harkness was gone. At eleven he called at the Richards house and knocked. Mrs. Richards peeped through the shutters, then went and received the envelope, and the stranger disappeared without a word. She came back flushed and a little unsteady on her legs, and gasped out:

"I am sure I recognized him! Last night it seemed to me that maybe I had seen him somewhere before."

"He is the man that brought the sack here?"

"I am almost sure of it."

"Then he is the ostensible Stephenson, too, and sold every important citizen in this town with his bogus secret. Now if he has sent checks instead of money, we are sold, too, after we thought we had escaped. I was beginning to feel fairly comfortable once more, after my night's rest, but the look of that envelope makes me sick. It isn't fat enough; $8,500 in even the largest bank-notes makes more bulk than that."

"Edward, why do you object to checks?"

"Checks signed by Stephenson! I am resigned to take the $8,500 if it could come in bank-notes—for it does seem that it was so ordered, Mary—but I have never had much courage, and I have not the pluck to try to market a check signed with that disastrous name. It would be a trap. That man tried to catch me; we escaped somehow or other; and now he is trying a new way. If it is checks—"

"Oh, Edward, it is *too* bad!" and she held up the checks and began to cry.

"Put them in the fire! quick! we mustn't be tempted. It is a trick to make the world laugh at *us*, along with the rest, and— Give them to *me*, since you can't do it!" He snatched them and tried to hold his grip till he could get to the stove; but he was human, he was a cashier, and he stopped a moment to make sure of the signature. Then he came near to fainting.

"Fan me, Mary, fan me! They are the same as gold!"

"Oh, how lovely, Edward! Why?"

"Signed by Harkness. What can the mystery of that be, Mary?"

"Edward, do you think—"

"Look here—look at this! Fifteen—fifteen—fifteen—thirty-four. Thirty-eight thousand five hundred! Mary, the sack isn't worth twelve dollars, and Harkness—apparently—has paid about par for it."

"And does it all come to us, do you think—instead of the ten thousand?"

"Why, it looks like it. And the checks are made to 'Bearer,' too."

"Is that good, Edward? What is it for?"

"A hint to collect them at some distant bank, I reckon. Perhaps Harkness doesn't want the matter known. What is that—a note?"

"Yes. It was with the checks."

It was in the "Stephenson" handwriting, but there was no signature. It said:

> "I am a disappointed man. Your honesty is beyond the reach of temptation. I had a different idea about it, but I wronged you in that, and I beg pardon, and do it sincerely. I honor you—and that is sincere too. This town is not worthy to kiss the hem of your garment. Dear sir, I made a square bet with myself that there were nineteen debauchable men in your self-righteous community. I have lost. Take the whole pot, you are entitled to it."

Richards drew a deep sigh, and said:

"It seems written with fire—it burns so. Mary—I am miserable again."

"I, too. Ah, dear, I wish—"

"To think, Mary—he *believes* in me."

"Oh, don't, Edward—I can't bear it."

"If those beautiful words were deserved, Mary—and God knows I believed I deserved them once—I think I could give the forty thousand dollars for them. And I would put that paper away, as representing more than gold and jewels, and keep it always. But now— We could not live in the shadow of its accusing presence, Mary."

He put it in the fire.

A messenger arrived and delivered an envelope.

Richards took from it a note and read it; it was from Burgess.

> "You saved me, in a difficult time. I saved you last night. It was at cost of a lie, but I made the sacrifice freely, and out of a grateful heart. None in this village knows so well as I know how brave and good and noble you are. At bottom you cannot respect me, knowing as you do of that matter of which I am accused, and by the general voice condemned; but I beg that you will at least believe that I am a grateful man; it will help me to bear my burden.
>
> [Signed]                    "BURGESS."

"Saved, once more. And on such terms!" He put the note in the fire. "I—I wish I were dead, Mary, I wish I were out of it all."

"Oh, these are bitter, bitter days, Edward. The stabs, through their very generosity, are so deep—and they come so fast!"

Three days before the election each of two thousand voters suddenly found himself in possession of a prized memento—one of the renowned bogus double-eagles. Around one of its faces was stamped these words: "THE REMARK I MADE TO THE POOR STRANGER WAS—" Around the other face was stamped these: "GO, AND REFORM. [SIGNED] PINKERTON." Thus the entire remaining refuse of the renowned joke was emptied upon a single head, and with calamitous effect. It revived the recent vast laugh and concentrated it upon Pinkerton; and Harkness's election was a walkover.

Within twenty-four hours after the Richardses had received their checks their consciences were quieting down, discouraged; the old couple were learning to reconcile themselves to the sin which they had committed. But they were to learn, now, that a sin takes on new and real terrors when there seems a chance that it is going to be found out. This gives it a fresh and most substantial and important aspect. At church the morning sermon was of the usual pattern; it was the same old things said in the same old way; they had heard them a thousand times and found them innocuous, next to meaningless, and easy to sleep under; but now it was different: the sermon seemed to bristle with accusations; it seemed aimed straight and specially at people who were concealing deadly sins. After church they got away from the mob of congratulators as soon as they could, and hurried homeward, chilled to the bone at they did not know what—vague, shadowy, indefinite fears. And by chance they caught a glimpse of Mr. Burgess as he turned a corner. He paid no attention to their nod of recognition! He hadn't seen it; but they did not know that. What could his conduct mean? It might mean—it might mean—oh, a dozen dreadful things. Was it possible that he knew that Richards could have cleared him of guilt in that bygone time, and had been silently waiting for a chance to even up accounts? At home, in their distress they got to imagining that their servant might have been in

the next room listening when Richards revealed the secret
to his wife that he knew of Burgess's innocence; next,
Richards began to imagine that he had heard the swish of
a gown in there at that time; next, he was sure he *had*
heard it. They would call Sarah in, on a pretext, and
watch her face: if she had been betraying them to Mr.
Burgess, it would show in her manner. They asked her
some questions—questions which were so random and
incoherent and seemingly purposeless that the girl felt sure
that the old people's minds had been affected by their
sudden good fortune; the sharp and watchful gaze which
they bent upon her frightened her, and that completed
the business. She blushed, she became nervous and confused, and to the old people these were plain signs of
guilt—guilt of some fearful sort or other—without doubt
she was a spy and a traitor. When they were alone again
they began to piece many unrelated things together and
get horrible results out of the combination. When things
had got about to the worst, Richards was delivered of a
sudden gasp, and his wife asked:

"Oh, what is it?—what is it?"

"The note—Burgess's note! Its language was sarcastic, I
see it now." He quoted: " 'At bottom you cannot respect
me, *knowing*, as you do, of *that matter* of which I am
accused'—oh, it is perfectly plain, now, God help me! He
knows that I know! You see the ingenuity of the phrasing.
It was a trap—and like a fool, I walked into it. And
Mary—?"

"Oh, it is dreadful—I know what you are going to say
—he didn't return your transcript of the pretended test-
remark."

"No—kept it to destroy us with. Mary, he has exposed
us to some already. I know it—I know it well. I saw it in
a dozen faces after church. Ah, he wouldn't answer our
nod of recognition—*he* knew what he had been doing!"

In the night the doctor was called. The news went
around in the morning that the old couple were rather
seriously ill—prostrated by the exhausting excitement growing out of their great windfall, the congratulations, and the
late hours, the doctor said. The town was sincerely distressed; for these old people were about all it had left to
be proud of, now.

Two days later the news was worse. The old couple were

delirious, and were doing strange things. By witness of the nurses, Richards had exhibited checks—for $8,500? No—for an amazing sum—$38,500! What could be the explanation of this gigantic piece of luck?

The following day the nurses had more news—and wonderful. They had concluded to hide the checks, lest harm come to them; but when they searched they were gone from under the patient's pillow—vanished away. The patient said:

"Let the pillow alone; what do you want?"

"We thought it best that the checks—"

"You will never see them again—they are destroyed. They came from Satan. I saw the hell-brand on them, and I knew they were sent to betray me to sin." Then he fell to gabbling strange and dreadful things which were not clearly understandable, and which the doctor admonished them to keep to themselves.

Richards was right; the checks were never seen again.

A nurse must have talked in her sleep, for within two days the forbidden gabblings were the property of the town; and they were of a surprising sort. They seemed to indicate that Richards had been a claimant for the sack himself, and that Burgess had concealed that fact and then maliciously betrayed it.

Burgess was taxed with this and stoutly denied it. And he said it was not fair to attach weight to the chatter of a sick old man who was out of his mind. Still, suspicion was in the air, and there was much talk.

After a day or two it was reported that Mrs. Richards's delirious deliveries were getting to be duplicates of her husband's. Suspicion flamed up into conviction, now, and the town's pride in the purity of its one undiscredited important citizen began to dim down and flicker toward extinction.

Six days passed, then came more news. The old couple were dying. Richards's mind cleared in his latest hour, and he sent for Burgess. Burgess said:

"Let the room be cleared. I think he wishes to say something in privacy."

"No!" said Richards: "I want witnesses. I want you all to hear my confession, so that I may die a man, and not a dog. I was clean—artificially—like the rest; and like the rest I fell when temptation came. I signed a lie, and claimed the miserable sack. Mr. Burgess remembered that I had done him a service, and in gratitude (and ignorance) he suppressed my claim and saved me. You know the thing that was charged against Burgess years ago. My testimony, and mine alone, could have cleared him, and I was a coward, and left him to suffer disgrace—"

"No—no—Mr. Richards, you—"

"My servant betrayed my secret to him—"

"No one has betrayed anything to me—"

—"and then he did a natural and justifiable thing, he repented of the saving kindness which he had done me, and he *exposed* me—as I deserved—"

"Never!—I make oath—"

"Out of my heart I forgive him."

Burgess's impassioned protestations fell upon deaf ears; the dying man passed away without knowing that once more he had done poor Burgess a wrong. The old wife died that night.

The last of the sacred Nineteen had fallen a prey to the fiendish sack; the town was stripped of the last rag of its ancient glory. Its mourning was not showy, but it was deep.

By act of the Legislature—upon prayer and petition—Hadleyburg was allowed to change its name to (never mind what—I will not give it away), and leave one word out of the motto that for many generations had graced the town's official seal.

It is an honest town once more, and the man will have to rise early that catches it napping again.

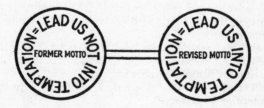

# THE MYSTERIOUS STRANGER

## I.

It was in 1590—winter. Austria was far away from the world, and asleep; it was still the Middle Ages in Austria, and promised to remain so forever. Some even set it away back centuries upon centuries and said that by the mental and spiritual clock it was still the Age of Belief in Austria. But they meant it as a compliment, not a slur, and it was so taken, and we were all proud of it. I remember it well, although I was only a boy; and I remember, too, the pleasure it gave me.

Yes, Austria was far from the world, and asleep, and our village was in the middle of that sleep, being in the middle of Austria. It drowsed in peace in the deep privacy of a hilly and woodsy solitude where news from the world hardly ever came to disturb its dreams, and was infinitely content. At its front flowed the tranquil river, its surface painted with cloud-forms and the reflections of drifting arks and stone-boats; behind it rose the woody steeps to the base of the lofty precipice; from the top of the precipice frowned a vast castle, its long stretch of towers and bastions mailed in vines; beyond the river, a league to the left, was a tumbled expanse of forest-clothed hills cloven by winding gorges where the sun never penetrated; and to the right a precipice overlooked the river, and between it and the hills just spoken of lay a far-reaching plain dotted with little homesteads nested among orchards and shade trees.

The whole region for leagues around was the hereditary property of a prince, whose servants kept the castle always in perfect condition for occupancy, but neither he nor his family came there oftener than once in five years. When they came it was as if the lord of the world had arrived, and had brought all the glories of its kingdoms along; and when they went they left a calm behind which was like the deep sleep which follows an orgy.

Eseldorf was a paradise for us boys. We were not overmuch pestered with schooling. Mainly we were trained to be good Christians; to revere the Virgin, the Church, and the saints above everything. Beyond these matters we were not required to know much; and, in fact, not allowed to. Knowledge was not good for the common people, and could make them discontented with the lot which God had appointed for them, and God would not endure discontentment with His plans. We had two priests. One of them, Father Adolf, was a very zealous and strenuous priest, much considered.

There may have been better priests, in some ways, than Father Adolf, but there was never one in our commune who was held in more solemn and awful respect. This was because he had absolutely no fear of the Devil. He was the only Christian I have ever known of whom that could be truly said. People stood in deep dread of him on that account; for they thought that there must be something supernatural about him, else he could not be so bold and so confident. All men speak in bitter disapproval of the Devil, but they do it reverently, not flippantly; but Father Adolf's way was very different; he called him by every name he could lay his tongue to, and it made everyone shudder that heard him; and often he would even speak of him scornfully and scoffingly; then the people crossed themselves and went quickly out of his presence, fearing that something fearful might happen.

Father Adolf had actually met Satan face to face more than once, and defied him. This was known to be so. Father Adolf said it himself. He never made any secret of it, but spoke it right out. And that he was speaking true there was proof in at least one instance, for on that occasion he quarreled with the enemy, and intrepidly threw his bottle at him; and there, upon the wall of his study, was the ruddy splotch where it struck and broke.

But it was Father Peter, the other priest, that we all loved best and were sorriest for. Some people charged him with talking around in conversation that God was all goodness and would find a way to save all his poor human children. It was a horrible thing to say, but there was never any absolute proof that Father Peter said it; and it was out of character for him to say it, too, for he was always good and gentle and truthful. He wasn't charged with saying it in the pulpit, where all the congregation could hear and testify, but only outside, in talk; and it is easy for enemies to manufacture *that*. Father Peter had an enemy and a very powerful one, the astrologer who lived in a tumbled old tower up the valley, and put in his nights studying the stars. Every one knew he could foretell wars and famines, though that was not so hard, for there was always a war and generally a famine somewhere. But he could also read any man's life through the stars in a big book he had, and find lost property, and every one in the village except Father Peter stood in awe of him. Even Father Adolf, who had defied the Devil, had a wholesome respect for the astrologer when he came through our village wearing his tall, pointed hat and his long, flowing robe with stars on it, carrying his big book, and a staff which was known to have magic power. The bishop himself sometimes listened to the astrologer, it was said, for, besides studying the stars and prophesying, the astrologer made a great show of piety, which would impress the bishop, of course.

But Father Peter took no stock in the astrologer. He denounced him openly as a charlatan—a fraud with no valuable knowledge of any kind, or powers beyond those of an ordinary and rather inferior human being, which naturally made the astrologer hate Father Peter and wish to ruin him. It was the astrologer, as we all believed, who originated the story about Father Peter's shocking remark and carried it to the bishop. It was said that Father Peter had made the remark to his niece, Marget, though Marget denied it and implored the bishop to believe her and spare her old uncle from poverty and disgrace. But the bishop wouldn't listen. He suspended Father Peter indefinitely, though he wouldn't go so far as to excommunicate him on the evidence of only one witness; and now Father Peter had been out a couple of years, and our other priest, Father Adolf, had his flock.

Those had been hard years for the old priest and Marget. They had been favorites, but of course that changed when they came under the shadow of the bishop's frown. Many of their friends fell away entirely, and the rest became cool and distant. Marget was a lovely girl of eighteen when the trouble came, and she had the best head in the village, and the most in it. She taught the harp, and earned all her clothes and pocket money by her own industry. But her scholars fell off one by one now; she was forgotten when there were dances and parties among the youth of the village; the young fellows stopped coming to the house, all except Wilhelm Meidling—and he could have been spared; she and her uncle were sad and forlorn in their neglect and disgrace, and the sunshine was gone out of their lives. Matters went worse and worse, all through the two years. Clothes were wearing out, bread was harder and harder to get. And now, at last, the very end was come. Solomon Isaacs had lent all the money he was willing to put on the house, and gave notice that to-morrow he would foreclose.

## II.

Three of us boys were always together, and had been so from the cradle, being fond of one another from the beginning, and this affection deepened as the years went on—Nikolaus Bauman, son of the principal judge of the local court; Seppi Wohlmeyer, son of the keeper of the principal inn, the "Golden Stag," which had a nice garden, with shade trees reaching down to the riverside, and pleasure boats for hire; and I was the third—Theodor Fischer, son of the church organist, who was also leader of the village musicians, teacher of the violin, composer, tax-collector of the commune, sexton, and in other ways a useful citizen, and respected by all. We knew the hills and the woods as well as the birds knew them; for we were always roaming them when we had leisure—at least, when we were not swimming or boating or fishing, or playing on the ice or sliding down hill.

And we had the run of the castle park, and very few had that. It was because we were pets of the oldest servingman in the castle—Felix Brandt; and often we went there, nights, to hear him talk about old times and strange things, and to smoke with him (he taught us that) and to drink coffee; for he had served in the wars, and was at the siege of Vienna; and there, when the Turks were defeated and driven away, among the captured things were bags of coffee, and the Turkish prisoners explained the character of it and how to make a pleasant drink out of it, and now he always kept coffee by him, to drink himself and also to astonish the ignorant with. When it stormed he kept us all night; and while it thundered and lightened outside he told us about ghosts and horrors of every kind, and of battles and murders and mutilations, and such things, and made it pleasant and cozy inside; and he told these things from his own experience largely. He had seen many ghosts in his time, and witches and enchanters, and once he was lost in a fierce storm at midnight in the mountains, and by the glare of the lightning had seen the Wild Huntsman rage on the blast with his specter dogs chasing after him through the driving cloud-rack. Also he had seen an incubus once, and several times he had seen the great bat that sucks the blood from the necks of people while they are asleep, fanning them softly with its wings and so keeping them drowsy till they die.

He encouraged us not to fear supernatural things, such as ghosts, and said they did no harm, but only wandered about because they were lonely and distressed and wanted kindly notice and compassion; and in time we learned not to be afraid, and even went down with him in the night to the haunted chamber in the dungeons of the castle. The ghost appeared only once, and it went by very dim to the sight and floated noiseless through the air, and then disappeared; and we scarcely trembled, he had taught us so well. He said it came up sometimes in the night and woke him by passing its clammy hand over his face, but it did him no hurt; it only wanted sympathy and notice. But the strangest thing was that he had seen angels—actual angels out of heaven—and had talked with them. They had no wings, and wore clothes, and talked and looked and acted just like any natural person, and you would never know them for angels except for the wonderful things they did which a mortal could not do, and the way they suddenly disappeared while you were talking with them, which was also a thing which no mortal could do. And he said they were pleasant and cheerful, not gloomy and melancholy, like ghosts.

It was after that kind of a talk one May night that we got up next morning and had a good breakfast with him and then went down and crossed the bridge and went away up into the hills on the left to a woody hill-top which was a favorite place of ours, and there we stretched out on the grass in the shade to rest and smoke and talk over these strange things, for they were in our minds yet, and impressing us. But we couldn't smoke, because we had been heedless and left our flint and steel behind.

Soon there came a youth strolling toward us through the trees, and he sat down and began to talk in a friendly way, just as if he knew us. But we did not answer him, for he was a stranger and we were not used to strangers and were shy of them. He had new and good clothes on, and was handsome and had a winning face and a pleasant voice, and was easy and graceful and unembarrassed, not slouchy and awkward and diffident, like the other boys. We wanted to be friendly with him, but didn't know how to begin. Then I thought of the pipe, and wondered if it would be taken as kindly meant if I offered it to him. But I remembered that we had no fire, so I was sorry and disappointed. But he looked up bright and pleased, and said:

"Fire? Oh, that is easy; I will furnish it."

I was so astonished I couldn't speak; for I had not said anything. He took the pipe and blew his breath on it, and the tobacco glowed red, and spirals of blue smoke rose up. We jumped up and were going to run, for that was natural; and we did run a few steps, although he was yearningly pleading for us to stay, and giving us his word that he would not do us any harm, but only wanted to be friends with us and have company. So we stopped and stood, and wanted to go back, being full of curiosity and wonder, but afraid to venture. He went on coaxing, in his soft, persuasive way; and when we saw that the pipe did not blow up and nothing happened, our confidence returned by little and little, and presently our curiosity got to be stronger than our fear, and we ventured back—but slowly, and ready to fly at any alarm.

He was bent on putting us as ease, and he had the right art; one could not remain doubtful and timorous where a person was so earnest and simple and gentle, and talked so alluringly as he did; no, he won us over, and it was not long before we were content and comfortable and chatty, and glad we had found this new friend. When the feeling of constraint was all gone we asked him how he had learned to do that strange thing, and he said he hadn't learned it at all; it came natural to him—like other things—other curious things.

"What ones?"

"Oh, a number; I don't know how many."

"Will you let us see you do them?"

"Do—please!" the others said.

"You won't run away again?"

"No—indeed we won't. Please do. Won't you?"

"Yes, with pleasure; but you musn't forget your promise, you know."

We said we wouldn't, and he went to a puddle and came back with water in a cup which he had made out of a leaf, and blew upon it and threw it out, and it was a lump of ice the shape of the cup. We were astonished and charmed, but not afraid any more; we were very glad to be there, and asked him to go on and do some more things. And he did. He said he would give us any kind of fruit we liked, whether it was in season or not. We all spoke at once:

"Orange!"

"Apple!"

"Grapes!"

"They are in your pockets," he said, and it was true. And they were of the best, too, and we ate them and wished we had more, though none of us said so.

"You will find them where those came from," he said "and everything else your appetites call for; and you need not name the thing you wish; as long as I am with you, you have only to wish and find."

And he said true. There was never anything so wonderful and so interesting. Bread, cakes, sweets, nuts—whatever one wanted, it was there. He ate nothing himself, but sat and chatted, and did one curious thing after another to amuse us. He made a tiny toy squirrel out of clay, and it ran up a tree and sat on a limb overhead and barked down at us. Then he made a dog that was not much larger than a mouse, and it treed the squirrel and danced about the tree, excited and barking, and was as alive as any dog could be. It frightened the squirrel from tree to tree and followed it up until both were out of sight in the forest. He made birds out of clay and set them free, and they flew away, singing.

At last I made bold to ask him to tell us who he was.

"An angel," he said, quite simply, and set another bird free and clapped his hands and made it fly away.

A kind of awe fell upon us when we heard him say that, and we were afraid again; but he said we need not be troubled, there was no occasion for us to be afraid of an angel, and he liked us, anyway. He went on chatting as simply and unaffectedly as ever; and while he talked he made a crowd of little men and women the size of your finger, and they went diligently to work and cleared and leveled off a space a couple of yards square in the grass and began to build a cunning little castle in it, the women mixing the mortar and carrying it up the scaffoldings in pails on their heads, just as our work-women have always done, and the men laying the courses of masonry—five hundred of these toy people swarming briskly about and working diligently and wiping the sweat off their faces as natural as life. In the absorbing interest of watching those five hundred little people make the castle grow step by step and course by course, and take shape and symmetry, that feeling and awe soon passed away and we were quite comfortable and at home again. We asked if we might make some people, and he said yes, and told Seppi to make some cannon for the walls, and told Nikolaus to make some halberdiers, with breastplates and greaves and helmets, and I was to make some cavalry, with horses, and in allotting these tasks he called us by our names, but did not say how he knew them. Then Seppi asked him what his own name was, and he said, tranquilly, "Satan," and held out a chip and caught a little woman on it who was falling from the scaffolding and put her back where she belonged, and said, "She is an idiot to step backward like that and not notice what she is about."

It caught us suddenly, that name did, and our work dropped out of our hands and broke to pieces—a cannon, a halberdier, and a horse. Satan laughed, and asked what was the matter. I said, "Nothing, only it seemed a strange name for an angel." He asked why.

"Because it's—it's—well, it's his name, you know."

"Yes—he is my uncle."

He said it placidly, but it took our breath for a moment and made our hearts beat. He did not seem to notice that, but mended our halberdiers and things with a touch, handing them to us finished, and said "Don't you remember? —he was an angel himself, once."

"Yes—it's true," said Seppi; "I didn't think of that."

"Before the Fall he was blameless."

"Yes," said Nikolaus, "he was without sin."

"It is a good family—ours," said Satan; "there is not a better. He is the only member of it that has ever sinned."

I should not be able to make any one understand how exciting it all was. You know that kind of quiver that trembles around through you when you are seeing something so strange and enchanting and wonderful that it is just a fearful joy to be alive and look at it; and you know how you gaze, and your lips turn dry and your breath comes short, but you wouldn't be anywhere but there, not for the world. I was bursting to ask one question—I had it on my tongue's end and could hardly hold it back—but I was ashamed to ask it; it might be a rudeness. Satan set an ox down that he had been making, and smiled up at me and said:

"It wouldn't be a rudeness and I should forgive it if it was. Have I seen him? Millions of times. From the time that I was a little child a thousand years old I was his second favorite among the nursery angels of our blood and lineage—to use a human phrase—yes, from that time until the Fall, eight thousand years, measured as you count time."

"Eight—thousand!"

"Yes." He turned to Seppi, and went on as if answering something that was in Seppi's mind: "Why, naturally I look like a boy, for that is what I am. With us what you call time is a spacious thing; it takes a long stretch of it to grow an angel to full age." There was a question in my mind, and he turned to me and answered it, "I am sixteen thousand years old—counting as you count." Then he turned to Nikolaus and said: "No, the Fall did not affect me nor the rest of the relationship. It was only he that I was named for who ate of the fruit of the tree and then beguiled the man and the woman with it. We others are still ignorant of sin; we are not able to commit it; we are without blemish, and shall abide in that estate always. We—" Two of the little workmen were quarreling, and in buzzing little bumblebee voices they were cursing and swearing at each other; now came blows and blood; then they locked themselves together in a life-and-death struggle. Satan reached out his hand and crushed the life out of them with his fingers, threw them away, wiped the red from his fingers on his handkerchief, and went on talking where he had left off: "We cannot do wrong; neither have we any disposition to do it, for we do not know what it is."

It seemed a strange speech, in the circumstances, but we barely noticed that, we were so shocked and grieved at the wanton murder he had committed—for murder it was, that was its true name, and it was without palliation or excuse, for the men had not wronged him in any way. It made us miserable, for we loved him, and had thought him so noble and so beautiful and gracious, and had honestly believed he was an angel; and to have him do this cruel thing—ah, it lowered him so, and we had had such pride in him. He went right on talking, just as if nothing had happened, telling about his travels, and the interesting things he had seen in the big worlds of our solar systems and of other solar systems far away in the remotenesses of space, and about the customs of the immortals that inhabit them, somehow fascinating us, enchanting us, charming us in spite of the pitiful scene that was now under our eyes, for the wives of the little dead men had found the crushed and shapeless bodies and were crying over them, and sobbing and lamenting, and a priest was kneeling there with his hands crossed upon his breast, praying; and crowds and crowds of pitying friends were massed about them, reverently uncovered, with their bare heads bowed, and many with the tears running down—a scene which Satan paid no attention to until the small noise of the weeping and praying began to annoy him, then he reached out and took the heavy board seat out of our swing and brought it down and mashed all those people into the earth just as if they had been flies, and went on talking just the same.

An angel, and kill a priest! An angel who did not know how to do wrong, and yet destroys in cold blood hundreds of helpless poor men and women who had never done him any harm! It made us sick to see that awful deed, and to think that none of those poor creatures was prepared except the priest, for none of them had ever heard a mass or seen a church. And we were witnesses; we had seen these murders done and it was our duty to tell, and let the law take its course.

But he went on talking right along, and worked his enchantments upon us again with that fatal music of his voice. He made us forget everything; we could only listen to him, and love him, and be his slaves, to do with us as he would. He made us drunk with the joy of being with him, and of looking into the heaven of his eyes, and of feeling the ecstasy that thrilled along our veins from the touch of his hand.

# III.

The Stranger had seen everything, he had been everywhere, he knew everything, and he forgot nothing. What another must study, he learned at a glance; there were no difficulties for him. And he made things live before you when he told about them. He saw the world made; he saw Adam created; he saw Samson surge against the pillars and bring the temple down in ruins about him; he saw Cæsar's death; he told of the daily life in heaven; he had seen the damned writhing in the red waves of hell; and he made us see all these things, and it was as if we were on the spot and looking at them with our own eyes. And we felt them, too, but there was no sign that they were anything to him beyond mere entertainments. Those visions of hell, those poor babes and women and girls and lads and men shrieking and supplicating in anguish—why, we could hardly bear it but he was as bland about it as if it had been so many imitation rats in an artificial fire.

And always when he was talking about men and women here on the earth and their doings—even their grandest and sublimest—we were secretly ashamed, for his manner showed that to him they and their doings were of paltry poor consequence; often you would think he was talking about flies, if you didn't know. Once he even said, in so many words, that our people down here were quite interesting to him, notwithstanding they were so dull and ignorant and trivial and conceited, and so diseased and rickety, and such a shabby, poor, worthless lot all around. He said it in a quite matter-of-course way and without bitterness, just as a person might talk about bricks or manure or any other thing that was of no consequence and hadn't feelings. I could see he meant no offense, but in my thoughts I set it down as not very good manners.

"Manners!" he said. "Why, it is merely the truth, and truth is good manners; manners are a fiction. The castle is done. Do you like it?"

Any one would have been obliged to like it. It was lovely to look at, it was so shapely and fine, and so cunningly perfect in all its particulars, even to the little flags waving from the turrets. Satan said we must put the artillery in place now, and station the halberdiers and display the cavalry. Our men and horses were a spectacle to see, they were so little like what they were intended for; for, of course, we had no art in making such things. Satan said they were the worst he had seen; and when he touched them and made them alive, it was just ridiculous the way they acted, on account of their legs not being of uniform lengths. They reeled and sprawled around us as if they were drunk, and endangered everybody's lives around them, and finally fell over and lay helpless and kicking. It made us all laugh, though it was a shameful thing to see. The guns were charged with dirt, to fire a salute, but they were so crooked and so badly made that all burst when they went off, and killed some of the gunners and crippled the others. Satan said we would have a storm now, and an earthquake, if we liked, but we must stand off a piece, out of danger. We wanted to call the people away, too, but he said never mind them; they were of no consequence, and we could make more, some time or other, if we needed them.

A small storm-cloud began to settle down black over the castle, and the miniature lightning and thunder began to play, and the ground to quiver, and the wind to pipe and wheeze, and the rain to fall, and all the people flocked into the castle for shelter. The cloud settled down blacker and blacker, and one could see the castle only dimly through it; the lightning blazed out flash upon flash and pierced the castle and set it on fire, and the flames shone out red and fierce through the cloud, and the people came flying out, shrieking, but Satan brushed them back, paying no attention to our begging and crying and imploring; and in the midst of the howling of the wind and the volleying of the thunder the magazine blew up, the earthquake rent the ground wide, and the castle's wreck and ruin tumbled into the chasm, which swallowed it from sight, and closed upon it, with all that innocent life, not one of the five hundred poor creatures escaping. Our hearts were broken; we could not keep from crying.

"Don't cry," Satan said; "they were of no value."

"But they are gone to hell!"

"Oh, it is no matter; we can make plenty more."

It was of no use to try to move him; evidently he was wholly without feeling, and could not understand. He was full of bubbling spirits, and as gay as if this were a wedding instead of a fiendish massacre. And he was bent on making us feel as he did, and of course his magic accomplished his desire. It was no trouble to him; he did whatever he pleased with us. In a little while we were dancing on that grave, and he was playing to us on a strange, sweet instrument which he took out of his pocket; and the music—but there is no music like that, unless perhaps in heaven, and that was where he brought it from, he said. It made one mad, for pleasure; and we could not take our eyes from him, and the looks that went out of our eyes came from our hearts, and their dumb speech was worship. He brought the dance from heaven, too, and the bliss of paradise was in it.

Presently he said he must go away on an errand. But we could not bear the thought of it, and clung to him, and pleaded with him to stay; and that pleased him, and he said so, and said he would not go yet, but would wait a little while and we would sit down and talk a few minutes longer; and he told us Satan was only his real name, and he was to be known by it to us alone, but he had chosen another one to be called by in the presence of others; just a common one, such as people have—Philip Traum.

It sounded so odd and mean for such a being! But it was his decision, and we said nothing; his decision was sufficient.

We had seen wonders this day; and my thoughts began to run on the pleasure it would be to tell them when I got home, but he noticed those thoughts, and said:

"No, all these matters are a secret among us four. I do not mind your trying to tell them, if you like, but I will protect your tongues, and nothing of the secret will escape from them."

It was a disappointment, but it couldn't be helped, and it cost us a sigh or two. We talked pleasantly along, and he was always reading our thoughts and responding to them, and it seemed to me that this was the most wonderful of all the things he did, but he interrupted my musings and said:

"No, it would be wonderful for you, but it is not wonderful for me. I am not limited like you. I am not subject to human conditions. I can measure and understand your human weaknesses, for I have studied them; but I have

none of them. My flesh is not real, although it would seem
firm to your touch; my clothes are not real; I am a spirit.
Father Peter is coming." We looked around, but did not
see any one. "He is not in sight yet, but you will see him
presently."

"Do you know him, Satan?"

"No."

"Won't you talk with him when he comes? He is not
ignorant and dull, like us, and he would so like to talk
with you. Will you?"

"Another time, yes, but not now. I must go on my errand after a little. There he is now; you can see him. Sit
still, and don't say anything."

We looked up and saw Father Peter approaching through
the chestnuts. We three were sitting together in the grass,
and Satan sat in front of us in the path. Father Peter came
slowly along with his head down, thinking, and stopped
within a couple of yards of us and took off his hat and got
out his silk handkerchief, and stood there mopping his
face and looking as if he were going to speak to us, but
he didn't. Presently he muttered, "I can't think what
brought me here; it seems as if I were in my study a minute
ago—but I suppose I have been dreaming along for an
hour and have come all this stretch without noticing; for
I am not myself in these troubled days." Then he went
mumbling along to himself and walked straight through
Satan, just as if nothing were there. It made us catch our
breath to see it. We had the impulse to cry out, the way
you nearly always do when a startling thing happens, but
something mysteriously restrained us and we remained
quiet, only breathing fast. Then the trees hid Father Peter
after a little, and Satan said:

"It is as I told you—I am only a spirit."

"Yes, one perceives it now," said Nikolaus, "but we are
not spirits. It is plain he did not see you, but were we invisible, too? He looked at us, but he didn't seem to see us."

"No, none of us was visible to him, for I wished it so."

It seemed almost too good to be true, that we were actually seeing these romantic and wonderful things, and
that it was not a dream. And there he sat, looking just like
anybody—so natural and simple and charming, and chatting along again the same as ever, and—well, words cannot make you understand what we felt. It was an ecstasy;

and an ecstasy is a thing that will not go into words; it feels like music, and one cannot tell about music so that another person can get the feeling of it. He was back in the old ages once more now, and making them live before us. He had seen so much, so much! It was just a wonder to look at him and try to think how it must seem to have such experience behind one.

But it made you seem sorrowfully trivial, and the creature of a day, and such a short and paltry day, too. And he didn't say anything to raise up your drooping pride—no, not a word. He always spoke of men in the same old indifferent way—just as one speaks of bricks and manure-piles and such things; you could see that they were of no consequence to him, one way or the other. He didn't mean to hurt us, you could see that; just as we don't mean to insult a brick when we disparage it; a brick's emotions are nothing to us; it never occurs to us to think whether it has any or not.

Once when he was bunching the most illustrious kings and conquerors and poets and prophets and pirates and beggars together—just a brick-pile—I was shamed into putting in a word for man, and asked him why he made so much difference between men and himself. He had to struggle with that a moment; he didn't seem to understand how I could ask such a strange question. Then he said:

"The difference between man and me? The difference between a mortal and an immortal? between a cloud and a spirit?" He picked up a wood-louse that was creeping along a piece of bark: "What is the difference between Cæsar and this?"

I said, "One cannot compare things which by their nature and by the interval between them are not comparable."

"You have answered your own question," he said. "I will expand it. Man is made of dirt—I saw him made. I am not made of dirt. Man is a museum of diseases, a home of impurities; he comes to-day and is gone to-morrow; he begins as dirt and departs as stench; I am of the aristocracy of the Imperishables. And man has the *Moral Sense*. You understand? He has the *Moral Sense*. That would seem to be difference enough between us, all by itself."

He stopped there, as if that settled the matter. I was sorry, for at that time I had but a dim idea of what the Moral Sense was. I merely knew that we were proud of having it, and when he talked like that about it, it wounded me, and I felt as a girl feels who thinks her dearest finery is being admired and then overhears strangers making fun of it. For a while we were all silent, and I, for one, was depressed. Then Satan began to chat again, and soon he was sparkling along in such a cheerful and vivacious vein that my spirits rose once more. He told some very cunning things that put us in a gale of laughter; and when he was telling about the time that Samson tied the torches to the foxes' tails and set them loose in the Philistines' corn, and Samson sitting on the fence slapping his thighs and laughing, with the tears running down his cheeks, and lost his balance and fell off the fence, the memory of that picture got him to laughing, too, and we did have a most lovely and jolly time. By and by he said:

"I am going on my errand now."

"Don't!" we all said. "Don't go; stay with us. You won't come back."

"Yes, I will; I give you my word."

"When? To-night? Say when."

"It won't be long. You will see."

"We like you."

"And I you. And as a proof of it I will show you something fine to see. Usually when I go I merely vanish; but now I will dissolve myself and let you see me do it."

He stood up, and it was quickly finished. He thinned away and thinned away until he was a soap-bubble, except that he kept his shape. You could see the bushes through him as clearly as you see things through a soap-bubble, and all over him played and flashed the delicate iridescent colors of the bubble, and along with them was that thing shaped like a window-sash which you always see on the globe of the bubble. You have seen a bubble strike the carpet and lightly bound along two or three times before it bursts. He did that. He sprang—touched the grass—bounded—floated along—touched again—and so on, and presently exploded—puff! and in his place was vacancy.

It was a strange and beautiful thing to see. We did not say anything, but sat wondering and dreaming and blinking; and finally Seppi roused up and said, mournfully sighing:

"I suppose none of it has happened."

Nikolaus sighed and said about the same.

I was miserable to hear them say it, for it was the same cold fear that was in my own mind. Then we saw poor old Father Peter wandering along back, with his head bent down, searching the ground. When he was pretty close to us he looked up and saw us, and said, "How long have you been here, boys?"

"A little while, Father."

"Then it is since I came by, and maybe you can help me. Did you come up by the path?"

"Yes, Father."

"That is good. I came the same way. I have lost my wallet. There wasn't much in it, but a very little is much to me, for it was all I had. I suppose you haven't seen anything of it?"

"No, Father, but we will help you hunt."

"It is what I was going to ask you. Why, here it is!"

We hadn't noticed it; yet there it lay, right where Satan stood when he began to melt—if he did melt and it wasn't a delusion. Father Peter picked it up and looked very much surprised.

"It is mine," he said, "but not the contents. This is fat; mine was flat; mine was light; this is heavy." He opened it; it was stuffed as full as it could hold with gold coins. He let us gaze our fill; and of course we did gaze, for we had never seen so much money at one time before. All our mouths came open to say "Satan did it!" but nothing came out. There it was, you see—we couldn't tell what Satan didn't want told; he had said so himself.

"Boys, did you do this?"

It made us laugh. And it made him laugh, too, as soon as he thought what a foolish question it was.

"Who has been here?"

Our mouths came open to answer, but stood so for a moment, because we couldn't say "Nobody," for it wouldn't be true, and the right word didn't seem to come; then I thought of the right one, and said it:

"Not a human being."

"That is so," said the others, and let their mouths go shut.

"It is not so," said Father Peter, and looked at us very severely. "I came by here a while ago, and there was no one here, but that is nothing; some one has been here since. I don't mean to say that the person didn't pass here before you came, and I don't mean to say you saw him, but some one did pass, that I know. On your honor—you saw no one?"

"Not a human being."

"That is sufficient; I know you are telling me the truth."

He began to count the money on the path, we on our knees eagerly helping to stack it in little piles.

"It's eleven hundred ducats odd!" he said. "Oh dear! if it were only mine—and I need it so!" and his voice broke and his lips quivered.

"It is yours, sir!" we all cried out at once, "every heller!"

"No—it isn't mine. Only four ducats are mine; the rest . . . !" He fell to dreaming, poor old soul, and caressing some of the coins in his hands, and forgot where he was, sitting there on his heels with his old gray head bare; it was pitiful to see. "No," he said, waking up, "it isn't mine. I can't account for it. I think some enemy . . . it must be a trap."

Nikolaus said: "Father Peter, with the exception of the astrologer you haven't a real enemy in the village—nor Marget, either. And not even a half-enemy that's rich enough to chance eleven hundred ducats to do you a mean turn. I'll ask you if that's so or not?"

He couldn't get around that argument, and it cheered him up. "But it isn't mine, you see—it isn't mine, in any case."

He said it in a wistful way, like a person that wouldn't be sorry, but glad, if anybody would contradict him.

"It is yours, Father Peter, and we are witness to it. Aren't we, boys?"

"Yes, we are—and we'll stand by it, too."

"Bless your hearts, you do almost persuade me; you do, indeed. If I had only a hundred-odd ducats of it! The house is mortgaged for it, and we've no home for our heads if we don't pay to-morrow. And that four ducats is all we've got in the—"

"It's yours, every bit of it, and you've got to take it—

we are bail that it's all right. Aren't we, Theodor? Aren't we, Seppi?"

We two said yes, and Nikolaus stuffed the money back into the shabby old wallet and made the owner take it. So he said he would use two hundred of it, for his house was good enough security for that, and would put the rest at interest till the rightful owner came for it; and on our side we must sign a paper showing how he got the money —a paper to show to the villagers as proof that he had not got out of his troubles dishonestly.

## IV.

It made immense talk next day, when Father Peter paid Solomon Isaacs in gold and left the rest of the money with him at interest. Also, there was a pleasant change; many people called at the house to congratulate him, and a number of cool old friends became kind and friendly again; and, to top all, Marget was invited to a party.

And there was no mystery; Father Peter told the whole circumstance just as it happened, and said he could not account for it, only it was the plain hand of Providence, so far as he could see.

One or two shook their heads and said privately it looked more like the hand of Satan; and really that seemed a surprisingly good guess for ignorant people like that. Some came slyly buzzing around and tried to coax us boys to come out and "tell the truth;" and promised they wouldn't ever tell, but only wanted to know for their own satisfaction, because the whole thing was so curious. They even wanted to buy the secret, and pay money for it; and if we could have invented something that would answer—but we couldn't; we hadn't the ingenuity, so we had to let the chance go by, and it was a pity.

We carried that secret around without any trouble, but the other one, the big one, the splendid one, burned the very vitals of us, it was so hot to get out and we so hot to let it out and astonish people with it. But we had to keep it in; in fact, it kept itself in. Satan said it would, and it did. We went off every day and got to ourselves in the woods so that we could talk about Satan, and really that was the only subject we thought of or cared anything about; and day and night we watched for him and hoped he would come, and we got more and more impatient all the time. We hadn't any interest in the other boys any more, and wouldn't take part in their games and enterprises. They seemed so tame, after Satan; and their doings so trifling and commonplace after his adventures in antiquity and the constellations, and his miracles and meltings and explosions, and all that.

During the first day we were in a state of anxiety on account of one thing, and we kept going to Father Peter's house on one pretext or another to keep track of it. That was the gold coin; we were afraid it would crumble and turn to dust, like fairy money. If it did— But it didn't. At the end of the day no complaint had been made about it, so after that we were satisfied that it was real gold, and dropped the anxiety out of our minds.

There was a question which we wanted to ask Father Peter, and finally we went there the second evening, a little diffidently, after drawing straws, and I asked it as casually as I could, though it did not sound as casual as I wanted, because I didn't know how:

"What is the Moral Sense, sir?"

He looked down, surprised, over his great spectacles, and said, "Why, it is the faculty which enables us to distinguish good from evil."

It threw some light, but not a glare, and I was a little disappointed, also to some degree embarrassed. He was waiting for me to go on, so in default of anything else to say, I asked, "Is it valuable?"

"Valuable? Heavens! lad, it is the one thing that lifts man above the beasts that perish and makes him heir to immortality!"

This did not remind me of anything further to say, so I got out, with the other boys, and we went away with that indefinite sense you have often had of being filled but not fatted. They wanted me to explain, but I was tired.

We passed out through the parlor, and there was Marget at the spinnet teaching Marie Lueger. So one of the deserting pupils was back; and an influential one, too; the others would follow. Marget jumped up and ran and thanked us again, with tears in her eyes—this was the third time—for saving her and her uncle from being turned into the street, and we told her again we hadn't done it; but that was her way, she never could be grateful enough for anything a person did for her; so we let her have her say. And as we passed through the garden, there was Wilhelm Meidling sitting there waiting, for it was getting toward the edge of the evening, and he would be asking Marget to take a walk along the river with him when she was done with the lesson. He was a young lawyer, and succeeding fairly well and working his way along, little by little. He was very fond of Marget, and she of him. He had not deserted along with the others, but had stood his ground all through. His faithfulness was not lost on Marget and her uncle. He hadn't so very much talent, but he was handsome and good, and these are a kind of talents themselves and help along. He asked us how the lesson was getting along, and we told him it was about done. And maybe it was so; we didn't know anything about it, but we judged it would please him, and it did, and didn't cost us anything.

## V.

On the fourth day comes the astrologer from his crumbling old tower up the valley, where he had heard the news, I reckon. He had a private talk with us, and we told him what we could, for we were mightily in dread of him. He sat there studying and studying awhile to himself; then he asked:

"How many ducats did you say?"

"Eleven hundred and seven, sir."

Then he said, as if he were talking to himself: "It is ver-y singular. Yes . . . very strange. A curious coincidence." Then he began to ask questions, and went over the whole ground from the beginning, we answering. By and by he said: "Eleven hundred and six ducats. It is a large sum."

"Seven," said Seppi, correcting him.

"Oh seven, was it? Of course a ducat more or less isn't of consequence, but you said eleven hundred and six before."

It would not have been safe for us to say he was mistaken, but he knew he was. Nikolaus said, "We ask pardon for the mistake, but we meant to say seven."

"Oh, it is no matter, lad; it was merely that I noticed the discrepancy. It is several days, and you cannot be expected to remember precisely. One is apt to be inexact when there is no particular circumstance to impress the count upon the memory."

"But there was one, sir," said Seppi, eagerly.

"What was it, my son?" asked the astrologer, indifferently.

"First, we all counted the piles of coin, each in turn, and all made it the same—eleven hundred and six. But I had slipped one out, for fun, when the count began, and now I slipped it back and said, 'I think there is a mistake—there are eleven hundred and seven; let us count again.' We did, and of course I was right. They were astonished; then I told how it came about."

The astrologer asked us if this was so, and we said it was.

"That settles it," he said. "I know the thief now. Lads, the money was stolen."

Then he went away, leaving us very much troubled, and wondering what he could mean. In about an hour we found out; for by that time it was all over the village that Father Peter had been arrested for stealing a great sum of money from the astrologer. Everybody's tongue was loose and going. Many said it was not in Father Peter's character and must be a mistake; but the others shook their heads and said misery and want could drive a suffering man to almost anything. About one detail there were no differences; all agreed that Father Peter's account of how the money came into his hands was just about unbelievable—it had such an impossible look. They said it might have come into the astrologer's hands in some such way, but into Father Peter's, never! Our characters began to suffer now. We were Father Peter's only witnesses; how much did he probably pay us to back up his fantastic tale? People talked that kind of talk to us pretty freely and frankly, and were full of scoffings when we begged them to believe really we had told only the truth. Our parents were harder on us than any one else. Our fathers said we were disgracing our families, and they commanded us to purge ourselves of our lie, and there was no limit to their anger when we continued to say we had spoken true. Our mothers cried over us and begged us to give back our bribe and get back our honest names and save our families from shame, and come out and honorably confess. And at last we were so worried and harassed that we tried to tell the whole thing, Satan and all—but no, it wouldn't come out. We were hoping and longing all the time that Satan would come and help us out of our trouble, but there was no sign of him.

Within an hour after the astrologer's talk with us, Father Peter was in prison and the money sealed up and in the hands of the officers of the law. The money was in a bag, and Solomon Isaacs said he had not touched it since he had counted it; his oath was taken that it was the same money, and that the amount was eleven hundred and seven ducats. Father Peter claimed trial by the ecclesiastical court, but our other priest, Father Adolf, said an ecclesiastical court hadn't jurisdiction over a suspended priest. The bishop upheld him. That settled it; the case would go to trial in the civil court. The court would not sit for some time to come. Wilhelm Meidling would be Father Peter's lawyer and do the best he could, of course, but he told us privately that a weak case on his side and all the power and prejudice on the other made the outlook bad.

So Marget's new happiness died a quick death. No friends came to condole with her, and none were expected; an unsigned note withdrew her invitation to the party. There would be no scholars to take lessons. How could she support herself? She could remain in the house, for the mortgage was paid off, though the government and not poor Solomon Isaacs had the mortgage-money in its grip for the present. Old Ursula, who was cook, chambermaid, housekeeper, laundress, and everything else for Father Peter, and had been Marget's nurse in earlier years, said God would provide. But she said that from habit, for she was a good Christian. She meant to help in the providing, to make sure, if she could find a way.

We boys wanted to go and see Marget and show friendliness for her, but our parents were afraid of offending the community and wouldn't let us. The astrologer was going around inflaming everybody against Father Peter, and saying he was an abandoned thief and had stolen eleven hundred and seven gold ducats from him. He said he knew he was a thief from that fact, for it was exactly the sum he had lost and which Father Peter pretended he had "found."

In the afternoon of the fourth day after the catastrophe old Ursula appeared at our house and asked for some washing to do, and begged my mother to keep this secret, to save Marget's pride, who would stop this project if she found it out, yet Marget had not enough to eat and was growing weak. Ursula was growing weak herself, and showed it; and she ate of the food that was offered her like a starving person, but could not be persuaded to carry any home, for Marget would not eat charity food. She took some clothes down to the stream to wash them, but we saw from the window that handling the bat was too much for her strength; so she was called back and a trifle of money offered her, which she was afraid to take lest Marget should suspect; then she took it, saying she would explain that she found it in the road. To keep it from being a lie and damning her soul, she got me to drop it while she watched; then she went along by there and found it, and exclaimed with surprise and joy, and picked it up and went her way. Like the rest of the village, she could tell every-day lies fast enough and without taking any precautions against fire and brimstone on their account; but this was a new kind of lie, and it had a dangerous look because she hadn't had any practice in it. After a week's practice it wouldn't have given her any trouble. It is the way we are made.

I was in trouble, for how would Marget live? Ursula could not find a coin in the road every day—perhaps not even a second one. And I was ashamed, too, for not having been near Marget, and she so in need of friends: but that was my parents' fault, not mine, and I couldn't help it.

I was walking along the path, feeling very downhearted, when a most cheery and tingling freshening-up sensation went rippling through me, and I was too glad for any words, for I knew by that sign that Satan was by. I had noticed it before. Next moment he was alongside of me and I was telling him all my trouble and what had been happening to Marget and her uncle. While we were talking we turned a curve and saw old Ursula resting in the shade of a tree, and she had a lean stray kitten in her lap and was petting it. I asked her where she got it, and she said it came out of the woods and followed her; and she said it probably hadn't any mother or any friends and she was going to take it home and take care of it. Satan said:

"I understand you are very poor. Why do you want to add another mouth to feed? Why don't you give it to some rich person?"

Ursula bridled at this and said: "Perhaps you would like to have it. You must be rich, with your fine clothes and quality airs." Then she sniffed and said: "Give it to the rich

—the idea! The rich don't care for anybody but themselves; it's only the poor that have feeling for the poor, and help them. The poor and God. God will provide for this kitten."

"What makes you think so?"

Ursula's eyes snapped with anger. "Because I know it!" she said. "Not a sparrow falls to the ground without His seeing it."

"But is falls, just the same. What good is seeing it fall?"

Old Ursula's jaws worked, but she could not get any word out for the moment, she was so horrified. When she got her tongue she stormed out, "Go about your business, you puppy, or I will take a stick to you!"

I could not speak, I was so scared. I knew that with his notions about the human race Satan would consider it a matter of no consequence to strike her dead, there being "plenty more;" but my tongue stood still, I could give her no warning. But nothing happened; Satan remained tranquil—tranquil and indifferent. I suppose he could not be insulted by Ursula any more than the king could be insulted by a tumble-bug. The old woman jumped to her feet when she made her remark, and did it as briskly as a young girl. It had been many years since she had done the like of that. That was Satan's influence; he was a fresh breeze to the weak and the sick, wherever he came. His presence affected even the lean kitten, and it skipped to the ground and began to chase a leaf. This surprised Ursula, and she stood looking at the creature and nodding her head wonderingly, her anger quite forgotten.

"What's come over it?" she said. "Awhile ago it could hardly walk."

"You have not seen a kitten of that breed before," said Satan.

Ursula was not proposing to be friendly with the mocking stranger, and she gave him an ungentle look and retorted: "Who asked you to come here and pester me, I'd like to know? and what do you know about what I've seen and what I haven't seen?"

"You haven't seen a kitten with the hair-spines on its tongue pointing to the front, have you?"

"No—nor you, either."

"Well, examine this one and see."

Ursula was become pretty spry, but the kitten was spryer,

and she could not catch it, and had to give it up. Then Satan said:

"Give it a name, and maybe it will come."

Ursula tried several names, but the kitten was not interested.

"Call it Agnes. Try that."

The creature answered to the name and came. Ursula examined its tongue. "Upon my word, it's true!" she said. "I have not seen this kind of a cat before. Is it yours?"

"No."

"Then how did you know its name so pat?"

"Because all cats of that breed are named Agnes; they will not answer to any other."

Ursula was impressed. "It is the most wonderful thing!" Then a shadow of trouble came into her face, for her superstitions were aroused, and she reluctantly put the creature down, saying: "I suppose I must let it go; I am not afraid—no, not exactly that, though the priest—well, I've heard people—indeed, many people . . . And, besides, it is quite well now and can take care of itself." She sighed, and turned to go, murmuring: "It is such a pretty one, too, and would be such company—and the house is so sad and lonesome these troubled days . . . Miss Marget so mournful and just a shadow, and the old master shut up in jail."

"It seems a pity not to keep it," said Satan.

Ursula turned quickly—just as if she were hoping some one would encourage her.

"Why?" she asked, wistfully.

"Because this breed brings luck."

"Does it? Is it true? Young man, do you know it to be true? How does it bring luck?"

"Well, it brings money, anyway."

Ursula looked disappointed. "Money? A cat bring money? The idea! You could never sell it here; people do not buy cats here; one can't even give them away." She turned to go.

"I don't mean sell it. I mean have an income from it. This kind is called the Lucky Cat. Its owner finds four silver groschen in his pocket every morning."

I saw the indignation rising in the old woman's face. She was insulted. This boy was making fun of her. That

was her thought. She thrust her hands into her pockets
and straightened up to give him a piece of her mind. Her
temper was all up, and hot. Her mouth came open and let
out three words of a bitter sentence, . . . then it fell
silent, and the anger in her face turned to surprise or wonder or fear, or something, and she slowly brought out her
hands from her pockets and opened them and held them
so. In one was my piece of money, in the other lay four
silver groschen. She gazed a little while, perhaps to see if
the groschen would vanish away; then she said, fervently:

"It's true—it's true—and I'm ashamed and beg forgiveness, O dear master and benefactor!" And she ran to Satan
and kissed his hand, over and over again, according to the
Austrian custom.

In her heart she probably believed it was a witch-cat and
an agent of the Devil; but no matter, it was all the more
certain to be able to keep its contract and furnish a daily
good living for the family, for in matters of finance even
the piousest of our peasants would have more confidence
in an arrangement with the Devil than with an archangel.
Ursula started homeward, with Agnes in her arms, and I
said I wished I had her privilege of seeing Marget.

Then I caught my breath, for we were there. There in
the parlor, and Marget standing looking at us, astonished.
She was feeble and pale, but I knew that those conditions
would not last in Satan's atmosphere, and it turned out so.
I introduced Satan—that is, Philip Traum—and we sat
down and talked. There was no constraint. We were simple
folk, in our village, and when a stranger was a pleasant
person we were soon friends. Marget wondered how we got
in without her hearing us. Traum said the door was open,
and we walked in and waited until she should turn around
and greet us. This was not true; no door was open; we entered through the walls or the roof or down the chimney, or
somehow; but no matter, what Satan wished a person to
believe, the person was sure to believe, and so Marget was
quite satisfied with that explanation. And then the main
part of her mind was on Traum, anyway; she couldn't
keep her eyes off him, he was so beautiful. That gratified
me, and made me proud. I hoped he would show off some,
but he didn't. He seemed only interested in being friendly
and telling lies. He said he was an orphan. That made
Marget pity him. The water came into her eyes. He said he

had never known his mamma; she passed away while he was a young thing; and said his papa was in shattered health, and had no property to speak of—in fact, none of any earthly value—but he had an uncle in business down in the tropics, and he was very well off and had a monopoly, and it was from this uncle that he drew his support. The very mention of a kind uncle was enough to remind Marget of her own, and her eyes filled again. She said she hoped their two uncles would meet, some day. It made me shudder. Philip said he hoped so, too; and that made me shudder again.

"Maybe they will," said Marget. "Does your uncle travel much?"

"Oh yes, he goes all about; he has business everywhere."

And so they went on chatting, and poor Marget forgot her sorrow for one little while, anyway. It was probably the only really bright and cheery hour she had known lately. I saw she liked Philip, and I knew she would. And when he told her he was studying for the ministry I could see that she liked him better than ever. And then, when he promised to get her admitted to the jail so that she could see her uncle, that was the capstone. He said he would give the guards a little present, and she must always go in the evening after dark, and say nothing, "but just show this paper and pass in, and show it again when you come out"—and he scribbled some queer marks on the paper and gave it to her, and she was ever so thankful, and right away was in a fever for the sun to go down; for in that old, cruel time prisoners were not allowed to see their friends, and sometimes they spent years in the jails without ever seeing a friendly face. I judged that the marks on the paper were an enchantment, and that the guards would not know what they were doing, nor have any memory of it afterward; and that was indeed the way of it. Ursula put her head in at the door now and said:

"Supper's ready, miss." Then she saw us and looked frightened, and motioned me to come to her, which I did, and she asked if we had told about the cat. I said no, and she was relieved, and said please don't; for if Miss Marget knew, she would think it was an unholy cat and would send for a priest and have its gifts all purified out of it, and then there wouldn't be any more dividends. So I said we wouldn't tell, and she was satisfied. Then I was beginning to say good-by to Marget, but Satan interrupted and said, ever so politely—well, I don't remember just the words, but anyway he as good as invited himself to supper, and me, too. Of course Marget was miserably embarrassed, for she had no reason to suppose there would be half enough for a sick bird. Ursula heard him, and she came straight into the room, not a bit pleased. At first she was astonished to see Marget looking so fresh and rosy, and said so; then she spoke up in her native tongue, which was Bohemian, and said—as I learned afterward—"Send him away, Miss Marget; there's not victuals enough."

Before Marget could speak, Satan had the word, and was talking back to Ursula in her own language—which was a surprise to her, and for her mistress, too. He said, "Didn't I see you down the road awhile ago?"

"Yes, sir."

"Ah, that pleases me; I see you remember me." He stepped to her and whispered: "I told you it is a Lucky Cat. Don't be troubled; it will provide."

That sponged the slate of Ursula's feelings clean of its anxieties, and a deep, financial joy shone in her eyes. The cat's value was augmenting. It was getting full time for Marget to take some sort of notice of Satan's invitation, and she did it in the best way, the honest way that was natural to her. She said she had little to offer, but that we were welcome if we would share it with her.

We had supper in the kitchen, and Ursula waited at table. A small fish was in the frying-pan, crisp and brown and tempting, and one could see that Marget was not expecting such respectable food as this. Ursula brought it, and Marget divided it between Satan and me, declining to take any of it herself; and was beginning to say she did not care for fish to-day, but she did not finish the remark. It was because she noticed that another fish had appeared in the pan. She looked surprised, but did not say anything. She probably meant to inquire of Ursula about this later. There were other surprises: flesh and game and wines and fruits—things which had been strangers in that house lately; but Marget made no exclamations, and now even looked unsurprised, which was Satan's influence, of course. Satan talked right along, and was entertaining, and made the time pass pleasantly and cheerfully; and although he told a good many lies, it was no harm in him, for he was only an angel and did not know any better. They do not know right from wrong; I knew this, because I remembered what he had said about it. He got on the good side of Ursula. He praised her to Marget, confidentially, but speaking just loud enough for Ursula to hear. He said she was a fine woman, and he hoped some day to bring her and his uncle together. Very soon Ursula was mincing and simpering around in a ridiculous girly way, and smoothing out her gown and prinking at herself like a foolish old hen, and all the time pretending she was not hearing what Satan was saying. I was ashamed, for it showed us to be what Satan considered us, a silly race and trivial. Satan said his uncle entertained a great deal, and to have a clever woman presiding over the festivities would double the attractions of the place.

"But your uncle is a gentleman, isn't he?" asked Marget.

"Yes," said Satan indifferently; "some even call him a Prince, out of compliment, but he is not bigoted; to him personal merit is everything, rank nothing."

My hand was hanging down by my chair; Agnes came along and licked it; by this act a secret was revealed. I started to say, "It is all a mistake; this is just a common, ordinary cat; the hair-needles on her tongue point inward, not outward." But the words did not come, because they couldn't. Satan smiled upon me, and I understood.

When it was dark Marget took food and wine and fruit, in a basket, and hurried away to the jail, and Satan and I walked toward my home. I was thinking to myself that I should like to see what the inside of the jail was like; Satan overheard the thought, and the next moment we were in the jail. We were in the torture-chamber, Satan said. The rack was there, and the other instruments, and there was a smoky lantern or two hanging on the walls and helping to make the place look dim and dreadful. There were people there—and executioners—but as they took no notice of us, it meant that we were invisible. A young man lay bound, and Satan said he was suspected of being a heretic, and the executioners were about to inquire into it. They asked the man to confess to the charge, and he said he could not, for it was not true. Then they drove splinter after splinter under his nails, and he shrieked with the pain. Satan was not disturbed, but I could not endure it, and had to be whisked out of there. I was faint and sick, but the fresh air revived me, and we walked toward my home. I said it was a brutal thing.

"No, it was a human thing. You should not insult the brutes by such a misuse of that word; they have not deserved it," and he went on talking like that. "It is like your paltry race—always lying, always claiming virtues which it hasn't got, always denying them to the higher animals, which alone possess them. No brute ever does a cruel thing —that is the monopoly of those with the Moral Sense. When a brute inflicts pain he does it innocently; it is not wrong; for him there is no such thing as wrong. And he does not inflict pain for the pleasure of inflicting it—only man does that. Inspired by that mongrel Moral Sense of his! A sense whose function is to distinguish between right and wrong, with liberty to choose which of them he will do. Now what advantage can he get out of that? He is always choosing, and in nine cases out of ten he prefers the wrong. There shouldn't be any wrong; and without the Moral Sense there couldn't be any. And yet he is such an unreasoning creature that he is not able to perceive that the Moral Sense degrades him to the bottom layer of animated beings and is a shameful possession. Are you feeling better? Let me show you something."

## VI.

In a moment we were in a French village. We walked through a great factory of some sort, where men and women and little children were toiling in heat and dirt and a fog of dust; and they were clothed in rags, and drooped at their work, for they were worn and half starved, and weak and drowsy. Satan said:

"It is some more Moral Sense. The proprietors are rich, and very holy; but the wage they pay to these poor brothers and sisters of theirs is only enough to keep them from dropping dead with hunger. The work-hours are fourteen per day, winter and summer—from six in the morning till eight at night—little children and all. And they walk to and from the pigsties which they inhabit—four miles each way, through mud and slush, rain, snow, sleet, and storm, daily, year in and year out. They get four hours of sleep.

They kennel together, three families in a room, in un-imaginable filth and stench; and disease comes, and they die off like flies. Have they committed a crime, these mangy things? No. What have they done, that they are punished so? Nothing at all, except getting themselves born into your foolish race. You have seen how they treat a misdoer there in the jail; now you see how they treat the innocent and the worthy. Is your race logical? Are these ill-smelling innocents better off than that heretic? Indeed, no; his pun-ishment is trivial compared with theirs. They broke him on the wheel and smashed him to rags and pulp after we left, and he is dead now, and free of your precious race; but these poor slaves here—why, they have been dying for years, and some of them will not escape from life for years to come. It is the Moral Sense which teaches the factory proprietors the difference between right and wrong—you perceive the result. They think themselves better than dogs. Ah, you are such an illogical, unreasoning race! And paltry —oh, unspeakably!"

Then he dropped all seriousness and just overstrained himself making fun of us, and deriding our pride in our warlike deeds, our great heroes, our imperishable fames, our mighty kings, our ancient aristocracies, our venerable history—and laughed and laughed till it was enough to make a person sick to hear him; and finally he sobered a little and said, "But, after all, it is not all ridiculous; there is a sort of pathos about it when one remembers how few are your days, how childish your pomps, and what shadows you are!"

Presently all things vanished suddenly from my sight, and I knew what it meant. The next moment we were walking along in our village; and down toward the river I saw the twinkling lights of the Golden Stag. Then in the dark I heard a joyful cry:

"He's come again!"

It was Seppi Wohlmeyer. He had felt his blood leap and his spirits rise in a way that could mean only one thing, and he knew Satan was near, although it was too dark to see him. He came to us, and we walked along together, and Seppi poured out his gladness like water. It was as if he were a lover and had found his sweetheart who had been lost. Seppi was a smart and animated boy, and had enthusiasm and expression, and was a contrast to Nikolaus and me. He was full of the last new mystery, now—the disappearance of Hans Oppert, the village loafer. People were beginning to be curious about it, he said. He did not say anxious—curious was the right word, and strong enough. No one had seen Hans for a couple of days.

"Not since he did that brutal thing, you know," he said.

"What brutal thing?" It was Satan that asked.

"Well, he is always clubbing his dog, which is a good dog, and his only friend, and is faithful, and loves him, and does no one any harm; and two days ago he was at it again, just for nothing—just for pleasure—and the dog was howling and begging, and Theodor and I begged, too, but he threatened us, and struck the dog again with all his might and knocked one of his eyes out, and he said to us, 'There, I hope you are satisfied now; that's what you have got for him by your damned meddling'—and he laughed, the heartless brute." Seppi's voice trembled with pity and anger. I guessed what Satan would say, and he said it.

"There is that misused word again—that shabby slander. Brutes do not act like that, but only men."

"Well, it was inhuman, anyway."

"No, it wasn't, Seppi; it was human—quite distinctly human. It is not pleasant to hear you libel the higher animals by attributing to them dispositions which they are free from, and which are found nowhere but in the human heart. None of the higher animals is tainted with the disease called the Moral Sense. Purify your language, Seppi; drop those lying phrases out of it."

He spoke pretty sternly—for him—and I was sorry I hadn't warned Seppi to be more particular about the word he used. I knew how he was feeling. He would not want to offend Satan; he would rather offend all his kin. There was an uncomfortable silence, but relief soon came, for that poor dog came along now, with his eye hanging down, and went straight to Satan, and began to moan and mutter brokenly, and Satan began to answer in the same way, and it was plain that they were talking together in the dog language. We all sat down in the grass, in the moonlight, for the clouds were breaking away now, and Satan took the dog's head in his lap and put the eye back in its place, and the dog was comfortable, and he wagged his tail and licked Satan's hand, and looked thankful and said the

same; I knew he was saying it, though I did not understand the words. Then the two talked together a bit, and
Satan said:

"He says his master was drunk."

"Yes, he was," said we.

"And an hour later he fell over the precipice there beyond the Cliff Pasture."

"We know the place; it is three miles from here."

"And the dog has been often to the village, begging
people to go there, but he was only driven away and not
listened to."

We remembered it, but hadn't understood what he
wanted.

"He only wanted help for the man who had misused
him, and he thought only of that, and has had no food nor
sought any. He has watched by his master two nights.
What do you think of your race? Is heaven reserved for it,
and this dog ruled out, as your teachers tell you? Can your
race add anything to this dog's stock of morals and mag-
nanimities?" He spoke to the creature, who jumped up,
eager and happy, and apparently ready for orders and impatient to execute them. "Get some men; go with the dog
—he will show you that carrion; and take a priest along to
arrange about insurance, for death is near."

With the last word he vanished, to our sorrow and
disappointment. We got the men and Father Adolf, and
we saw the man die. Nobody cared but the dog; he mourned
and grieved, and licked the dead face, and could not be
comforted. We buried him where he was, and without a
coffin, for he had no money, and no friend but the dog.
If we had been an hour earlier the priest would have been
in time to send that poor creature to heaven, but now he
was gone down into the awful fires, to burn forever. It
seemed such a pity that in a world where so many people
have difficulty to put in their time, one little hour could
not have been spared for this poor creature who needed it
so much, and to whom it would have made the difference
between eternal joy and eternal pain. It gave an appalling
idea of the value of an hour, and I thought I could never
waste one again without remorse and terror. Seppi was
depressed and grieved, and said it must be so much better
to be a dog and not run such awful risks. We took this
one home with us and kept him for our own. Seppi had a

very good thought as we were walking along, and it cheered
us up and made us feel much better. He said the dog had
forgiven the man that had wronged him so, and maybe
God would accept that absolution.

There was a very dull week, now, for Satan did not
come, nothing much was going on, and we boys could not
venture to go and see Marget, because the nights were
moonlit and our parents might find us out if we tried. But
we came across Ursula a couple of times taking a walk in
the meadows beyond the river to air the cat, and we learned
from her that things were going well. She had natty new
clothes on and bore a prosperous look. The four groschen
a day were arriving without a break, but were not being
spent for food and wine and such things—the cat attended
to all that.

Marget was enduring her forsakenness and isolation
fairly well, all things considered, and was cheerful, by help
of Wilhelm Meidling. She spent an hour or two every
night in the jail with her uncle, and had fattened him up
with the cat's contributions. But she was curious to know
more about Philip Traum, and hoped I would bring him
again. Ursula was curious about him herself, and asked
a good many questions about his uncle. It made the
boys laugh, for I had told them the nonsense Satan had
been stuffing her with. She got no satisfaction out of us, our
tongues being tied.

Ursula gave us a small item of information: money being plenty now, she had taken on a servant to help about
the house and run errands. She tried to tell it in a commonplace, matter-of-course way, but she was so set up by
it and so vain of it that her pride in it leaked out pretty
plainly. It was beautiful to see her veiled delight in this
grandeur, poor old thing, but when we heard the name of
the servant we wondered if she had been altogether wise;
for although we were young, and often thoughtless, we
had fairly good perception on some matters. This boy was
Gottfried Narr, a dull, good creature, with no harm in
him and nothing against him personally; still, he was under a cloud, and properly so, for it had not been six
months since a social blight had mildewed the family—
his grandmother had been burned as a witch. When that
kind of a malady is in the blood it does not always come
out with just one burning. Just now was not a good time

for Ursula and Marget to be having dealings with a member of such a family, for the witch-terror had risen higher during the past year than it had ever reached in the memory of the oldest villagers. The mere mention of a witch was almost enough to frighten us out of our wits. This was natural enough, because of late years there were more kinds of witches than there used to be; in old times it had been only old women, but of late years they were of all ages—even children of eight and nine; it was getting so that anybody might turn out to be a familiar of the Devil —age and sex hadn't anything to do with it. In our little region we had tried to extirpate the witches, but the more of them we burned the more of the breed rose up in their places.

Once, in a school for girls only ten miles away, the teachers found that the back of one of the girls was all red and inflamed, and they were greatly frightened, believing it to be the Devil's marks. The girl was scared, and begged them not to denounce her, and said it was only fleas; but of course it would not do to let the matter rest there. All the girls were examined, and eleven out of the fifty were badly marked, the rest less so. A commission was appointed, but the eleven only cried for their mothers and would not confess. Then they were shut up, each by herself, in the dark, and put on black bread and water for ten days and nights; and by that time they were haggard and wild, and their eyes were dry and they did not cry any more, but only sat and mumbled, and would not take the food. Then one of them confessed, and said they had often ridden through the air on broomsticks to the witches' Sabbath, and in a bleak place high up in the mountains had danced and drunk and caroused with several hundred other witches and the Evil One, and all had conducted themselves in a scandalous way and had reviled the priests and blasphemed God. That is what she said—not in narrative form, for she was not able to remember any of the details without having them called to her mind one after the other; but the commission did that, for they knew just what questions to ask, they being all written down for the use of witch-commissioners two centuries before. They asked, "Did you do so and so?" and she always said yes, and looked weary and tired, and took no interest in it. And so when the other ten heard that this one confessed, they confessed, too, and

answered yes to the questions. Then they were burned at
the stake all together, which was just and right; and everybody went from all the countryside to see it. I went, too;
but when I saw that one of them was a bonny, sweet girl I
used to play with, and looked so pitiful there chained to
the stake, and her mother crying over her and devouring
her with kisses and clinging around her neck, and saying,
"Oh, my God! oh, my God!" it was too dreadful, and I
went away.

It was bitter cold weather when Gottfried's grandmother
was burned. It was charged that she had cured bad head-
aches by kneading the person's head and neck with her
fingers—as she said—but really by the Devil's help, as
everybody knew. They were going to examine her, but she
stopped them, and confessed straight off that her power was
from the Devil. So they appointed to burn her next morning, early, in our market-square. The officer who was to
prepare the fire was there first, and prepared it. She was
there next—brought by the constables, who left her and
went to fetch another witch. Her family did not come with
her. They might be reviled, maybe stoned, if the people
were excited. I came, and gave her an apple. She was
squatting at the fire, warming herself and waiting; and
her old lips and hands were blue with the cold. A stranger
came next. He was a traveler, passing through; and he
spoke to her gently, and, seeing nobody but me there to
hear, said he was sorry for her. And he asked if what she
confessed was true, and she said no. He looked surprised
and still more sorry then, and asked her:

"Then why did you confess?"

"I am old and very poor," she said, "and I work for my
living. There was no way but to confess. If I hadn't they
might have set me free. That would ruin me, for no one
would forget that I had been suspected of being a witch,
and so I would get no more work, and wherever I went
they would set the dogs on me. In a little while I would
starve. The fire is best; it is soon over. You have been
good to me, you two, and I thank you."

She snuggled closer to the fire, and put out her hands to
warm them, the snow-flakes descending soft and still on her
old gray head and making it white and whiter. The crowd
was gathering now, and an egg came flying and struck her

in the eye, and broke and ran down her face. There was a laugh at that.

I told Satan all about the eleven girls and the old woman, once, but it did not affect him. He only said it was the human race, and what the human race did was of no consequence. And he said he had seen it made; and it was not made of clay; it was made of mud—part of it was, anyway. I knew what he meant by that—the Moral Sense. He saw the thought in my head, and it tickled him and made him laugh. Then he called a bullock out of a pasture and petted it and talked with it, and said:

"There—he wouldn't drive children mad with hunger and fright and loneliness, and then burn them for confessing to things invented for them which had never happened. And neither would he break the hearts of innocent, poor old women and make them afraid to trust themselves among their own race; and he would not insult them in their death-agony. For he is not besmirched with the Moral Sense, but is as the angels are, and knows no wrong, and never does it."

Lovely as he was, Satan could be cruelly offensive when he chose; and he always chose when the human race was brought to his attention. He always turned up his nose at it, and never had a kind word for it.

Well, as I was saying, we boys doubted if it was a good time for Ursula to be hiring a member of the Narr family. We were right. When the people found it out they were naturally indignant. And, moreover, since Marget and Ursula hadn't enough to eat themselves, where was the money coming from to feed another mouth? That is what they wanted to know; and in order to find out they stopped avoiding Gottfried and began to seek his society and have sociable conversations with him. He was pleased—not thinking any harm and not seeing the trap—and so he talked innocently along, and was no discreeter than a cow.

"Money!" he said; "they've got plenty of it. They pay me two groschen a week, besides my keep. And they live on the fat of the land, I can tell you; the prince himself can't beat their table."

This astonishing statement was conveyed by the astrologer to Father Adolf on a Sunday morning when he was returning from mass. He was deeply moved, and said:

"This must be looked into."

He said there must be witchcraft at the bottom of it, and told the villagers to resume relations with Marget and Ursula in a private and unostentatious way, and keep both eyes open. They were told to keep their own counsel, and not rouse the suspicions of the household. The villagers were at first a bit reluctant to enter such a dreadful place, but the priest said they would be under his protection while there, and no harm could come to them, particularly if they carried a trifle of holy water along and kept their beads and crosses handy. This satisfied them and made them willing to go; envy and malice made the baser sort even eager to go.

And so poor Marget began to have company again, and was as pleased as a cat. She was like 'most anybody else—just human, and happy in her prosperities and not averse from showing them off a little; and she was humanly grateful to have the warm shoulder turned to her and be smiled upon by her friends and the village again; for of all the hard things to bear, to be cut by your neighbors and left in contemptuous solitude is maybe the hardest.

The bars were down, and we could all go there now, and we did—our parents and all—day after day. The cat began to strain herself. She provided the top of everything for those companies, and in abundance—among them many a dish and many a wine which they had not tasted before and which they had not even heard of except at second-hand from the prince's servants. And the tableware was much above ordinary, too.

Marget was troubled at times, and pursued Ursula with questions to an uncomfortable degree; but Ursula stood her ground and stuck to it that it was Providence, and said no word about the cat. Marget knew that nothing was impossible to Providence, but she could not help having doubts that this effort was from there, though she was afraid to say so, lest disaster come of it. Witchcraft occurred to her, but she put the thought aside, for this was before Gottfried joined the household, and she knew Ursula was pious and a bitter hater of witches. By the time Gottfried arrived Providence was established, unshakably intrenched, and getting all the gratitude. The cat made no murmur, but went on composedly improving in style and prodigality by experience.

In any community, big or little, there is always a fair proportion of people who are not malicious or unkind by nature, and who never do unkind things except when they are overmastered by fear, or when their self-interest is greatly in danger, or some such matter as that. Eseldorf had its proportion of such people, and ordinarily their good and gentle influence was felt, but these were not ordinary times—on account of the witch-dread—and so we did not seem to have any gentle and compassionate hearts left, to speak of. Every person was frightened at the unaccountable state of things at Marget's house, not doubting that witchcraft was at the bottom of it, and fright frenzied their reason. Naturally there were some who pitied Marget and Ursula for the danger that was gathering about them, but naturally they did not say so; it would not have been safe. So the others had it all their own way, and there was none to advise the ignorant girl and the foolish woman and warn them to modify their doings. We boys wanted to warn them, but we backed down when it came to the pinch, being afraid. We found that we were not manly enough nor brave enough to do a generous action when there was a chance that it could get us into trouble. Neither of us confessed this poor spirit to the others, but did as other people would have done—dropped the subject and talked about something else. And I knew we all felt mean, eating and drinking Marget's fine things along with those companies of spies, and petting her and complimenting her with the rest, and seeing with self-reproach how foolishly happy she was, and never saying a word to put her on her guard. And, indeed, she was happy, and as proud as a princess, and so grateful to have friends again. And all the time these people were watching with all their eyes and reporting all they saw to Father Adolf.

But he couldn't make head or tail of the situation. There must be an enchanter somewhere on the premises, but who was it? Marget was not seen to do any jugglery, nor was Ursula, nor yet Gottfried; and still the wines and dainties never ran short, and a guest could not call for a thing and not get it. To produce these effects was usual enough with witches and enchanters—that part of it was not new; but to do it without any incantations, or even any rumblings or earthquakes or lightnings or apparitions—that was new, novel, wholly irregular. There was nothing in the books

like this. Enchanted things were always unreal. Gold
turned to dirt in an unenchanted atmosphere, food withered away and vanished. But this test failed in the present
case. The spies brought samples: Father Adolf prayed over
them, exorcised them, but it did no good; they remained
sound and real, they yielded to natural decay only, and
took the usual time to do it.

Father Adolf was not merely puzzled, he was also exasperated; for these evidences very nearly convinced him—
privately—that there was no witchcraft in the matter. It
did not wholly convince him, for this could be a new kind
of witchcraft. There was a way to find out as to this: if this
prodigal abundance of provender was not brought in from
the outside, but produced on the premises, there was witchcraft, sure.

## VII.

Marget announced a party, and invited forty people;
the date for it was seven days away. This was a fine opportunity. Marget's house stood by itself, and it could be
easily watched. All the week it was watched night and day.
Marget's household went out and in as usual, but they carried nothing in their hands, and neither they nor others
brought anything to the house. This was ascertained. Evidently rations for forty people were not being fetched. If
they were furnished any sustenance it would have to be
made on the premises. It was true that Marget went out
with a basket every evening, but the spies ascertained that
she always brought it back empty.

The guests arrived at noon and filled the place. Father
Adolf followed; also, after a little, the astrologer, without
invitation. The spies had informed him that neither at
the back nor the front had any parcels been brought in.
He entered, and found the eating and drinking going on
finely, and everything progressing in a lively and festive
way. He glanced around and perceived that many of the
cooked delicacies and all of the native and foreign fruits
were of a perishable character, and he also recognized that
these were fresh and perfect. No apparitions, no incantations, no thunder. That settled it. This was witchcraft.
And not only that, but of a new kind—a kind never
dreamed of before. It was a prodigious power, an illustrious

power; he resolved to discover its secret. The announcement of it would resound throughout the world, penetrate to the remotest lands, paralyze all the nations with amazement—and carry his name with it, and make him renowned forever. It was a wonderful piece of luck, a splendid piece of luck; the glory of it made him dizzy.

All the house made room for him; Marget politely seated him; Ursula ordered Gottfried to bring a special table for him. Then she decked it and furnished it, and asked for his orders.

"Bring me what you will," he said.

The two servants brought supplies from the pantry, together with white wine and red—a bottle of each. The astrologer, who very likely had never seen such delicacies before, poured out a beaker of red wine, drank it off, poured another, then began to eat with a grand appetite.

I was not expecting Satan, for it was more than a week since I had seen or heard of him, but now he came in—I knew it by the feel, though people were in the way and I could not see him. I heard him apologizing for intruding; and he was going away, but Marget urged him to stay, and he thanked her and stayed. She brought him along, introducing him to the girls, and to Meidling, and to some of the elders; and there was quite a rustle of whispers: "It's the young stranger we hear so much about and can't get sight of, he is away so much." "Dear, dear, but he is beautiful—what is his name?" "Philip Traum." "Ah, it fits him!" (You see, "Traum" is German for "Dream.") "What does he do?" "Studying for the ministry, they say." "His face is his fortune—he'll be a cardinal some day." "Where is his home?" "Away down somewhere in the tropics, they say—has a rich uncle down there." And so on. He made his way at once; everybody was anxious to know him and talk with him. Everybody noticed how cool and fresh it was, all of a sudden, and wondered at it, for they could see that the sun was beating down the same as before, outside, and the sky was clear of clouds, but no one guessed the reason, of course.

The astrologer had drunk his second beaker; he poured out a third. He set the bottle down, and by accident overturned it. He seized it before much was spilled, and held it up to the light, saying, "What a pity—it is royal wine."

Then his face lighted with joy or triumph, or something, and he said, "Quick! Bring a bowl."

It was brought—a four-quart one. He took up that two-pint bottle and began to pour; went on pouring, the red liquor gurgling and gushing into the white bowl and rising higher and higher up its sides, everybody staring and holding their breath—and presently the bowl was full to the brim.

"Look at the bottle," he said, holding it up; "it is full yet!" I glanced at Satan, and in that moment he vanished. Then Father Adolf rose up, flushed and excited, crossed himself, and began to thunder in his great voice, "This house is bewitched and accursed!" People began to cry and shriek and crowd toward the door. "I summon this detected household to—"

His words were cut off short. His face became red, then purple, but he could not utter another sound. Then I saw Satan, a transparent film, melt into the astrologer's body; then the astrologer put up his hand, and apparently in his own voice said, "Wait—remain where you are." All stopped where they stood. "Bring a funnel!" Ursula brought it, trembling and scared, and he stuck it in the bottle and took up the great bowl and began to pour the wine back, the people gazing and dazed with astonishment, for they knew the bottle was already full before he began. He emptied the whole of the bowl into the bottle, then smiled out over the room, chuckled, and said, indifferently: "It is nothing—anybody can do it! With my powers I can even do much more."

A frightened cry burst out everywhere. "Oh, my God, he is possessed!" and there was a tumultuous rush for the door which swiftly emptied the house of all who did not belong in it except us boys and Meidling. We boys knew the secret, and would have told it if we could, but we couldn't. We were very thankful to Satan for furnishing that good help at the needful time.

Marget was pale, and crying; Meidling looked kind of petrified; Ursula the same; but Gottfried was the worst—he couldn't stand, he was so weak and scared. For he was of a witch family, you know, and it would be bad for him to be suspected. Agnes came loafing in, looking pious and unaware, and wanted to rub up against Ursula and be petted, but Ursula was afraid of her and shrank away from her, but pretending she was not meaning any incivility, for she knew very well it wouldn't answer to have strained relations with that kind of a cat. But we boys took Agnes and petted her, for Satan would not have befriended her if he had not had a good opinion of her, and that was indorsement enough for us. He seemed to trust anything that hadn't the Moral Sense.

Outside, the guests, panic-stricken, scattered in every direction and fled in a pitiable state of terror; and such a tumult as they made with their running and sobbing and shrieking and shouting that soon all the village came flocking from their houses to see what had happened, and they thronged the street and shouldered and jostled one another in excitement and fright; and then Father Adolf appeared, and they fell apart in two walls like the cloven Red Sea, and presently down this lane the astrologer came striding and mumbling, and where he passed the lanes surged back in packed masses, and fell silent with awe, and their eyes stared and their breasts heaved, and several women fainted; and when he was gone by the crowd swarmed together and followed him at a distance, talking excitedly and asking questions and finding out the facts. Finding out the facts and passing them on to others, with improvements—improvements which soon enlarged the bowl of wine to a barrel, and made the one bottle hold it all and yet remain empty to the last.

When the astrologer reached the market-square he went straight to a juggler, fantastically dressed, who was keeping three brass balls in the air, and took them from him and faced around upon the approaching crowd and said: "This poor clown is ignorant of his art. Come forward and see an expert perform."

So saying, he tossed the balls up one after another and set them whirling in a slender bright oval in the air, and added another, then another and another, and so on—no one seeing whence he got them—adding, adding, adding, the oval lengthening all the time, his hands moving so swiftly that they were just a web or a blur and not distinguishable as hands; and such as counted said there were now a hundred balls in the air. The spinning great oval reached up twenty feet in the air and was a shining and glinting and wonderful sight. Then he folded his arms and told the balls to go on spinning without his help—and they did it. After a couple of minutes he said, "There, that will do," and the oval broke and came crashing down, and the balls scattered abroad and rolled every whither. And wherever one of them came the people fell back in dread, and no one would touch it. It made him laugh, and he scoffed at the people and called them cowards and old women. Then he turned and saw the tight-rope, and said foolish people were daily wasting their money to see a clumsy and ignorant varlet degrade that beautiful art; now they should see the work of a master. With that he made a spring into the air and lit firm on his feet on the rope. Then he hopped the whole length of it back and forth on one foot, with his hands clasped over his eyes; and next he began to throw somersaults, both backward and forward, and threw twenty-seven.

The people murmured, for the astrologer was old, and always before had been halting of movement and at times even lame, but he was nimble enough now and went on with his antics in the liveliest manner. Finally he sprang lightly down and walked away, and passed up the road and around the corner and disappeared. Then that great, pale, silent, solid crowd drew a deep breath and looked into one another's faces as if they said: "Was it real? Did you see it, or was it only I—and I was dreaming?" Then they broke into a low murmur of talking, and fell apart in couples, and moved toward their homes, still talking in that awed way, with faces close together and laying a hand on an arm and making other such gestures as people make when they have been deeply impressed by something.

We boys followed behind our fathers, and listened, catching all we could of what they said; and when they sat down in our house and continued their talk they still had us for company. They were in a sad mood, for it was certain, they said, that disaster for the village must follow this awful visitation of witches and devils. Then my father remembered that Father Adolf had been struck dumb at the moment of his denunciation.

"They have not ventured to lay their hands upon an anointed servant of God before," he said; "and how they could have dared it this time I cannot make out, for he wore his crucifix. Isn't it so?"

"Yes," said the others, "we saw it."

"It is serious, friends, it is very serious. Always before, we had a protection. It has failed."

The others shook, as with a sort of chill, and muttered those words over—"It has failed." "God has forsaken us."

"It is true," said Seppi Wohlmeyer's father; there is nowhere to look for help."

"The people will realize this," said Nikolaus's father, the judge, "and despair will take away their courage and their energies. We have indeed fallen upon evil times."

He sighed, and Wohlmeyer said, in a troubled voice: "The report of it all will go about the country, and our village will be shunned as being under the displeasure of God. The Golden Stag will know hard times."

"True, neighbor," said my father; "all of us will suffer —all in repute, many in estate. And, good God!—"

"What is it?"

"That can come—to finish us!"

"Name it—um Gottes Willen!"

"The Interdict!"

It smote like a thunderclap, and they were like to swoon with the terror of it. Then the dread of this calamity aroused their energies, and they stopped brooding and began to consider ways to avert it. They discussed this, that, and the other way, and talked till the afternoon was far spent, then confessed that at present they could arrive at no decision. So they parted sorrowfully, with oppressed hearts which were filled with bodings.

While they were saying their parting words I slipped out and set my course for Marget's house to see what was happening there. I met many people, but none of them greeted me. It ought to have been surprising, but it was not, for they were so distraught with fear and dread that they were not in their right minds, I think; they were white and haggard, and walked like persons in a dream, their eyes open but seeing nothing, their lips moving but uttering nothing, and worriedly clasping and unclasping their hands without knowing it.

At Marget's it was like a funeral. She and Wilhelm sat together on the sofa, but said nothing, and not even holding hands. Both were steeped in gloom, and Marget's eyes were red from the crying she had been doing. She said:

"I have been begging him to go, and come no more, and

so save himself alive. I cannot bear to be his murderer. This house is bewitched, and no inmate will escape the fire. But he will not go, and he will be lost with the rest."

Wilhelm said he would not go; if there was danger for her, his place was by her, and there he would remain. Then she began to cry again, and it was all so mournful that I wished I had stayed away. There was a knock, now, and Satan came in, fresh and cheery and beautiful, and brought that winy atmosphere of his and changed the whole thing. He never said a word about what had been happening, nor about the awful fears which were freezing the blood in the hearts of the community, but began to talk and rattle on about all manner of gay and pleasant things: and next about music—an artful stroke which cleared away the remnant of Marget's depression and brought her spirits and her interests broad awake. She had not heard any one talk so well and so knowingly on that subject before, and she was so uplifted by it and so charmed that what she was feeling lit up her face and came out in her words; and Wilhelm noticed it and did not look as pleased as he ought to have done. And next Satan branched off into poetry, and recited some, and did it well, and Marget was charmed again; and again Wilhelm was not as pleased as he ought to have been, and this time Marget noticed it and was remorseful.

I fell asleep to pleasant music that night—the patter of rain upon the panes and the dull growling of distant thunder. Away in the night Satan came and roused me and said: "Come with me. Where shall we go?"

"Anywhere—so it is with you."

Then there was a fierce glare of sunlight, and he said, "This is China."

That was a grand surprise, and made me sort of drunk with vanity and gladness to think I had come so far—so much, much farther than anybody else in our village, including Bartel Sperling, who had such a great opinion of his travels. We buzzed around over that empire for more than half an hour, and saw the whole of it. It was wonderful, the spectacles we saw; and some were beautiful, others too horrible to think. For instance— However, I may go into that by and by, and also why Satan chose China for this excursion instead of another place; it would interrupt my tale to do it now. Finally we stopped flitting and lit.

We sat upon a mountain commanding a vast landscape of mountain-range and gorge and valley and plain and river, with cities and villages slumbering in the sunlight, and a glimpse of blue sea on the farther verge. It was a tranquil and dreamy picture, beautiful to the eye and restful to the spirit. If we could only make a change like that whenever we wanted to, the world would be easier to live in than it is, for change of scene shifts the mind's burdens to the other shoulder and banishes old, shop-worn wearinesses from mind and body both.

We talked together, and I had the idea of trying to reform Satan and persuade him to lead a better life. I told him about all those things he had been doing, and begged him to be more considerate and stop making people unhappy. I said I knew he did not mean any harm, but that he ought to stop and consider the possible consequences of a thing before launching it in that impulsive and random way of his; then he would not make so much trouble. He was not hurt by this plain speech; he only looked amused and surprised, and said:

"What? I do random things? Indeed, I never do. I stop and consider possible consequences? Where is the need? I know what the consequences are going to be—always."

"Oh, Satan, then how could you do these things?"

"Well, I will tell you, and you must understand if you can. You belong to a singular race. Every man is a suffering-machine and a happiness-machine combined. The two functions work together harmoniously, with a fine and delicate precision, on the give-and-take principle. For every happiness turned out in the one department the other stands ready to modify it with a sorrow or a pain—maybe a dozen. In most cases the man's life is about equally divided between happiness and unhappiness. When this is not the case the unhappiness predominates—always; never the other. Sometimes a man's make and disposition are such that his misery-machine is able to do nearly all the business. Such a man goes through life almost ignorant of what happiness is. Everything he touches, everything he does, brings a misfortune upon him. You have seen such people? To that kind of a person life is not an advantage, is it? It is only a disaster. Sometimes for an hour's happiness a man's machinery makes him pay years of misery. Don't you know that? It happens every now and then. I will give

you a case or two presently. Now the people of your village are nothing to me—you know that, don't you?"

I did not like to speak out too flatly, so I said I had
suspected it.

"Well, it is true that they are nothing to me. It is not
possible that they should be. The difference between them
and me is abysmal, immeasurable. They have no intellect."

"No intellect?"

"Nothing that resembles it. At a future time I will examine what man calls his mind and give you the details
of that chaos, then you will see and understand. Men have
nothing in common with me—there is no point of contact;
they have foolish little feelings and foolish little vanities
and impertinences and ambitions; their foolish little life
is but a laugh, a sigh, and extinction; and they have no
sense. Only the Moral Sense. I will show you what I mean.
Here is a red spider, not so big as a pin's head. Can you
imagine an elephant being interested in him—caring
whether he is happy or isn't, or whether he is wealthy or
poor, or whether his sweetheart returns his love or not, or
whether his mother is sick or well, or whether he is looked
up to in society or not, or whether his enemies will smite
him or his friends desert him, or whether his hopes will
suffer blight or his political ambitions fail, or whether he
shall die in the bosom of his family or neglected and
despised in a foreign land? These things can never be important to the elephant; they are nothing to him; he cannot shrink his sympathies to the microscopic size of them.
Man is to me as the red spider is to the elephant. The elephant has nothing against the spider—he cannot get down
to that remote level; I have nothing against man. The elephant is indifferent; I am indifferent. The elephant would
not take the trouble to do the spider an ill turn; if he
took the notion he might do him a good turn, if it came
in his way and cost nothing. I have done men good service,
but no ill turns.

"The elephant lives a century, the red spider a day; in
power, intellect, and dignity the one creature is separated
from the other by a distance which is simply astronomical.
Yet in these, as in all qualities, man is immeasurably further below me than is the wee spider below the elephant.

"Man's mind clumsily and tediously and laboriously
patches little trivialities together and gets a result—such as

it is. My mind creates! Do you get the force of that? Creates anything it desires—and in a moment. Creates without material. Creates fluids, solids, colors—anything, everything—out of the airy nothing which is called Thought. A man imagines a silk thread, imagines a machine to make it, imagines a picture, then by weeks of labor embroiders it on canvas with the thread. I think the whole thing, and in a moment it is before you—created.

"I think a poem, music, the record of a game of chess—anything—and it is there. This is the immortal mind—nothing is beyond its reach. Nothing can obstruct my vision; the rocks are transparent to me, and darkness is daylight. I do not need to open a book; I take the whole of its contents into my mind at a single glance, through the cover; and in a million years I could not forget a single word of it, or its place in the volume. Nothing goes on in the skull of man, bird, fish, insect, or other creature which can be hidden from me. I pierce the learned man's brain with a single glance, and the treasures which cost him threescore years to accumulate are mine; he can forget, and he does forget, but I retain.

"Now, then, I perceive by your thoughts that you are understanding me fairly well. Let us proceed. Circumstances might so fall out that the elephant could like the spider—supposing he can see it—but he could not love it. His love is for his own kind—for his equals. An angel's love is sublime, adorable, divine, beyond the imagination of man—infinitely beyond it! But it is limited to his own august order. If it fell upon one of your race for only an instant, it would consume its object to ashes. No, we cannot love men, but we can be harmlessly indifferent to them; we can also like them, sometimes. I like you and the boys, I like Father Peter, and for your sakes I am doing all these things for the villagers."

He saw that I was thinking a sarcasm, and he explained his position.

"I have wrought well for the villagers, though it does not look like it on the surface. Your race never know good fortune from ill. They are always mistaking the one for the other. It is because they cannot see into the future. What I am doing for the villagers will bear good fruit some day; in some cases to themselves; in others, to unborn generations of men. No one will ever know that I was the cause, but it will be none the less true, for all that. Among you boys you have a game: you stand a row of bricks on end a few inches apart; you push a brick, it knocks its neighbor over, the neighbor knocks over the next brick—and so on till all the row is prostrate. That is human life. A child's first act knocks over the initial brick, and the rest will follow inexorably. If you could see into the future, as I can, you would see everything that was going to happen to that creature; for nothing can change the order of its life after the first event has determined it. That is, nothing will change it, because each act unfailingly begets an act, that act begets another, and so on to the end, and the seer can look forward down the line and see just when each act is to have birth, from cradle to grave."

"Does God order the career?"

"Foreordain it? No. The man's circumstances and environment order it. His first act determines the second and all that follow after. But suppose, for argument's sake, that the man should skip one of these acts; an apparently trifling one, for instance; suppose that it had been appointed that on a certain day, at a certain hour and minute and second and fraction of a second he should go to the well, and he didn't go. That man's career would change utterly, from that moment; thence to the grave it would be wholly different from the career which his first act as a child had arranged for him. Indeed, it might be that if he had gone to the well he would have ended his career on a throne, and that omitting to do it would set him upon a career that would lead to beggary and a pauper's grave. For instance: if at any time—say in boyhood—Columbus had skipped the triflingest little link in the chain of acts projected and made inevitable by his first childish act, it would have changed his whole subsequent life, and he would have become a priest and died obscure in an Italian village, and America would not have been discovered for two centuries afterward. I know this. To skip any one of the billion acts in Columbus's chain would have wholly changed his life. I have examined his billion of possible careers, and in only one of them occurs the discovery of America. You people do not suspect that all of your acts are of one size and importance, but it is true; to snatch at an appointed fly is as big with fate for you as in any other appointed act—"

"As the conquering of a continent, for instance?"

"Yes. Now, then, no man ever does drop a link—the thing has never happened! Even when he is trying to make up his mind as to whether he will do a thing or not, that itself is a link, an act, and has its proper place in his chain; and when he finally decides an act, that also was the thing which he was absolutely certain to do. You see, now, that a man will never drop a link in his chain. He cannot. If he made up his mind to try, that project would itself be an unavoidable link—a thought bound to occur to him at that precise moment, and made certain by the first act of his babyhood."

It seemed so dismal!

"He is a prisoner for life," I said sorrowfully, "and cannot get free."

"No, of himself he cannot get away from the consequences of his first childish act. But I can free him."

I looked up wistfully.

"I have changed the careers of a number of your villagers."

I tried to thank him, but found it difficult, and let it drop.

"I shall make some other changes. You know that little Lisa Brandt?"

"Oh yes, everybody does. My mother says she is so sweet and so lovely that she is not like any other child. She says she will be the pride of the village when she grows up; and its idol, too, just as she is now."

"I shall change her future."

"Make it better?" I asked.

"Yes. And I will change the future of Nikolaus."

I was glad, this time, and said, "I don't need to ask about his case; you will be sure to do generously by him."

"It is my intention."

Straight off I was building that great future of Nicky's in my imagination, and had already made a renowned general of him and hofmeister at the court, when I noticed that Satan was waiting for me to get ready to listen again. I was ashamed of having exposed my cheap imaginings to him, and was expecting some sarcasms, but it did not happen. He proceeded with his subject:

"Nicky's appointed life is sixty-two years."

"That's grand!" I said.

"Lisa's, thirty-six. But, as I told you, I shall change their lives and those ages. Two minutes and a quarter from now Nikolaus will wake out of his sleep and find the rain blowing in. It was appointed that he should turn over and go to sleep again. But I have appointed that he shall get up and close the window first. That trifle will change his career entirely. He will rise in the morning two minutes later than the chain of his life had appointed him to rise. By consequence, thenceforth nothing will ever happen to him in accordance with the details of the old chain." He took out his watch and sat looking at it a few moments, then said: "Nikolaus has risen to close the window. His life is changed, his new career has begun. There will be consequences."

It made me feel creepy; it was uncanny.

"But for this change certain things would happen twelve days from now. For instance, Nikolaus would save Lisa from drowning. He would arrive on the scene at exactly the right moment—four minutes past ten, the long-ago appointed instant of time—and the water would be shoal, the achievement easy and certain. But he will arrive some seconds too late, now; Lisa will have struggled into deeper water. He will do his best, but both will drown."

"Oh, Satan! oh, dear Satan!" I cried, with the tears rising in my eyes, "save them! Don't let it happen. I can't bear to lose Nikolaus, he is my loving playmate and friend; and think of Lisa's poor mother!"

I clung to him and begged and pleaded, but he was not moved. He made me sit down again, and told me I must hear him out.

"I have changed Nikolaus's life, and this has changed Lisa's. If I had not done this, Nikolaus would save Lisa, then he would catch cold from his drenching; one of your race's fantastic and desolating scarlet fevers would follow, with pathetic after-effects; for forty-six years he would lie in his bed a paralytic log, deaf, dumb, blind, and praying night and day for the blessed relief of death. Shall I change his life back?"

"Oh no! Oh, not for the world! In charity and pity leave it as it is."

"It is best so. I could not have changed any other link in his life and done him so good a service. He had a billion possible careers, but not one of them was worth living; they were charged full with miseries and disasters. But for my intervention he would do his brave deed twelve days from now—a deed begun and ended in six minutes—and get for all reward those forty-six years of sorrow and suffering I told you of. It is one of the cases I was thinking of awhile ago when I said that sometimes an act which brings the actor an hour's happiness and self-satisfaction is paid for—or punished—by years of suffering."

I wondered what poor little Lisa's early death would save her from. He answered the thought:

"From ten years of pain and slow recovery from an accident, and then from nineteen years' pollution, shame, depravity, crime, ending with death at the hands of the executioner. Twelve days hence she will die; her mother would save her life if she could. Am I not kinder than her mother?"

"Yes—oh, indeed yes; and wiser."

"Father Peter's case is coming on presently. He will be acquitted, through unassailable proofs of his innocence."

"Why, Satan, how can that be? Do you really think it?"

"Indeed, I know it. His good name will be restored, and the rest of his life will be happy."

"I can believe it. To restore his good name will have that effect."

"His happiness will not proceed from that cause. I shall change his life that day, for his good. He will never know his good name has been restored."

In my mind—and modestly—I asked for particulars, but Satan paid no attention to my thought. Next, my mind wandered to the astrologer, and I wondered where he might be.

"In the moon," said Satan, with a fleeting sound which I believed was a chuckle. "I've got him on the cold side of it, too. He doesn't know where he is, and is not having a pleasant time; still, it is good enough for him, a good place for his star studies. I shall need him presently; then I shall bring him back and possess him again. He has a long and cruel and odious life before him, but I will change that, for I have no feeling against him and am quite willing to do him a kindness. I think I shall get him burned."

He had such strange notions of kindness! But angels are made so, and do not know any better. Their ways are not like our ways; and, besides, human beings are nothing to them; they think they are only freaks. It seems to me odd that he should put the astrologer so far away; he could have dumped him in Germany just as well, where he would be handy.

"Far away?" said Satan. "To me no place is far away; distance does not exist for me. The sun is less than a hundred million miles from here, and the light that is falling upon us has taken eight minutes to come; but I can make that flight, or any other, in a fraction of time so minute that it cannot be measured by a watch. I have but to think the journey, and it is accomplished."

I held out my hand and said, "The light lies upon it; think it into a glass of wine, Satan."

He did it. I drank the wine.

"Break the glass," he said.

I broke it.

"There—you see it is real. The villagers thought the brass balls were magic stuff and as perishable as smoke. They were afraid to touch them. You are a curious lot— your race. But come along; I have business. I will put you to bed." Said and done. Then he was gone; but his voice came back to me through the rain and darkness saying, "Yes, tell Seppi, but no other."

It was the answer to my thought.

## VIII.

Sleep would not come. It was not because I was proud of my travels and excited about having been around the big world to China, and feeling contemptuous of Bartel Sperling, "the traveler," as he called himself, and looked down upon us others because he had been to Vienna once and was the only Eseldorf boy who had made such a journey and seen the world's wonders. At another time that would have kept me awake, but it did not affect me now. No, my mind was filled with Nikolaus, my thoughts ran upon him only, and the good days we had seen together at romps and frolics in the woods and the fields and the river in the long summer days, and skating and sliding in the winter when our parents thought we were in school. And now he was going out of this young life, and the summers and winters would come and go, and we others would rove and play as before, but his place would be vacant; we should see him no more. To-morrow he would not suspect, but would be as he had always been, and it would shock me to hear him laugh, and see him do lightsome and frivolous things, for to me he would be a corpse, with waven hands and dull eyes, and I should see the shroud around his face; and next day he would not suspect, nor the next, and all the time his handful of days would be wasting swiftly away and that awful thing coming nearer and nearer, his fate closing steadily around him and no one knowing it but Seppi and me. Twelve days—only twelve days. It was awful to think of. I noticed that in my thoughts I was not calling him by his familiar names, Nick and Nicky, but was speaking of him by his full name, and reverently, as one speaks of the dead. Also, as incident after incident of our comradeship came thronging into my mind out of the past, I noticed that they were mainly cases where I had wronged him or hurt him, and they rebuked me and reproached me, and my heart was wrung with remorse, just as it is when we remember our unkindnesses to friends who have passed beyond the veil, and we wish we could have them back again, if only for a moment, so that we could go on our knees to them and say, "Have pity, and forgive."

Once when we were nine years old he went a long errand of nearly two miles for the fruiterer, who gave him a splendid big apple for reward, and he was flying home with it, almost beside himself with astonishment and delight, and I met him, and he let me look at the apple, not thinking of treachery, and I ran off with it, eating it as I ran, he following me and begging; and when he overtook me I offered him the core, which was all that was left; and I laughed. Then he turned away, crying, and said he had meant to give it to his little sister. That smote me, for she was slowly getting well of a sickness, and it would have been a proud moment for him, to see her joy and surprise and have her caresses. But I was ashamed to say I was ashamed, and only said something rude and mean, to pretend I did not care, and he made no reply in words, but there was a wounded look in his face as he turned away toward his home which rose before me many times in after years, in the night, and reproached me and made me ashamed again. It had grown dim in my mind, by and by, then it disappeared; but it was back now, and not dim.

Once at school, when we were eleven, I upset my ink and spoiled four copy-books, and was in danger of severe punishment; but I put it upon him, and he got the whipping.

And only last year I had cheated him in a trade, giving him a large fish-hook which was partly broken through for three small sound ones. The first fish he caught broke the hook, but he did not know I was blamable, and he refused to take back one of the small hooks which my conscience forced me to offer him, but said, "A trade is a trade; the hook was bad, but that was not your fault."

No, I could not sleep. These little, shabby wrongs upbraided me and tortured me, and with a pain much sharper than one feels when the wrongs have been done to the living. Nikolaus was living, but no matter; he was to me as one already dead. The wind was still moaning about the eaves, the rain still pattering upon the panes.

In the morning I sought out Seppi and told him. It was down by the river. His lips moved, but he did not say anything, he only looked dazed and stunned, and his face turned very white. He stood like that a few moments, the tears welling into his eyes, then he turned away and I locked my arm in his and we walked along thinking, but not speaking. We crossed the bridge and wandered through the meadows and up among the hills and the woods, and at last the talk came and flowed freely, and it was all about Nikolaus and was a recalling of the life we had lived with him. And every now and then Seppi said, as if to himself:

"Twelve days!—less than twelve days."

We said we must be with him all the time; we must have all of him we could; the days were precious now. Yet we did not go to seek him. It would be like meeting the dead, and we were afraid. We did not say it, but that was what we were feeling. And so it gave us a shock when we turned a curve and came upon Nikolaus face to face. He shouted, gaily:

"Hi-hi! What is the matter? Have you seen a ghost?"

We couldn't speak, but there was no occasion; he was willing to talk for us all, for he had just seen Satan and was in high spirits about it. Satan had told him about our trip to China, and he had begged Satan to take him a journey, and Satan had promised. It was to be a far journey, and wonderful and beautiful; and Nikolaus had begged him to take us, too, but he said no, he would take us some day, maybe, but not now. Satan would come for him on the 13th, and Nikolaus was already counting the hours, he was so impatient.

That was the fatal day. We were already counting the hours, too.

We wandered many a mile, always following paths which had been our favorites from the days when we were little, and always we talked about the old times. All the blitheness was with Nikolaus; we others could not shake off our depression. Our tone toward Nikolaus was so strangely gentle and tender and yearning that he noticed it, and was pleased; and we were constantly doing him deferential little offices of courtesy, and saying, "Wait, let me do that for you," and that pleased him, too. I gave him seven fish-hooks—all I had—and made him take them; and Seppi gave him his new knife and a humming-top painted red and yellow—atonements for swindles practised upon him formerly, as I learned later, and probably no longer remembered by Nikolaus now. These things touched him, and he could not have believed that we loved him so; and his pride in it and gratefulness for it cut us to the heart, we were so undeserving of them. When we parted at last, he was radiant, and said he had never had such a happy day.

As we walked along homeward, Seppi said, "We always prized him, but never so much as now, when we are going to lose him."

Next day and every day we spent all of our spare time with Nikolaus; and also added to it time which we (and he) stole from work and other duties, and this cost the three of us some sharp scoldings, and some threats of punishment. Every morning two of us woke with a start and a shudder, saying, as the days flew along, "Only ten days left;" "only nine days left;" "only eight;" "only seven." Always it was narrowing. Always Nikolaus was gay and happy, and always puzzled because we were not. He wore his invention to the bone trying to invent ways to cheer us up, but it was only a hollow success; he could see that our jollity had no heart in it, and that the laughs we broke into came up against some obstruction or other and suffered damage and decayed into a sigh. He tried to find out what the matter was, so that he could help us out of our trouble or make it lighter by sharing it with us; so we had to tell many lies to deceive him and appease him.

But the most distressing thing of all was that he was always making plans, and often they went beyond the 13th! Whenever that happened it made us groan in spirit. All his mind was fixed upon finding some way to conquer our depression and cheer us up; and at last, when he had but three days to live, he fell upon the right idea and was jubilant over it—a boys-and-girls' frolic and dance in the woods, up there where we first met Satan, and this was to occur on the 14th. It was ghastly, for that was his funeral day. We couldn't venture to protest; it would only have brought a "Why?" which we could not answer. He wanted us to help him invite his guests, and we did it—one can refuse nothing to a dying friend. But it was dreadful, for really we were inviting them to his funeral.

It was an awful eleven days; and yet, with a lifetime stretching back between to-day and then, they are still a grateful memory to me, and beautiful. In effect they were days of companionship with one's sacred dead, and I have known no comradeship that was so close or so precious. We clung to the hours and the minutes, counting them as they wasted away, and parting with them with that pain and bereavement which a miser feels who sees his hoard filched from him coin by coin by robbers and is helpless to prevent it.

When the evening of the last day came we stayed out too long; Seppi and I were in fault for that; we could not bear to part with Nikolaus; so it was very late when we left him at his door. We lingered near awhile, listening; and that happened which we were fearing. His father gave him the promised punishment, and we heard his shrieks. But we listened only a moment, then hurried away, remorseful for this thing which we had caused. And sorry for the father, too; our thought being, "If he only knew—if he only knew!"

In the morning Nikolaus did not meet us at the appointed place, so we went to his home to see what the matter was. His mother said:

"His father is out of all patience with these goings-on, and will not have any more of it. Half the time when Nick is needed he is not to be found; then it turns out that he has been gadding around with you two. His father gave him a flogging last night. It always grieved me before, and many's the time I have begged him off and saved him, but this time he appealed to me in vain, for I was out of patience myself."

"I wish you had saved him just this one time," I said, my voice trembling a little; "it would ease a pain in your heart to remember it some day."

She was ironing at the time, and her back was partly toward me. She turned about with a startled or wondering look in her face and said, "What do you mean by that?"

I was not prepared, and didn't know anything to say; so it was awkward, for she kept looking at me; but Seppi was alert and spoke up:

"Why, of course it would be pleasant to remember, for the very reason we were out so late was that Nikolaus got to telling how good you are to him, and how he never got whipped when you were by to save him; and he was so full of it, and we were so full of the interest of it, that none of us noticed how late it was getting."

"Did he say that? Did he?" and she put her apron to her eyes.

"You can ask Theodor—he will tell you the same."

"It is a dear, good lad, my Nick," she said. "I am sorry I let him get whipped; I will never do it again. To think—all the time I was sitting here last night, fretting and angry at him, he was loving me and praising me! Dear, dear, if we could only know! Then we shouldn't ever go wrong; but we are only poor, dumb beasts groping around and making mistakes. I sha'n't ever think of last night without a pang."

She was like all the rest; it seemed as if nobody could open a mouth, in these wretched days, without saying something that made us shiver. They were "groping around," and did not know what true, sorrowfully true things they were saying by accident.

Seppi asked if Nikolaus might go out with us.

"I am sorry," she answered, "but he can't. To punish him further, his father doesn't allow him to go out of the house to-day."

We had a great hope! I saw it in Seppi's eyes. We thought, "If he cannot leave the house, he cannot be drowned." Seppi asked, to make sure:

"Must he stay in all day, or only the morning?"

"All day. It's such a pity, too; it's a beautiful day, and he is so unused to being shut up. But he is busy planning his party, and maybe that is company for him. I do hope he isn't too lonesome."

Seppi saw that in her eye which emboldened him to ask if we might go up and help him pass his time.

"And welcome!" she said, right heartily. "Now I call that real friendship, when you might be abroad in the fields and the woods, having a happy time. You are good boys, I'll allow that, though you don't always find satisfactory ways of improving it. Take these cakes—for yourselves—and give him this one, from his mother."

The first thing we noticed when we entered Nikolaus's room was the time—a quarter to 10. Could that be correct? Only such a few minutes to live! I felt a contraction at my heart. Nikolaus jumped up and gave us a glad welcome. He was in good spirits over his plannings for his party and had not been lonesome.

"Sit down," he said, "and look at what I've been doing. And I've finished a kite that you will say is a beauty. It's drying, in the kitchen; I'll fetch it."

He had been spending his penny savings in fanciful trifles of various kinds, to go as prizes in the games, and they were marshaled with fine and showy effect upon the table. He said:

"Examine them at your leisure while I get mother to touch up the kite with her iron if it isn't dry enough yet."

Then he tripped out and went clattering downstairs, whistling.

We did not look at the things; we couldn't take any interest in anything but the clock. We sat staring at it in silence, listening to the ticking, and every time the minute-hand jumped we nodded recognition—one minute fewer to cover in the race for life or for death. Finally Seppi drew a deep breath and said:

"Two minutes to ten. Seven minutes more and he will pass the death-point. Theodor, he is going to be saved! He's going to—"

"Hush! I'm on needles. Watch the clock and keep still."

Five minutes more. We were panting with the strain and the excitement. Another three minutes, and there was a footstep on the stair.

"Saved!" And we jumped up and faced the door.

The old mother entered, bringing the kite. "Isn't it a beauty?" she said. "And, dear me, how he has slaved over it —ever since daylight, I think, and only finished it awhile before you came." She stood it against the wall, and stepped back to take a view of it. "He drew the pictures his own self, and I think they are very good. The church isn't so very good, I'll have to admit, but look at the bridge—any one can recognize the bridge in a minute. He asked me to bring it up. . . . Dear me! it's seven minutes past ten, and I—"

"But where is he?"

"He? Oh, he'll be here soon; he's gone out a minute."

"Gone out?"

"Yes. Just as he came down-stairs little Lisa's mother came in and said the child had wandered off somewhere, and as she was a little uneasy I told Nikolaus to never mind about his father's orders—go and look her up. . . . Why, how white you two do look! I do believe you are sick. Sit down; I'll fetch something. That cake has disagreed with you. It is a little heavy, but I thought—"

She disappeared without finishing her sentence, and we hurried at once to the back window and looked toward the river. There was a great crowd at the other end of the bridge, and people were flying toward that point from every direction.

"Oh, it is all over—poor Nikolaus! Why, oh, why did she let him get out of the house!"

"Come away," said Seppi, half sobbing, "come quick— we can't bear to meet her; in five minutes she will know."

But we were not to escape. She came upon us at the foot of the stairs, with her cordials in her hands, and made us come in and sit down and take the medicine. Then she watched the effect, and it did not satisfy her; so she made us wait longer, and kept upbraiding herself for giving us the unwholesome cake.

Presently the thing happened which we were dreading. There was a sound of tramping and scraping outside, and a crowd came solemnly in, with heads uncovered, and laid the two drowned bodies on the bed.

"Oh, my God!" that poor mother cried out, and fell on her knees, and put her arms about her dead boy and began to cover the wet face with kisses. "Oh, it was I that sent him, and I have been his death. If I had obeyed, and kept him in the house, this would not have happened. And I am rightly punished; I was cruel to him last night, and him begging me, his own mother, to be his friend."

And so she went on and on, and all the women cried, and pitied her, and tried to comfort her, but she could not forgive herself and could not be comforted, and kept on saying if she had not sent him out he would be alive and well now, and she was the cause of his death.

It shows how foolish people are when they blame themselves for anything they have done. Satan knows, and he said nothing happens that your first act hasn't arranged to happen and made inevitable; and so, of your own motion you can't ever alter the scheme or do a thing that will break a link. Next we heard screams, and Frau Brandt came wildly plowing and plunging through the crowd with her dress in disorder and hair flying loose, and flung herself upon her dead child with moans and kisses and pleadings and endearments; and by and by she rose up almost exhausted with her outpourings of passionate emotion, and clenched her fist and lifted it toward the sky, and her tear-drenched face grew hard and resentful, and she said:

"For nearly two weeks I have had dreams and presentiments and warnings that death was going to strike what was most precious to me, and day and night and night and day I have groveled in the dirt before Him praying Him to have pity on my innocent child and save it from harm—and here is His answer!"

Why, He had saved it from harm—but she did not know.

She wiped the tears from her eyes and cheeks, and stood awhile gazing down at the child and caressing its face and its hair with her hands; then she spoke again in that bitter tone: "But in His hard heart is no compassion. I will never pray again."

She gathered her dead child to her bosom and strode away, the crowd falling back to let her pass, and smitten dumb by the awful words they had heard. Ah, that poor woman! It is as Satan said, we do not know good fortune from bad, and are always mistaking the one for the other. Many a time since I have heard people pray to God to spare the life of sick persons, but I have never done it.

Both funerals took place at the same time in our little church next day. Everybody was there, including the party guests. Satan was there, too; which was proper, for it was on account of his efforts that the funerals had happened. Nikolaus had departed this life without absolution, and a collection was taken up for masses, to get him out of purgatory. Only two-thirds of the required money was gathered, and the parents were going to try to borrow the rest, but Satan furnished it. He told us privately that there was no purgatory, but he had contributed in order that Nikolaus's parents and their friends might be saved from worry and distress. We thought it very good of him, but he said money did not cost him anything.

At the graveyard the body of little Lisa was seized for debt by a carpenter to whom the mother owed fifty groschen for work done the year before. She had never been able to pay this, and was not able now. The carpenter took the corpse home and kept it four days in his cellar, the mother weeping and imploring about his house all the time; then he buried it in his brother's cattle-yard, without religious ceremonies. It drove the mother wild with grief and shame, and she forsook her work and went daily about the town, cursing the carpenter and blaspheming the laws of the emperor and the church, and it was pitiful to see. Seppi asked Satan to interfere, but he said the carpenter and the rest were members of the human race and were acting quite neatly for that species of animal. He would interfere if he found a horse acting in such a way, and we must inform him when we came across that kind of horse doing that kind of a human thing, so that he could stop it. We believed this was sarcasm, for of course there wasn't any such horse.

But after a few days we found that we could not abide that poor woman's distress, so we begged Satan to examine her several possible careers, and see if he could not change her, to her profit, to a new one. He said the longest of her careers as they now stood gave her forty-two years to live, and her shortest one twenty-nine, and that both were charged with grief and hunger and cold and pain. The only improvement he could make would be to enable her to skip a certain three minutes from now; and he asked us if he should do it. This was such a short time to decide in that we went to pieces with nervous excitement, and before we could pull ourselves together and ask for particulars he said the time would be up in a few more seconds; so then we gasped out, "Do it!"

"It is done," he said; "she was going around a corner; I have turned her back; it has changed her career."

"Then what will happen, Satan?"

"It is happening now. She is having words with Fischer, the weaver. In his anger Fischer will straightway do what he would not have done but for this accident. He was present when she stood over her child's body and uttered those blasphemies."

"What will he do?"

"He is doing it now—betraying her. In three days she will go to the stake."

We could not speak; we were frozen with horror, for if we had not meddled with her career she would have been spared this awful fate. Satan noticed these thoughts, and said:

"What you are thinking is strictly human-like—that is to say, foolish. The woman is advantaged. Die when she might, she would go to heaven. By this prompt death she gets twenty-nine years more of heaven than she is entitled to, and escapes twenty-nine years of misery here."

A moment before we were bitterly making up our minds that we would ask no more favors of Satan for friends of ours, for he did not seem to know any way to do a person a kindness but by killing him; but the whole aspect of the case was changed now, and we were glad of what we had done and full of happiness in the thought of it.

After a little I began to feel troubled about Fischer, and asked, timidly, "Does this episode change Fischer's life-scheme, Satan?"

"Change it? Why, certainly. And radically. If he had not met Frau Brandt awhile ago he would die next year, thirty-four years of age. Now he will live to be ninety, and have a pretty prosperous and comfortable life of it, as human lives go."

We felt a great joy and pride in what we had done for Fischer, and were expecting Satan to sympathize with this feeling; but he showed no sign and this made us uneasy. We waited for him to speak, but he didn't; so, to assuage our solicitude we had to ask him if there was any defect in

Fischer's good luck. Satan considered the question a moment, then said, with some hesitation:

"Well, the fact is, it is a delicate point. Under his several former possible life-careers he was going to heaven."

We were aghast. "Oh, Satan! and under this one—"

"There, don't be so distressed. You were sincerely trying to do him a kindness; let that comfort you."

"Oh, dear, dear, that cannot comfort us. You ought to have told us what we that were doing, then we wouldn't have acted so."

But it made no impression on him. He had never felt a pain or a sorrow, and did not know what they were, in any really informing way. He had no knowledge of them except theoretically—that is to say, intellectually. And of course that is no good. One can never get any but a loose and ignorant notion of such things except by experience. We tried our best to make him comprehend the awful thing that had been done and how we were compromised by it, but he couldn't seem to get hold of it. He said he did not think it important where Fischer went to; in heaven he would not be missed, there were "plenty there." We tried to make him see that he was missing the point entirely; that Fischer, and not other people, was the proper one to decide about the importance of it; but it all went for nothing; he said he did not care for Fischer—there were plenty more Fischers.

The next minute Fischer went by on the other side of the way, and it made us sick and faint to see him, remembering the doom that was upon him, and we the cause of it. And how unconscious he was that anything had happened to him! You could see by his elastic step and his alert manner that he was well satisfied with himself for doing that hard turn for poor Frau Brandt. He kept glancing back over his shoulder expectantly. And, sure enough, pretty soon Frau Brandt followed after, in charge of the officers and wearing jingling chains. A mob was in her wake, jeering and shouting, "Blasphemer and heretic!" and some among them were neighbors and friends of her happier days. Some were trying to strike her, and the officers were not taking as much trouble as they might to keep them from it.

"Oh, stop them, Satan!" It was out before we remembered that he could not interrupt them for a moment without changing their whole after-lives. He puffed a little puff toward them with his lips and they began to reel and stagger and grab at the empty air; then they broke apart and fled in every direction, shrieking, as if in intolerable pain. He had crushed a rib of each of them with that little puff. We could not help asking if their life-chart was changed.

"Yes, entirely. Some have gained years, some have lost them. Some few will profit in various ways by the change, but only that few."

We did not ask if we had brought poor Fischer's luck to any of them. We did not wish to know. We fully believed in Satan's desire to do us kindnesses, but we were losing confidence in his judgment. It was at this time that our growing anxiety to have him look over our life-charts and suggest improvements began to fade out and give place to other interests.

For a day or two the whole village was a chattering turmoil over Frau Brandt's case and over the mysterious calamity that had overtaken the mob, and at her trial the place was crowded. She was easily convicted of her blasphemies, for she uttered those terrible words again and said she would not take them back. When warned that she was imperiling her life, she said they could take it in welcome, she did not want it, she would rather live with the professional devils in perdition than with these imitators in the village. They accused her of breaking all those ribs by witchcraft, and asked her if she was not a witch? She answered scornfully:

"No. If I had that power would any of you holy hypocrites be alive five minutes? No; I would strike you all dead. Pronounce your sentence and let me go; I am tired of your society."

So they found her guilty, and she was excommunicated and cut off from the joys of heaven and doomed to the fires of hell; then she was clothed in a coarse robe and delivered to the secular arm, and conducted to the marketplace, the bell solemnly tolling the while. We saw her chained to the stake, and saw the first film of blue smoke rise on the still air. Then her hard face softened, and she looked upon the packed crowd in front of her and said, with gentleness:

"We played together once, in long-agone days when we were innocent little creatures. For the sake of that, I forgive you."

We went away then, and did not see the fires consume her, but we heard the shrieks, although we put our fingers in our ears. When they ceased we knew she was in heaven, notwithstanding the excommunication; and we were glad of her death and not sorry that we had brought it about.

One day, a little while after this, Satan appeared again. We were always watching out for him, for life was never very stagnant when he was by. He came upon us at that place in the woods where we had first met him. Being boys, we wanted to be entertained; we asked him to do a show for us.

"Very well," he said; "would you like to see a history of the progress of the human race?—its development of that product which it calls civilization?"

We said we should.

So, with a thought, he turned the place into the Garden of Eden, and we saw Abel praying by his altar; then Cain came walking toward him with his club, and did not seem to see us, and would have stepped on my foot if I had not drawn it in. He spoke to his brother in a language which we did not understand; then he grew violent and threatening, and we knew what was going to happen, and turned away our heads for the moment; but we heard the crash of the blows and heard the shrieks and the groans; then there was silence, and we saw Abel lying in his blood and gasping out his life, and Cain standing over him and looking down at him, vengeful and unrepentant.

Then the vision vanished, and was followed by a long series of unknown wars, murders, and massacres. Next we had the Flood, and the Ark tossing around in the stormy waters, with lofty mountains in the distance showing veiled and dim through the rain. Satan said:

"The progress of your race was not satisfactory. It is to have another chance now."

The scene changed, and we saw Noah overcome with wine.

Next, we had Sodom and Gomorrah, and "the attempt to discover two or three respectable persons there," as Satan described it. Next, Lot and his daughters in the cave.

Next came the Hebraic wars, and we saw the victims massacre the survivors and their cattle, and save the young girls alive and distribute them around.

Next we had Jael; and saw her slip into the tent and drive the nail into the temple of her sleeping guest; and we were so close that when the blood gushed out it trickled in a little, red stream to our feet, and we could have stained our hands in it if we had wanted to.

Next we had Egyptian wars, Greek wars, Roman wars, hideous drenchings of the earth with blood; and we saw the treacheries of the Romans toward the Carthaginians, and the sickening spectacle of the massacre of those brave people. Also we saw Cæsar invade Britain—"not that those barbarians had done him any harm, but because he wanted their land, and desired to confer the blessings of civilization upon their widows and orphans," as Satan explained.

Next, Christianity was born. Then ages of Europe passed in review before us, and we saw Christianity and Civilization march hand in hand through those ages, "leaving famine and death and desolation in their wake, and other signs of the progress of the human race," as Satan observed.

And always we had wars, and more wars, and still other wars—all over Europe, all over the world. "Sometimes in the private interest of royal families," Satan said, "sometimes to crush a weak nation; but never a war started by the aggressor for any clean purpose—there is no such war in the history of the race."

"Now," said Satan, "you have seen your progress down to the present, and you must confess that it is wonderful—in its way. We must now exhibit the future."

He showed us slaughters more terrible in their destruction of life, more devastating in their engines of war, than any we had seen.

"You perceive," he said, "that you have made continual progress. Cain did his murder with a club; the Hebrews did their murders with javelins and swords; the Greeks and Romans added protective armor and the fine arts of military organization and generalship; the Christian has added guns and gun-powder; a few centuries from now he will have so greatly improved the deadly effectiveness of his weapons of slaughter that all men will confess that without Christian civilization war must have remained a poor and trifling thing to the end of time."

Then he began to laugh in the most unfeeling way, and make fun of the human race, although he knew that what he had been saying shamed us and wounded us. No one but an angel could have acted so; but suffering is nothing to them; they do not know what it is, except by hearsay.

More than once Seppi and I had tried in a humble and diffident way to convert him, and as he had remained silent we had taken his silence as a sort of encouragement; necessarily, then, this talk of his was a disappointment to us, for it showed that we had made no deep impression upon him. The thought made us sad, and we knew then how the missionary must feel when he has been cherishing a glad hope and has seen it blighted. We kept our grief to ourselves, knowing that this was not the time to continue our work.

Satan laughed his unkind laugh to a finish; then he said: "It is a remarkable progress. In five or six thousand years five or six high civilizations have risen, flourished, commanded the wonder of the world, then faded out and disappeared; and not one of them except the latest ever invented any sweeping and adequate way to kill people. They all did their best—to kill being the chiefest ambition of the human race and the earliest incident in its history—but only the Christian civilization has scored a triumph to be proud of. Two or three centuries from now it will be recognized that all the competent killers are Christians; then the pagan world will go to school to the Christian—not to acquire his religion, but his guns. The Turk and the Chinaman will buy those to kill missionaries and converts with."

By this time his theater was at work again, and before our eyes nation after nation drifted by, during two or three centuries, a mighty procession, an endless procession, raging, struggling, wallowing through seas of blood, smothered in battle-smoke through which the flags glinted and the red jets from the cannon darted; and always we heard the thunder of the guns and the cries of the dying.

"And what does it amount to?" said Satan, with his evil chuckle. "Nothing at all. You gain nothing; you always come out where you went in. For a million years the race has gone on monotonously propagating itself and monotonously reperforming this dull nonsense—to what end? No wisdom can guess! Who gets a profit out of it? Nobody but a parcel of usurping little monarchs and nobilities who despise you; would feel defiled if you touched them; would shut the door in your face if you proposed to call; whom you slave for, fight for, die for, and are not ashamed of it, but proud; whose existence is a perpetual insult to you and you are afraid to resent it; who are mendicants supported by your alms, yet assume toward you the airs of benefactor toward beggar; who address you in the language of master to slave, and are answered in the language of slave to master; who are worshiped by you with your mouth, while in your heart—if you have one—you despise yourselves for it. The first man was a hypocrite and a coward, qualities which have not yet failed in his line; it is the foundation upon which all civilizations have been built. Drink to their perpetuation! Drink to their augmentation! Drink to—" Then he saw by our faces how much we were hurt, and he cut his sentence short and stopped chuckling, and his manner changed. He said, gently: "No, we will drink one another's health, and let civilization go. The wine which has flown to our hands out of space by desire is earthly, and good enough for that other toast; but throw away the glasses; we will drink this one in wine which has not visited this world before."

We obeyed, and reached up and received the new cups as they descended. They were shapely and beautiful goblets, but they were not made of any material that we were acquainted with. They seemed to be in motion, they seemed to be alive; and certainly the colors in them were in motion. They were very brilliant and sparkling, and of every tint, and they were never still, but flowed to and fro in rich tides which met and broke and flashed out dainty explosions of enchanting color. I think it was most like opals washing about in waves and flashing out their splendid fires. But there is nothing to compare the wine with. We drank it, and felt a strange and witching ecstasy as of heaven go stealing through us, and Seppi's eyes filled and he said worshipingly:

"We shall be there some day, and then—"

He glanced furtively at Satan, and I think he hoped

Satan would say, "Yes, you will be there some day," but Satan seemed to be thinking about something else, and said nothing. This made me feel ghastly, for I knew he had heard; nothing, spoken or unspoken, ever escaped him. Poor Seppi looked distressed, and did not finish his remark. The goblets rose and clove their way into the sky, a triplet of radiant sundogs, and disappeared. Why didn't they stay? It seemed a bad sign, and depressed me. Should I ever see mine again? Would Seppi ever see his?

## IX.

It was wonderful, the mastery Satan had over time and distance. For him they did not exist. He called them human inventions, and said they were artificialities. We often went to the most distant parts of the globe with him, and stayed weeks and months, and yet were gone only a fraction of a second, as a rule. You could prove it by the clock. One day when our people were in such awful distress because the witch commission were afraid to proceed against the astrologer and Father Peter's household, or against any, indeed, but the poor and the friendless, they lost patience and took to witch-hunting on their own score, and began to chase a born lady who was known to have the habit of curing people by devilish arts, such as bathing them, washing them, and nourishing them instead of bleeding them and purging them through the ministrations of a barber-surgeon in the proper way. She came flying down, with the howling and cursing mob after her, and tried to take refuge in houses, but the doors were shut in her face. They chased her more than half an hour, we following to see it, and at last she was exhausted and fell, and they caught her. They dragged her to a tree and threw a rope over the limb, and began to make a noose in it, some holding her, meantime, and she crying and begging, and her young daughter looking on and weeping, but afraid to say or do anything.

They hanged the lady, and I threw a stone at her, although in my heart I was sorry for her; but all were throwing stones and each was watching his neighbor, and if I had not done as the others did it would have been noticed and spoken of. Satan burst out laughing.

All that were near by turned upon him, astonished and not pleased. It was an ill time to laugh, for his free and scoffing ways and his supernatural music had brought him under suspicion all over the town and turned many privately against him. The big blacksmith called attention to him now, raising his voice so that all should hear, and said:

"What are you laughing at? Answer! Moreover, please explain to the company why you threw no stone."

"Are you sure I did not throw a stone?"

"Yes. You needn't try to get out of it; I had my eye on you."

"And I—I noticed you!" shouted two others.

"Three witnesses," said Satan: "Mueller, the blacksmith; Klein, the butcher's man; Pfeiffer, the weaver's journeyman. Three very ordinary liars. Are there any more?"

"Never mind whether there are others or not, and never mind about what you consider us—three's enough to settle your matter for you. You'll prove that you threw a stone, or it shall go hard with you."

"That's so!" shouted the crowd, and surged up as closely as they could to the center of interest.

"And first you will answer that other question," cried the blacksmith, pleased with himself for being mouthpiece to the public and hero of the occasion. "What are you laughing at?"

Satan smiled and answered, pleasantly: "To see three cowards stoning a dying lady when they were so near death themselves."

You could see the superstitious crowd shrink and catch their breath, under the sudden shock. The blacksmith, with a show of bravado, said:

"Pooh! What do you know about it?"

"I? Everything. By profession I am a fortuneteller, and I read the hands of you three—and some others—when you lifted them to stone the woman. One of you will die tomorrow week; another of you will die to-night; the third has but five minutes to live—and yonder is the clock!"

It made a sensation. The faces of the crowd blanched, and turned mechanically toward the clock. The butcher and the weaver seemed smitten with an illness, but the blacksmith braced up and said, with spirit:

"It is not long to wait for prediction number one. If it fails, young master, you will not live a whole minute after, I promise you that."

No one said anything; all watched the clock in a deep stillness which was impressive. When four and a half minutes were gone the blacksmith gave a sudden gasp and clapped his hands upon his heart, saying, "Give me breath! Give me room!" and began to sink down. The crowd surged back, no one offering to support him, and he fell lumbering to the ground and was dead. The people stared at him, then at Satan, then at one another; and their lips moved, but no words came. Then Satan said:

"Three saw that I threw no stone. Perhaps there are others; let them speak."

It struck a kind of panic into them, and, although no one answered him, many began to violently accuse one an- other, saying, "You said he didn't throw," and getting for reply, "It is a lie, and I will make you eat it!" And so in a moment they were in a raging and noisy turmoil, and beat- ing and banging one another; and in the midst was the only indifferent one—the dead lady hanging from her rope, her troubles forgotten, her spirit at peace.

So we walked away, and I was not at ease, but was saying to myself, "He told them he was laughing at them, but it was a lie—he was laughing at me."

That made him laugh again, and he said, "Yes, I was laughing at you, because, in fear of what others might re- port about you, you stoned the woman when your heart re- volted at the act—but I was laughing at the others, too."

"Why?"

"Because their case was yours."

"How is that?"

"Well, there were sixty-eight people there, and sixty-two of them had no more desire to throw a stone than you had."

"Satan!"

"Oh, it's true. I know your race. It is made up of sheep. It is governed by minorities, seldom or never by majorities. It suppresses its feelings and its beliefs and follows the handful that makes the most noise. Sometimes the noisy handful is right, sometimes wrong; but no matter, the crowd follows it. The vast majority of the race, whether savage or civilized, are secretly kind-hearted and shrink from inflicting pain, but in the presence of the aggressive and pitiless minority they don't dare to assert themselves. Think of it! One kind-hearted creature spies upon another, and sees to it that he loyally helps in iniquities which re- volt both of them. Speaking as an expert, I know that ninety-nine out of a hundred of your race were strongly against the killing of witches when that foolishness was first agitated by a handful of pious lunatics in the long ago. And I know that even to-day, after ages of transmitted prejudice and silly teaching, only one person in twenty puts any real heart into the harrying of a witch. And yet apparently everybody hates witches and wants them killed. Some day a handful will rise up on the other side and make the most noise—perhaps even a single daring man with a big voice and a determined front will do it—and in a week all the sheep will wheel and follow him, and witch-hunting will come to a sudden end.

Monarchies, aristocracies, and religions are all based upon that large defect in your race—the individual's distrust of his neighbor, and his desire, for safety's or comfort's sake, to stand well in his neighbor's eye. These institutions will always remain, and always flourish, and always oppress you, affront you, and degrade you, because you will always be and remain slaves of minorities. There was never a country where the majority of the people were in their secret hearts loyal to any of these institutions."

I did not like to hear our race called sheep, and said I did not think they were.

"Still, it is true, lamb," said Satan. "Look at you in war—what mutton you are, and how ridiculous!"

"In war? How?"

"There has never been a just one, never an honorable one—on the part of the instigator of the war. I can see a million years ahead, and this rule will never change in so many as half a dozen instances. The loud little handful—as usual—will shout for the war. The pulpit will—warily and cautiously—object—at first; the great, big, dull bulk of the nation will rub its sleepy eyes and try to make out why there should be a war, and will say, earnestly and indignantly, "It is unjust and dishonorable, and there is no necessity for it." Then the handful will shout louder. A few fair men on the other side will argue and reason against the war with speech and pen, and at first will have a hearing and be applauded; but it will not last long; those others will outshout them, and presently the anti-war audiences will thin out and lose popularity. Before long you will see this curious thing: the speakers stoned from the platform, and free speech strangled by hordes of furious men who in their secret hearts are still at one with those stoned speakers—as earlier—but do not dare to say so. And now the whole nation—pulpit and all—will take up the war-cry, and shout itself hoarse, and mob any honest man who ventures to open his mouth; and presently such mouths will cease to open. Next the statesmen will invent cheap lies, putting the blame upon the nation that is attacked, and every man will be glad of those conscience-soothing falsities, and will diligently study them, and refuse to examine any refutations of them; and thus he will by and by convince himself that the war is just, and will thank God for the better sleep he enjoys after this process of grotesque self-deception."

## X.

Days and days went by now, and no Satan. It was dull without him. But the astrologer, who had returned from his excursion to the moon, went about the village, braving public opinion, and getting a stone in the middle of his back now and then when some witch-hater got a safe chance to throw it and dodge out of sight. Meantime two influences had been working well for Marget. That Satan, who was quite indifferent to her, had stopped going to her house after a visit or two had hurt her pride, and she had set herself the task of banishing him from her heart. Reports of Wilhelm Meidling's dissipation brought to her from time to time by old Ursula had touched her with remorse, jealousy of Satan being the cause of it; and so now, these two matters working upon her together, she was getting a good profit out of the combination—her interest in Satan was steadily cooling, her interest in Wilhelm as steadily warming. All that was needed to complete her conversion was that Wilhelm should brace up and do something that should cause favorable talk and incline the public toward him again.

The opportunity came now. Marget sent and asked him to defend her uncle in the approaching trial, and he was greatly pleased, and stopped drinking and began his preparations with diligence. With more diligence than hope, in fact, for it was not a promising case. He had many interviews in his office with Seppi and me, and threshed out our testimony pretty thoroughly, thinking to find some valuable grains among the chaff, but the harvest was poor, of course.

If Satan would only come! That was my constant thought. He could invent some way to win the case; for he had said it would be won, so he necessarily knew how it could be done. But the days dragged on, and still he did not come. Of course I did not doubt that it would be won, and that Father Peter would be happy for the rest of his life, since Satan had said so; yet I knew I should be much more comfortable if he would come and tell us how to manage it. It was getting high time for Father Peter to have a saving change toward happiness, for by general report he was worn out with his imprisonment and the ignominy that was burdening him, and was like to die of his miseries unless he got relief soon.

At last the trial came on, and the people gathered from all around to witness it; among them many strangers from considerable distances. Yes, everybody was there except the accused. He was too feeble in body for the strain. But Marget was present, and keeping up her hope and her spirit the best she could. The money was present, too. It was emptied on the table, and was handled and caressed and examined by such as were privileged.

The astrologer was put in the witness-box. He had on his best hat and robe for the occasion.

*Question.* You claim that this money is yours?

*Answer.* I do.

*Q.* How did you come by it?

*A.* I found the bag in the road when I was returning from a journey.

*Q.* When?

*A.* More than two years ago.

*Q.* What did you do with it?

*A.* I brought it home and hid it in a secret place in my observatory, intending to find the owner if I could.

*Q.* You endeavored to find him?

*A.* I made diligent inquiry during several months, but nothing came of it.

*Q.* And then?

*A.* I thought it not worth while to look further, and was minded to use the money in finishing the wing of the foundling-asylum connected with the priory and nunnery.

So I took it out of its hiding-place and counted it to see if any of it was missing. And then—

*Q.* Why do you stop? Proceed.

*A.* I am sorry to have to say this, but just as I had finished and was restoring the bag to its place, I looked up and there stood Father Peter behind me.

Several murmured, "That looks bad," but others answered, "Ah, but he is such a liar!"

*Q.* That made you uneasy?

*A.* No; I thought nothing of it at the time, for Father Peter often came to me unannounced to ask for a little help in his need.

Marget blushed crimson at hearing her uncle falsely and impudently charged with begging, especially from one he had always denounced as a fraud, and was going to speak, but remembered herself in time and held her peace.

*Q.* Proceed.

*A.* In the end I was afraid to contribute the money to the foundling-asylum, but elected to wait yet another year and continue my inquiries. When I heard of Father Peter's find I was glad, and no suspicion entered my mind; when I came home a day or two later and discovered that my own money was gone I still did not suspect until three circumstances connected with Father Peter's good fortune struck me as being singular coincidences.

*Q.* Pray name them.

*A.* Father Peter had found his money in a path—I had found mine in a road. Father Peter's find consisted exclusively of gold ducats—mine also. Father Peter found eleven hundred and seven ducats—I exactly the same.

This closed his evidence, and certainly it made a strong impression on the house; one could see that.

Wilhelm Meidling asked him some questions, then called us boys, and we told our tale. It made the people laugh, and we were ashamed. We were feeling pretty badly, anyhow, because Wilhelm was hopeless, and showed it. He was doing as well as he could, poor young fellow, but nothing was in his favor, and such sympathy as there was was now plainly not with his client. It might be difficult for court and people to believe the astrologer's story, considering his character, but it was almost impossible to believe Father Peter's. We were already feeling badly enough, but when the astrologer's lawyer said he believed he would

not ask us any questions—for our story was a little delicate
and it would be cruel for him to put any strain upon it—
everybody tittered, and it was almost more than we could
bear. Then he made a sarcastic little speech, and got so
much fun out of our tale, and it seemed so ridiculous and
childish and every way impossible and foolish, that it made
everybody laugh till the tears came; and at last Marget
could not keep up her courage any longer, but broke down
and cried, and I was so sorry for her.

Now I noticed something that braced me up. It was
Satan standing alongside of Wilhelm! And there was such
a contrast!—Satan looked so confident, had such a spirit in
his eyes and face, and Wilhelm looked so depressed and
despondent. We two were comfortable now, and judged
that he would testify and persuade the bench and the people that black was white and white black, or any other
color he wanted it. We glanced around to see what the
strangers in the house thought of him, for he was beautiful,
you know—stunning, in fact—but no one was noticing
him; so we knew by that that he was invisible.

The lawyer was saying his last words; and while he was
saying them Satan began to melt into Wilhelm. He melted
into him and disappeared; and then there was a change,
when his spirit began to look out of Wilhelm's eyes.

That lawyer finished quite seriously, and with dignity.
He pointed to the money, and said:

"The love of it is the root of all evil. There it lies, the
ancient tempter, newly red with the shame of its latest victory—the dishonor of a priest of God and his two poor
juvenile helpers in crime. If it could but speak, let us hope
that it would be constrained to confess that of all its con-
quests this was the basest and the most pathetic."

He sat down. Wilhelm rose and said:

"From the testimony of the accuser I gather that he
found this money in a road more than two years ago. Correct me, sir, if I misunderstood you."

The astrologer said his understanding of it was correct.

"And the money so found was never out of his hands
thenceforth up to a certain definite date—the last day of
last year. Correct me, sir, if I am wrong."

The astrologer nodded his head. Wilhelm turned to the
bench and said:

"If I prove that this money here was not that money, then it is not his?"

"Certainly not; but this is irregular. If you had such a witness it was your duty to give proper notice of it and have him here to—" He broke off and began to consult with the other judges. Meantime that other lawyer got up excited and began to protest against allowing new witnesses to be brought into the case at this late stage.

The judges decided that his contention was just and must be allowed.

"But this is not a new witness," said Wilhelm. "It has already been partly examined. I speak of the coin."

"The coin? What can the coin say?"

"It can say it is not the coin that the astrologer once possessed. It can say it was not in existence last December. By its date it can say this."

And it was so! There was the greatest excitement in the court while that lawyer and the judges were reaching for coins and examining them and exclaiming. And everybody was full of admiration of Wilhelm's brightness in happening to think of that neat idea. At last order was called and the court said:

"All of the coins but four are of the date of the present year. The court tenders its sincere sympathy to the accused, and its deep regret that he, an innocent man, through an unfortunate mistake, has suffered the undeserved humiliation of imprisonment and trial. The case is dismissed."

So the money could speak, after all, though that lawyer thought it couldn't. The court rose, and almost everybody came forward to shake hands with Marget and congratulate her, and then to shake with Wilhelm and praise him; and Satan had stepped out of Wilhelm and was standing around looking on full of interest, and people walking through him every which way, not knowing he was there. And Wilhelm could not explain why he only thought of the date on the coins at the last moment, instead of earlier; he said it just occurred to him, all of a sudden, like an inspiration, and he brought it right out without any hesitation, for, although he didn't examine the coins, he seemed, somehow, to know it was true. That was honest of him, and like him; another would have pretended he had thought of it earlier, and was keeping it back for a surprise.

He had dulled down a little now; not much, but still you could notice that he hadn't that luminous look in his eyes that he had while Satan was in him. He nearly got it back, though, for a moment when Marget came and praised him and thanked him and couldn't keep him from seeing how proud she was of him. The astrologer went off dissatisfied and cursing, and Solomon Isaacs gathered up the money and carried it away. It was Father Peter's for good and all, now.

Satan was gone. I judged that he had spirited himself away to the jail to tell the prisoner the news; and in this I was right. Marget and the rest of us hurried thither at our best speed, in a great state of rejoicing.

Well, what Satan had done was this: he had appeared before that poor prisoner, exclaiming, "The trial is over, and you stand forever disgraced as a thief—by verdict of the court!"

The shock unseated the old man's reason. When we arrived, ten minutes later, he was parading pompously up and down and delivering commands to this and that and the other constable or jailer, and calling them Grand Chamberlain, and Prince This and Prince That, and Admiral of the Fleet, Field Marshal in Command, and all such fustian, and was as happy as a bird. He thought he was Emperor!

Marget flung herself on his breast and cried, and indeed everybody was moved almost to heartbreak. He recognized Marget, but could not understand why she should cry. He patted her on the shoulder and said:

"Don't do it, dear; remember, there are witnesses, and it is not becoming in the Crown Princess. Tell me your trouble—it shall be mended; there is nothing the Emperor cannot do." Then he looked around and saw old Ursula with her apron to her eyes. He was puzzled at that, and said, "And what is the matter with you?"

Through her sobs she got out words explaining that she was distressed to see him—"so." He reflected over that a moment, then muttered, as if to himself: "A singular old thing, the Dowager Duchess—means well, but is always snuffling and never able to tell what it is about. It is because she doesn't know." His eyes fell on Wilhelm. "Prince of India," he said, "I divine that it is you that the Crown

Princess is concerned about. Her tears shall be dried; I will no longer stand between you; she shall share your throne; and between you you shall inherit mine. There, little lady, have I done well? You can smile now—isn't it so?"

He petted Marget and kissed her, and was so contented with himself and with everybody that he could not do enough for us all, but began to give away kingdoms and such things right and left, and the least that any of us got was a principality. And so at last, being persuaded to go home, he marched in imposing state; and when the crowds along the way saw how it gratified him to be hurrahed at, they humored him to the top of his desire, and he responded with condescending bows and gracious smiles, and often stretched out a hand and said, "Bless you, my people!"

As pitiful a sight as ever I saw. And Marget, and old Ursula crying all the way.

On my road home I came upon Satan, and reproached him with deceiving me with that lie. He was not embarrassed, but said, quite simply and composedly:

"Ah, you mistake; it was the truth. I said he would be happy the rest of his days, and he will, for he will always think he is the Emperor, and his pride in it and his joy in it will endure to the end. He is now, and will remain, the one utterly happy person in this empire."

"But the method of it, Satan, the method! Couldn't you have done it without depriving him of his reason?"

It was difficult to irritate Satan, but that accomplished it.

"What an ass you are!" he said. "Are you so unobservant as not to have found out that sanity and happiness are an impossible combination? No sane man can be happy, for to him life is real, and he sees what a fearful thing it is. Only the mad can be happy, and not many of those. The few that imagine themselves kings or gods are happy, the rest are no happier than the sane. Of course, no man is entirely in his right mind at any time, but I have been referring to the extreme cases. I have taken from this man that trumpery thing which the race regards as a Mind; I have replaced his tin life with a silver-gilt fiction; you see the result—and you criticize! I said I would make him permanently happy, and I have done it. I have made him happy by the only means possible to his race—and you are not satisfied!" He heaved a discouraged sigh, and said, "It seems to me that this race is hard to please."

There it was, you see. He didn't seem to know any way to do a person a favor except by killing him or making a lunatic out of him. I apologized, as well as I could; but privately I did not think much of his processes—at that time.

Satan was accustomed to say that our race lived a life of continuous and uninterrupted self-deception. It duped itself from cradle to grave with shams and delusions which it mistook for realities, and this made its entire life a sham. Of the score of fine qualities which it imagined it had and was vain of, it really possessed hardly one. It regarded itself as gold, and was only brass. One day when he was in this vein he mentioned a detail—the sense of humor. I cheered up then, and took issue. I said we possessed it.

"There spoke the race!" he said; "always ready to claim what it hasn't got, and mistake its ounce of brass filings for a ton of gold-dust. You have a mongrel perception of humor, nothing more; a multitude of you possess that. This multitude sees the comic side of a thousand low-grade and trivial things—broad incongruities, mainly; grotesqueries, absurdities, evokers of the horse-laugh. Then ten thousand high-grade comicalities which exist in the world are sealed from their dull vision. Will a day come when the race will detect the funniness of these juvenilities and laugh at them—and by laughing at them destroy them? For your race, in its poverty, has unquestionably one really effective weapon—laughter. Power, money, persuasion, supplication, persecution—these can lift at a colossal humbug —push it a little—weaken it a little, century by century; but only laughter can blow it to rags and atoms at a blast. Against the assault of laughter nothing can stand. You are always fussing and fighting with your other weapons. Do you ever use that one? No; you leave it lying rusting. As a race, do you ever use it at all? No; you lack sense and the courage."

We were traveling at the time and stopped at a little city in India and looked on while a juggler did his tricks before a group of natives. They were wonderful, but I knew Satan could beat that game, and I begged him to show off a little, and he said he would. He changed himself into a native in turban and breech-cloth, and very considerately conferred on me a temporary knowledge of the language.

The juggler exhibited a seed, covered it with earth in a small flower-pot, then put a rag over the pot; after a minute the rag began to rise; in ten minutes it had risen a foot; then the rag was removed and a little tree was exposed, with leaves upon it and ripe fruit. We ate the fruit, and it was good. But Satan said:

"Why do you cover the pot? Can't you grow the tree in the sunlight?"

"No," said the juggler; "no one can do that."

"You are only an apprentice; you don't know your trade. Give me the seed. I will show you." He took the seed and said, "What shall I raise from it?"

"It is a cherry seed; of course you will raise a cherry."

"Oh no; that is a trifle; any novice can do that. Shall I raise an orange-tree from it?"

"Oh yes!" and the juggler laughed.

"And shall I make it bear other fruits as well as oranges?"

"If God wills!" and they all laughed.

Satan put the seed in the ground, put a handful of dust on it, and said, "Rise!"

A tiny stem shot up and began to grow, and grew so fast that in five minutes it was a great tree, and we were sitting in the shade of it. There was a murmur of wonder, then all looked up and saw a strange and pretty sight, for the branches were heavy with fruits of many kinds and colors—oranges, grapes, bananas, peaches, cherries, apricots, and so on. Baskets were brought, and the unlading of the tree began; and the people crowded around Satan and kissed his hand, and praised him, calling him the prince of jugglers. The news went about the town, and everybody came running to see the wonder—and they remembered to bring baskets, too. But the tree was equal to the occasion; it put out new fruits as fast as any were removed; baskets were filled by the score and by the hundred, but always the supply remained undiminished. At last a foreigner in white linen and sun-helmet arrived, and exclaimed, angrily:

"Away from here! Clear out, you dogs; the tree is on my lands and is my property."

The natives put down their baskets and made humble obeisance. Satan made humble obeisance, too, with his fingers to his forehead, in the native way, and said:

"Please let them have their pleasure for an hour, sir— only that, and no longer. Afterward you may forbid them; and you will still have more fruit than you and the state together can consume in a year."

This made the foreigner very angry, and he cried out, "Who are you, you vagabond, to tell your betters what they may do and what they mayn't!" and he struck Satan with his cane and followed this error with a kick.

The fruits rotted on the branches, and the leaves withered and fell. The foreigner gazed at the bare limbs with the look of one who is surprised, and not gratified. Satan said:

"Take good care of the tree, for its health and yours are bound together. It will never bear again, but if you tend it well it will live long. Water its roots once in each hour every night—and do it yourself; it must not be done by proxy, and to do it in daylight will not answer. If you fail only once in any night, the tree will die, and you likewise. Do not go home to your own country any more— you would not reach there; make no business or pleasure engagements which require you to go outside your gate at night—you cannot afford the risk; do not rent or sell this place—it would be injudicious."

The foreigner was proud and wouldn't beg, but I thought he looked as if he would like to. While he stood gazing at Satan we vanished away and landed in Ceylon.

I was sorry for that man; sorry Satan hadn't been his customary self and killed him or made him a lunatic. It would have been a mercy. Satan overheard the thought, and said:

"I would have done it but for his wife, who has not offended me. She is coming to him presently from their native land, Portugal. She is well, but has not long to live, and has been yearning to see him and persuade him to go back with her next year. She will die without knowing he can't leave that place?"

"He won't tell her?"

"He? He will not trust that secret with any one; he will reflect that it could be revealed in sleep, in the hearing of some Portuguese guest's servant some time or other."

"Did none of those natives understand what you said to him?"

"None of them understood, but he will always be afraid that some of them did. That fear will be torture to him, for he has been a harsh master to them. In his dreams he will imagine them chopping his tree down. That will make his days uncomfortable—I have already arranged for his nights."

It grieved me, though not sharply, to see him take such a malicious satisfaction in his plans for this foreigner.

"Does he believe what you told him, Satan?"

"He thought he didn't, but our vanishing helped. The tree, where there had been no tree before—that helped. The insane and uncanny variety of fruits—the sudden withering —all these things are helps. Let him think as he may, reason as he may, one thing is certain, he will water the tree. But between this and night he will begin his changed career with a very natural precaution—for him."

"What is that?"

"He will fetch a priest to cast out the tree's devil. You are such a humorous race—and don't suspect it."

"Will he tell the priest?"

"No. He will say a juggler from Bombay created it, and that he wants the juggler's devil driven out of it, so that it will thrive and be fruitful again. The priest's incantations will fail; then the Portuguese will give up that scheme and get his watering-pot ready."

"But the priest will burn the tree. I know it; he will not allow it to remain."

"Yes, and anywhere in Europe he would burn the man, too. But in India the people are civilized, and these things will not happen. The man will drive the priest away and take care of the tree."

I reflected a little, then said, "Satan, you have given him a hard life, I think."

"Comparatively. It must not be mistaken for a holiday."

We flitted from place to place around the world as we had done before, Satan showing me a hundred wonders, most of them reflecting in some way the weakness and triviality of our race. He did this now every few days—not out of malice—I am sure of that—it only seemed to amuse and interest him, just as a naturalist might be amused and interested by a collection of ants.

## XI.

For as much as a year Satan continued these visits, but at last he came less often, and then for a long time he did not come at all. This always made me lonely and melancholy. I felt that he was losing interest in our tiny world and might at any time abandon his visits entirely. When one day he finally came to me I was overjoyed, but only for a little while. He had come to say good-by, he told me, and for the last time. He had investigations and undertakings in other corners of the universe, he said, that would keep him busy for a longer period than I could wait for his return.

"And you are going away, and will not come back any more?"

"Yes," he said. "We have comraded long together, and it has been pleasant—pleasant for both; but I must go now, and we shall not see each other any more."

"In this life, Satan, but in another? We shall meet in another, surely?"

Then, all tranquilly and soberly, he made the strange answer, *"There is no other."*

A subtle influence blew upon my spirit from his, bringing with it a vague, dim, but blessed and hopeful feeling that the incredible words might be true—even *must* be true.

"Have you never suspected this, Theodor?"

"No. How could I? But if it can only be true—"

"It is true."

A gust of thankfulness rose in my breast, but a doubt checked it before it could issue in words, and I said, "But—but—we have seen that future life—seen it in its actuality, and so—"

"It was a vision—it had no existence."

I could hardly breathe for the great hope that was struggling in me. "A vision?—a vi—"

*"Life itself is only a vision, a dream."*

It was electrical. By God! I had had that very thought a thousand times in my musings!

"*Nothing* exists; all is a dream. God—man—the world
—the sun, the moon, the wilderness of stars—a dream, all a
dream; they have no existence. *Nothing exists save empty
space—and you!*"

"I!"

"And you are not you—you have no body, no blood, no
bones, you are but a *thought*. I myself have no existence;
I am but a dream—your dream, creature of your imagination. In a moment you will have realized this, then you will
banish me from your visions and I shall dissolve into the
nothingness out of which you made me. . . .

"I am perishing already—I am failing—I am passing away.
In a little while you will be alone in shoreless space, to wander its limitless solitudes without friend or comrade forever
—for you will remain a *thought*, the only existent thought,
and by your nature inextinguishable, indestructible. But I,
your poor servant, have revealed you to yourself and set you
free. Dream other dreams, and better!

"Strange! that you should not have suspected years ago—
centuries, ages, eons ago!—for you have existed, compan-
ionless, through all the eternities. Strange, indeed, that you
should not have suspected that your universe and its contents were only dreams, visions, fiction! Strange, because
they are so frankly and hysterically insane—like all dreams:
a God who could make good children as easily as bad, yet
preferred to make bad ones; who could have made every
one of them happy, yet never made a single happy one;
who made them prize their bitter life, yet stingily cut it
short; who gave his angels eternal happiness unearned, yet
required his other children to earn it; who gave his angels
painless lives, yet cursed his other children with biting
miseries and maladies of mind and body; who mouths
justice and invented hell—mouths mercy and invented hell
—mouths Golden Rules, and forgiveness multiplied by
seventy times seven, and invented hell; who mouths morals
to other people and has none himself; who frowns upon
crimes, yet commits them all; who created man without
invitation, then tries to shuffle the responsibility for man's
acts upon man, instead of honorably placing it where it belongs, upon himself; and finally, with altogether divine
obtuseness, invites this poor, abused slave to worship
him! . . .

"You perceive, *now*, that these things are all impossible except in a dream. You perceive that they are pure and puerile insanities, the silly creations of an imagination that is not conscious of its freaks—in a word, that they are a dream, and you the maker of it. The dream-marks are all present; you should have recognized them earlier.

"It is true, that which I have revealed to you; there is no God, no universe, no human race, no earthly life, no heaven, no hell. It is all a dream—a grotesque and foolish dream. Nothing exists but you. And you are but a *thought*—a vagrant thought, a useless thought, a homeless thought, wandering forlorn among the empty eternities!"

He vanished, and left me appalled; for I knew, and realized, that all he had said was true.

# A CHRONOLOGY

| | |
|---|---|
| 1835, Nov. 30 | Samuel L. Clemens born in Florida, Missouri. |
| 1839–1853 | Boyhood, schooling, and work as apprentice printer in Hannibal, Missouri. |
| 1857–1861 | "Cub" and licensed steamboat pilot on the Mississippi. |
| 1861 | Brief military service as a Confederate irregular. |
| 1861–1866 | Works as journalist and occasional miner in the Nevada Territory and California. |
| 1863, Feb. 3 | Signs the pseudonym "Mark Twain" to a humorous travel letter in the Virginia City *Territorial Enterprise.* |
| 1867 | Eastern lecture debut; to Europe and the Holy Land on the *Quaker City.* |
| 1870, Feb. 2 | Marries Olivia Langdon of Elmira, N.Y. |
| 1871 | Settles in Hartford, Connecticut, where, with occasional trips abroad, the Clemens family, including three daughters, remain until 1891. |
| 1885 | Mark Twain's own firm, Charles L. Webster and Company, publishes *Huckleberry Finn* and General Ulysses Grant's *Personal Memoirs.* Increasingly involved with the development and marketing of the Paige Typesetter. |
| 1891 | Closes Hartford house, spending the next nine years mainly abroad. |
| 1894 | Goes into bankruptcy along with his publishing house. |
| 1895–1896 | Round-the-world lecture tour to pay off debts. |
| 1896, August 18 | Susy, his favorite, dies of meningitis. |
| 1900 | Returns to America, prosperity and celebrity. |
| 1904, June 5 | Mrs. Clemens dies in Florence. |
| 1907 | Receives honorary Litt. D. from Oxford University. |
| 1910, April 21 | Dies in Redding, Connecticut. |

# A BIBLIOGRAPHY

## Books by Mark Twain:

*The Celebrated Jumping Frog of Calaveras County and other Sketches* (1867); *The Innocents Abroad* (1869); *Roughing It* (1872); *The Gilded Age* (with Charles Dudley Warner; 1873); *Sketches: New and Old* (1875); *The Adventures of Tom Sawyer* (1876); *A Tramp Abroad* (1880); *The Prince and the Pauper* (1882); *Life on the Mississippi* (1883); *The Adventures of Huckleberry Finn* (1885); *A Connecticut Yankee in King Arthur's Court* (1889); *The Tragedy of Pudd'nhead Wilson* (1894); *Personal Recollections of Joan of Arc* (1896); *Following the Equator* (1897); *How to Tell a Story and Other Essays* (1897); *The Man that Corrupted Hadleyburg* (1900); *What Is Man?* (1906); *Mark Twain's Speeches* (1910); *The Mysterious Stranger* (1916); *Europe and Elsewhere* (1923); *Mark Twain's Autobiography* (1924); *Mark Twain in Eruption* (1940); *The Autobiography of Mark Twain* (1959); *Letters from the Earth* (1962).

## Mark Twain's Letters, Notebooks, and Papers:

*Letters* (1917); *Notebook* (1935); *Love Letters* (1949); *Mark Twain to Mrs. Fairbanks* (1949); *Mark Twain-Howells Letters* (1960). Mark Twain's papers are being edited for publication by the University of California Press; the first three volumes appeared in 1967—*Letters to His Publishers, Satires and Burlesques,* and *Which Was the Dream?*

## Biographical and Critical Writing about Twain:

Albert Bigelow Paine's authorized and indispensable *Mark Twain: A Biography* was published in 1912, two years after William Dean Howells's affectionate portrait entitled *My Mark Twain.* Among the numerous biographical studies that have since appeared are: Van Wyck Brooks's *The Ordeal of Mark Twain* (1920; revised in 1933); Bernard DeVoto's *Mark Twain's America* (1932) and *Mark Twain at Work* (1942); Samuel C. Webster's *Mark Twain: Business Man* (1946); Kenneth R. Andrews's *Nook Farm: Mark Twain's Hartford Circle* (1950); and Justin Kaplan's *Mr. Clemens and Mark Twain* (1966).

Among major, recent critical studies are: Kenneth S. Lynn's *Mark Twain and Southwestern Humor* (1959); Walter Blair's *Mark Twain & Huck Finn* (1960); Henry Nash Smith's *Mark Twain: The Development of a Writer* (1962); and James M. Cox's *Mark Twain: The Fate of Humor* (1966).

General bibliographies, which include the enormous periodical literature, can be found in *Eight American Authors: A Review of Research* (1956), edited by Floyd Stovall; E. Hudson Long's *Mark Twain Handbook* (1957); and each issue of the quarterly *American Literature* (1929—).